'Claire Lowdon has written the definitive novel of a generation of Londoners. So involved did I become in their lives, so closely did I feel I knew them, that the note of disquiet that carries through the pages like the eerie mewl of a tuning fork absolutely levelled me when finally it reached its full glass-shattering resonance three-quarters of the way through' Gavin Corbett

'Attuned to the nuances of social interaction that lie above the threshold of awareness and elude articulation, Lowdon observes interpersonal relationships with a satirist's sharp eye. Her narrator pierces façades and parses hybrid, often contradictory, cocktails of emotion with an efficiency reminiscent of Alan Hollinghurst's early novels … Peeling the layers of her characters' drives and desires demands a precision that, as the subtlety of these observations attests, Lowdon possesses' Lindsay Gail Gibson, *Times Literary Supplement*

'A startlingly assured debut, chronicling the lives of twenty-somethings in contemporary London. (I read it in the same fevered excitement as I read Claire Messud's *The Emperor's Children*.) It's a social commentary, a page-turner and it's packed with beautiful sentences' *Sunday Business Post*

'All the way through what is essentially a realist novel about young Londoners runs an edge of tension, of suppressed panic. You await the explosion, never quite knowing what form it will take … Minor events all seem to take place in the shadow of the loaded gun we know must be about to go off, in "those vacuum-packed, suspended seconds" before the obscure but inevitable bang … The characters' moral wranglings and the machinery of the plot spiral inexorably inwards, into the bedroom. It's there that everything will eventually go bang' Lidija Haas, *Guardian*

'Lowdon has Evelyn Waugh's willingness to inflict gruesome plot twists on her Bright Young Things' *Literary Review*

CLAIRE LOWDON

Left of the Bang

4th ESTATE • *London*

Fourth Estate
An imprint of HarperCollins*Publishers*
1 London Bridge Street,
London SE1 9GF
4thestate.co.uk

This Fourth Estate paperback edition published in 2016

First published in Great Britain in 2015 by Fourth Estate

1

A catalogue record for this book
is available from the British Library

ISBN 978-0-00-810216-6

Song lyrics quoted from: 'Hey Jude' by John Lennon and Paul McCartney (Sony/
ATV); 'The Nearness of You', music by Hoagy Carmichael, lyrics by Ned
Washington (Sony/ATV); 'Only Girl (In The World)', by Crystal Johnson, Mikkel S. Eriksen,
Tor Erik Hermansen, Sandy Wilhelm (Sony/ATV); 'S&M', by Ester Dean, Mikkel S. Eriksen,
Tor Erik Hermansen, Sandy Wilhelm (Sony/ATV); 'We Are the Champions', by Freddie
Mercury (Sony/ATV); 'You're Not the Only Oyster in the Stew', music by Harold Spina,
lyrics by Johnny Burke (Warner/Chappell Music)

Typeset in Sabon by Palimpsest Book Production Limited,
Falkirk, Stirlingshire

Printed and bound in Great Britain by
Clays Ltd, St Ives plc

For my grandmothers, D.E.M. and G.M.M.L.

Left of the bang: a military term for the build-up to an explosion. On a left–right time line, preparation and prevention are left of the bang; right of the bang refers to the aftermath.

One

Her father's arms around her. His voice vibrating through his chest and into hers.

'I'm here, tinker. I'm here.'

Her bleeding toenail, open like a birthday card.

Two

When Tamsin Jarvis was twelve, she saw her father kissing another woman.

The whole family was up in Manchester to hear him conduct a celebration of British music at the Bridgewater Hall. It was a treat, at the end of the concert, for Tamsin to go to his dressing room all by herself. Her mother had to put ten-year-old Serena to bed in the Jurys Inn Hotel across the road. 'Tell Daddy not to hang around chatting, the restaurant's booked for nine forty-five.'

Backstage, everything was hushed. All the doors had leather quilting. The carpet was very thick. A stagehand with his radio earpiece hooked round his neck pointed her towards the end of the corridor. Tamsin pushed her father's door open, enjoying its weight and the smooth, silent swing of the hinges.

Three seconds later she closed it again, just as silently. The lovers had been kissing with their eyes shut. Neither of them knew they'd been seen.

The woman was Valery Fischer, the mezzo from the concert. Val and her husband Patrick were old friends of the Jarvises. Their only son, a stocky, sporty eleven-year-old called Alex, played viola in the same youth orchestra as Serena. Last summer, the two families had even spent a long weekend together in a rented cottage in Suffolk.

Tamsin walked slowly back up the corridor, seeing it all over again. Bertrand's left hand gripping Val's bottom through the stiff satin of her turquoise strapless dress. His right hand crushing her loosely permed curls. A large raised mole in the middle of Val's back, pale, like a Rice Krispie. The kiss itself: muscular, forceful, almost angry, as if they were fighting one another with their mouths.

In the foyer, she sat down on the floor next to the ice-cream stand and tried to think. When she closed her eyes, she could hear the sound of her own blood. She could feel it, too, each pulse a tight squirting sensation. Around her, adult chatter thinned to a trickle as the concert-goers left the building. Tamsin stayed where she was, eyes still closed. A Hoover began its melancholy drone.

'Tamsin?'

It was her father. He was still wearing his black trousers, but he'd swapped his tux and dress shirt for a loose grey tunic. He held out one of his big hands for Tamsin to haul herself up with.

'What are you doing down there?'

'We have to go,' said Tamsin. 'We'll be late for supper.'

* * *

For five years she told no one.

Tamsin was frightened: of the pain that disclosure would cause her mother, of the possibility of divorce (a condition that ranked, in her twelve-year-old mind, as second only to cancer). Most of all she was frightened of her father's anger – which, she realised, would no longer be the familiar, beneficent anger of grown-up to child, father to daughter, but real, unbounded, adult anger.

She hated being alone with him. Car journeys were the worst: prisoner in the passenger seat on the way home from school, her father asking about her day, trying to make her laugh. He was his usual garrulous, ebullient self, fond of hyperbole, susceptible to sentiment, domineering, opinionated, funny, warm. Tamsin could see nothing in his demeanour to suggest that here was a man with a terrible secret. And this was what made him truly monstrous.

Bertrand wasn't as relaxed as he appeared. He was worried – by Tamsin, about Tamsin. Before, the two of them had been a team. Now she was nervy and skittish, slow in conversation, unwilling to meet his eye. If he hugged her, she hugged back, but she no longer initiated contact between them. On more than one occasion, he had the impression that his touch was actually unpleasant to her.

Before – but before what? Bertrand didn't know; he couldn't even really say when the change had occurred. He wondered if some male authority figure had behaved inappropriately towards her – a teacher, or perhaps one of the gap-year students who helped out at her summer music school. When he suggested this to his wife, however, she dismissed it as a typical piece of melodrama. 'She's growing up, that's all. She can't be your little girl for ever.' They were in the bedroom, getting ready to go out for the evening. Roz spritzed perfume onto her left wrist, then drew her right wrist across her left in a sawing motion. 'She'll be thirteen soon. It's just hormones,' she said decisively, meeting her husband's doubtful frown with a brisk, case-closed sort of look.

Bertrand also wondered whether Tamsin knew about his affair. Somehow, it seemed to him that she might. No matter how firmly he told himself that his anxiety was unfounded, he felt increasingly uneasy in his daughter's presence; and in time, he found he was unable to prevent unease from translating into mild aversion. He was ashamed of this feeling, and did everything he could to conceal it – to the point where he appeared, if anything, even more affectionate and indulgent towards Tamsin than before.

As far as her mother was concerned, Tamsin was a textbook teenager: surly and non-responsive at home, perpetually in trouble at school. She collected detentions, missed curfews, got a tattoo. At fourteen she spent a night in A&E with a stomach full of vodka and caffeine tablets. At fifteen she pierced her own bellybutton. 'Hormones' became Roz's buzzword, mouthed unsubtly over Tamsin's head to sympathetic friends. Secretly, she was a little frightened of her eldest daughter. Tamsin at sixteen was a good six inches taller than her mother and almost ethereally thin, with angular shoulders and no hips or breasts to speak of. Cropped halterneck tops exposed the bejewelled bellybutton, elongated by the tautness of her stomach and embellished, more often than not, with a purplish crust of infection.

On the rare occasions that her parents argued, Tamsin lay awake in bed, monitoring the muffled sounds coming up from the kitchen for any change in register that might signal the end. The end: expected and dreaded yet also, in a small, hard way, longed for. But the rapid cadences of blame and recrimination always rallentandoed into a truce, followed, a few minutes later, by her mother's face at the bedroom door, flushed with guilt and tenderness.

'*Darling*. All couples argue. There's nothing to worry about, I promise. Your father and I love each other. And we love you. Love you love you *love* you.'

Roz perched her small frame on the edge of the bed. Her daughter's large-lidded eyes – Bertrand's eyes – were round and wide, a precious glimpse of the little girl who had long since morphed into this difficult, untouchable half-woman.

And so the silence continued, as if it might go on for ever. But later, when Tamsin looked back at that time, she would recall very clearly a sense of anticipation. A firework mutely blossoming, Concorde ripping noiselessly across the sky: those vacuum-packed, suspended seconds before the bang.

Three

Five fifteen on a Tuesday evening in late November: the crowded southbound Bakerloo line. Tamsin Jarvis, now seventeen, still very skinny, had a seat. Even better, she had the end seat. This meant she could lean right away from the woman on her left and press her hot cheek onto the pane of glass dividing the seats from the standing section. She had shrugged off her parka at Marylebone to reveal a faded black Nirvana T-shirt bearing the slogan 'flower sniffin kitty pettin baby kissin corporate rock whore'. In her lap, a book of Beethoven piano sonatas, open at No. 21. Tamsin had been tracing the melody with a chewed-down fingernail, pleasantly conscious of the incongruity: a grungy-looking teenage girl absorbed in classical music, performing the indisputable miracle of turning black marks on the page into sounds in her head.

She didn't notice the suitcase until the train was pulling out of Piccadilly Circus. It was a pine-green, hard-shelled case with wheels and an extendable handle, pushed up against the other side of the glass panel. How long had it been there? At Charing Cross, she looked to see if somebody claimed it. People jostled past it on their way out, irritated by the obstacle. A small woman with a scrappy high ponytail banged her knee on it and let out a bleat of pain. The woman scowled around for the owner, but no one came forward.

Almost as soon as the train had left the station, it stopped. Tamsin looked at the suitcase. Then through the window behind her at the tunnel blackness with its dirty arcana of wires and pipes. Then back at the suitcase. Someone was watching her: a tall boy about her own age, with broad shoulders and something slightly Asian, Chinese or Japanese maybe, about the eyes. He was standing in the middle of the carriage, holding the hand-rail with both hands, elbows flexed as if about to do a chin-up.

The boy nodded towards the suitcase.

'Is that yours?'

Tamsin shook her head. 'Is it yours?' she asked, stupidly.

'No.' The boy leaned forward and tapped the shoulder of an older man in a pale grey trench coat. 'Excuse me, sir: does that case belong to you?' His voice was respectful and refined, the accent upper class without a hint of arrogance.

The man frowned, shook a no, turned back to his paper.

Tamsin and the boy each read the same thoughts in the other's face. When the train jolted, they both jumped. But it was just a false start; another jerk and they were moving again. Tamsin looked away, suddenly sheepish. No one else seemed concerned about the case; surely they were both being paranoid.

But her gaze was drawn back. Tamsin's mind played forward to the blast, the train carriage crumpled like a Coke can. Though of course, she wouldn't see that. She was sitting next to the suitcase; she would be killed outright. *Tamsin Jarvis, daughter of the conductor*

Bertrand Jarvis, was killed outright in the attacks of 25 November. Unless the pane of glass was thick enough to protect her, just to begin with. Maybe it would shatter, or melt down onto her, sticking her clothes to her skin...

At Embankment, the same thing again: one lot of passengers shuffling off, the next lot starting to push their way on prematurely. And all the time the suitcase squatting there, unclaimed. At the last minute, Tamsin stood up and burrowed to the exit. Two seconds later the tall boy followed her out. Neither of them said anything.

In the bustle of the platform, Tamsin felt their fears start to shrink into silliness. The boy headed decisively for the help-point phone, only to find it was broken. As they discussed what to do, their convictions gave way to embarrassment. At last Tamsin said, quite firmly, that she thought they had both overreacted.

The boy laughed nervously. 'Right. Bloody hell. Don't know about you, but I could really do with a drink.'

'I was meant to be meeting friends in Camberwell...' She looked up at him. There was a charming, improbable smattering of freckles across the bridge of his very straight nose. 'But yes, a drink would be lovely, yes.'

He held out his hand, smiling for the first time. 'I'm Chris.'

On the escalator, Tamsin felt the elation she associated with playing truant, but there was something else, too: an intimacy thrown over them first by fear and now, increasingly, foolishness. Yet at the entrance to the station, they both paused and breathed in deeply, tasting concrete in the damp November air. The world was newly sweet.

Chris took her to Gordon's Wine Bar on Villiers Street. 'A real gem of a place,' he said loudly, as they made their way down the little stone staircase. The bar had low-vaulted ceilings and red candles stuck into old wine bottles, each with a dusty ruff of stalactites. The clientele was mostly male and middle-aged; but there were also some groups of younger drinkers playing for sophistication, and a fair-haired couple with matching hiking boots and a *Rough Guide*. Tamsin was nervous about her fake ID – thus far, she'd done most of her underage drinking in Camden pubs – so Chris, already eighteen, went up to buy the drinks. As she waited, she gazed round at the framed newspaper clippings, the cobwebs (evidently encouraged), the line-up of bottles behind the bar.

Tamsin was indulging in an old, childish game of deciding which instrument each wine bottle would be – some were square-shouldered like violins, others sloped gently from the neck like double basses – when the fear she'd felt in the tube rose up again. What if, at this very moment, people were dying because she and Chris had been too – too what? too selfish? too shy? – to act?

'How will we know what's happened?' she asked Chris, as he placed a little carafe of red and two glasses on the table in front of her.

Chris shrugged. He started to pour out their wine, still standing, not meeting her eyes.

'It was definitely nothing.' He sat down opposite her, tucking his long legs under the table with difficulty. Tamsin waited for him to settle, then lifted her wine glass and tipped her head to one side.

'Cheers.'

The clink of their glasses registered as a punctuation mark. Somehow, it had been agreed that neither of them would mention the suitcase again.

Their conversation was unremarkable: where they lived, what A-levels, how many siblings. Hearing in each other's voices the same expensive educations, he confessed, a little shyly, to Rugby ('but on a bursary, you know'), she to St Paul's. They ascertained that, aged fourteen, they had both been to the same teenage charity ball, where a friend of Tamsin's had kissed a record twenty-five boys in the space of two hours. Perhaps Chris had been one of them? Tamsin described her friend: tallish, dyed blonde hair, heavy eyeliner? Chris didn't think so; the girl he had kissed that night – the first girl he had ever kissed – was a brunette with traintracks. And so to kisses, first kisses, bad kisses, aborted kisses, swapping horror stories with that world-weariness peculiar to late adolescence, dismissive and vaunting at the same time. Tamsin referenced a one-night stand, ever-so-casually, and watched Chris's eyes widen briefly, telling against his knowing nod.

'Right.' Tamsin emptied the last of the carafe into Chris's glass. 'My turn,' she said, bending for her handbag. 'Wait a moment ... here it is ... no, *fuck*. Fuck, I was sure I had twenty quid.'

Chris was already on his feet. 'It's fine, really, I've got plenty – I'll get it. Please, allow me,' he added as Tamsin made to protest. 'It would be my pleasure.'

These last words seemed an absurd imitation of someone older. Tamsin started to laugh; but when she saw the discomfort in Chris's face, she softened the laugh to a giggle that was inescapably flirtatious – becoming, without quite meaning to, a girl being bought a drink by a boy who wanted to buy it for her.

He came back with a bottle this time. 'Friend of mine, he did a gap year working in Bordeaux, just picking grapes to start with, bloody hard work ... anyway, we're meant to be tasting, what was it, blackberries, and some sort of spice, oh, it was clove, and something else a bit weird – leather, I think...'

Tamsin watched Chris's mouth while he talked. She

was trying to work out whether she fancied him. He was undoubtedly good looking and, to her, a little exotic – his Japanese father, his Hong Kong childhood. But in spite of Chris's charm and the off-beat romance of this impromptu date, she wasn't entirely sure she liked him. There was something in him that couldn't function without outside approval. He wasn't a show-off, exactly, but he needed an audience.

(Later, she would forget this. In the edited version, only the romance would remain.)

Chris's hand hovered near the book of Beethoven Sonatas, now lying on the table underneath Tamsin's bag. 'Uh, may I?'

He opened it gently. 'All these notes … I tried once, but I was no good. Think I just about made Grade 5.' He shook his head in admiration. 'I'd love to hear you play. Seriously, I think musicians must be the closest thing to angels.'

For a moment Tamsin thought it was a bad pick-up line; but one look at Chris's face told her he was in earnest. She decided that she didn't fancy him.

'Are you going to be a professional?'

Tamsin nodded, then remembered to add a modest grimace. 'If I make it. It's pretty tough.'

Chris was impressed. 'What about the rest of your family? Are they musical, too?'

'My – yes, my mum's a singer, actually. And my sister plays the oboe.' Tamsin found herself reluctant to say who her father was.

Chris's thoughts were rather more straightforward. He did fancy Tamsin, and he wanted to kiss her. She was tough and edgy and – a word that had powerful mystique for Chris – *artistic*. He was entranced. The more they talked, the more certain he felt that they had been brought together by fate and irresistible mutual attraction.

Everything about the evening seemed tinged with inevitability.

They had had nothing to eat. By 9 p.m. when they stood up to leave, they were both fairly drunk. On the stairs, Chris dared a hand in the small of her back. Not wanting to embarrass him, Tamsin let it stay there; though she had a dim premonition that this would mean more serious embarrassment for both of them later.

But later never came. As soon as they reached ground level, Tamsin's phone began to buzz.

'Shit, loads of missed calls. Sorry—'

Tamsin wedged the phone between ear and hunched right shoulder, leaving her hands free to fumble with the zip on her parka. Chris could hear the low chirrup of the dial tone.

'Mummy? Mummy, is that you?'

Her face went tight as she listened. 'Okay. I'm coming home.'

Tamsin pocketed her phone and started on the zip for a second time. 'I have to go.' Her voice was hard and strangely adult, different from any other tone he'd heard her use that evening.

'Is everything all right?' Something warned him not to touch her again.

'I can't explain. Sorry. I have to go.' It was a pedestrian-only road but she checked for cars out of habit, three quick pecks of the head. Chris called after her but she was already gone, over the street and into the bright tiled mouth of the tube station.

He didn't have her phone number. He didn't even know her surname.

And so for Chris – who never had the chance to discover that Tamsin didn't want to be kissed – the evening retained all the allure of unrealised possibility. Time magnified her charms in his memory. Tamsin informed his type; he looked for her height in other women, her slightness, those small, widely spaced breasts that had barely nudged the fabric of her T-shirt. To say he thought about her constantly would be an exaggeration, but she was, in a sense, always there – as an ideal, a measure against which everyone else was found wanting.

* * *

On the phone, her mother had been unintelligible. Tamsin assumed she had somehow uncovered the affair, but in fact, her father had simply announced that he was leaving and that he had been planning to leave for years. The trigger? Serena's sixth-form scholarship to the Purcell School: Bertrand had wanted to wait until both his daughters had a secure future ahead of them before disrupting their home environment. Now that Serena's musical career was more or less assured, he felt free to leave.

This was what he was explaining to his wife, for the fourth time that evening, as Tamsin came through the front door.

'My god. My fucking god.' Roz's voice was muted with disbelief. 'You actually think you've been *considerate*, don't you, you *shit*—'

In the hall, Tamsin hung up her coat; she felt as if she were preparing for an interview. The house smelled like it always did: wood polish, old suppers, stargazer lilies, home.

When she stepped into the sitting room, both her parents turned to look at her. Her mother was dressed, incongruously, in a ritzy black cocktail number with a swishy little fringe of bugle beads around the hem. Her usual five-inch heels had been kicked off; standing in her bare feet on the thick carpet, Roz looked very small indeed. The corn on her middle right toe shone in the lamplight.

'Your father's leaving us. He can't wait to get away, apparently. He's been sick of us for years, apparently.'

Bertrand took a step towards his wife, one hand raised. 'Roz, that's not fair, that's not what I said—'

'But luckily for you, he's deigned to stick around till now. So as *not to disrupt your home environment*. Now, isn't that nice of him, Tamsin? Aren't you going to say thank you to your father?'

'Roz, this is between you and me. I won't have you using Tam like this—'

'He says there's no one else, but I almost wish there was. I almost wish there was.' Roz fought down a knot of hysteria. 'I think I could understand that better than this, this *dismissal*—'

'Valerie Fischer.' Tamsin kept her voice as clear and steady as she could. Even in her anger, she was aware of the need to enjoy this longed-for consummation. 'It's Valerie Fischer, isn't it, Dad?'

Father and daughter held one another's gaze like lovers for three, four, five seconds before they remembered Roz.

She was motionless, a visionary staring through them to a strange new past.

* * *

From then on, everything was different. Roz was unable even to choose between red and green pesto without consulting her daughter. There was no longer any question of Tamsin leaving home; Roz needed her too much. She attended the Royal College of Music as planned, but stayed in her old childhood bedroom at home in Holland Park. After years of friction, mother and daughter were now inseparable. Tamsin acted as spokesperson, supplying all the fury and indignation and disgust that Roz herself couldn't seem to muster.

'Tamsin's my sellotape,' Roz would tell her friends. 'She's the only thing holding me together.' She gave her mirthless laugh.

Tamsin's friends were wary of her, unnerved by the thought of her long silence. She was newly inscrutable. She even looked different: gone were the Nirvana T-shirts and the belly-button rings. At first, her new role – as her mother's counsellor, comforter, guard dog – felt like dressing up. Then she became it, and it grew harder and harder to remember a time when she and Roz hadn't been bound to each other in this way. The scar above her belly button faded, from aubergine through lavender to a little raised sickle-shape the colour of clotted cream.

It was around this time that Roz retired from singing, after twenty-four years as a soprano soloist. When she and Bertrand first met, Roz had been a rising star in the opera world, already well known for her unexpectedly powerful vibrato. Her size was her USP: it seemed extraordinary that such a small person could make such a big noise with apparently so little effort. It also helped that she was beautiful. 'Aha. Roz Andersen, the siren with the siren,' Bertrand had quipped when they were introduced. Two weeks before their wedding, *The Sunday Times* ran a picture of Roz on the cover of the colour supplement, playing Desdemona in a big-budget ROH production of Verdi's *Otello*. Then Bertrand's career really took off, and together they became moderately famous. They were the golden-haired golden couple of music, rarely absent from *Tatler*.

Cigarettes had always been an occasional pleasure for Roz, a guilty secret kept carefully hidden from the agency that insured her voice. After the break-up,

16

though, she took up smoking in earnest. A pack a day, then two packs. Everyone was worried. Roz lost count of the times she was warned about ruining her voice. Her response was unvarying: 'I know. I don't care.' She took grim solace in this deliberate self-sabotage, which seemed to her to correspond with the magnitude of Bertrand's crime.

(In fact, Roz's voice was going anyway. Killing it off with a nicotine addiction induced by the trauma of separation was marginally preferable to watching her reputation fall into a slow, age-related decline.)

It was Tamsin, with her own unlimited supply of anger, who finally persuaded her mother to convert grief into rage. After three months of crying and smoking, Roz put on her sequinned Louboutins and climbed up onto the roof of Bertrand's precious Merc, with a steely Tamsin and two fearful, admiring neighbours (both women) looking on. The next day, she distributed his wine cellar amongst her friends.

During the divorce process the *Daily Mail* got in touch, hoping for photographs. Together, Roz and Tamsin sifted through two decades' worth of holiday snaps to find the perfect pose: Bertrand on the beach, off-duty, paunch relaxed, clutching a can of Boddingtons. The amphitheatre of his gut. In a second photograph he and his moobs reclined on a deckchair. A third showed him sad-arsed under a beach shower, muffin-tops slopping over the waistband of his designer trunks. The *Mail* ran all three. The headline was 'Conductor in the Odium'.

When Roz moved out, Tamsin moved with her. Bertrand offered to pay the rent on a separate flat, closer to the Royal College; but this, like all his attempts at rapprochement, was met by the cool, almost professional hatred that had come to define Tamsin's relations with him.

There were no boyfriends during the Royal College

years. On her one, brief visit to Roz's therapist, in the immediate aftermath of the divorce, Tamsin had been diagnosed with 'trust issues'. 'That's unoriginal,' Tamsin had told the shrink, feeling herself equally unoriginal even as she said it: the privileged rich kid from a broken home, wisecracking back to her jaded psych. Since then, several of her friends had suggested the same thing – that her father's behaviour made it hard for her to have any faith in men. Tamsin had another explanation: the Royal College boys simply weren't to her taste. They were too precious, too aware of their own talent. She slept with a couple of them, but more out of a sense of obligation to a hedonistic student lifestyle than any real desire. Mostly, though, she was at home with Roz, or working at her piano.

Occasionally she still thought about the boy on the train. The faint aversion was gone. She remembered only that he had been good looking, and that there had been wine, and candlelight, and an exhilarating sense of adventure. Most of all she remembered herself, with the disconcerting feeling she was remembering someone else.

Then she graduated from the College, fell in love with a history teacher several years her senior, and forgot about Chris completely.

* * *

When Tamsin was nineteen, her shoulders lost their angles; her arms and legs filled out; her nose and jaw took on a solidity that was unmistakably Bertrand's. Her hair darkened to his exact shade of dirty gold, and even her newly swollen breasts appeared to belong more to her father's side of the family than her mother's.

Alarmed by the weight gain, Tamsin went to see her GP. She certainly wasn't fat, but she was a lot bigger than she had been six months ago. Was it the Pill? Dr Lott didn't think so. She scrolled briskly back up through her notes, rows of Listerine-green data on a convex black screen giving their laconic account of Tamsin's life. Menstruation had started late, hadn't it? This was probably just the tail-end of a mildly delayed puberty. 'It happens sometimes. Nothing to be worried about. You're a healthier weight for your height now, actually. It's really not a problem.'

But it was. The mirror gave her back her father's face, leonine, handsome, hated.

Four

The history teacher was called Callum Dempster. He and
Tamsin met in the canteen of St Timothy's, the East
London comprehensive where Callum was deputy head
of humanities. Newly graduated from the Royal College,
Tamsin was playing keyboard in an Arts Council-funded
workshop designed to introduce children from disadvan-
taged backgrounds to classical music. Callum was embarrassed that he'd never heard of her famous father; she
was delighted.

After five years at Cambridge, one year in Berlin and
nearly a decade in London, Callum's Glaswegian accent was
as strong as it had been when he left home. He hadn't
consciously held on to it, but he'd never tried to lose it,
either: in his experience, it had always been a social advantage. At Cambridge, many of his privately educated peers
felt reassured by his background. If someone like Callum
could make it from a high rise on the banks of the Clyde
to rooms in King's, then the system wasn't entirely unfair.
He also added colour. Making assumptions based chiefly
on *Trainspotting*, people would talk to him about drugs –
only to learn that he didn't even smoke. But a paracriminal
prestige had clung to him anyway. Callum was tough, Callum

20

was authentic, Callum was somehow more real than anyone who came from Wiltshire or Surrey or Hampstead.

Tamsin was a member of the Socialist Workers Party – something Callum teased her about so mercilessly that, six months into their relationship, she stopped going to the meetings. But she still read the email newsletters, and Callum still represented, for her, a vague yet unequivocally positive concept she called 'the Real World'.

So she was disappointed when he landed his dream job: teaching Classics at a prep school near Chalfont St Peter, about an hour's fast cycle ride outside London.

'I don't understand why you don't want to make a difference. Those children at your school, what's going to happen to them if people like you give up on them?' She was washing up, something she only did when she was angry.

Callum explained, patiently, that he wasn't making a difference at St Timothy's, he was just marking time. 'And anyhow, Tam, even if I could make a difference, it would never be big enough to justify how shite the job is. I'm not interested in crowd control. I'm interested in teaching. I'm not being defeatist here, I'm being realistic. And honest. I want to enjoy my life.'

The job at the prep school, Denham Hall, provided him with small classes of well-behaved children and a salary that meant he could finally put down a deposit on a flat. In the long holidays, he had time to start writing a book he'd been thinking about since his Masters: a study of the culture of combat in Roman society, and its impact on modern conceptions of warfare.

Once again, his accent came in handy. It was as classless at Denham Hall as it had been at St Timothy's. In both schools, it won him unworked-for respect.

* * *

Callum's Cambridge friends had long since abandoned their Braudel and taken jobs as bankers, lawyers, management consultants. All of them were home-owners; and, with a few exceptions (Will Heatherington, devoted playboy; Colin Warner, probably gay; Leo Goulding, fledging neurosurgeon and workaholic), all of them were married.

And then Leo got engaged, to a pretty, plump anaesthetist called Bex. They celebrated with drinks at their new house in Herne Hill. Tamsin went to the party with Callum, a little reluctantly. She was eight years younger than him and she found his clever, older friends intimidating.

She also resented the ridiculous fancy dress that Callum's friends found so amusing. It seemed absurd that all these intelligent people, now mostly in their thirties, should want to make themselves foolish in this way. Tonight's theme was A&E: many guests had simply come in lab coats or pilfered scrubs, but there were also plenty of full-blown head wounds, pregnancies, crutches and stethoscopes. The room was decorated with crepe bandages and surgical masks. Even the playpen set up in the corner for the few couples who already had babies had been draped with a Red Cross flag. Tamsin had let Callum stick a plaster on her cheek, but that was as far as she was prepared to go.

'No no no that's pre*cise*ly the problem. The privileging of a university degree over all other forms of higher education,' said a short girl wearing a tight white tank top covered in fake blood. Tamsin had met her several times before but she couldn't remember her name. 'If that doesn't encourage elitism, then...'

Leo, their host, shook his head impatiently. 'I just don't think we can begin to understand what the world might look like to someone without certain basic advantages. And I'm not just talking financially.'

Tamsin had been stuck in this conversation for over twenty minutes and she was bored. Neither the girl, whom she didn't like, nor Leo, whom she did, had thought to ask her opinion at any point. She went to drink her wine but her glass was empty. Callum was nowhere to be seen.

'Tamsin Jarvis! Looking as ravishing as ever!'

Will Heatherington inserted himself between the girl and Tamsin and deposited a loud kiss on each of Tamsin's cheeks. He was one of Callum's closest friends; for three years at Cambridge, they had been on the university water polo team together.

For once, Tamsin was pleased to see Will. She actually knew him independently of Callum: his family had lived near hers in Holland Park, and Tamsin had encountered Will at intervals throughout her childhood, mostly at their parents' parties. She remembered him as a boisterous teenager, teasing her unkindly about her skinny legs. Now thirty-two, Will was good-looking in the most obvious way: tall, with naturally olive skin, glossy dark blond hair, Bambi eyes and strong cheekbones. He could have been a mid-nineties boy-band pin-up. Only the full mouth was out of register. There was a hint of the predator about his pout, a complacency that was somehow aggressively expectant.

'Tamsin, you're dry, we can't have that.' Will produced a bottle of champagne and started to fill her glass. These days he was scrupulously polite to Tamsin; but there was always something in his tone that gave her the impression he was secretly laughing at her. 'Hope you don't mind, Leo, I invited some reinforcements for later. Including two hot lesbians,' he went on, turning to the girl in the blood-stained tank top.

'I'm not gay any more,' she said.

Will grinned and ruffled her carefully styled hair, which was already sparked with grey at the sides. 'I'll believe that when I see it, darling.'

'Reinforcements, yes, that's fine,' said Leo, detaching himself from the little group. 'Sorry – got to go rescue Bex – she's been cornered by those orthopods she was too nice not to invite—'

'Sooooo,' said Will, resting one forearm on Tamsin's shoulder and the other on the un-lesbian lesbian's, as if they were all jolly chums. 'Isn't this nice? Leo and Bex, the beating of two tender hearts as one, the unimpeded marriage of true minds, etcetera, etcetera?'

'Mmmm,' said Tamsin, who never quite knew how to respond to Will's florid speaking style.

'Talking of true love,' he went on, 'has my secretary managed to keep her paws off your boyfriend?'

'Leah's not your secretary,' Tamsin replied evenly. She was remembering why she disliked Will so much.

'Leah?' asked the un-lesbian, suddenly interested. 'As in Jonno-and-Baz-in-one-weekend Leah?'

'The same.' Will bowed his head.

'Has she been trying it on with Callum?' the girl asked Tamsin. She looked amused.

'No, she's just his flatmate.'

'What, like they *live* together?'

'Mm-hmm.'

The girl raised one dark eyebrow. 'And how do you feel about that?'

Leah was a PR officer at Will's law firm, referred to by Will either as his secretary or 'our resident serial shagger'. But despite the girl's reputation, Tamsin didn't feel threatened. In fact, Tamsin never felt threatened by anyone where Callum was concerned: he adored her, and she knew it. Now, though, under the pressure of scrutiny, Tamsin found herself incapable of communicating this conviction. She took an overlarge gulp of champagne and blinked to clear the tears that the fizz brought to her eyes.

'Leah's cool, we don't see that much of her, but she seems cool,' she heard herself say, lamely. The un-lesbian stared at her for a moment, then turned back to Will.

'I heard she fucked Charlie Huffman.'

Tamsin held out her empty glass for more champagne. She was, if possible, having even less fun than she'd anticipated.

Callum, on the other hand, had been having a wonderful evening. He was not generally prone to sentiment, but tonight, fondly, tipsily, surely, he felt everyone he loved in the world was here, in this room. There was little Jake Simonson, excitedly telling everyone about his first architectural commission. There were Victor and Caitlin, a serious, hard-working pair of actuaries, deeply bronzed and full of stories from the year-long trip to India that everyone thought they'd never make; Zander Pownall, messing about in the playpen with his two-year-old son, no trace of the long depression he'd suffered in his mid-twenties; Antoine Namani, another neurosurgeon, making everyone laugh with his medically inflected rap ('I'm malignant, you're benign, when I lay down a rhyme, I metastasise straight into yo' spine'). And, of course, Tamsin, his Tamsin, beautiful tonight in a long wrap skirt tied high at the waist, her sulkiness visible only to him – which in itself felt like something precious. It was, thought Callum fuzzily, a roomful of happy endings.

Fetching a fresh beer from the drinks table, Callum noticed a tall man he'd never met before, dressed in a vamped-up nurse's outfit: tiny white skirt, choppy blonde wig, lumpily stuffed fake breasts. Under a grainy layer of foundation, the ghosts of several large freckles were visible. It was easily the most outrageous costume of the evening. When Callum complimented him on it, the man thanked him by lifting up the skirt to display a pair of women's knickers, his penis squashed obscenely behind the sheer fabric.

'Practically standard issue these days,' the nurse-man said cheerfully. 'No self-respecting officer seen dead at a party without see-through panties.'

'You're in the army?' Callum was immediately interested.

'Yes, sir. Just finished at Sandhurst,' said the man with irrepressible pride. He tugged off the wig, revealing a full head of closely-cropped black hair, which he proceeded to scratch with the innocent abandon of a dog shaking itself after a swim.

'And how did you find Sandhurst?'

'Still recovering from the final exercise. It was a total CF.'

'Is that the ten-day one? Diamond Victory?'

'Dynamic Victory. It's a beast.' The boy looked impressed. 'How do you know that?'

Callum smiled, pleased with the compliment. 'I'm writing a book, a sort of military history thing ... Sorry – what's a "CF"?'

'CF, charlie foxtrot – means "cluster fuck", basically a major beasting. Also a verb, as in, I got cluster-fucked. Which you do, at Sandhurst. That's the whole point.'

The two men laughed and clinked beer bottles properly this time, acknowledging their approval of one another.

'Is it true that you lot are using "muggle" for "civilian" now?'

They were fifteen minutes into a discussion on military slang when Callum noticed Tamsin watching them from across the room with an uninterpretable expression on her face. Callum waved her over, eager to show off his new find.

'Here, Tam, come on, I want you to meet—'

'Chris.' Tamsin said the name at the same time as Callum. 'It is Chris, isn't it?'

'Have we...?' The boy was embarrassed. Then his

soft mouth pulled tight in an enormous grin. 'My god – it's Tamsin!'

'Do you know each other?' Callum asked, unnecessarily.

'I can't believe you recognised me under all this shit!' Chris was still grinning broadly. 'How do you guys—'

'Callum's my boyfriend.' As if to illustrate this, Tamsin kissed Callum on the cheek. There was a longish pause. 'So ... what are you up to these days, Chris?'

'Well, actually, I'm in the army—' Chris began, but he was interrupted by a violent thump on his shoulder. Leo's brother Edwin, a small, smooth-faced man with thick dark eyebrows, had come to claim his friend.

'Sorry to interrupt, but we've been waiting for this bastard to come and do shots with us for over half an hour.'

'Great to meet you.' Chris shook Callum's hand vigorously. 'And – and to see you too, Tamsin,' he added, looking slightly confused.

'Right fucker, your first one's a triple,' said Edwin, as he marched Chris over to their friends.

'Where do you know him from?' Callum asked Tamsin.

She looked vague. 'Ages ago. I don't know him at all, really.' Tamsin's unusually large eyelids gave her face a sleepy, sensual expression. When she had been drinking it sometimes seemed to Callum as if it cost her a physical effort to keep her eyes from closing altogether.

'Callum, you dirty great faggot, where have you been all my life?' It was Will again, pulling Callum into a back-slapping hug. Tamsin made a face at Callum over Will's shoulder, but allowed herself to be led off to meet Will's 'reinforcements', who were busy re-stocking the drinks table with stronger stuff. The playpen was being packed away.

* * *

Tamsin woke from a dream about Bolognese sauce to the smell of Bolognese sauce. Then she remembered it was Sunday, and the smell modulated to bacon. She squinted at the other side of the bed. Callum was already up. Hoping to defer her hangover for another five minutes, she pulled the duvet over her head and settled back down into the pillow.

The flush of the toilet woke her again. Tamsin came out from under the duvet and the smell adjusted itself for a third and final time. The door to the little en suite bathroom was ajar.

'Callum. God. You could at least shut the door,' she croaked.

Callum emerged from the bathroom with an apologetic grin. He opened the window, filling the room with the fumes of the Edgware Road and the sickly strawberry scent from the shisha bar on the ground floor.

'Shit, I feel rough.' Tamsin pressed three fingers to each temple and glared up at Callum. 'Why aren't you in more pain?'

Callum sat down on the bed. 'Because I wasn't half as full of it as you were, you nugget.' He leaned in for a kiss, but Tamsin clamped her lips shut.

'Mm-mmm.' She shook her head. 'I don't taste good. And I'm not kissing you while this room still stinks. En suite. Jesus. Maybe the least romantic proposition *ever*.'

'All right, all right,' he laughed, running a hand over his khaki-coloured hair, which immediately sprang back to attention. 'I'll get us some coffee.'

Callum came back with coffee, toast and yesterday's newspapers, the cutlery jittering on the tray as he bent to settle it in Tamsin's lap. He perched on the windowsill with his own mug, watching Tamsin through steam lit white by the morning sun. Her loose cotton vest sagged in the middle and he could see the two parallel lines marking the start of her breasts. In the beginning, Tamsin had been embarrassed by her breasts, which were full and heavy and sat low on her chest. It had taken Callum a long time to get her to sleep without her bra on, and even longer to persuade her to stand up naked in front of him. Her left breast was noticeably larger than her right, something she hated and he adored.

'You perving?' asked Tamsin, without looking up from her paper.

'Who, me? Never.'

There was a longish silence. Then Callum said, 'Chris seems like a nice guy.' The words had a slightly processed, unnatural timbre. This was because Callum had been preparing to say them ever since Tamsin woke up.

'Mmm?' Tamsin glanced up distractedly. 'Oh yeah. Yeah, he does.'

'How did you say you knew him?'

'I didn't say, did I?' Now Tamsin put the paper down, frowning slightly. 'I don't remember if I said. I don't think I did.' She paused. 'It was my first year at College. He was going out with a friend of mine for a bit. So I saw him a couple of times, through her. Then they broke up and I didn't see him again. Until last night.'

Tamsin was surprised by both the lie and the facility with which she'd invented it.

'Which friend?' Callum wanted to know.

'Girl called Kitty,' Tamsin said. 'Don't think you ever met her.'

'You didn't know him biblically?'

'What?'

'Did you – sorry.' Callum winced at his own question.

'Christ, Callum!' Tamsin shook her head in exasperation. 'No. No I did not sleep with him.'

'Okay. Sorry. Tam, I'm sorry. I just wondered. I don't

29

know why.' Smiling sheepishly, Callum padded over to the bed and got in beside Tamsin.

'Am I allowed to kiss you yet?' he asked.

Tamsin put two fingers to his lips. 'Only if you promise to stop being an idiot,' she said, looking stern. 'And be gentle, okay? My head *hurts*.'

Callum made a little growling noise and pretended to bite her fingers. Then he kissed her, very softly, on the upper lip. The blue-and-green-checked duvet had slipped halfway down the bed. Callum tugged it up over their shoulders and drew Tamsin towards him for a hug, tucking her head under his chin. Her hair smelled of Herbal Essences shampoo and Marlboro Lights.

'I love you,' Tamsin said to Callum's collarbone. 'I love you and I really should get up. I'm so behind with my practice it's not even funny.' She yawned and stretched, then drew in for another kiss. 'Right. That's it. I'm up.'

Callum lay with his hands behind his head and watched her dress. Halfway through the process – pale yellow cotton bra and faded jeans, no T-shirt – she went into the bathroom to clean her teeth and came back with a thick white blob of moisturiser above each corner of her upper lip. This was a preventative measure, talisman against the two deep lines flanking her father's mouth. He watched her twisting the dome of her deodorant into her armpits. As she waited for it to dry, she held her arms away from her sides in a slightly simian pose. Callum knew all of this by heart and he loved it.

* * *

On the way from Callum's flat to the bus stop, Tamsin stopped between the Halal Fish'n'Chip shop and the Discount Drug Co. She wanted to undo it all, to go back and tell Callum the truth about Chris. She had never lied to him about anything like this before, and she wasn't entirely sure why she had now.

But then, she thought, she had never told anyone about what happened – or rather, what didn't happen – on the tube that day. At first, the enormity of her parents' break-up had simply displaced everything around it. Later, when she remembered the incident, she felt no compulsion to turn it into an anecdote. As a little girl, one of Tamsin's greatest pleasures was to eat an apple and throw away the core, in the knowledge that she was the first and last human being ever to set eyes on the sleek mahogany pips at its centre. A similar impulse had governed her silence on the subject of Chris and the suitcase. The story formed a secret fold in the fabric of her life, and it seemed that to talk about it would be to spoil it, somehow.

Tamsin had been staring unseeingly into the window of the Discount Drug Co. – which, inexplicably, sold nothing even remotely pharmaceutical, just fake Gucci handbags and Louis Vuitton luggage sets. The salesman saw her looking and came to the door. 'You want real leather, I give you good price.'

Tamsin shook her head and moved away. She couldn't confess to Callum now. The fact that she'd lied in the first place would only create grounds for suspicion when really, she knew, there were none.

On the bus, the Edgware Road moved past jerkily, in instalments. Starbucks, M&S, Tesco Metro, traffic lights. Four newsagents all offering money transfer and mobile phone unlocking. More traffic lights. The man sitting in front of her got off at Paddington. Tamsin watched him down the street, thinking that his short, tight Afro had looked like a black version of one of those green kitchen scourers. She wondered whether it felt anything like a scourer, then wondered if that was a terrible thing to wonder. She realised that she'd never touched a black person's hair and the thought suddenly seemed very shameful to her.

This was the sort of thing that bothered Tamsin. It also bothered her that she was twenty-five and still living with her mother in Notting Hill. Notting Hill itself bothered her. Taking the bus, she saw the Burberry hijabs and oil-black puffa jackets steadily giving way to faded denim and Havaiana flip flops. And then, when she got off, the walk down from the relative buzz of Pembridge Road into the hush of the side streets with their milk-white villas and dense green gardens. In central London, quiet like this has a direct correlation with money.

Quietest of all was Ashcombe Mews, where Tamsin lived with Roz, and, some of the time, her younger sister Serena (Beanie). Tamsin unlocked the door of Number 8 and stepped from the sunny street into the dark hallway. When her mother bought the house five years ago with the money from the divorce settlement, she had immediately painted all of the ground-floor rooms a rich midnight blue. She also coloured her long, naturally white-blonde hair black with a home-dye kit from Boots. *Colour therapy*, she had snapped at anyone who dared to wonder why. Then the dye grew out, leaving a ragged chevron of blonde and grey down the middle of her head. Smoking in dark glasses, Roz had looked like Ozzy Osbourne.

All this was before she discovered her new vocation. It was her friend Meredith Sykes (fifty-four, twice divorced, CEO of a successful lingerie chain) who first came up with the idea of the lectures. Initially, Roz was unconvinced. Her experience of heartbreak seemed too private to be of interest to anyone else. 'But these are powerful universal tropes you've tapped into,' Meredith had urged. 'What you did to Bertrand – people dream about that sort of stuff all the time, but you actually went ahead and did it. Of course people will want to hear about it.'

She was right. Within a year, Roz was giving several talks a month on the healing properties of revenge. The audiences were small and exclusive: she advertised solely through word of mouth, and charged a considerable amount for her time. Roz found she liked the work. It went some way to filling the gap that singing had left in her life. She was still performing, after all, and she was still very good at it: her audiences loved her for the way she tempered the rhetoric of empowerment with just the right amount of self-irony. Grateful clients would send her photographs and even videos of their own acts of retribution, which Roz incorporated into her PowerPoint slideshow. She was especially popular with divorce parties.

These days Roz's hair was still black, but she had it done professionally now, by Errol at Matthew Hershington's in Maida Vale. Every three weeks, Errol 'curated' her hair (his word) into an inky bob shaped steeply at the back. Tamsin had been the one to encourage these visits in the first place ('You need to start looking after yourself, Mummy, spend some time on *you* for a change'), but she didn't like the cut. It was too severe. Her mother's neck was unforgivingly exposed, rigged with tendons that longer hair had kept hidden. She looked harder, as well as older.

But Roz was not quite the indomitable ideal she endorsed in her lectures. Her anger, unlike Tamsin's, contained impurities. It kept reverting back to a baser metal: sadness.

Today Tamsin found her mother hunched over her laptop, engrossed in a website with a familiar mid-blue banner at the top of the page.

'*Facebook?* Mummy, what are you doing on there? Please don't tell me you've signed up, it's really naff when older people—'

'It's fine, I'm using a different name, she doesn't even know I'm looking.' Roz spoke quickly, with a low intensity to her voice that Tamsin dreaded.

'Who doesn't know you're looking?' Tamsin asked, although there could be only one answer.

'Tammy, look, it's *her* page. I can see everything about her – all her photos, all the stupid things she posts on her board—'

'Wall,' Tamsin murmured, bending forward so that she could see over her mother's shoulder.

'God, but she's a shameless self-promoter,' Roz went on. 'Every bloody concert … here, listen to this: "Glyndebourne rehearsals start tomorrow, so excited! Adès might just be my number one all-time hero, can't believe I get to work with him!" Who cares? Why does she think anyone's interested in her stupid little life?'

'Okay, that's enough. Let me have it.' Tamsin put out a hand for the laptop.

Roz hesitated, momentarily defiant; but then her shoulders sagged in defeat and she relinquished the laptop meekly. She applied her index fingers to the corners of her eyes to stop two tears that were forming there. 'I just don't understand how he can bear to be with someone like that. Why her? *Why her?*'

'What *I* don't understand,' said Tamsin, grimly, 'is why you're still asking yourself these pointless questions. No, really, I don't get it. How can you still be giving headspace to someone who treated you so badly? Think about it, Roz' – Tamsin reserved her mother's name for moments like this – 'it just doesn't make any sense, does it? Well, does it?'

They had arrived, with practised speed, at an old impasse in an old argument. Roz shrugged helplessly. She couldn't explain why she still thought about Bertrand so much. Her daughter's fierce logic left no room for the fact that he was there in her dreams every other night, being kind.

Tamsin raked her shoulder-length hair away from her face with her fingertips and held it scrunched at the back of her head. 'Sometimes it's almost as if you've forgotten what he did,' she said, sitting down heavily on the sofa next to Roz.

These were the opening lines of a story they both knew very well indeed, a story that began with the basic facts of Bertrand's betrayal and ended, by way of a list (not comprehensive) of the lies he had told, with a series of exhortations to emotional strength and independence. The trajectory of her mother's response – from silent tears through increasingly resolute sniffs to the desired declarations of outrage and contempt – was as familiar to Tamsin as the story itself.

'Shall I tell you something, Tamsin? I'm *glad* that what happened happened. I really am. To think that I lived with a monster like that for so many years with *no idea* of his capacity for *cruelty*—'

When the initial fervour of her renewed indignation had subsided, Roz gripped her daughter tightly around the waist and leaned her head sideways onto Tamsin's shoulder.

'What would I do without you.' It was a statement, not a question.

'Mmmm.' Tamsin's features contracted briefly in a frown her mother couldn't see. Then she stood up and smiled brightly at Roz. 'Right. Cup of tea and a cigarette?'

Serena was in the kitchen, eating a bowl of artisan ravioli.

'That stuff's expensive, you know,' Tamsin told her sister as she filled the kettle. 'You're not meant to eat it like it's cereal.'

'So?' said Serena through a mouthful of the pasta. 'It's not like you paid for it.'

Serena was wearing nothing but a navy-blue polo shirt belonging to an old boyfriend. On her tiny frame, it functioned as a dress: the sleeves reached past her elbows, the hem skimmed her pinkish knees. Like Roz, Serena was just five foot two. She had fine silvery-blonde hair, which she wore pinned up high in a smooth, glossy twist. Her top two front teeth protruded very slightly, resting behind her lower lip and pushing it forward into a permanent pout. All of this – the hair, the teeth, the twenty-three inch waist – was Roz's. Roz was privately ashamed of how much more strongly she felt the genetic allegiance between herself and her younger daughter. But again and again, she found herself both comforted and moved by the perpetual surprise of this everyday miracle.

Tamsin pushed a cup of tea towards Roz, who was holding her mobile phone away from her at arm's length like a hand mirror in order to read a text message. Her glasses were on the counter, within easy reach. Tamsin bit back her irritation at this and turned it instead on Serena.

'What are you doing here, anyway?' she wanted to know. Serena, who had none of Tamsin's scruples about accepting Bertrand's money, shared a town house in Clapham with three girlfriends. Generally, she only came home if she wanted Roz to look after her in the run-up to a big concert.

'Nice to see you too. I had my driving test yesterday, didn't I? And before you ask' – Serena got up and scraped the last two ravioli into the bin – 'I didn't pass.'

'Bad luck.' Tamsin spoke without a trace of sympathy. 'What happened?'

'I ran over a squirrel.'

Tamsin laughed and some tea exploded out through her nose. She wiped her dripping face on her sleeve, still sniggering.

'It's not funny.' Serena looked upset.

'It is if you have a sense of humour.'

'I don't have time for this.' Serena stalked across the reclaimed flagstones towards the door. 'I've got to practise.'

Tamsin slumped into the chair where her sister had been sitting. In a vase at the centre of the table, six dying tulips formed a histrionic tableau, their heads hanging heavily from the s-bends of their stems. A few petals, faded from red to a weak tea brown, were stuck to the tabletop. From the music room came the sound of Serena warming up her reed in fast, staccato bursts.

Roz tucked her mobile phone into the pocket of her tight black jeans and sat down at the table next to Tamsin. 'You could try to be a bit nicer to Beanie, Tam. She's very disappointed. She really needed to pass that test.'

'No, she didn't. She lives in London. There are buses and tubes and pavements. She doesn't *need* to drive.'

Tamsin was aware that this was the conversational equivalent of picking a newly formed scab, but she said it anyway. She scraped at one of the decomposing tulip petals with her thumbnail as she waited for the reply she didn't want to hear.

'Bean's got a lot of touring coming up this summer. You know that.' Her mother's voice was maddeningly gentle. 'Having a car would make her life a lot easier.'

'Sure. Like it's not easy enough already,' said Tamsin, moving her hand out of reach of a solicitous pat.

'Tammy. Look at me.' Roz pulled her chair closer to the table. She felt slightly awkward, as she often did when called on to play mother to her eldest daughter. 'It *is* easier for her. You *know* it's a specialism, she's a rare commodity. You're one of an overwhelming majority. It was always going to be harder for you.'

This was an excuse that had long since lost its power to comfort Tamsin, even though, outwardly, it still made sense. Serena was a baroque musician; she played the recorder and the oboe d'amore. In the tiny, closed world of Early Music, she was a big talent. It was statistically much more difficult to make it as a concert pianist – as Tamsin was trying to do.

The real reason Tamsin wasn't making it, wasn't ever going to make it, was that although she was very good indeed, very good indeed wasn't quite good enough. Serena was more than good enough. She was indisputably the better musician. Roz's attempts to prevent this unacknowledged fact from coming between her two daughters were proving ineffective. Tamsin's envy, once furtive and self-censoring, no longer bothered to conceal itself. Increasingly, Serena felt the weight of this envy and resented it. It was boring for her to have to downplay her successes the whole time. She was sick of being sensitive.

Tamsin rubbed a bit of petal between her thumb and middle finger and flicked it sulkily across the table. 'I don't care if she's got a concert, she can't have the music room all day. I do have work to do too, you know.' She pushed her chair back from the table with some force and stood up, annoyed by her own petulance yet unable to move away from it.

'Tammy—'

But her daughter was already gone. The kitchen door swung slowly shut behind her, muting the sound of Serena's playing.

*   *   *

Two pints of Foster's, a gin and tonic, the best part of a bottle of wine, a bottle of Beck's, a triple shot of tequila, some more wine, a Jägerbomb, a pint of Stella and a good deal of whisky: it is hardly surprising that the following morning, Chris Kimura remembered very little about his encounter with Tamsin and Callum. In fact, he didn't remember it at all until he was on the train back to Bulford. Chris had spent the night at Edwin's house in Islington, waking early to the aftertaste of the raw onion garnish on one of Pitta the Great's finest doner kebabs. In the bathroom he vomited deliberately and efficiently. Fragments of the night before presented themselves to him as he showered, in no particular order: a taxi ride, a fight outside the kebab shop, Edwin trying to convince everyone to go to Spearmint Rhino, some girls on a bus. Brushing his teeth for the second time, Chris discovered a sadness in himself. He lowered the toothbrush and frowned at his foamy-mouthed reflection for a few moments, trying to locate the origin of this feeling. He spat, rinsed, brushed his teeth again. The onion prevailed.

No one else was up, so Chris let himself out as quietly as he could. He searched his iPod for a song to match the sadness, settling on 'The Boxer' by Simon and Garfunkel, from his playlist 'Bluemood 3'. Despite the title, it was not at all unusual for Chris to listen to this playlist when he was feeling perfectly happy. Chris's favourite songs dealt exclusively with heartbreak and loneliness and futility and loss. Although he had no personal experience of these conditions, the music people wrote about them seemed to him not only the most beautiful, but also the most vital and profound. Learning the piano as a child, he had been fascinated by the minor scales, by the way two simple semitone shifts suffused the dumb bright landscape of the major with a mysterious sorrow. He would practise his minor arpeggios very slowly with his right foot jammed down hard on the sustaining pedal, relishing the sweet ache that swelled at his sternum as the palimpsest of notes gathered and built. Now, at twenty-five, Chris never felt more alive than when a Chopin nocturne or a Coldplay ballad kindled this same unparsable tightness in his chest, full of heft and feeling, signifying *something*.

As the train was pulling out of Waterloo, he remembered talking to an affable man with a Scottish accent, and, much more clearly, that this man was the boyfriend of Tamsin. *Tamsin*. He hadn't recognised her at first. His instinctive reaction, last night and again now, was one of disappointment bordering on distaste. The Tamsin of his memory was otherwordly, sylphlike, radiantly blonde. Now that ideal had been declared invalid by this older girl with darker, coarser hair and large breasts that seemed to pull her shoulders round and down in sad submission to gravity. The lodestar he'd been fixed on for seven years had turned out to be a microlight.

As soon as Chris articulated these thoughts he felt ashamed of them. Then it occurred to him that Tamsin was no longer a girl but a Woman; and, having fitted a word to her new state, Chris found his old admiration returning with fresh force. A Woman. Of *course* that was what she was. He felt a buzz of contempt for his younger self, obsessing over a teenage girl, unequal, till now, to the fuller, sweeter reality of Woman.

Oddly enough, the fact of her boyfriend concerned him less than the difference in her appearance had done. Chris was so accustomed to the idea of not having Tamsin that her unavailability felt somehow expected. Besides, the boyfriend's presence left him in a position that he immediately appreciated as both noble and poignant. The third Schubert Impromptu came on his headphones, then Jeff Buckley's 'Hallelujah'. By the end of 'Bittersweet Symphony' by the Verve, Chris was resolved: the only decent thing to do was nothing. He wouldn't ask Edwin for Tamsin's number. He would make no attempt to find her on Facebook. He would make the sacrifice, he thought, smiling a bittersweet smile at his own benevolence. He would leave their happiness untainted.

When his phone bleeped with a text message inviting him for supper next weekend, it took him several minutes to work out who 'Callum' was.

* * *

Callum genuinely did want to see Chris again. The guy was smart, and he had plenty to say about the army. Mostly, though, the invitation was a gesture of goodwill towards Tamsin – to show he was sorry for being so suspicious, to prove that he had set aside his insecurity about Chris.

Jealousy is never rational; it zooms in, it enlarges, it distorts. In Callum's case, it focused solely on men that Tamsin had slept with. Occasionally this annoyed Tamsin. She found herself wanting to reason with him, to point out that the men she *hadn't* slept with – the what-ifs – were surely far more of a threat to him that the ones she had tried and rejected.

This, however, would have been cruel, and she knew it. When it came to Callum and sex, any sort of challenge was liable to be read as an attack.

There had been just one, ostensibly definitive discussion between the two of them on the subject of Callum's penis. A bold move on Callum's part, this conversation had taken place nearly three years ago, before they had ever even slept together.

It was their fourth date and they were walking along Grand Union Canal after a chilly picnic lunch on Primrose Hill. Inside a plum-coloured houseboat with apricot detailing, someone was frying onions.

Callum kicked a beech mast. It skittered along the path then dropped, almost noiselessly, into the canal. 'There's something you should know about me.'

'MI6?' Tamsin had joked, laughing at his sudden seriousness. She tried to imitate his accent. 'The neem's Deimpster, Cahllum Deimpster.'

'It's about sex.' Callum was straight-faced.

For a terrible moment, Tamsin wanted to giggle. She blew her nose instead. When she looked at Callum again, the urge had passed. 'Go on,' she said, doing her best to sound soberly mature.

'Well – it's difficult for me. I mean really difficult. Please' – he stopped her question with a look – 'hear me out, okay?'

He assured her that there would be sex, just not much of the traditional penetrative kind. His fingers and tongue, he said with a wry smile, were used to compensating for his incompetent penis. 'And it isn't totally defunct. It works maybe forty per cent of the time. Okay, maybe more like thirty. If only I'd kept the receipt for the damn thing.'

Tamsin understood that he was making a joke, but she couldn't laugh at the bitterness in his voice. Instead, she squeezed his hand and said, gently, 'Doesn't it depend a bit on who you're with? I mean, if you feel comfortable...' Already she was thinking that she would be the one to make the difference.

'Yes, actually.' Callum let out a dry chuckle. 'The more I care about a girl, the less likely it is to work. In fact, you can take it as a definite compliment if my penis hates you.'

Tamsin looked around; there was no one in sight apart from a lone dog-walker, over a hundred yards ahead of them and safely out of earshot. 'So ... can you ... masturbate?' she asked, bringing out the last word with difficulty.

Although she had slept with several people, this was the first time she had talked directly about sex with a man.

Callum nodded. 'That's never been an issue.'

A duck laughed in the distance.

'And can I – can I do that to you?'

'Perhaps. You can try.' He frowned. 'Look, it's the same deal. Sometimes it works. Mostly it doesn't.'

Then he had explained that his problem didn't entail infertility. He wanted her to have all the facts so that she could make an informed decision. 'I'm not asking for any guarantee of commitment or anything like that.' Callum coughed to clear the formality from his voice. 'I just didn't want you to find out and be shocked. And you see, the thing is, my last—' He stopped. He'd promised himself that he wasn't going to go into specifics. 'Some women have been cool with it, but others haven't. It's boring for both of us if you have to make excuses later on to spare my feelings. If you're just not up for it, say now and I'll understand.' He sounded almost angry and he couldn't meet her eyes.

Tamsin was moved by his vulnerability. 'Oh, Callum, don't be ridiculous. Of course, of course I don't mind. Of course it's not a problem.'

(And anyway: what else could she say?)

They had stopped under a bridge, its damp bricks padded with the bright olive velvet of moss. Callum cupped Tamsin's face in his hands. It was a long kiss, fuelled by their relief at reaching the end of a difficult discussion.

* * *

Callum was one of those men who cook competitively, with loud remarks about 'plating up' and the joys of offal. He bought his olive oil in huge square cans and shopped in Borough Market at least once a fortnight. This evening he was doing one of his staple dinner party menus: scallops on a minted pea puree followed by slow-cooked rabbit ragout, with panacotta (*dead simple, actually*) for dessert. When the buzzer buzzed, he was up to his elbows in rabbit, picking through the mess of meat to check for the smaller bones.

'I'll get it,' said Tamsin quickly, even though Callum was already wiping his hands clean.

Tamsin had managed to keep her face neutral when Callum told her he'd invited Chris round for supper. Really, she was terrified – terrified that Chris might recount, as an amusing anecdote, the real story of how they met, and expose her version of their history for a fiction. She needed to tell him not to tell – but she had no idea how to communicate this with Callum in the room. Now she hurried over to answer the door, half-hoping to whisper a warning to Chris before he entered the flat.

'Hi, hello,' said Chris, stepping towards her. He paused, moved his head from left to right like a tennis player waiting to return a serve, coughed twice, then thrust out his hand.

'Hi,' said Tamsin, as they shook. She felt afresh the strangeness of seeing this figure from the almost-forgotten past. Without the makeup and the nurse's outfit, he looked much more like the boy she remembered, although he was older now, with a man's broader frame and a strong neck thickened by exercise. There was something unnatural about his physique, as if his muscles had been inflated very suddenly: Clark Kent transformed into Superman. His T-shirt had clearly been bought for a scrawnier version of himself.

Impossible, she realised, to say anything to Chris now. 'It's, er, nice to see you,' she told him. 'Again.'

Chris nodded fervently. 'I know, it's so weird, it's one of the strangest things that's ever—'

'Come on through, come on through,' she said loudly, desperate to prevent his sentence from heading any further in that particular direction.

'Chris, hi, good to see you again, mate.' Callum waved to them from the little open kitchen, jovial but distracted. 'Tam, I can't find the bloody mint leaves. They're not in the fridge, they should be in the fridge.'

Tamsin stepped over to the fridge and produced the packet of mint, eyebrows arched.

'God, I hate it when you do that,' said Callum, coming up behind her and putting his arms round her waist.

Tamsin twisted round in his arms so that she was facing him. 'It's because your peripheral vision's no good.' Her tone was pertly flirtatious. 'Men didn't need it, you see, when they were chasing woolly mammoths.'

Usually, Callum had scant patience with Tamsin's penchant for evolutionary psychology. But right now they were performing, as couples do in company, a pat double act. Callum tucked his hands up under his armpits and capered like an ape until Tamsin pretended to cuff him round the head.

'Right,' he said, turning to Chris. 'Enough of all that. Let me get you a drink.'

This little routine wasn't wasted on Chris. He had accepted Callum's invitation out of a sense of kismet: because he barely remembered giving Callum his number, the text message seemed, somehow, to be a call to destiny, a prompt it would be foolish to ignore. His initial resolution to leave Tamsin and Callum in peace had dissolved in a froth of conjecture (was she unhappy with Callum? was Callum unhappy with her? how had she felt, meeting him again after all those years?). Now he was here and he could see the situation for what it was – domestic bliss

– his role was very clear. There were no decisions to make, no moral dilemmas to brood over. He would talk to Callum, eat his supper, adore Tamsin from afar, then go back to barracks life.

What he hadn't bargained on was liking Callum quite as much as he did. Chris would meet his few non-army friends at the weekends for sixteen hours of expensive hedonism before crawling back to Bulford. In contrast, Callum and his compact little flat were, as Chris pronounced loudly over pudding, 'the peak of civilisation'. It was all wonderful: Callum's cooking, the canvas photo prints of Moroccan souks and Scottish islands (all Callum's own work), the complete set of Loeb classics on the homemade bookshelves, the electric drum kit in the corner of the room on which Callum let him mess about and finally, after much protesting, demonstrated a short but breathtaking burst of eight against nine.

'Our Callum's something of a Renaissance man,' Tamsin remarked, drollery a poor mask for her pride.

Best of all, Callum appeared to be fascinated by Chris. He asked question after question about the army, and actually took out a small notebook when they got started on the history of the machine gun.

'Can you believe it? Gatling, the guy who was basically responsible for the machine gun mark two – after the Maxim, that is – genuinely thought he was saving lives. One soldier kills a hundred times more people, so you need a hundred times less soldiers. I mean, go figure.'

Tamsin watched them as they talked, feeling relieved that they had not, so far, approached the question of her history with Chris. Yet she was also feeling curiously excluded. She had been dreading conversation about Afghanistan or Iraq, two subjects on which she felt herself to be embarrassingly under-informed. But neither Chris nor Callum seemed interested in what she thought.

'You think of bullets, you think of bangs, right?' Chris was saying. ''S'nothing like that at all. More of a whipcrack sound, a sort of stinging, high-pitched whine, peeow, peeeow.'

He had his head dipped low as if he were actually in a trench, sheltering from rifle fire. Callum was leaning back in his chair, legs crossed at the ankle and hands behind his head, nodding slowly with an expression of shrewd attention on his face.

Finally, Callum left to go to the toilet and Tamsin took her chance.

'Listen,' she said, keeping her voice low. 'I hope this doesn't sound too crazy, but I haven't actually told Callum that whole thing about how we met. It just seemed ... I told him you used to date a friend of mine, years ago, and that I met you once or twice through her. Shit, this does sound crazy, doesn't it?'

But to her surprise, Chris was immediately compliant, even grateful, for this alternative version of events. He didn't appear to think it was odd that she hadn't told Callum the real story of how they knew one another.

'God no, of course, that's much better,' he said. 'We met through your friend, perfect. Thanks. Seriously, thanks.' He sounded relieved.

(Chris was embarrassed: by what he now perceived as unforgivable cowardice that day on the tube. It didn't look too hot for Second Lieutenant Kimura to be running away from a suitcase. Tamsin's lie allowed him to save face. Was she just as ashamed, he wondered? Or was it something else she was hiding from Callum? Even as he rejected this interpretation as absurd, he found himself feeling faintly, pleasantly hopeful.)

They finished the meal with port and Stilton. It had been a boozy evening. Halfway through his second glass of port, Chris became almost tearful.

47

'People, they ask me, they ask me all the time why I joined the army. I wish I could show them this, all this.' He flung his arms open to indicate the room. 'This is my answer. People like you two, all this decency, and culture – this is *exactly* what I'm fighting for. We're fighting the bastards who'll throw acid in the eyes of schoolgirls so that this, this *paradise* – because, for all its faults, the UK really is paradise – this *paradise* that allows people like you guys to just *be*, to do your thing...' He raised his glass in a reverent toast. 'I wish you all the best. I really do.'

Callum reached over to plunge the coffee, hiding a smile at the younger man's emotion.

Later, at the door, Chris kissed Tamsin on both cheeks, then pulled Callum into a backslapping hug. 'Great evening. Pukka scran.'

Callum laughed. 'Pleasure. Like I say, you're welcome any time.'

A door banged somewhere in the flat, making them all start. A moment later, a girl in a pure white towelling dressing gown and fluffy blue slippers appeared in the kitchen and shuffled over to the sink. Long dark hair obscured her face.

'Leah, I'm so sorry – I didn't realise you were here, you should have come out – you could have joined us—' Callum was embarrassed.

Leah produced an apple from the pocket of her dressing gown. 'S'okay, I was sleeping.' She squeezed a generous blob of Fairy Liquid into her palm and began to wash the apple under the tap.

Chris looked at Tamsin, who crossed her eyes and grinned at him. He stifled an urge to laugh. Leah squirted another dose of Fairy Liquid onto her apple. When she put the bottle back down on the kitchen counter, two tiny oily bubbles puffed out, twinkled, burst. They were all watching her.

Callum stepped awkwardly towards her. 'Erm, Chris, this is Leah, my flatmate, Leah, this is Chris, a friend.'

Leah took a clean tea towel from a drawer and dried her apple on it. At last she turned to face them.

'Hello, Chris. Hi, Tamsin.'

She was very beautiful. Her glossy hair hung from a neat centre parting, two straight sheets of onyx that reflected the kitchen lights. Apart from one flat, irregularly shaped mole on her right cheek, her biscuit-coloured skin was blemish-free.

'Uh, hi,' said Chris. 'Actually, I'm just going, but, er, nice to meet you.'

Leah smiled unconvincingly and bit into her apple.

Five

Like all small, enclosed communities, Denham Hall –
where Callum had now been working for nearly a year
– had its own mores and cultural codes. At the core of
the school's identity was a nostalgia – fiercely subscribed
to by most of the pupils – for the rigours of the bad old
days. Many children in the top two years remembered
the previous headmaster and his deputy speaking Latin
together over lunch and in the corridors. Corporal punishment had ceased only when it was made illegal in 1999,
a fact often repeated among the pupils with a mixture of
horror and pride.

Until quite recently, Denham Hall had been boys-only;
even now, boys outnumbered girls in a ratio of 2:1. This
discrepancy had two effects. The first was a general
feeling, cheerfully shared by both sexes, that boys were
standard issue, whereas girls were an anomalous deviation
from the norm. The second effect was that each year, the
school's position on puberty was determined by the rela-
tively small number of girls in the top forms. If most of
these girls had developed discernible breasts, then adulthood was in vogue. But this year, only two out of the
twenty-five pupils in the incipient eighth form – boys and

girls – had started puberty with any real conviction. There was Des Kapoor, who had an unreliable glitch in his voice and faint inverted commas above the corners of his upper lip; and there was Sophie Witrand, cup size 32A and growing, fast. Neither Des nor Sophie had any social heft. The cool kids in their year-group were Milly Urquhart, Ludo Hall, and little Rhiannon Jenkins – all still small and slim and smooth-skinned, their snub noses only just beginning to morph into more distinctive shapes.

These three set the tone: for now, the currency at Denham Hall was immaturity. The children seemed innately to understand that their un-sprouted bodies were approaching expiry date, and that this made them all the more valuable. Theirs was a clean, clear beauty, crystalline in comparison to the maculate adult world with its coarse dark body hair and pendulous flesh. Menstruation was regarded with particular disgust. Yet paradoxically, the accoutrements of puberty were *de rigueur*: bras were worn, legs were shaved, deodorant ostentatiously applied. The ideal was to display all the sophistication of adolescence, while maintaining the physical purity of childhood. Anyone who actually needed the deodorant would have been 'minging'.

Sophie Witrand, the only person in the whole year who could have done with a bra, was one of the few girls who didn't have one. She had shaved her legs just once, with a razor stolen from her father. The act itself had been executed in the airing cupboard (there was no lock on the Witrands' bathroom door), without shaving foam or even water. Sophie's leg hair was blonde and almost invisible, but once this soft nap had been harvested by the razor's four-blade grille it formed a little heap the colour of silt, dry yet silky when she rubbed it between thumb and forefinger. Her mother, a keen gardener, used the bottom shelf of the airing cupboard to germinate the seeds of delicate plants. Sophie pushed a finger into the gateau-black soil of *verbena bonariensis* and planted her pinchful of evidence. A tray of white Italian sunflowers had just germinated, the tips of the little shoots still hooded by the old humbug-striped seed casings. For a silly second Sophie wondered what her leg hair would look like if it grew. A snatch of Edward Lear came into her head: 'I answered him as I thought good / As many red herrings as grow in the wood.'

Her idea was to replace the razor and tell no one, but two hours later she was down in the kitchen wearing her longest nightie, tremulous yet ready to confess. Sophie was obsessively truthful. When she was younger her parents had imposed a rule to prevent her from tiring herself out by reading late into the night: book closed and lights out at 8 p.m. If Sophie exceeded this deadline by just five minutes, she would lie awake worrying until the guilt grew too great to bear, at which point she would have to get up and go downstairs to admit her transgression to her mother.

Now she sat on her mother's lap and hid her face as she explained what she had done. Mrs Witrand rubbed her daughter's back, alternating strokes with little pats as if she were burping a baby. She let the theft of the razor pass without comment. Then she took Sophie up to the bathroom and gave her some of her Body Shop moisturiser. She explained how shaving made the hairs grow back thicker, and how – look, see those little white flakes? – Sophie's skin had already been ravaged by the razor. 'If you like, I'll take you to get them waxed, you only have to ask. But I think your legs are just fine. I'd give anything to have lovely soft hair like that again. You do know you can hardly see it, darling?'

Sophie thought of her mother's legs with their squiggly veins. The backs of her big calves had dimples like sand that had been rained on. Once Sophie had poked one of these strange dents and been surprised to find it firm and unresisting. Mrs Witrand was large but not flabby; her flesh was tightly packed under her skin, as if bursting to get out. Everything about her was slightly oversized, from her size nine feet to the fat brown plait that hung down her back to her waist. Underneath her thick, straight-cut fringe, her pale blue eyes were permanently narrowed by the upward pressure of her glacé cheeks.

Both mother and daughter knew that Sophie would never ask to have her legs waxed. Although no hint of reproach had entered Mrs Witrand's voice, a judgement had, implicitly, been passed: Sophie's error was forgiven but not to be repeated. It had been the same when she had mentioned the possibility of a bra. Mrs Witrand was briskly implacable: 'You don't need one yet, sweet pea, you're only twelve. There'll be plenty of time for all that later.'

* * *

'Mr Love's wearing a bra, pass it on!'

Rhiannon Jenkins, nearly thirteen but no bigger than a nine-year-old, short dark hair, a face-full of cappuccino freckles. She was the smallest girl in the class and something of a mascot. Teachers found her faux-naïve manner infuriating; her peers found it hilarious.

Predictably, it was Sophie Witrand who had been left to sit next to Mr Dempster in the double passenger seat at the front of the bus. She squirmed round and squeezed her neck past the headrest, desperate to join in with her classmates' banter. Callum decided not to comment on her twisted seatbelt.

Next year's scholarship form at Denham Hall, 8S, were stuck in Friday afternoon traffic on the M25. It was the final day of a week-long summer programme designed to introduce scholarship candidates to real-world applications of subjects they were studying. Parents invariably thought it was a fantastic opportunity. Their children tended to disagree. This week had been the hottest of the year so far and they had spent most of it in a minibus. They were overheated and sticky and sunburnt and fed up.

Today's itinerary had been Geography (Chichester Harbour) and Latin (Fishbourne Roman Palace). Mr Love the Geography master was melting in the driving seat, sweaty kiss-curls of thin brown hair clinging to his forehead. The front of his pale blue double-cuff shirt was now translucent with sweat. Through the damp cotton, Mr Love's chest hair did look like a black lace bra.

Callum was wearing Hawaiian board shorts and a tight V-neck T-shirt with the logo 'NBX Burnout' – just as open to ridicule, in its way, as Mr Love's outfit. But 8S had granted Mr Dempster immunity. There was a certain toughness about him that made them wary of taking the piss. He was also going to be their form teacher next year. It was preferable to have him as an ally.

The snickering was getting louder. Callum turned to face the class with one eyebrow raised and his head slightly cocked. Could he have seen it, Mr Love would not have thanked him for this look. But it worked. There was one more titter, and then 8S were silent.

'Mr Love won't play our CD, though.'

The speaker sounded aggrieved. Ludo Hall was head of choir; he had tightly waved marmalade hair and a pure treble voice reputed to have made several of the male members of staff weep. Because of this, and in spite of a staffroom mantra 'not to let Ludo Hall think he's special', he was treated, ever so slightly, like a celebrity. Women of all ages responded to his fine, pale features, and Ludo had already begun to respond to this response.

In class he was subtly disruptive, with a keen sense of injustice and a talent for figuring himself as the wronged party when caught.

Callum eyed him evenly then smiled before the boy could see him weighing his decision. 'Ah, Charles?' he said, turning back to Mr Love.

The CD was *Loud* by Rihanna, and it kept everyone happy all the way back to Denham Hall. Everyone except for Mr Love (*Sex in the air, I don't care I love the smell of it*) and Sophie Witrand. Callum watched her with a mixture of pity and interest. She was twisted right round to face the class, trying to sing along with song lyrics she didn't really know. After five minutes of being ignored she flopped back into her seat. But then she would pick herself up and start again.

During one of her 'time-outs', she asked him a question.

'So the Romans, they didn't believe in God, did they, sir?'

'The Romans had lots of gods. You know that, Sophie.' She was one of the brightest students in the class.

'No, but not *God* God, like the Christian God – they didn't even really know about him till the three hundreds ay dee, did they.'

'Until the fourth century, that's right. Very good. Emperor?'

'Emperor Constantine. But, sir...' Sophie was distracted by a chorus she evidently knew. She wriggled away from their conversation and launched herself back into Rihanna. '*Want you to MAKE ME FEEL – like I'm the only girl in the world – like I'm the only one that you'll ever luh-uv...*'

Back at school, however, she stayed sitting in the bus long after the others had piled out. Callum held the door open for her, but she didn't budge.

'Sir, do *you* believe in God?'

'Whew.' Callum drummed his fingers on the top of the minibus door, looking up for inspiration. The bright flat blue sky was softer now, tinged with mauve and graduating to a clear eau de Nil at the horizon. 'Well ... let's just say, on an evening like this, it's hard not to feel something, eh?'

She was too intelligent to take this as a yes. Callum felt the reproach in her gaze and found himself apologising.

'Sorry.' He glanced at his watch. They were meeting Will for drinks at nine. Chris would be arriving at eight. 'Sophie, I'm afraid I don't really have time for this now. Ask me again some other day, I promise I'll give you a better answer.'

Sophie nodded sadly and got out of the bus, ducking under his arm with a mumbled 'Bye, sir'.

Her baggy shorts, rumpled from the long bus ride, had ridden up between her bum cheeks; unselfconsciously, she tugged the material free. The evening sun lit the downy hair of her legs in a soft halo. Callum thought of plant stems, brightly outlined by their greenly glowing fibres.

* * *

At ten o'clock that morning, Tamsin had known exactly what she'd be wearing for an evening in the pub with Callum, Will, and various of Will's cronies: jeans and a T-shirt, minimal makeup. At midday, Callum had texted to say that Chris would be joining them. Now it was 6 p.m. and Tamsin was in her bedroom, deliberating between her two shortest dresses.

Tamsin tugged the dress up over her head and stood in her underwear for a moment, contemplating her near-naked reflection. The stretch marks encircling her breasts glinted slug-trail silver in the early evening sunlight. She forced herself to think dispassionately about Chris. He was good-looking and intelligent, but then she knew plenty of good-looking, intelligent people. Compared to Callum, he seemed unattractively young. Really, the thrill she felt at the thought of seeing him again made no sense at all.

It didn't occur to her that just his reappearance might be enough to pique her interest in him. Tamsin prided herself on her pragmatism; unlike Chris, she had no time for fate or destiny or kismet. But coincidence is a powerful aphrodisiac. After their first encounter seven years ago, Tamsin remembered Chris chiefly because of the unusual circumstances in which they met. Then she forgot him, because he had been uninteresting to her. When she saw him again at Leo's party, there was suddenly a pair of coincidences, mutually amplifying their significance. Then there had been that supper at Callum's, and now here he was again, in town for the weekend, apparently, just wondering what she and Callum were up to, whether he could join them for supper, perhaps even stay the night ... The effect of these repetitions was, subtly but surely, one of emphasis added, *his name in italics in her mind*.

As Tamsin struggled with the zip on dress number two, virtue abruptly won out. She loved Callum, very much: she had no business baring her legs for Chris, or anyone else. In the top left-hand corner of the mirror was a small sticker collection, comprising three holographic hearts in shades of puce, six fuzzy-felt teddy bears, a parakeet and a hamburger, placed there by the eight-year-old Tamsin. For years, Tamsin had barely even noticed the stickers; now, suddenly, she found herself irritated by them. She peeled them all off, crumpled them into a tacky ball, and rubbed ineffectually at their gummy ghosts with spit.

When she went down to the sitting room to say goodbye

to her mother, Tamsin was wearing jeans, a plain white collared shirt and just a little more makeup than usual. She walked briskly, as in the wake of a job well done, though in fact the opposite was true: by identifying her attraction and labelling it forbidden, she had only succeeded in augmenting it. (Just as the impulsive, insignificant lie she had told Callum lent her dealings with Chris an element of the clandestine that contributed to his growing mystique.)

'Mummy?'

Roz was absorbed in a text message. At the sound of her name, she started.

'I'm just off. Who's the message from?' Tamsin tried to look but her mother whisked the phone out of sight.

'Oh, no one, it's nothing important.'

As they kissed goodbye, Tamsin felt a surprising heat radiating from her mother's powdered cheek.

* * *

When Tamsin arrived at the Edgware Road flat at seven thirty, Callum wasn't back – but Chris was there, sitting on the sofa, flicking through one of Callum's sketchbooks. He looked up guiltily.

'Sorry – Callum's flatmate, she let me in – I hope it's okay if I—'

'No, of course, it's fine, go ahead. You just – I'll just go and say hi to Leah—' They were both talking too loudly.

'Um, I think she's in the shower.'

'Oh right, cool. Do you, can I get you a drink?'

Tamsin retreated to the kitchen to fetch some beers and to collect her thoughts. She hadn't expected to find herself alone with Chris.

When she returned he held up the sketchbook to show

a page featuring four little charcoal drawings of Tamsin sleeping, just a few lines in each, swiftly and skilfully done.

'These ones of you – it is you, isn't it? – they're amazing. This one, here – this one's the best.' Chris pointed to the biggest of the four sketches. The charcoal Tamsin was on her back, her arms thrown up above her head and her eyes lightly closed as if she were resting briefly rather than actually sleeping. Tamsin liked it, too, but she loyally nominated Callum's favourite, a less flattering rendition of her asleep on her side, her lower cheek slightly sagged by gravity.

'And this is all Callum's own work, right?'

'Yup. He paints a little, too, but basically he likes pencil best.'

'Is there anything the guy doesn't do?'

Tamsin smiled. The conversation felt horribly stiff and formal, but Chris's appreciation of Callum was genuine, and it endeared him to her even further.

'I mean, he could sell these.' Chris passed his open palm over the sketches very slowly, holding it an inch above the surface. Tamsin was surprised by his hands: they were older than they should be, with dry, split nails and dirt that lay so deep in the seams of his knuckles it looked as if it had been sewn in. Her gaze strayed up his torso to the collar of his shirt (finely woven cotton, with pink-white-blue stripes that reminded her of toothpaste). The top two buttons were undone. There were three soft hairs in the notch at the base of his throat, sweetly exposed.

To quash this alarming thought Tamsin began talking, at speed.

'He does, actually. Sell them. At his school, he does portraits – from photographs of the children, usually just a simple head-and-shoulders thing, but sometimes he'll do group ones with siblings, even pets. Personally I think it's a bit of a waste. But the parents are willing to pay silly money for it, so...'

59

She trailed off. This wasn't right at all. She hadn't meant to criticise Callum to Chris; having done so, she felt guilty of a small betrayal.

They lapsed into silence again. Tamsin took the remote control from the coffee table and fiddled for a while with the black plastic cover of the battery compartment.

'Listen, I just want to say—'

She looked up, startled by the urgency in Chris's voice. He was sitting right forward on the edge of the sofa.

'Last time,' he went on, 'when we had supper – I think I might've drunk a bit too much – I'm sorry about the speech.'

Tamsin smiled. 'It's fine, we were all quite—'

'To tell the truth I was a bit nervous about meeting you again.' He paused for a moment as if waiting for permission to continue. Outside in the street, someone honked a car horn once, twice, then a third time, long and loud. The sound bent and died. Tamsin avoided Chris's gaze but he didn't seem to notice her discomfort.

'The thing is...' he began again, then stopped. He didn't even know what he was trying to say. That he had been thinking about her for seven years? That he loved her? That he was just glad to see her, and to see her happy? All absurd, Chris thought, blushing to himself as he heard and rejected each of these options.

'Hello hello!'

Callum was at the door, red-faced from his long ride home. The tangerine sheen of his orange lycra cycling gear was darkly stained with sweat at the crotch and armpits, while a larger stain formed a peninsula tapering from his neckline down to his navel. Tamsin launched herself on him, mindless of the sweat.

* * *

The Duke's Head was an old South London pub that had recently been subjected to a trendy makeover. Tamsin found herself sitting between Chris and Will on a reclaimed church pew, presided over by a working set of traffic lights. She was horribly conscious of her proximity to Chris. Each time she relaxed, her knee drifted over to touch his thigh. She couldn't tell whether Chris was aware of this, too, but judging from his awkwardness in Callum's flat, it seemed likely that he was. Her buttocks ached with the effort of avoiding contact.

Across the table, Leah was looking terrific in a navy-blue bandeau dress and a pair of gold earrings shaped like Celtic knots. Leah rarely drank alcohol; this evening she was sipping grapefruit juice through a straw, carefully preserving the pearly gloss that coated her lips. 'Mmm, very smart,' Tamsin had said when Leah emerged from the bedroom in her high heels and immaculate makeup. Not quite a compliment – the implication being that Leah was overdressed for an evening in the pub. Leah had replied, in her habitual tone of sullen apathy, that she was going out later. She always had somewhere else to go on to, though they never met the friends she went with.

Sitting next to Leah were Big Mac (Ollie Macfarlane) and his girlfriend Suze. Big Mac was a consultant at Deloitte. He had a fine bass voice; at Cambridge, he had been a King's choral scholar. His intention had been to work at Deloitte for a few years to build up his savings, then make a go of it as a singer – a plan he talked about with decreasing conviction as each year went by. Big Mac identified as Scottish: despite a fruity Home Counties accent, he wore his kilt more often than Callum did. He was extremely fat and suffered from a minor addiction to cheese-and-onion crisps. Right now he was irritated because the pub only served chilli cashews and wasabi nuts; but also because Suze was making no attempt to disguise her admiration for Second Lieutenant Kimura and his daredevil tales from the Rifles' recent training exercise in the Kenyan wilderness.

'And there it was, right in front of us, the monster itself' – Chris paused for effect; Suze appeared to be holding her breath – 'a zebra, munching on some leaves!'

Apart from Big Mac, everyone laughed. Chris was the man of the moment – a fresh face with an exciting job and a large backlog of anecdotes that nobody had heard before.

'Oh my god, it sounds so frightening!' Suze panted, still recovering from the suspense before the punchline.

Suze was what Will unkindly referred to as a 'stealth moose' – gorgeous from a distance, with her catwalk figure and long blonde hair, but alarmingly ugly up close. She had a bad squint and her features were out-of-focus with the worst acne scars Chris had ever seen. Now she leaned even further across the table towards him, her smallish breasts squeezed awkwardly together by her upper arms. She evidently expected some sort of response, but Chris couldn't think of anything to say. He blinked, uncomfortable under the blaze of her admiration. He was still getting used to the effect of his military persona on some women.

'What about women?' It was as if Will had read his mind. 'Surely certain, how can I put this, *needs* arise?'

Chris nodded. 'Yes, that's a real problem, actually – we had a few days' leave in the local town at the end of the jungle training and the guys had to be given a fairly in-depth refresher session on sexual health. I was worried that the doctor's spiel had been a wee bit too technical for some of the younger guys, so I took a bunch of them aside to paraphrase.' Now Chris adopted a slow, too-loud tone, as if he were talking to someone mentally impaired.

'If you get AIDS, you will die. All the hookers have AIDS. If you don't want AIDS, do not stick any part of your body into any part of their bodies. If you're going to be a real retard about it, though, bag up.'

He chuckled drily. 'One young lad invited me to join him and his friends back at their room for "some fun". Turned out they'd taken my lesson to heart: they'd paid a girl to strip and lie there naked while they all stood round and wanked on her.'

There was a brief silence while everyone decided whether to be interested or shocked or coolly unfazed. Suze was no longer leaning over towards Chris. She glanced round at the others, trying to gauge their reactions.

'And you – what did you do?' demanded Big Mac.

At last Chris heard the personal hostility in Big Mac's tone. 'I went back to my hotel room and watched porn on my laptop,' he said evenly.

'How old were these guys, on average?' Callum asked. It was the first time he'd spoken in a while.

Chris sat a little straighter in his seat, lighting up at the pleasure of talking to Callum. 'Uh, the youngest was about seventeen, oldest mid thirties, I guess. But mostly late teens, early twenties.'

'And how do you feel about these men, these boys, being exposed to that sort of scenario so young?'

This was something Tamsin usually admired about Callum – the interest he took in other people, the quiet, intelligent way he collected information, asking his careful questions, storing up the answers to think about later, at length. He rarely offered personal opinions during casual conversation. But just now this trait struck Tamsin as bloodless, even a little unfair – as if he were trying to catch Chris out over a subject on which he, Callum, had no real authority.

'Obviously it's not ideal. But to be frank, it's better than the alternative – which is jail, for most of them. Most of these young guys, they're illiterate, they've got problems with money, family problems. The army offers them a way out of all that.'

'Some people might feel that that's a rather defeatist position,' Callum said neutrally. 'Sorry. I'm playing devil's advocate. Well, I sort of am.'

'I disagree. I strongly disagree.' Chris's ardour was a sharp contrast to Callum's coolness. He wasn't angry, but his dark eyes were big with conviction. 'I know what I'm saying might not be all that palatable, but at least it's realistic.' (Tamsin murmured in automatic approval: 'realistic' was something of a trigger-word for her, an uncontested good, regardless of context.) 'Fact of the matter is that the army educates them, it provides financial guidance, pastoral care … It isn't perfect, but it's by far the best of a pretty shabby set of options. And in the end, when you look at the camaraderie, the sense of purpose, the *brotherhood* – I'm really not exaggerating when I say that joining the army is the best decision that most of these guys will ever make.' Chris nodded fervently.

Bored, Will waved the debate away. 'Well, that's all very Agincourt of you, Chris. But I'm more interested in your cocks. In the jungle, when and where do you masturbate? I want specifics.'

'Will!' Tamsin turned on him.

Will feigned hurt. 'These things are terribly important.'

'It's okay, I don't mind,' said Chris.

'That's not the point.'

Will tapped the tabletop impatiently with the flat of his hand. 'Come on, Chris, don't be shy, you're among friends.'

'I'm not shy, it's just…' Chris looked to Tamsin for consent.

'Oh, don't mind her,' said Will, draping an arm round Tamsin's shoulders. 'Tam and I go way back, don't we?'

Tamsin wriggled out from under his arm. Will was always claiming for them an intimacy that had never existed, and it irked her.

'Basically,' Chris began, uncertainly, 'men will always find a way. Problem with the jungle was that we were all sleeping in hammocks, at fairly close quarters. I suppose after a while it just happens.'

'So you were effectively jerking off in public,' said Will.

Chris hesitated before continuing. 'The, uh, the wanker does his best to be discreet, and everyone else does their best to ignore it. That is, depending on the guy. There was one lad who made a bit of a thing about it. Dave Gaskin – though everyone called him Gashbag. He had, er, some innovative solutions to the problem of waste disposal.'

'As in – what exactly?'

'He either rubbed it into his chest – said it was good for the skin – or' – Chris's mouth puckered in amused distaste – 'or he ate the stuff. Sorry, ladies,' he finished, remembering Tamsin.

'Don't worry,' said Tamsin stiffly.

Chris was embarrassed. 'Sorry, bit far.' He stood up, looking flustered. 'My round, isn't it? Sorry. Same again? Three Peroni, two Pinot Grigio, and a – a grapefruit juice?'

'Actually, I'll just have water,' said Leah. The background noise forced her to raise her voice. For the first time, Chris heard the gluey consonants of a Birmingham accent lurking behind her carefully clipped speech.

As he queued for drinks, Chris experienced a familiar deflation. He had been riding high on attention all evening, but now he felt sadly empty. Much as he loved performing, these days it so often felt like the only mode available to him. He was always 'the army guy'. People's responses were getting boringly predictable. Suze's adoration, Big Mac's cynicism, Will's covert bid to prove that he, too, could be one of the boys – they were such *types*.

Of course he knew he encouraged it. He put himself on display, and by putting himself on display, he fairly volunteered for exclusion. The civilian world was becoming another country. He didn't quite belong here any more – and yet he didn't quite belong in the army, either. He was too sensitive; he could do tough, when it was required, but it was always a bit of an act. Even the cigarettes he smoked after dinner in the mess felt like props. Same as being mixed-race, Chris thought morosely: Japanese in England, English in Japan...

Two boys were blocking his way, leaning on the bar and sipping at their pints of Guinness.

'Excuse me,' Chris said. 'If you wouldn't mind, I think—'

'No, excuse *me*,' said taller boy, boldly impersonating Chris's plummy vowels. 'I am most *terribly* sorry.' He had a tidemark of foam on his upper lip. They shuffled over to make room for Chris, the short one laughing sycophantically at his companion's joke.

No, thought Chris as he ordered, it had not been a good night. He had a growing suspicion that he'd made himself ridiculous to Tamsin in the flat; and just now he had surely offended her with that stupid story about Dave Gaskin.

(As it happened, Tamsin wasn't at all bothered by the talk about masturbation. Her objection to Will's question had been entirely arbitrary, an expression of her general frustration with the evening. For no very good reason, she felt cross, with Callum, with Chris, with herself; so for no very good reason, she got angry with Will.)

'That'll be twenny-six-sixty,' the barman told him.

'Really?' Chris was surprised; he had never been much good with numbers. 'Hang on, I might have to give you most of that in change...'

'London prices, eh?' said the barman, conspiratorially. 'It's the Peroni what does it, that's four pound fifty a pint.'

'Really?' Chris said again, contorting his torso as he strained to access the more remote corners of his jeans pockets.

'You're not from round here, are you?'

'Well, not exactly.' Chris wondered if this was going to be one of those 'No-but-what-country-do-you-*really*-come-from*' conversations. 'I'm living near Salisbury at the moment.'

'I knew it!' The barman was triumphant. 'Takes one to know one, but honestly, that haircut – dead giveaway every time. You must be, what, Rifles? or is it Paras? And with a posh voice like that ... Captain?' This last speculation was made entirely without malice or resentment.

'I wish,' Chris grinned. 'Still very much a crow-bag second lieutenant, though.'

Well, you should try being a crow-bag private, *sir*,' joked the barman. 'Fusiliers,' he added, with pride.

Chris looked at the barman more closely. Early forties, certainly no older than forty-five. 'Gulf War?' he asked, holding out a palm-full of coins and notes.

The barman nodded. 'That's right. Best years of my life.'

The two men exchanged a look of perfect understanding. Chris wanted to laugh.

He took the Pinot Grigios and the water back to their table and came back for the three Peronis.

'You know that bird with the black hair, then?' The taller of the two boys was looking at him again.

'What?' It was a moment before Chris understood that he was talking about Leah. 'Oh, yes.'

'She's well fit.'

'She's—' Chris said, then stopped, realising he knew almost nothing about Leah. She was beautiful, certainly, but she also seemed dull and stuck-up.

'How old is she?'

'I don't know. I'll ask her,' Chris told him, amused.

'We were just discussing phase two of this evening's revels,' Will explained when Chris returned. 'Leah knows some chap who's DJing at the Hoxton Pony, he can get us free entry. No queuing. You up for it?'

'Yeah, definitely, count me in.' Chris slurped at his pint of beer, his good mood returning. 'Oh, by the way, Leah – you've got an admirer over at the bar. Tall boy with the grubby T-shirt. Don't worry, he is legal. Just.'

For a moment, Leah looked annoyed. Then she realised Chris was joking and her face softened into a brief smile. Her top lip tucked under as the smile widened, revealing a surprising amount of pale pink gum above her teeth.

Suze touched Big Mac's hand. 'I'm keen for a bit of dancing,' she said. 'That is, if you are, babes?'

Big Mac shook his head. 'No way. Can't stand Shoreditch.'

'I'm coming,' said Tamsin, brightly. 'I haven't been out, as in *out* out, in like forever.'

Callum looked surprised. 'But you hate clubs.'

'Who said that?' Tamsin frowned at him. 'I hate *some* clubs, not *all* clubs. And I *love* the Hoxton Pony.' She produced a small hand mirror from her bag and set about checking her makeup, pinching her eyelashes between thumb and forefinger to get rid of any stray clumps of mascara.

'Sorry, guys, breaking news.' Will was reading a text message. 'Have to take a rain check, I'm afraid. I've, ah, got to go see a man about a dog.'

'Booty call?' asked Big Mac.

Will passed the phone to Big Mac, who read the message, snickered, and passed it back.

Chris did a round-up, ticking off the names on his fingers. 'So that's me, Leah, Tamsin – Callum?'

Callum glanced at Tamsin uncertainly, then turned back to Chris. 'Yeah, sure. Why not?'

'My friends are waiting for me.' Leah pushed her glass of water away, untouched. 'You lot can come if you want, but I have to get going now.'

She sounded as if she were bored by all of them; and this, somehow, commanded a certain power. Everyone, even Will, hurried to finish their drinks.

Callum helped Tamsin into her fitted corduroy jacket. 'Tam, you quite sure about this? Last time we went clubbing, remember, in Shunt? You said to remind you next time – about how much you hated it.' He turned her round to face him. 'So this is me reminding you.'

'Stop being so patronising,' Tamsin muttered, shrugging his hands away. She raised her voice. 'I'm just going to the loo, okay? Meet you all outside in a sec.'

'Ooh, wait for me, I'm coming too,' called Suze, rushing to catch up with Tamsin as she picked her way through to the toilets. 'It's been such a nice evening, hasn't it? It's sooo good to see you all.' Suze had a tendency to gush when she was nervous, which was almost always the case, especially around other women: she was very aware of her own physical inferiority. 'And Chris, I mean, it's just so amazing to have the opportunity to talk to someone like that. He's just *such* an interesting guy, isn't he?'

The spotlights in the bathroom were too bright. As the girls entered the two empty toilet stalls, the conversation broke off; they only knew each other slightly, and it seemed a little odd to carry on talking.

Tamsin's skin was hot, flushed from four big glasses of wine. The toilet seat felt pleasantly cool against her thighs. She leaned forward with her elbows on her knees and her hands clasped in front of her, waiting. In the other stall Suze's long stream of piss chirruped and hissed, then shushed itself to a whisper. Rustle of toilet paper, louder rustle of the flush. Tamsin still couldn't go. She pushed a fist into her bladder and tried to relax. Someone had written 'I'll be right back' in black permanent marker on the toilet-roll dispenser and signed it 'Godot'.

After a bit Tamsin gave up and joined Suze at the sinks.

'God. *Please* tell me this is an unflattering mirror,' Suze grimaced.

'Yeah, it's pretty bad,' said Tamsin, distractedly. She was unhappy with her shirt; it looked frumpy, the fabric stretched awkwardly over her large chest. She undid a button. Now the neckline was just a little too low, exposing the black lace trim of her bra. Tamsin left it undone and reached up to re-do her ponytail. She knew she was behaving badly, but all her former resolve had vanished. Anyway, so what if she only wanted to go to the club because of Chris? That impulse wasn't wrong in itself; it was only a crime if she acted on it. Which of course she wasn't going to.

'And I know I shouldn't say this,' Suze went on, as if they'd never stopped talking about Chris, 'but isn't he *gorgeous*?'

'Mmmm,' said Tamsin. 'If you like that sort of thing.'

'You mean Chinesey? But he's so tall it doesn't really count, does it?' Suze rubbed at her eyebrows to clear them of foundation. 'Do you reckon he and Leah will...?'

'Probably. After all, that's what Leah does best, isn't it?' Tamsin was shocked by the venom in her own voice. So that was it, she realised. She wanted to go to the club with Chris – but more than that, she didn't want Chris and Leah going to the club without her. Tamsin pushed the thought all the way to its conclusion: she didn't want

Chris, but she didn't want anyone else to have him, either. The unfairness of this was obvious. She felt ashamed, contrite.

'I didn't mean that, it came out a bit harsher than I meant it. I meant that she's just so beautiful, any guy would be crazy not to want her.'

'I know,' Suze sighed. 'She's maybe the most beautiful person I've ever met. But you, you're stunning too, Tamsin.' Suze gave her reflection a rueful look and smiled, via the mirror, at Tamsin's guilty face.

* * *

At Waterloo, Tamsin, Callum and Leah waited while Chris topped up his Oyster card. Callum turned his face to his shoulder to hide a yawn.

'Actually, you know what, I think maybe I won't come after all,' Tamsin said suddenly.

Callum laughed. 'I won't say I told you so.'

'Right, all set.' Chris was back, brandishing his Oyster card.

'Ah, Chris mate, change of plan,' Callum explained. 'Tam and me're going to call it a night.'

'Oh, right.' Chris couldn't hide his disappointment. 'Maybe I should just come back with you guys, I won't be able to get in—'

'No, no, no problem, you can have Tam's key. All right, Tam?'

Tamsin dug in her handbag for the key. 'Here you go.'

Chris looked dubious. 'I don't know, I still think it's simpler if I just come back now…'

'Well, it's up to you—' Callum began.

'No, Chris should go.' Tamsin cut in with more force than she'd intended. 'You go, go and have fun with Leah. Really.' She gave Chris a significant look, vaguely

71

imagining, in her tipsy state, that he understood the full import of her decision to go straight back to Callum's.

'If you're really sure...' Chris took the key, somewhat reluctantly, and passed through the barrier to join Leah.

Waiting on the Bakerloo line platform, Tamsin and Callum kissed like teenagers. Tamsin took Callum's hand and pushed it up under her shirt, onto the skin of her stomach. Usually she disliked public displays of affection, but just now she was conscious of a need to test something, and was relieved when she felt her body responding to Callum's touch.

'Nice empty flat, no one to hear us,' Callum crooned into her ear. 'Though you do know ... as soon as you're ready to move in ... Leah'll go when I say, it could be just the two of us always—'

Tamsin pulled away. 'We were having such a nice time,' she said, preparing to mount the podium of their favourite argument; but she was interrupted by a shout from the other end of the platform.

'Hey there! Tamsin, Callum!'

Bounding towards them with irregular, exhausted strides was a very red-faced Chris.

'Changed my mind,' he panted, raising his voice above the incoming train. 'Whew. Didn't think I'd catch you, I had to run all the way back up the escalators.'

'You didn't have to, we really didn't mind you going,' Tamsin told him as they shuffled onto the train.

'I know, I just somehow didn't feel like it any more,' Chris said; and Tamsin experienced a guilty throb of triumph.

'So what do you think of the American system?' Callum said to Chris once the doors had closed, continuing an earlier conversation about the pros and cons of six-month deployments.

Tamsin let them talk. Too tired and tipsy to follow the

arguments, she stared idly up at a poster informing her she was 'living proof that posters get read'. She only zoned back into the conversation at Charing Cross, when Callum needed her to remember a name.

'You know Tam, that little wine bar just above the station here – the one you took me to on our second date.' He turned to Chris. 'Sort of a cellar, very dark and atmospheric.'

'Do you mean Gordon's?' Chris asked.

'Gordon's, that's it! So you know it then. Isn't it fantastic?'

'Yes, a real gem,' agreed Chris, with a quick wink at Tamsin. The secret about their long-ago meeting on the tube seemed like a private joke to him now.

Tamsin looked away, feeling sick; but once again, Chris failed to notice her discomfort. He saw only her beauty and her freshness, the satin sheen on her heavy eyelids, the simplicity of her plain white shirt (so much more appealing to him than Leah's dressed-up look). She hadn't noticed that one of her buttons had come undone; from his superior vantage point, Chris could see the scalloped edge of her bra. It was his turn to look away. With this girl, even a glimpse of her underwear made him feel guilty. He recalled her squeamishness during the conversation about wanking: it signalled a fundamental purity, the saint-like status she held for him. She and Callum formed the perfect couple, the bond between them inevitable, unshakeable.

Chris smiled fuzzily down at his new friends. 'I don't know what you guys are up to,' he began, 'but I've got a fortnight's leave coming up, starting Tuesday. I'm with family for the second week, but next week – perhaps I could take you both out to dinner...?'

'Sorry, we're going on holiday,' Tamsin said quickly.

'Bad timing,' agreed Callum. 'Otherwise we'd have

loved ... And you know, we still haven't had that chat about the army, I mean more formally, without assistance from Will.'

Chris and Callum both chuckled.

'That's a shame,' said Chris. 'I was really—'

'You're going to be in London all week – where are you staying?' Callum interrupted him.

'Well, Edwin has a house up in Islington, there's a sofa there, or I might—'

'No, listen, this is silly, my bed's going to be empty all week – you might as well keep Tam's key and use the flat as and when you want it.'

'Seriously, you mean that?' Chris stammered.

'No problem at all,' Callum smiled. 'It's good to have you around, Chris. You're a great guy.'

Chris looked down at his feet. People often found this disconcerting in Callum: his ability to state personal affection quite candidly, without avoiding eye-contact or employing any self-protective irony. Tamsin thought it the most un-English thing about him, though she didn't know that it was particularly Scottish, either. When they first met, she had been impressed by this directness; but lately, she had begun to find it embarrassing.

* * *

Back at the flat, Tamsin used the bathroom while Callum helped Chris with the sofa bed. Her first idea was to pretend to be asleep when Callum lay down beside her.

'Tam?' he said softly, then went on without waiting for a reply. 'About earlier ... I'm sorry.'

'It's not just that.' Tamsin sat up in bed, unable, after all, to stay silent. 'What about Chris?'

'What *about* Chris?'

'You're suddenly so pally. We've only just met him.'

'You knew him before, didn't you?' said Callum, reasonably.

'What? What do you mean?' Tamsin tripped on the possibility that somehow, Callum had found out the truth about her and Chris. Then she realised what he was referring to. 'Oh, you mean from College. Well, I didn't know him very well. You can't just go offering your flat to people like that.'

'Actually, I can. It being *my flat*,' said Callum, injecting the last two words with uncharacteristic bitterness.

'What's that supposed to mean?'

'What's what supposed to mean?'

'You know what.'

'Well, only...' Callum shrugged unhappily. 'Only that – sometimes it seems as if you don't actually *want* to live with me.'

'*Fuck* that's unfair. You *know* I do. You know it's just a question of—'

'—financial stability,' Callum finished with her. He sounded very tired.

This was the reason Tamsin always gave: that she wanted to be able to pay her rent without accepting help from either Callum or her father.

'You know I don't mind if you can't always make rent,' Callum said now. 'It just seems to me that it's the perfect way for you to make the, the leap.'

'*Fuck*,' Tamsin said again. 'I've heard this so many times, Cal. It's like being stuck in a fucking feedback loop.'

'Right.'

Callum shuffled onto his side so that he was facing away from her and reached down for a book. He took *Our Man in Havana* from the top of a precarious pagoda of half-read books and began to read. In this quietly devastating way, he brought the argument to a close.

Tamsin listened to three page turns before she began to cry. Callum put the book down and took her into his arms.

'I'm sorry,' she snuffled. 'I'm so sorry. I know I'm being a bitch, I don't know why ... I think it's just ... my period's on its way, that's probably...'

'Ssshhh, sshhh.' Callum hooked his leg over her hip and drew her closer to him. 'I love you.'

Six

Sophie Witrand was squashed into the back seat of the Fiat Bravo with her brother James and her sister Harriet. Her swollen chest jounced painfully over the potholes of the Cornish back roads. The Witrands were on their way to Penderick Manor, a dilapidated country house about a mile from Padstow where they holidayed every year.

'Soph? So-oph.' Six-year-old Harriet waved her chubby hand in front of Sophie's blank face, just like she'd seen their mother do. 'Soph, let's say the car's a chocolate factory. Here's where the chocolate gets mixed.' She reached down between her legs and mimed vigorous stirring. 'And this is the pipe' – she made two loose tunnels from her fingers and thumbs and sketched out a pipe leading up to the headrest in front of Sophie – 'and *here*'s the tap where it comes running out. Mmmm, mmmm, it's sooo good.' Harriet turned on an imaginary tap and leaned forward to lap at the chocolate.

Sophie pulled down on her seatbelt, which was digging into the new hard bit underneath her left nipple, and wriggled away from her sister. 'Mum, Harry won't sit still. She's being really annoying.'

'Darling, she just wants to play with you.'

'Harriet, quick, there's a fire at the chocolate factory!' James yelled, waving his hands to signify flames. 'Nee-naw nee-naw nee-naw!'

'Shut your gob, James,' said Sophie.

'Sophie!' Mrs Witrand raised her voice. 'I've told you before, I won't have you using that unkind expression.'

Harriet started to cry; James's flailing elbow had caught her on the side of her head.

'Right!' shouted Mr Witrand. 'Sleeping Lions, the lot of you!'

For a moment, Sophie considered objecting to the childishness of this, but the idea of closing her eyes and disappearing from the chaos of siblings and parents was very appealing. She leaned her head against her seatbelt strap and tried to get comfortable.

Next thing she knew, she was being gently shaken awake by her father.

'Sophie, Sophie, we're here.'

He was squatting in the gravel driveway outside the West Wing, his face just level with hers. Francis Witrand was tall and lanky with prominent knees. He favoured brown deck shoes without socks, and Aertex polo shirts in navy blue and racing green. His perfectly round, tortoiseshell spectacles never came off, even when he was in the sea.

'Well, I reckon you won that round,' he smiled. 'You didn't even hear us taking the bags in, did you?' He helped her gently to her feet. 'James and Harriet are in the kitchen – I think they're waiting for you.'

'Why?' Sophie was confused. Then she remembered. 'Oh, that.' Usually, Sophie led her siblings in an inventory of their favourite things: the big bed in the girls' room, with the enormous scrolled footboard that made it feel like a ship; a chipped rocking horse with real horse hair in its tail; the old bread oven in the kitchen wall, where

James had once hidden during their most epic game of hide-and-seek; the picnic tree, a hollow oak in the garden big enough for all three of them to fit inside.

'Actually, I think I'd rather just go and unpack,' Sophie told her father. 'Tell the others they can do it without me this time.' She scrunched across the gravel to the house, her puffy nipples chafing from the friction of her T-shirt. It felt hot between her legs, and a little bit itchy.

In the bedroom, she lay down on the big ship-bed and took out her mp3 player. Sophie's parents disapproved of all pop music expect those bands with 'real musical merit', which amounted to Sting, Dory Previn and the Beatles. Sophie selected track 09 on *The Best of the Beatles*, 'Hey Jude'. All of the Beatles songs, in fact all songs ever, were really about Ludo Hall, with his coppery hair and his golden voice. 'Hey Jude' clearly foretold the moment at which Ludo's chilly chorister façade would soften and melt. *The minute you can let her under your skin, then you begin to make it better...*

* * *

About a hundred miles north along the coast, Tamsin and Callum were spending the week at a bed-and-breakfast in Ilfracombe. They had driven down in a rented Vauxhall the day after their evening in the pub with Will and Chris. For the first hour of the journey, it rained. Neither of them said much. They were mildly hung-over, and still a little subdued by their argument the night before. Callum turned the radio on; Tamsin turned it off. 'You know I hate Rob Cowan. Sorry.'

They stopped at a service station for coffee and petrol. While Tamsin waited for Callum to pay, the sun came out, electroplating the puddles on the station forecourt.

Callum emerged, squinting at the sunlight, and Tamsin was surprised by a sudden surge of affection for him.

'I missed you,' she told him as he got back into the car. It was an odd thing to say, but Callum seemed to understand. He set their coffees down on the dashboard and kissed her, tenderly, carefully, on the mouth.

As they sped along the A303, the novelty of the venture began to excite them both. This was only their second holiday together; their first – a week's skiing in Austria last year – had lacked this thrilling element of escape. Tamsin leaned her head against the window frame, watching, faintly mesmerised, as the countryside unspooled itself. The further they drove from London, the more impossible it seemed that Chris Kimura could pose any kind of threat to her happiness with Callum. Last night had been a temporary derangement, a few hours of doubt brought on by tiredness and alcohol (a conclusion which neatly omitted the fact that her problems with Chris had begun *before* she started drinking). They passed Stonehenge, dark and dumbly significant. After Taunton, the road began to narrow and the place names became pleasingly alien: Sampford Peverell, Uffculme, Trull. They were still in England, only four hours' drive from the Edgware Road; yet it felt as if they had travelled out of place and time.

By the time they reached Ilfracombe, Tamsin was buzzing. She hammed up her enthusiasm, wriggling in her seat and demanding Callum drive the car straight down to the sea.

'Let's dump our bags. Then we'll have all afternoon to play. And if you're a very good girl, I might even buy you an ice cream.'

The Armeria Guesthouse was the cheapest B&B in town, because that was all that Tamsin, who had insisted on splitting the bill, could afford. 'Anyway, all these little places are just the same – greasy breakfasts, chintzy furniture. Naff, but also sort of charming.'

But the Armeria was too downmarket even to bother with chintz. The look was more Holiday-Inn-on-a-budget, with beige-grey walls and 'natural effect' imitation-linen curtains, attached to their rails by loops of fabric rather than curtain rings. The bed slanted sideways into a rhomboid if you so much as sat on it, and there was a pervasive stench of gas on the stairs. In the bathroom, the complimentary soap was small enough to be an after-dinner mint.

Tamsin shrugged her backpack to the ground, irritated to find herself close to tears.

Callum put his arms round her. 'Hey, who needs seaside kitsch when you could have, erm, what is this exactly, shall we say, a post-modern subversion of utilitarian design? Just as ugly, yet totally useless.'

Tamsin giggled into his T-shirt. She loved this about Callum: that he was never a point-scorer, even when patently in the right.

*　　*　　*

On Tuesday, the first day of his fortnight's leave, Chris Kimura was detained in Bulford by the hospitalisation of one of his men. (Nothing serious: Private Justin Cooley, too drunk to find his own pockets, had swallowed £2.77 in loose change after a win on the fruit machine.) On Wednesday morning he overslept. By the time he arrived in London, it was too late to drop off his big kitbag at Callum's flat: he had promised to meet Doug Ronson, an old friend from Sandhurst, in the Argyll Street Bella Pasta at 6 p.m. sharp.

Doug was based at Wrexham in North Wales. As a dedicated 'night-bomber', this was very hard on him; shags in Wrexham were in short supply, the local girls having long since wised up to the wiles of young men with cam-cream behind their ears. Doug spent most of his free time on uniformdating.com, 'the number one online dating site for anyone looking to date a soldier'. Women from as far away as Stoke-on-Trent were prepared to travel to Wrexham for a night of unconditional pleasure with Second Lieutenant Ronson, especially if he agreed to keep his combat boots on.

But tonight it was Doug making the journey and the effort. He had fallen not for an army-o-phile but for one of the uniforms: Helen, a lab technician at AstraZeneca. Helen's profile picture on uniformdating.com showed her posing goofily with a test-tube, dressed in lab coat and plastic safety goggles. Doug had messaged her with a suggestive remark about what she got up to with the test-tube and had been soundly reprimanded. Compellingly, it was the banality of his humour she had objected to, not the smut. Doug was hooked; they exchanged emails, more pictures, a phone call; and three weeks later, here he was in Bella Pasta, nervously checking the garlic-festooned entrance every ten seconds to see if Helen and her friend Lara had arrived.

'Doug, mate, relax. They're hardly going to miss us.' Chris gestured to his kitbag, which was propped up on a little tiled ledge right underneath the specials black-board: the staff, suspicious of its bulk, had insisted on keeping it in full sight. 'So tell me – what does this Laura look like?'

'Lara. Her name is Lara. You have to get that right, or Helen'll think I haven't been listening.'

Chris was Doug's wingman, there to make him look good by talking him up, or, in the event of false adver-tising on Helen's part, to get him out as quickly as possible. Helen was bringing Lara for the same purpose, though there was a tacit understanding that, if all went well, the evening would turn into a double date.

'Lara, right, got it. Well? Is she fit?' Funny, thought Chris – this bluff, blokey turn of phrase he adopted with his army buddies. He never thought of girls as 'fit', or 'racked', and he often winced to hear these words in the mouths of others.

'I don't know exactly, I haven't seen a photo. But Helen says she looks just like her, says they get mistaken for sisters all the time. And Helen is eff eye tee *fit*.'

Helen, it transpired, was stunning. She had longish hair the colour of slate, cut in a side-swept fringe that exposed a sweet sliver of pale forehead. Her blue eyes were expertly outlined in liquid eyeliner. Everything about her was sharply drawn, from her eyebrows to her cupid's bow.

'This is me—' she said, turning her upper body from left to right and back as if modelling her own clothes.

'You look … I mean…' began Doug. Doug had a very red face that should have rendered him unattractive, yet somehow didn't; now, confronted with Helen's careless beauty, his cheeks darkened almost to burgundy. Chris looked at him in surprise. Doug was an evangelist of a pick-up manual that expounded the art of the 'neg' (a back-handed compliment, designed to hook a girl by lowering her self-esteem). He made a point of never being openly impressed by a woman.

'—and this is Lara,' finished Helen, giving her friend a light squeeze round the shoulders.

'Hiya, guys,' said Lara, with a little wave. She looked like Helen only in so far as she had dark hair cut in an identical style. The hair was obviously dyed. She was very short with a boyish torso, thrust outward to maximise the jut of her suspiciously high breasts. Where Helen was pale, Lara was tanned a deep ochre, although this colouring was mottled in places.

'You're, um, very brown,' Chris told her as she sat down, then instantly regretted saying this.

But Lara was unconcerned. 'Yeah, it's great, isn't it? Best thing is, I didn't even have to go on a sunbed, and it's all natural, it's all my own pigment, right? These injections you can do, you get the kit online, melanotan it's called. It's not actually legal, but you've got to live life to the edge, right?' She let out a laugh that stopped as abruptly as it had begun.

'Gosh.'

Chris looked over at Doug for help, but the bugger merely winked and readjusted his seat so that they were more obviously arranged into two couples. He turned resignedly back to Lara. The only thing for it was to get drunk, fast. Chris picked up the bottle of wine and poured himself a generous glass.

Lara held out her own wine glass. 'Oh yeah, please, fill me up. This is so fun, isn't it?' she said bossily. 'Tell me now, what's your name?'

'Chris,' said Chris. He wondered whether her eyelashes were fake, too.

'No, I mean in the army. What name do they call you? Like general or colonel or whatever.'

'I'm a second lieutenant.'

'So that's pretty high, right?' Lara sounded impressed.

'For an officer, it's the lowest rank.'

She frowned. 'But how old are you?'

'Twenty-six.'

'So how come you're still on the lowest one? Are you not very good or what?'

Chris smiled despite himself. If nothing else, she was refreshingly blunt. 'I only started my training eighteen months ago. I've been a second lieutenant for six months.'

'So what were you doing for all that time, before the army?'

'I was doing a degree.'

84

Lara laughed the laugh. 'Get off, you're shitting me! You did *not* do a degree.'

'Why is that so unbelievable?'

'Because you're in the *army*,' said Lara. 'Go on, then, what did you study?'

'French and Italian.'

'You're just trying to chat me up. No *way* can you speak French. No *way*.'

'I don't know what to say,' said Chris flatly. 'Ask Doug if you don't believe me.'

'No, I want you to prove it. Say something in French.'

Chris shrugged, giving himself up to the utter absurdity of this conversation. 'All right then ... let's think ... *C'est un trou de verdure où chante une rivière, accrochant follement aux herbes des haillons d'argent; où le soleil, de la montagne fière, luit; c'est un petit val qui mousse de rayons.*'

It came out perfectly: no trips, no hesitations, plenty of Gallic panache. All three of them were looking at him as if he'd just levitated.

When Helen and Doug turned back to their conversation, Lara leaned across the table and asked, in an undertone,

'Will you say that when you're fucking me?'

* * *

Three pubs, one cocktail bar and a long, costly taxi ride later, Chris found himself fumbling with the clasp on Lara's heavily padded bra, surrounded by a galaxy of pink-tinted fairy lights.

From the moment Lara had posed her audacious question – *Will you say that when you're fucking me?* – there had been no doubt that they would end up sleeping together. Chris simply didn't have it in him to refuse. It had been months since he'd slept with anyone, and now here was a girl offering him unconditional sex in a tone which implied that, despite her unpromising exterior, she was something of an expert in the bedroom. Add to this the alchemy of alcohol and the transformation – from overdone Essex girl to petite and sultry sack artist with a great pair of tits – was complete.

Up in Lara's Ikea-filled bedroom, however, the charm was rapidly wearing off.

'Fuck it,' breathed Chris. Then: 'Sorry. Sorry. It's this clasp – I can't seem to—'

Lara made no attempt to help him. 'Doesnmatter, leave it on,' she mumbled, flopping back onto the bed. 'Ow! Scratchy.' She tossed a sequinned cushion to the floor with a hiccuppy giggle. Chris was kneeling over her, wearing nothing but his boxers and a single sock. Unsteadily, Lara lifted a leg until her foot was in line with his crotch. There was a large verruca on her big toe, surrounded by an escarpment of hardened skin.

'Mashage?' she asked.

Chris was confused. 'You – you want me to give you a massage?'

'Nooo,' she said impatiently, as if he were being very stupid; then, with surprising coordination for someone so drunk, she pressed her foot against his penis and began to stroke it up and down. It was unorthodox but not unpleasant. Chris closed his eyes.

Pain followed by vague nausea: Lara's foot had slipped, bringing her toes into contact with his balls. Chris opened his eyes and pulled her leg away from his crotch. He rubbed his subsiding erection, trying to ignore the ache in his balls. To his relief, he felt himself getting hard again. All he wanted now was to get this over with so he could sleep.

Still holding his cock with one hand, he tugged at

Lara's diamante-studded g-string. At this she became very animated, wriggling her legs enthusiastically to shuffle the g-string down and away and stroking her inner thighs in what was presumably meant to be a seductive, inviting manner.

'Oooooo,' she moaned. 'Ooooo, I want you so bad.'

Chris moistened his cock with spit and, after several false starts, succeeded in pushing it into her. She was very tight; even in his drunken state, it wouldn't take long for him to come like this. Lara accompanied his clumsy thrusting with a series of high-pitched sighs, each one slightly louder than the last.

Suddenly she went quiet and her features stiffened. For a moment, Chris thought she was about to orgasm; but then her cheeks bulged and she turned her head to vomit all over one of the sequined pillows. There was an extraordinary volume of the stuff, coloured a deep purple from all the red wine. Several strands of unchewed spaghetti glistened amongst the pulpy mess.

The vomit slithered slowly off the cushion and onto the mattress. Chris scrambled sideways, backing away from the sagging puddle as his cock softened and shrank.

* * *

In spite of the B&B, Tamsin and Callum were having a good time. They woke early each morning thanks to the ineffective curtains. While Callum showered, Tamsin knelt at the little table with the miniature kettle and the free sachets of Horlicks to make cheese and pâté sandwiches for their lunch. Then they would set out for a day on the beach, or a windy walk along the coast. Callum took his camera wherever they went. On the clifftop, he set up his tripod for a 360-degree panorama. He photographed the wildflowers in dazzling close-up, Tamsin's blurry form just visible in the background. When they were on the beach, he sketched while she read.

Most days they ate a pub supper, but Tamsin had promised to let Callum take her out for one meal in a restaurant of his choosing. Wednesday evening saw them dressed up for dinner at The Quay, a trendy harbour-side restaurant with a dining room decorated by Damien Hirst.

They started with gin and tonics in the bar, which they drank while flicking through that day's pictures, their heads pressed conspiratorially together over the camera screen. Halfway through the usual stock of wildflowers and seascapes, Tamsin shot out her hand to cover the camera.

Callum chuckled. 'It's okay, the coast's clear.'

'No, Callum, I don't want to see those, they're horrible,' Tamsin protested; but she let Callum prise her fingers off the screen.

'Look. Just look. You're beautiful.'

The pictures – three of them – showed Tamsin on a secluded beach, naked except for a pair of simple black bikini bottoms. In the first picture she was lying face-up on a towel that was also the New Zealand flag, sunbathing; in the second she was on her front, her buttocks stippled red by the texture of the towel; and in the third, she was actually posing for the camera. Callum had positioned her in front of the sea, then adjusted the aperture so that the background was nothing more than a grey-blue smudge. Tamsin's strident posture – shoulders back, chin held high – was at odds with the discomfort on her face. The corners of her mouth were tensed, as if hesitating between amusement and shame. Her hair, still wet from a recent swim, hung round her face in pointed clumps, and her knees and shoulders were dusted with the dull flat glitter of sand. Her heavy breasts swagged down and sideways; between them, the sun cast the undulations of her sternum into faint relief. One pale nipple was slightly stiffer than the other.

'Three graces for the price of one,' joked Callum, flicking back and forth between the pictures. He looked pleased.

'Okay, that's enough.' Tamsin took the camera from him and moved on to the next image: a cormorant on a rock, unfocused, just a little too far out for the zoom to reach. Then the signpost leading up from the beach: '104½ steps'. Then Tamsin eating an ice cream. Then Tamsin with the end of the ice-cream cone stuck to her nose, grinning clownishly. Then a flower, a bird, the sea.

'*God,*' said Tamsin suddenly, putting the camera down. 'I had no idea my tits looked that awful when I'm on my back. They were practically in my armpits. I look deformed.'

'Tam.' Callum shuffled round on his bar stool and took both of her hands in his. 'That's what breasts do.' He kissed her doubtful mouth. 'Look at me. You have very, very lovely breasts. There's a picture by Picasso – actually, a whole series of pictures – with a woman lying on the beach, just like that, tits all over the place. And it's lovely.'

'I bet she was big. I bet she was *Amazonian.*' This was a deliberate reproach: Callum had once used the word 'Amazonian' in praise of Tamsin, and had never been forgiven. 'Anyway, I don't even like Picasso. Why would I want to look like one of his weird disfigured women?'

'Well, Picasso likes you.' Callum was typically undeterred by the venom in Tamsin's voice. 'Picasso fancies you rotten. *I* fancy you rotten.'

A smile tweaked her cheeks.

The next picture was the last, and the only one of both Callum and Tamsin together. Callum had held the camera at arm's length, gripping Tamsin to him with his free hand. Their faces appeared at the very edge, as though the wind were blowing them out of the frame. Tamsin's hair had wrapped itself around her neck like a shawl. They were breathless from the wind and the exercise, lending the picture an atmosphere of jubilant spontaneity. This was not the case at all: the first four versions of this picture had been deleted right there on the clifftop, on the grounds that Callum looked too grumpy. 'You just made me pose naked. The least you could do is smile,' Tamsin had admonished him. Now, as the picture told its beneficent lie, they could both see that it had been a good idea.

'We look happy,' Tamsin said.

'We *are* happy,' Callum corrected, squeezing her softly round the waist.

* * *

In Penderick, the Witrands were playing dominoes. 'This whole game is basically just chance, isn't it?' Sophie asked her father in a superior tone, confident that he, too, would be bored by such a trivial pastime. The whole holiday had been a bit boring, so far. They had done all the usual things: trips to the beach, ice creams, crab fishing, barbecues, lazy afternoons by the salt-water swimming pool. Yet for Sophie, none of this was quite as much fun as it used to be. Also, the itching between her legs wouldn't go away. Terrified that it might be the onset of her first period, she kept dashing off to the bathroom to check; then, worried that her loo-trips were suspiciously frequent, she took to sliding a finger (under the table, behind a tree) down into her pants to see if it came up bloody. It didn't, but she still felt repulsed by the faint glisten of moisture on her fingertip. When she couldn't get to a tap to wash it off, she would hold the finger just in front of her mouth and allow a little gobbet of spittle to drip down onto it, then wipe it dry with a twist of her T-shirt.

'Hang on...' Mr Witrand was counting out dominoes. 'Three ... four ... five...' Then he turned over one of his tiles to reveal a one–two spot. 'Actually, it's not just chance. It's quite interesting, really. Imagine you've just played this domino, and there are no other two spots out on the table.'

'Dad, we can see your domino!' Harriet objected.

James slid right down in his seat so that his chin rested on the edge of the table. 'James, stop messing about,' Mrs Witrand told him.

James made his eyes bulge horribly. 'But I'm a headless man,' he said, hoarsely, his throat constricted by the pressure from the table.

'If you're headless, how come I can see your head?' Harriet wanted to know.

'Francis,' said Mrs Witrand, gently. 'The others want to play. Now,' she beamed round at her brood, 'who's got the double six?'

It was Sophie. She pushed the little tile over with her finger and flicked it out into the centre of the table, not bothering to straighten it when it came to rest at an angle.

'Wow, well done, Sophie.' Harriet was impressed.

'Don't be so dumb, it's just luck,' Sophie said crossly. 'So you shouldn't say well done. If I didn't actually do anything. Which I didn't.'

She cheered up a bit when she won the first round. Trying not to appear too pleased, Sophie sat back and watched her father scrambling the dominoes. For some reason, her eyes followed the back of the double six as it clinked around among the other tiles. She looked away, but not for long enough to lose it: when the time came to pick again, she selected the tile she thought she had been watching and was guiltily gratified to find that it was indeed the double six.

At the end of the second round she did it again.

'Gosh, Sophie, that's your third double six in a row!' her mother exclaimed. There was no hint of suspicion in her voice: everyone knew that Sophie never lied.

Sophie grinned. 'I know, isn't it cool?' She was enjoying herself now. It was intoxicating, the ease with which she had fooled them all. For the second time in her childhood, she realised that her reputation for absolute truthfulness entailed enormous power.

(The first time still troubled her conscience: when she was seven and James was five, Mrs Witrand had helped them to make plaster-of-Paris figurines of Peter Rabbit and one of the weasels from *The Wind in the Willows*. Peter was Sophie's; she had painted him beautifully, just like in the book, with a tiny orange carrot sticking out of his blue jacket pocket. James's weasel – painted royal blue with bright pink and green spots – had, unaccountably, won far greater acclaim from Mrs Witrand, who took to showing the little figurine to her friends with a tittered suggestion that she should 'enter it for the Turner prize'. Bored one afternoon, Sophie found herself overcome by a desire to see if she could snap the head off the Peter Rabbit. As soon as she had done so, she regretted it. In tears, she offered up the broken Peter to her mother, blaming the damage on James. She was comforted; James, who habitually told little white lies, was punished, and no amount of protesting on his part could clear his name. Several times in the intervening five years Sophie had been on the brink of confessing this lie; but she could never quite face the loss of credibility that would ensue.)

When Sophie turned up the double six for a fourth time in a row, everyone was amazed.

'My goodness, the chances of that—' Mr Witrand did some hurried calculations on the back of a Chinese take-away menu. 'So that's about ... nought point nought-

noughtnought one percent. *Astronomically* small. We have all just witnessed,' he announced solemnly, 'an extra*ordinary* probabilistic event.'

'Maybe Sophie's magic,' Harriet suggested.

'There's no such thing as magic.' The return of Sophie's bad mood coincided with a sudden increase in the intensity of the itching in her pants. This must be it, she thought: her dreaded period, here at last. 'I need the loo,' she told her family, pushing roughly past James in her haste to leave. 'You guys play this one without me, Harry can have my six.'

* * *

Tamsin and Callum were a little unsteady on their way back from the restaurant. They walked with their arms round each other's waists, hips bumping awkwardly together. There was a full moon and a freckling of stars. Callum half-sang, half-whistled snatches of a Fats Waller song they both liked. 'You're not the only oyster in the stew ... not the only Frenchman in Paree ... da dum da dum mmm but you're the only one for me.'

Back at the Armeria, they undressed in silence. They were both preoccupied with their own versions of the same very familiar problem. Callum was frantically cycling through mental picture after mental picture – not cormorants or wildflowers this time, but women, in all possible postures and combinations of depravity, hoping beyond hope that he would light on something that excited his groin as well as his mind. Tamsin, on the other side of the bed, was second-guessing this agitation.

Over the years Tamsin had become adept at calculating Callum's internal state from a number of subtle external factors. Right now, for example, it was nearly midnight – so he would be tired. There had been a lot of alcohol.

And a fair bit of boisterous sexual humour in the restaurant, she thought. He was like that, sometimes, when he was feeling nervous. Worst of all, the evening itself – the romantic dinner, that tipsy walk in the moonlight – expected sex; and Tamsin knew that, for Callum, expectation was fatal.

'Hold on, won't be a tick...' Callum muttered, and shuffled off into the bathroom, for the second time in fifteen minutes.

Now this was an unequivocal indication that he was delaying the moment of contact. Tamsin made her decision. Leaving her knickers on, she climbed into bed and waited for Callum to join her.

This was the real problem with Callum's problem: that he was completely unable to talk about it. His openness on that day by the canal three years ago had taken a colossal effort of will; since then, he and Tamsin had barely exchanged three words on the subject. It was this silence, rather than the problem itself, that previous girlfriends had been unable to cope with.

But it was an issue that also wasn't an issue – thanks, in large part, to Tamsin. Once she realised how much her attempts to talk about it upset him, she had stopped trying. She did something that none of his other girlfriends had ever done: she accepted his conditions. She made no further mention of counselling or Viagra or hypnosis. Instead of talking, she watched and listened. Like a bird-watcher returning to the same spot each day, her powers of observation had increased with time. She knew that her mouth – though far from infallible – was more effective than her hands or her vagina. She knew when he wanted to persevere, and when he wanted to give up. Crucially, she knew when he didn't want to try at all.

It would be wrong to suggest that Tamsin didn't mind all of this. The important thing was that she minded it less than she liked Callum. And then she got used to it, as human beings are helplessly bound to get used to anything, given enough time. What had once seemed strange and awkward to her now seemed almost normal. Without realising it, she began to enjoy Callum's voiceless gratitude, to enjoy looking after him, to enjoy being good at it. The silence was like a shared secret, binding them more closely together than easy, uncomplicated sex could ever have done.

And she was by no means unsatisfied. When sex itself failed, Callum was usually happy to bring her to orgasm another way. He was considerably better at doing so than anyone she had slept with before. Initially, Tamsin was uncomfortable about the asymmetry of this arrangement – how so often their time in bed would end with her contented and spent, yet without any possibility of recip-rocating. Before long, though, she found that this asym-metry had been subtly incorporated into the private culture of their sex life. In 'real life', she abhorred the differences between her background and Callum's, and did everything she could to reject the trappings of her privileged child-hood. But in the bedroom there was an unmistakable flavour of dominion and servitude – she lordly, reclining, he humbly tending to her needs. It was a dynamic that excited her more she than realised. And Callum sensed her excitement and found it deeply gratifying, even though he could only rarely match it with his own.

So most of the time sex, in some form, was possible; but there were nights – like tonight – when Tamsin under-stood that the humiliation of his impotence was simply too much for Callum – that any attempt at sex would be a cruelty. He had been in the bathroom for a long time. When he finally reappeared he slipped back into the bed and lay there, not saying anything, making no move to touch her. His misery was palpable.

Tamsin rolled over onto her side and pressed her lips against his cheek.

'I think I'd rather if we just stayed like this, you know, kissing, tonight,' she whispered. 'I've actually started my period. It's early this month. It's not that heavy, it's just – you know, sometimes you don't really feel like it.'

Callum shifted to face her, instantly animated by his relief. 'We don't have to do anything, hen, if you don't want to. You know that.' He touched a finger to her nose.

Tamsin kissed him then flipped round so that her body was cupped by his. Callum reached his hand over her waist and pressed his palm into her stomach.

'Does it hurt? Do you have cramp?

'A little,' Tamsin told him. 'It's not so bad.'

This sort of lie gave Tamsin no trouble at all. She liked that she could do this for Callum; she liked *knowing* him, and being known. They were specialists, she thought sleepily, specialists in each other.

'Cal?' Her resolve arrived suddenly, a free gift. 'When we get back, I want to move in with you.'

She felt his body stiffen. 'Really? You're sure?'

'Very sure. Look, I can take that Associated Board examining job. And another few hours of teaching. That'll take me up to, what, at least a grand each month.'

'But—' Callum was still wary of the good news. 'But I thought you said the AB job was drudge work. That it would take up too much of your practice time.'

'Callum, I really want to live with you.'

This time the emotion in her voice persuaded him.

* * *

Leah Chapman's Thursday-night swim always followed the same routine: ten lengths for the warm-up, then breast-stroke legs with no arms, then breast-stroke arms with no legs. Then a sort of interval training that she'd learned from her father. You did four lengths, then rested, then three lengths, then rested, then two lengths, then one length, then two again, then three again, then four. It was a way of tricking your body into working harder. On the way down you instinctively sped up, because you knew the distances were getting shorter. But somehow your body got stuck on the 'fast' setting, so that on the way back up you overdid it, and by the end you were exhausted.

Exhausted felt good. Leah was happiest in the shower once it was all over, clean, non-chlorinated water pulsing down over her neck and shoulders. She washed her hair with a product called Ultra Swim to combat the chlorine. The conditioner was thick and pearlescent and formed a stiff aquamarine worm cast as you squeezed it out into your palm. Leah had a special microfibre towel to dry herself on, no bigger than a facecloth: even on the short walk from the pool back to the flat, she disliked feeling the warm wet weight of a conventional towel, breeding germs in her sports bag.

On the way out of the ladies' changing room Leah passed two vending machines. One sold isotonic sports drinks in implausible shades of green and blue, but the other – the other never failed to sideswipe her with the big soft mitt of nostalgia. Crunchie, Twix, Mars, Refresher, Chomp ... When she was three, Leah's father had taught her to swim, then taken her, four times a week for eight years, to Dolphins swim club at the Moseley Road pool. If she was one of the fastest in her group, he would reward her with a chittery-bite from the vending machine. A chittery-bite was any chocolate bar you ate when you were feeling chittery – or, in her father's Brummie accent, 'chidderuh'. He had wanted her to swim in the Olympics.

Leah Chapman was twenty-four and she hadn't eaten a chittery-bite in over a decade. Usually she rewarded her efforts in the pool with a fresh pack of chewing gum. Leah had a serious chewing-gum habit, putting away in excess of one packet a day, and more when she was feeling stressed. It was not unusual for her to wake with jaw-ache the morning after a particularly intense chewing session. There were only five calories in a piece of sugar-free Wrigleys, and, better still, Leah had read that the motion of chewing triggered the digestive process in your stomach. You could trick your body, just like with the interval training.

It had been hot all week but, to Leah's relief, the pavements were dark with rainwater: a flash downpour while she had been in the pool. Any prolonged hot spell, even in August, counted for Leah as sinister evidence of global warming. She walked slowly, enjoying the freshness in the air.

At the newsagents, Leah bought a multi-pack of Spearmint Extra and a bottle of Evian. The good-looking Pakistani boy behind the counter gave her a special smile: 'Andhowareyoutoday?' She would have to start going to the next newsagents along, even though it smelled of fish food. Contrary to popular opinion, Leah often felt uncomfortable about the admiration her beauty provoked. What it amounted to was a frustrating lack of privacy. Men were constantly trying to engage with her on this privileged, intimate level, posing their silent questions, forcing her behaviour to read as invitation or discouragement.

Back at the flat, Leah put her swimming costume and the microfibre cloth to soak in hot water and antibacterial detergent. Then she changed into a pair of imitation-silk pyjamas and padded through to the kitchen to make supper: low-fat, low-sodium hummus spread over two rice cakes, with a sliced-up apple on top.

It was not until she carried this meal over to the television that she noticed Chris. He was asleep on the sofa, dressed in a dark green T-shirt and a pair of boxer shorts. She knew that he might be using Callum's room this week, and her initial shock was rapidly replaced by irritation. Now she would have to wake him, assuage his embarrassment, make conversation...

Then she was overcome by an embarrassment of her own. She had completely forgotten his name. She stared at him, trying to think. He was snoring lightly and there was a whitish patch of dried saliva in the corner of his mouth.

Leah put a hand on his shoulder and squeezed.

'Um – hi? Hello? Hello?'

For a few seconds he didn't respond – then woke abruptly, starting away from her touch and covering himself with a cushion as if he were actually naked. 'Oh god. I'm so sorry. I meant to text you – I must've fallen asleep. I used your shower – I was getting dressed – I just lay down for a moment, and then ... I'm so sorry.'

'It's okay.' Leah didn't bother to hide her annoyance. 'Why don't you go and get dressed?'

'Yes. Yes. I'm so sorry—' Chris stood up and backed away towards the door of Callum's bedroom.

Leah turned on the television. She found the twenty-four-hour news and gazed blankly at the scrolling red ribbon of text at the bottom of the screen. She thought his name was a P or maybe a D. David? Daniel? Peter?

When he came back he was wearing jeans and a T-shirt printed with a cartoon of a man in a striped full-body swimsuit under the words 'Hatfield College: Having A Jolly Good Time Since 1854'. He looked very tired, with lines around his mouth and eyes that Leah didn't remember from before.

'I'm so sorry,' he began again, then stopped, briefly

distracted by the news, which was showing pictures of Iranian detainees accused of conspiracy following Ahmadinejad's re-election. 'Sorry, I keep saying sorry. But I feel awful, I mean—'

'It's okay,' Leah said again, more sincerely.

'Is that – what's that?' He had noticed the tray of food on her lap. 'Because I thought – do you want to get a takeaway?'

'No, no, this is just a snack, I've already eaten,' Leah lied.

'Right. Right. Would it be okay, if I just sort of stayed here this evening? Because I'm – I had quite a heavy one last night. To say the least.' He tugged at the neck of his T-shirt and lowered his head slightly so that he had to glance upwards to meet her eye. It was a contrite, confessional gesture that made him look, for all his height and bulk, like a little boy.

Leah got to her feet, resigned now to an evening of his company. 'I'll get you some painkillers.'

On her way back from the bathroom, his name came to her at last.

'Here you go, Chris.' Pleased with herself, Leah held out the ibuprofen and a glass of water.

Chris gave her a grateful smile. 'Thanks. You don't drink, do you?'

'I try not to.'

'Sensible girl.' Then, more seriously: 'How come?'

'It's because...' Leah paused to weigh up her two answers, the pious press release (that alcohol was full of unrefined sugars, not to mention bad for the liver) and the real reason. Chris was looking up at her expectantly. 'It's because – well, I have eczema.'

She pushed back her sleeve and held her arm out to show him. In the crook of her elbow there was a lozenge of tough pink skin, flaky and slightly ribbed in texture.

'When I drink it itches more, and I scratch it. I can't seem to help myself. Not just here, but all over. I wake up the next morning and the sheets are all specky with blood. It's horrible.' This came out aggressively, as if she were somehow holding Chris responsible for the problem. She hurried to change the subject. 'Shall we – what do you want to watch? Callum's got loads of DVDs.'

'No, what do *you* want to watch?' Chris was reticent, unwilling to take the lead.

'I don't mind.' Leah knelt by the DVDs. 'What sort of thing do you like?'

'Well ... say if you're not – but I think, I think I'm in the mood for a bit of horror.'

'Horror?' Leah brightened, smiling for the first time. 'I love horror movies.'

Chris and Leah liked horror for different reasons: Leah for the way the sneaky camerawork and the creepy music never failed to quicken her heartbeat; and Chris for the crass predictability of the genre, the way everything, but everything, was signposted in advance (by the music, by the lighting, by the sheer stupidity of the victim-protagonists).

Nonetheless, a little patch of common ground had been exposed, and this, along with the fact that she had managed to remember his name, helped dissipate the last of Leah's irritation. As she settled herself on the sofa, she noticed that his cheeks were completely smooth; what stubble he had was very fine, and concentrated entirely around his chin and mouth. She decided that she disliked him less than she had done in the pub last Saturday. Then, he had been loud and alarmingly talkative. Confident, articulate people unsettled Leah, because they made her acutely aware of her own social failings. She was usually okay when it was just her and one other person, but in a group she knew she had no chance.

When she did manage to think of something to say, she hid her shyness behind a sardonic tone that came out sounding much ruder than she meant it to. Combined with her reputation for sleeping around, this brusqueness won her few female friends: she knew that the prevailing opinion among the girls at work was that Leah Chapman was out for herself, a loner, a predator, a slag.

It felt odd that anyone should think of her in this way. She actually thought that being a slag sounded quite nice: it implied hedonistic abandon. That wasn't her at all, because she didn't really like sex. Thanks to *Cosmo* and Hollywood, she had a shrewd idea of how it was meant to feel, but in her extensive experience, penetration resulted in pain or nothing at all – certainly not the kind of pleasure that could make you cry out with delight. Each time she slept with someone new, there would be a brief moment when it seemed as if things might go differently; but in the end it was always the same, boring and slightly uncomfortable. Sometimes she thought she would stop having sex altogether, and live out the rest of her life like the stick insects she had kept as a child, munching on leaves, making herself invisible. But these periods of abstinence never lasted more than two or three weeks. Sex was a habit with her now – a habit perpetuated by loneliness, and, bizarrely, a sense of obligation. Leah found it difficult to say no, and she had a dim superstition that, if she refused too many offers, there would come a point when no more offers would be made. Although she often felt oppressed by male attention, she could not imagine life without it.

Chris and Leah watched in companionable silence, both deriving from the movie's familiar trajectory that sense of achievement peculiar to well-loved books and films, which oblige us by meeting our expectations at every turn. Chris's mind was half on Leah's quiet presence beside him, the way her body tensed and relaxed as each scene built to its melodramatic climax. He realised that he was enjoying her company. There was something calming about her, which, after the messy debauchery of the night before, he was well-placed to appreciate. Certainly she was no longer standoffish, as she had seemed in the pub last weekend. And he was touched by her revelation about the eczema, which he read – correctly – as an uncharacteristic lowering of her guard.

Leah sat right forward in her seat for the closing sequence; then, when the credits rolled up, she sat back again, her shoulder brushing against Chris's as she did so. Chris half-shuddered, half-thrilled at this contact. He was in that strange, shivery phase of his hangover, when the skin's sensory abilities seem unnaturally heightened – not quite arousal, but something very similar. He turned to look properly at Leah. Her hair was almost dry now. The mole on her right cheek was flat and pale with ragged edges, a bit like a melted smudge of milk chocolate. Chris resisted an impulse to reach up and thumb it away.

'Good stuff, eh?' he said, inclining his head towards the television.

'Mmmm,' Leah agreed.

It happened almost by accident: their eyes met, casually, insignificantly. Chris looked away, then glanced back – to find that Leah was still looking at him. In fact, she too had looked away then looked back, and, meeting Chris's gaze for a second time, assumed that he had never taken his eyes off her.

Now it seemed to each of them as if the other were very deliberately maintaining this contact. The look lengthened, accrued meaning. So Chris wanted to kiss her, Leah thought; well, she had no particular objection to that. Chris was remembering, dimly, something Tamsin had said to him at the tube station the other night: *You go and have fun with Leah.* Had Tamsin known that Leah liked him?

With the first contact – soft and light on her upper lip, Chris's tongue felt faintly, as warmth rather than wetness – came a flicker of excitement in Leah's belly, and then another, deeper stirring lower down. Leah closed her eyes and willed her mind into these sensations, trying to keep them alight. It was a bit like being in bed when it was very cold, with one false move enough to destroy the thin aura of heat around your body. Chris increased the pressure of his lips and tongue; he had his hands in her hair, and she could hear, from his breathing, that he was becoming aroused. With effort, Leah kept contact with the feeling inside her.

But as they kissed their way through to her bedroom, and Chris's hands began to clutch more urgently at her pyjamas, the old disconnect started to set in. Fifteen minutes ago, they had been sitting on the sofa watching a horror movie. Now Chris was palming her breasts. Her mind caught on the weirdness of this and the tingling in her belly vanished. She tried for a few moments to get it back, though she knew very well it was gone for good. Chris started to unbutton her pyjama top. He held it closed until all the buttons were undone, then opened it with a movement that reminded Leah, absurdly, of someone spreading a newspaper. Holding the top open, he stared at her body with what she presumed was meant to be lust-filled awe. The gap between what she felt and what Chris was evidently experiencing widened further. But there was a protocol stronger than her apathy at work. Leah shrugged off her pyjama top then reached for the hem of Chris's T-shirt. Chris eagerly took the hint, tugging the T-shirt off over his head and flinging it to the floor.

'Lie down,' he commanded her.

Leah lay down on her back.

'No, like this – on your side.' Chris rolled her over so that she was facing away from him. 'I'm going to kiss your back, all over,' he announced, as if proposing a special treat.

'Mmmm,' said Leah, and Chris began to kiss her back, with feeling. Leah watched the wall, wondering why they were doing this. She was bored and a little bit cold. It was taking a long time. She moaned a bit, so as not to seem ungrateful.

And then she was back facing Chris, and he was kissing her mouth, her breasts, her belly, caressing her nipples, moving his hand down between her legs, back up to his mouth to moisten his fingers, down between her legs again, rubbing and stroking and dipping and poking, and all the while she heard herself, with a chill disappointment, providing the familiar backing track of groans and sighs, mood music for Chris's mounting excitement. She watched him fumble with the condom, his desire too quick for his fingers. It was strange, she thought, as he entered her, seeing someone so clearly *in the grip* of something, when she herself felt so little. As he approached his orgasm his lips puckered and stiffened and the tip of his tongue stuck out. His eyes were squeezed shut, like a little child playing peek-a-boo.

Chris *was* having a good time, though not quite so straightforwardly as Leah imagined. After the cosy clutter of the sitting room, Leah's spartan bedroom was a shock. It was a large room made larger by the fact that it was almost completely empty, apart from a wardrobe, a double futon, and a small table with a silver Mac laptop positioned in its centre. There were no photographs of friends or family. The only decoration on the walls was a huge mirror in a thick black plastic frame. Chris was relieved when they moved to the futon, so that he was no longer aware of his reflection, hulking boorishly over Leah's petite figure. But even on the futon he felt exposed.

Then there was Leah's breathtaking beauty. It seemed to Chris that a girl this good-looking must be accustomed to pyrotechnics in the bedroom; and the mere thought of this gave him stage fright. The malarkey with her back had partly been an attempt to appear sensitive and passionate, but mostly it was a chance for Chris to steady himself, to buy a little time before the breach.

When Leah started to respond out loud to his kisses, Chris's penis stiffened from a semi into a full-on erection. But it felt precarious. He was tired and horribly hungover; he knew he couldn't afford to take his time. Luckily, Leah's obvious arousal encouraged him to pick up the pace. Her dryness surprised him slightly, but it didn't seem to be diminishing her pleasure, and once he was inside her she started to buck and moan with real enthusiasm. Her excitement redoubled his; he was close, too close, he was going to come and there was nothing he could do about it, he was going to fail at this – but then, just as he began to tip over the edge she came too, loudly and joyfully, clawing at his back, mewling and panting as he emptied himself inside her.

Chris's hangover, kept temporarily at bay by the sex, returned with renewed force as soon as his orgasm subsided. His head was thick and sore and he felt overwhelmed by a crushing, full-body exhaustion. He managed to knot the condom and place it on the heel of his upturned shoe, which was lying next to the bed, and kiss Leah once on the mouth; then he put his arms around her, mumbled an unintelligible apology for being so tired, and promptly fell into a deep sleep.

Leah held him for a bit, feeling faintly disgusted at the stickiness created by flesh on flesh. She felt his body twitch, and shivered herself: the spasms of early sleep always gave her the creeps. When she was certain he was properly asleep she eased herself away from him and crept out to the bathroom to clean herself up. She ran a shallow bath and lay there for a long time.

She had a memory, blurred at the edges but bright in the centre, of being very small in a big room with lots of hexagonal tables. Each table had its own activity: drawing, painting, sticking, etc. At one table, the children were scribbling on sheets of paper with wax crayons; as Leah watched, beautiful patterns emerged from the scribble. The memory jumped forward: she was sitting at a table by herself, with a pile of paper in front of her, scribbling on sheet after sheet in an attempt to make the patterns come. A teacher, tall with alarming lipstick, had stooped to ask her what she was doing making such a mess – then explained, with a derisive laugh, that you had to put a lace doily under the paper before you rubbed it with the crayon.

The word 'stupid' had not actually been said, but Leah, aged two or three or four, had heard it anyway. It seemed to Leah that this was still her trouble – that she was stupid at sex. Obviously, she was missing something crucial, but she had no idea what that might be.

Chris was still asleep when she got up the next morning. Leah dressed as quietly as she could, but just as she was about to leave her phone pinged with an email alert and Chris sat up, blinking his confusion.

'Where – oh – you're going,' he said.

'I didn't want to wake you.'

Chris shook his head to clear it of sleep. 'Listen, tonight – I'm with friends tonight. But on Saturday, do you want to do dinner?'

'Saturday I'm busy,' Leah said automatically, shouldering her handbag and moving towards the door.

'Well – how about Saturday – in three weeks' time. Sorry it's so far ahead.'

The invitation, although Leah couldn't know this, was rooted in Chris's personal code of chivalry rather than any genuine desire to see her again. He was asking her out simply because he couldn't imagine not asking her out, now that he had slept with her. Chris had a strong conception of 'what sort of guy' he was, based on ideals of honour and courage and decency. He was *not* the sort of guy who slept with girls then never called them back. Really, casual sex sat uneasily with his deeply romantic nature. Whenever he fell short of this standard – as he had done two nights ago, with Lara – he would admonish himself sternly for a day or so, then do his best to forget the transgression completely.

Leah put her hand on the doorknob. Her instinct was to turn him down, as she had done with almost every other man she had ever slept with.

But then an idea came to her. She would see Chris again: she would sleep with him, and this time, for the first time ever, *she wouldn't lie*. No, she promised herself, she wouldn't make a single noise unless it escaped her lips of its own accord. She had no idea what would happen if she did this – just a sudden desire to do something different, to break the cycle of faking orgasm after orgasm with man after man.

'Okay,' she told him. 'Three weeks on Saturday. I'll see you then.'

* * *

On the last night of their holiday, the Witrands went to a pub in a nearby village. Sophie slurped her way through a pound of mussels, impressing both her parents.

Everyone but Harriet had finished their main courses. James was in the loo; Mrs Witrand was monitoring

Harriet's progress with her scampi; and Sophie and her father were using a shoelace to try out 'Grog's Index of Basic Knots', which was printed on the back of the menu.

Harriet let her knife and fork fall noisily to her plate. '*Now* can I have some ice cream?'

'Don't talk with your mouth full, please. We said half. You had ten to start with. So you've got one more to go.' Mrs Witrand turned a sun-reddened shoulder to her youngest daughter. 'Francis? James has been an awfully long time. Do you think you should go and check on him?'

But before Mr Witrand could answer, James was back.

'Mum, mum, there's a machine in the toilets selling lollipops, they're only one pound for *three*, can we get, I mean please can we get some?' He positioned himself next to his mother's chair, his head angled upwards. 'Pleeease?' he said again, twisting his features into a comical parody of an angelic child: eyelashes fluttering, grin peeled back to reveal gappy front teeth.

Mrs Witrand was flustered. 'Darling, I don't think those are lollipops. Just go and have another little look, okay?'

Sophie wondered why her mother was whispering; then, suddenly understanding, she let out a snirt of laughter.

'Soph, Soph, what's so funny?' Harriet wanted to know.

Mrs Witrand frowned at Sophie. 'Nothing. Nothing's funny.'

'Can we have ice cream *and* a lollipop? Look—' Harriet opened her mouth to demonstrate its emptiness, bar a few white flecks of scampi on her tongue.

'James made a mistake, there aren't any lollipops.'

'There are, there are!' James was back, his voice loud with the excitement of being right. 'I checked and there really are, they've got three flavours, strawberry chocolate and banana, *and* they say they're extra long lasting.'

109

Someone at a nearby table snickered.

'Francis.' Mrs Witrand's voice was ominously neutral. 'I thought you said you'd talked to him.

'Well—'

'I'm taking the children to the car. We'll wait for you there while you pay.'

'So we're not getting ice cream?'

'You can have two tomorrow. No arguing, okay?'

In bed that night the itching was worse than ever. Sophie's phantom period still hadn't started, but it was surely only a matter of time. She wished she could get to a computer to find out what the itching meant, how long she had left before her sentence began. She couldn't stop thinking about Elena, the German exchange student who'd attended the school last term. Elena had been very tall with lots of frizzy mouse-grey hair and biggish breasts made shapeless by a thick cotton sports bra. Everyone knew she had her period because sometimes she couldn't go swimming, and once after netball Rhiannon Jenkins had found some STs in her washbag – little plastic-packed squares printed with a pattern of polka dots. For some reason these squares had been codenamed 'biscuits'; for the rest of term it was all the rage to ask Elena if she wanted a biscuit then run off, giggling hysterically.

Maybe she could just pretend to be ill every time it was her period, Sophie thought. Then she wouldn't have to tell anyone about it, not even her mother. She could simply stay in bed for – how long did a period last, anyway? Two days? Three days? A whole week?

There was another twinge between her legs, the largest yet. Sophie glanced over at Harriet to check she was asleep and pushed her hand down under the bedclothes. She rubbed at the source of the itching. This time, she detected more than just moisture. There was something

110

squishy, almost solid. She brought her hand up again, carefully cupped to protect whatever it was from the bedclothes.

There, on her fingertip, was a tiny worm. There was just enough moonlight coming through the gap in the heavy velvet curtains for Sophie to see that its body was ridged and whitely translucent.

As she watched, its pointed tail waved gently from side to side.

Seven

The same combination of accident and inertia that had sparked their kiss ensured that Chris and Leah's first date led to a second – a development facilitated, in his well-meaning way, by Callum. On the afternoon of his return from Ilfracombe, he called Chris to arrange a time for the two of them to finally sit down together and talk about the army.

'Why don't we do Sunday week, so a fortnight today?' Chris suggested. 'You probably know this already, but – I'm actually going out with Leah that night, on the Saturday. So I'll be in town anyway.'

'No, I didn't know that.' Callum was surprised but pleased. 'That's great. I assume' – here his tone changed to one of good-natured salaciousness – 'I assume you've, ah, got a bed for the night?'

'Yes, barring the definite possibility that I completely balls things up,' Chris bantered back – feeling, not for the first time, that 'things' were gathering a disconcerting momentum of their own. He had suggested this date to Leah out of courtesy and even pity; and now here he was, casting himself as the clumsy supplicant, implying that beneath his chipper self-deprecation lay a genuine interest in Callum's flatmate.

Callum laughed, then grew serious again. 'I have to tell you, Chris, it's great to hear that Leah's finally going for a decent bloke.'

Chris was flattered, but he left the conversation with the worrying impression that a false move with Leah could well earn him the disapproval of Callum and, by extension, Tamsin. Up till now he had looked no further into the future than this upcoming date. Callum's enthusiasm seemed to suggest that more might be expected of him; that it might be very difficult to drop Leah without serious collateral damage.

That evening, Callum cooked supper for Leah, ostensibly as a thank-you for hosting Chris in his absence, but with the ulterior motive of quizzing her on the subject of this date. They ate a vegetable stir-fry with brown rice noodles, all the vegetables organic and seasonal and locally sourced. Callum was always considerate of Leah's esoteric eating habits, which were legion. He suspected that the real reason for her pickiness was a concern not for the greenhouse effect but for her weight, which she monitored twice daily on a futuristic pair of scales that also measured her BMI. Yet he said nothing. Despite her man-eating reputation, Leah lacked robustness. Callum thought of her in much the same way as he might think of a particularly diffident student, and this invoked in him the strong protective instinct that had prompted him to speak so warmly of her to Chris.

'There's more in the wok if you want it,' he said now, knowing that she would refuse.

Leah pushed her plate away. 'No thanks, I'm really full. Sort of a bit bloated, actually – rice does that to me, sometimes.' She tore a piece of glossy black plastic seal from the top of the soy sauce bottle and strummed it against her thumb.

'All going well at work, then?' Callum asked, for the

second time that evening. He and Leah never seemed to have much to say to one another. According to Tamsin, it was because Leah was fundamentally boring, but Callum couldn't agree. He thought of those wood-panelled rooms in old murder-mystery novels, where the tap-tapping of the detective's knuckles reveals a secret passage behind a certain section of the wall. Callum felt sure that there was more to Leah than her beauty and her food fads. It was just a question of finding the way in.

When Leah got up to clear the plates, Callum followed her into the kitchen.

'Chris says you're going on a date.'

'That's right.' Leah kept her head bowed over the dishwasher.

'You don't sound very excited.'

'Mmmm.' She shrugged, still facing away from him.

Callum was irritated by her nonchalance. He was, in a sense, her champion – one of the only people who thought of Leah as prey, not predator. Watching her slim back as she bent over the dirty plates, he saw the possibility that the other picture of her was correct. He felt abruptly uncomfortable about the encouragement he had given Chris.

'Leah?' he said, making no attempt to soften the school-room severity in his tone. 'Chris is a good guy. I hope you're not going to mess him around.'

Leah shook her head as if this were an absurd idea, smiling her gummy smile to hide a hurt that Callum saw anyway. He repressed the impulse to apologise: no harm in making her think a bit, he decided.

Then there was the date itself. Chris's first idea was to take Leah for a simple meal at some Italian chain restaurant, then hole up in a nearby pub for the rest of the evening. But in the micro-culture of the Bulford barracks, dating plans were subject to wild inflation. The objective was to impress not the girl but your fellow officers. In fact, the best stories often involved elaborate schemes that ended in disaster. The legend of Jon Jefford, for example, lived on three years after JJ had left the army. He had proposed to his girlfriend in a hot-air balloon – an ambitious romantic gesture that went badly wrong when she turned him down, sentencing them both to two hours of windy silence, with the picnic hamper and the bottle of unopened champagne reproaching them from the corner of the basket.

Thus in the three weeks leading up to his date with Leah, Chris found himself under considerable pressure to come up with something more exotic than Bella Pasta. Despite his good looks, he was known to be hopeless with women, so the mere fact of the date attracted a good deal of genial mockery. One of the guys managed to wrest Leah's name from him; when her Facebook page revealed her to be 'fucking hot', and 'way too good for a Cro-Magnon like Crimbo', interest in the date grew stronger still. Chris, enjoying the kudos, began to think big. By the time Saturday came round, he had an action-packed evening lined up: cocktails and animal face-painting at one of ZSL's 'Zoo Lates' before supper at Dans Le Noir (a novelty restaurant that served its diners in total darkness), then on to a pop-up roller disco in a disused Bermondsey warehouse.

Which was how he ended up in A&E at St Thomas's with a broken wrist, accompanied by a markedly sober Leah. Chris himself was drunk enough to ignore the pain; it was Leah, concerned by the rapid swelling, who had insisted on taking him to hospital. He kissed her in the waiting room. Their faces were still faintly streaked with tiger-stripes from the face-painting session at the zoo. Some of the paint leaked into the kiss, lending it a chalky, floral flavour.

'Christopher Kimura,' said the tannoy, and Chris got up to see the doctor.

He came back fifteen minutes later with his wrist band-aged and splinted, feeling euphoric. A wipe-out on the roller-dance floor and a kiss in A&E: he was already imagining how these antics would be received by his Bulford audience.

'Okay,' he told Leah as they left the hospital, unable to keep from grinning. 'I'm aware that, as first dates go, that was an unmitigated disaster. But if I promise, scout's honour, not to break any more bones, do you think you might let me make it up to you next weekend?'

Leah was confused; he almost sounded pleased about his injury. Nonetheless, turning him down in this condi-tion didn't seem to be an option. She remembered Callum in the kitchen, serious and stern. 'Sure,' she heard herself say. 'Sure. Next weekend. That would be nice.'

Besides, she had enjoyed herself, more or less. There had been so much to do – the animals, the face-painting, eating in the dark, roller-skating – that she had been spared the usual agonies of conversation. She remembered her last proper date, with a nervous little banker who had actually asked her, after a particularly long silence, what her favourite colour was. Chris, by contrast, was a showman with an endless fund of anecdote and repartee, providing a running commentary on everything from the sex habits of bonobos to the significance of the hijab in Western culture. Apart from the occasional smile, nothing much seemed to be required of Leah; and this, she decided, was nice. It was relaxing.

And there was something else about Chris, another point of difference between him and the men she usually dated. Leah's suitors tended to fall into two categories: those rendered mute by her beauty, and those who thought it granted them full groping rights, like greedy diners determined to get maximum value from an all-you-can-eat buffet. Chris, however, was neither nervous nor lecherous. He appeared to be entirely unbothered by her presence; there was no ogling, no inappropriate groping, not even in the pitch-dark restaurant. By the time they got to A&E, Leah wasn't sure if he even fancied her. They were having a good time, but his attitude towards her was friendly rather than flirtatious. It was this novel uncertainty that provoked her into putting her hand on his knee; when he responded by leaning in for a kiss, she felt a gratifying sense of relief.

* * *

August's dry heat continued into September, bleaching the grass of the Denham Hall playing fields. The new term began in summer uniform, with 'Shirt Sleeve Order' (a borrow from Army terminology) chalked up morning after morning on the big blackboard in the Assembly room. To younger pupils, not yet resigned to the relentless inevitability of the seasons, it began to seem possible that summer might go on for ever.

This was Callum's first year as Head of Latin. His predecessor, Dennis Bird, had retired last term after a set of school reports revealed the severity of his early-onset Alzheimer's. (The same paragraph written out fifty-four times in his elegant turquoise script, with only the name and gender altered.) Mr Bird had always taught the top sets, although his teaching methods were so ineffective that Callum's classes consistently out-performed their brighter peers. After three years of Mr Bird, 8S had a long way to go before sitting scholarship papers in the spring. Callum was more or less an instant hit. They chafed a little at his introductory lecture on the importance of the Classics to modern society; but they liked 'iDisco', the neat vocab app he'd developed for their smart phones, and the way he was unfazed by Ludo Hall's arsenal of 'innocent' questions ('Sir, sir, why do all the statues have tiny you-know-whats?'). Four members of the class – Karl Huber, Felicity Teasdale, Sophie Witrand and, to everyone's surprise, Ludo – signed up for the Greek lessons he was offering after school on Tuesdays and Thursdays.

Sophie had mixed feelings about her final year at Denham Hall. On the one hand, it was nice to be on top at last, one of the big kids, feared and adored by the younger years. Yet each day brought her closer to the end of her time at the school – synonymous, in Sophie's mind, with the end of her childhood. She saw more clearly than ever that time would continue to pass without her permission.

In the changing rooms, Sophie checked the other girls' chests for signs of growth. In some lights she thought she could see Poppy Ohlson's nipples protruding more than usual, but this was a minute change, visible only under the keenest scrutiny. Sophie kept her own body hidden, feeling its difference more shamefully than ever. The worms were a distant nightmare now. Her mother had taken her to see the GP, who admonished her for not washing her hands before meals and prescribed a course of mebendazole. But her period was only a deferred sentence, and in the meantime, her breasts were getting bigger. Every morning in chapel she prayed to a God she wasn't quite sure she believed in to take them away, to restore her chest to its old bony flatness.

She had come to dread bathtime with her siblings. It seemed wrong to be taking her clothes off in front of James, and Harriet was openly, cruelly curious about the now very visible changes to her big sister's body, pushing and flicking at Sophie's heat-softened nipples whenever

Mrs Witrand left the room. Sophie made no effort to retaliate or even resist: she wanted to pretend that the breasts weren't there, and objecting to Harriet's antics would mean admitting to the difference between their bodies. So bathtimes continued communal, and Harriet continued to poke and pinch, and Sophie submitted to this punishment in silence, feeling that it was, in a way, her due.

* * *

The light began to fade earlier in the evenings. On Tuesdays and Thursdays, after the extra Greek class, Callum found himself cycling back in near-darkness, arriving home as late as 8.30 or 9 p.m. Then there would be marking to do, and, at the weekends, school football matches that could take up a whole Saturday afternoon and sometimes the best part of the evening. This all meant that he had very little time left to spend with Tamsin, who seemed to have changed her mind about moving in with him. She hadn't categorically said that she wouldn't, but she refused to name a date when Callum suggested they tell Leah about their plans. Instead of taking the part-time Associated Board job as they had discussed, she was now working nearly full-time for Amad Health, giving recitals in their care homes for the elderly. 'You're not doing this because of the money, are you?' Callum ventured to ask her, just once. Her reply was ready and indignant. 'It's not about you and the flat. It's not even about me. This is about *other people*, about using my music to do something for *other people* at last.'

She sounded very sure of herself, but Callum was concerned. Two years ago, Tamsin had played at the Southbank Centre's Purcell Room. She worked towards the concert for months, telling everyone that if it went well it could be her 'big break'. Apart from her father, all her friends and family were invited. When the reviews unanimously declared her a competent yet mediocre player, she had renounced the piano completely and taken a job at McDonald's. It was a melodramatic overreaction that had irritated Callum. After two weeks, he and Roz succeeded in talking Tamsin back round to the idea of a career in music, albeit a slightly less glittery one. McDonald's was abandoned and the piano resumed, more soberly than before.

It seemed to Callum that the Amad Health job had the same flavour of self-sabotage. True, Tamsin was using her music, but she was mostly playing hits from a collection entitled '101 Golden Oldies'. The job was poorly paid and she spent hours travelling from care home to care home. Often she had to work with a violinist whose creative approach to pitch and timing was accompanied by an unshakeable conviction that he was the next Yehudi Menuhin. At the end of the day, she was too tired from all the travelling to practise properly; and last week, she had even turned down an opportunity to play in a new recital series in Islington.

Callum could think of no obvious trigger. Tamsin had never had another concert so high-profile as the Southbank gig, but she was hired as an accompanist on a fairly regular basis, and she was getting a reputation as a reliable guest soloist for concerto work on the amateur orchestra circuit. Not, by any means, the high-flying career she had dreamt of; not a career she could hold up with pride before her father; but not a complete failure, either.

So what, then, had made the difference?

Tamsin didn't know herself – which was partly why she became so shrewish whenever Callum tried to talk to her about it. For some time now she had been aware of a profound dissatisfaction. People kept telling her was doing fine; and she knew that, in so much as she still had a chance of making a living from performance, she *was* doing fine. But practising up to eight hours a day to maintain a standard which would forever fall short of her personal expectations seemed a grim way to spend one's life. Privately, she figured the Amad job as an epiphany. At last she had recognised her limitations and made the brave decision to free her music from its privileged bourgeois confines: instead, she would use her talents to bring light into the greyest of lives. The fact that both Callum and her mother were opposed to her new job gratified her, because it was exactly the reaction she had anticipated.

Yet none of this quite accounted for her renewed reluctance to move in with Callum. On this point, all Tamsin knew was that the certainty she had felt in Ilfracombe had vanished. There, she had barely thought about Chris Kimura. Now, though, the mere mention of his name was enough to leave her light-headed with excitement. Tamsin abhorred any kind of infidelity, no matter how abstract: it seemed contemptible that she should love Callum yet think of Chris.

She suffered her own conscience for a week or so, and then began to repackage her sharp-edged problem in softer, bulkier wrapping. The word she lit on, courtesy of pop psychology, was 'displacement': her crush on Chris must be a symptom of some deeper anxiety. Her current favourite was a theory involving her father's betrayal. It stood to reason that Bertrand's behaviour towards her mother should leave her with a distrust of men in general. Thus, just as she was on the brink of happiness with Callum, her latent insecurity about this happiness manifested itself in the form of an arbitrary attachment to a man whom she had met on fewer than ten occasions.

The truth, of course, was rather more straightforward. Tamsin had swerved very close to it on that night out with Will and Big Mac et al. Talking to Suze in the pub toilets, she had correctly identified her desire to go clubbing as an unwillingness to leave Chris alone with Leah. The attraction Chris held for her now was similarly rooted in his unavailability – which had become a reality. She had returned from Ilfracombe to find that Chris and Leah were, in Leah's words, 'sort of dating'; a month later, they were in an exclusive relationship. Tamsin professed herself delighted, both publically and privately. She never suspected that she fancied Chris largely because he belonged to someone else. Had that motivation occurred to her, she would have rejected it as too pedestrian, unequal to the intensity of her emotion. The father-hypothesis prevailed. Tamsin nursed her nascent love for Chris as a secret disability, grew increasingly short-tempered with Callum, and remained evasive on the question of when, if ever, she would move in with him.

* * *

Leah and Chris were as surprised as anyone else to find themselves together. Perversely, the deal-clincher was the disastrous sex. On the night of the roller-disco, Chris was too drunk and too wounded to engage in anything more complex than a kiss, so Leah put him to bed on the sofa in the sitting room with his arm propped up on the coffee table. Their next date was a quieter affair: a gastro-pub supper followed by drinks at a little-known jazz club. Boo's Basement had been recommended to Chris by Andre Fillion, a fellow Riflesman and Miles Davis enthusiast. Hours of aimless improvisation, with no lyrics or power chords to speak of, was hardly Chris's idea of a good night out. But Andre had insisted that you never really *got* jazz until you saw it live, and Chris, not wanting to seem uncultured, had taken down the address. 'You won't regret it,' Andre had said. 'Trust me, it's going to be magic.'

Half an hour in, Chris was still waiting for the magic to happen. Basically, he didn't like jazz, although he had affected connoisseurship to Leah. There was something inherently smug about the lazy late-night shuffle of the snare drum, Chris thought, a subtle taunt contained in the piano line tripping glibly over the top. He tried to tap his heel in a way that signalled unconscious connection with the music, but this took too much effort, so he gave up and concentrated instead on his double measure of single malt whisky. He looked at Leah looking at the jazz. Was she 'getting' it? Her face was, as almost always, unreadable. Chris realised how little he knew about her. He wasn't even entirely sure what her job was. At least, he had no idea what her days actually consisted of. Chris was briefly gripped by concern that he hadn't asked her enough about herself over supper, that he had talked solely of his platoon and his barracks and his ambitions. But no, he thought, he had asked plenty of questions. It was her answers that had been insufficient. She had grown animated just the once, during a conversation about her last job as a secretary at an investment bank – a job she quit when she saw her boss emptying a pocket full of small change into the wastepaper basket.

'Not just coppers, mind,' Leah had said, her residual Brummie thickening her consonants, as it did whenever she became heated. 'There were tens and twenties in there, too. About one pound fifty in total. I checked. And it was the paper bin. For *recycling*.' She fixed him with a wild-eyed glare. 'I *hate* waste. I hate unnecessary possessions. Sometimes I look around me and all I see is—' She stopped herself and began again, more calmly. 'I'm thinking of becoming a minimalist. There's this group online, they send you this fold-up crate, about this big' –

she gestured about three feet by four – 'and that's all you're meant to have, your whole life in that box.'

Chris had liked this change – the contrast between her habitual brevity and this sudden vigour, still waters stirred into turbulence. *Stirred*. He remembered what sex had done to her, the transformation that his penis had effected on her composure. Squinting through the gloom of the jazz club, Chris checked his watch. Another forty-five minutes, he reckoned, and it would be safe to suggest they head back. Boredom and alcohol were making him horny. He felt no very strong connection to Leah, physically or otherwise, but their one night together – now over a month ago – had become, in his mind, the best sex he had ever had. At the time, he had been tired and hungover, yet he had still managed to bring her to a noisy climax that coincided exactly with his own – a proud first for Chris. Tonight would be even better. They were going to do it over and over again, he thought happily, as many times as he possibly could, in every position known to man. He imagined grabbing those slim brown ankles and hoisting her legs up to rest on his shoulders as he buried himself deep inside her. Then he would pull out almost all the way and stay there, teasing her with his tip, until she begged for more.

The reality of their second sex scene was very different. There was some promising necking on the tube journey home, but that was where Leah's enthusiasm seemed to end. Back in her minimalist bedroom, once the sex began in earnest, Leah was disturbingly, dismayingly silent. Forget noisy climaxing or begging for more: she didn't so much as sigh. Chris watched her closely as he thumbed her nipples, expecting at least a frown of pleasure; but her face was as immobile as it had been at the jazz club. Chris did his best to stay calm. He spent a lonely twenty minutes down between her legs, with no idea whether what he was doing was even nice, let alone arousing. After almost an hour of this, he felt he had earned some action. And maybe, he thought, that was what Leah wanted. Yes: that was what had worked last time. She wanted penetration, she wanted depth. He rubbed his half-hard penis until it was stiff again and pushed it into Leah with renewed optimism.

For an instant, Leah's features tensed into something that looked suspiciously like a wince.

Chris froze. 'Are you okay?'

Leah nodded.

'Am I hurting you?'

'Not any more,' was the discomforting response. 'It's all right. Keep going.'

Now Leah had her eyes closed, lightly, so that Chris could almost think her asleep. He felt crassly mechanical, a loom shuttling back and forth. It took him a long time to come.

When it was over he rolled off her and lay on his back staring up at the ceiling. There was no need to ask Leah how it had been for her. He thought about apologising, but before he could marshal the courage to speak she was on her way to the bathroom. Chris tugged his boxer shorts back on, trying to put some distance between himself and his stickily wrinkled penis. Up till now, sex had seemed reasonably straightforward. He hadn't slept with many girls, but he was fairly certain that they had all enjoyed themselves – as Leah had, just four weeks ago, on this very same futon. He couldn't remember what he had done those other times; all he knew was that tonight, he had failed, completely and utterly, to replicate the formula of his previous successes. When Leah came back, he pretended to be asleep.

The next day, Chris was the last to wake. Hearing voices from the next room, he dressed hurriedly and stepped out to find Leah, Tamsin and Callum eating breakfast. Callum got up to fry him an egg, leaving Chris semi-alone with the girls. He hadn't expected Tamsin. She was sitting with her knees drawn up to her chin and her heels resting on the edge of the chair, her body enveloped in a huge yellow sports sweater.

'Well good morning, officer,' she said, popping her legs out of the sweater and stretching widely. It wasn't clear whether she was wearing anything underneath. The other two were in similar states of undress: Leah wore her white bathrobe, while Callum merrily tended the frying pan in nothing but a pair of rumpled cotton boxers. Chris, in his chinos and button-down shirt, felt naked. He wondered what Leah might have said about him. He wondered if Tamsin might guess, from his awkwardness, that last night had not ended well, and infer from that inference that he was clueless, amateur, a sexual incompetent.

In an attempt to look confidently loved-up, he put a hand out and squeezed Leah on the shoulder. Seeing Tamsin notice this, it struck him that a shoulder squeeze might not be enough, so he bent down and kissed Leah on the temple. Leah smiled briefly in response. Her failure to match contact with contact seemed to Chris to confirm his fears. His head treated him to a little movie clip of paranoia: Tamsin and Leah, snickering together as they dissected his abysmal performance in the bedroom last night. Wasn't that what women did? The thought made him suddenly desperate. He needed another chance, but after yesterday the odds of Leah agreeing to go out with him again were surely slim to none.

Then an idea came to him. 'Bon Jovi's coming to Hyde Park,' he said to Leah. 'I'm going with friends, there's a ticket spare if you'd like to join us.'

Asking her in front of her friends, deliberately omitting

to mention a date: Chris knew that this wasn't quite fair, but he needed – or so he thought – all the advantage he could get. Leah had a mouthful of food; it seemed to take for ever for her to chew and swallow. As he waited for her answer, Chris realised that the sensation in his stomach would probably qualify as 'butterflies'. Fleetingly he registered the irony of being so wound up about a girl he didn't even like. But this insight was quickly replaced by a simpler (though erroneous) supposition: that such a tangible physical response must mean that he did like Leah, much more than he had originally thought.

And Leah? She was even more surprised – and pleased – than she had been when he asked her out again at the end of their first date; she felt sure that her silence in bed last night must have been the ultimate turn-off, that Chris was never going to want to sleep with her again. She chased down her food with a sip of orange juice.

'Yeah, sure,' she nodded.

Leah sounded thoroughly unexcited by the idea, but Chris still had to stop himself thanking her out loud, so overwhelming was his gratitude. 'Awesome,' he grinned at her.

And so there was a third date at the festival in Hyde Park, a fortnight later, and Leah met several of Chris's friends, all of whom behaved as if she and Chris were a proper couple. Leah found that she didn't mind this. It was nice to hang out with a bunch of people who weren't a) hitting on her or b) hating her for getting hit on. By the end of the evening, a tipping point had been reached: they were now at the stage when breaking things off with each other would have required more energy than simply maintaining the status quo.

Leah began to refer to Chris as 'the guy I'm seeing', a sound bite so effective for discouraging unwanted attention that she couldn't think why she hadn't started using

127

it years ago. She liked the fact that Chris was away all week and sometimes not even free on the weekends. If they had seen more of each other, the relationship would probably have foundered. As it was, she was always pleased to see him, but never sad when they said goodbye. Chris, meanwhile, was wielding the term 'my girlfriend' with proprietorial relish. This, it turned out, was half the charm for him. He liked having a girlfriend, he liked being someone's boyfriend. If Leah texted him while he was in the Mess, he would roll his eyes before reading the message and mutter something about 'the missus', adoring every minute of his affected servitude. In this version of their relationship, he was a worthless dog on whom the beautiful, well-adjusted Leah had inexplicably taken pity. Her projected perfection provided Chris with the perfect foil for anecdotes about his own shortcomings, of which he was particularly fond. (For example: the story of how, under the twin corrupting influences of vodka Red Bull and Doug, he had pretended to hump one of the Trafalgar Square lions, with Leah and Helen looking on in long-suffering disbelief.)

The sex was still a problem. Leah wasn't enjoying herself, but she was happier in bed than she had ever been, because she no longer felt she was play-acting. She didn't realise how much her unresponsiveness bothered Chris. He always got hard and he always came, so Leah assumed that he was having a good time. It never occurred to her that her satisfaction might matter to him.

Although Chris was never so disturbed by her silence as he had been on the night of the jazz club, he was still horribly confused. He began to think that the problem might be Leah's rather than his, and this relaxed him somewhat; but their very first night together remained an unnerving anomaly. Had she come that night, or had she been faking it? He was obsessed with a question he felt unable to ask. If she had been faking it, he had been completely fooled; and if Leah had fooled him, then what of all the other girls? The fear that they too had been pretending made him more determined than ever to satisfy Leah, to wring from her, at whatever cost, a helpless, breathless, dry-throated orgasm. He tried everything he could think of, except talking. And the more Chris tried, the more hours he spent with his hand between her legs and his lips glued to her nipple (her preferred method of stimulation, he surmised, because she seemed willing to endure it longer than any other before pushing him away), the more certain Leah grew that she would never come, not with Chris, not with anyone.

They were happiest on double dates. Sometimes they hung out with Callum and Tamsin, but more often it was Doug and Helen who joined them at the cinema or in the pub. For Chris, the chief pleasure of these evenings was, once again, the act of being so conspicuously a boyfriend. He liked the legitimacy of being in a relationship, and the structure it lent to his otherwise formless existence outside of barracks. He knew that he wasn't in love with Leah – in fact, he was never more aware of this than in the company of Doug and Helen. When Doug implied that Helen was too good for him, he really meant it. Helen, for her part, managed the intricate trick of adoring Doug without ever really approving of him – exactly the sort of firm-handedness Doug needed. Chris saw in their happiness a promise of his own utopian future with a woman who still looked suspiciously like Tamsin Jarvis. And for now, he was content to play house with Leah. He had an unarticulated sense of rehearsal, of using this relationship as a trial run for the Real Thing.

Leah, too, appreciated the rare sensation of belonging. Her social anxiety was staunched by the fact that the roles within their little group were so clearly defined:

Doug and Chris would try their hardest to outdo each other with increasingly outrageous anecdotes, while Leah and Helen formed an audience that reacted, preferably with horror, to these stories.

'My men have really excelled themselves this week,' Chris would announce, feigning sadness. 'They had a tramp.' He paused to enjoy his audience's confusion. 'In a cupboard in the corridor. They actually had a tramp. They found him somewhere in Salisbury, and they were paying him – with food and shelter, in the cupboard – to do shit for them. Ironing, polishing their boots and so on.' Chris lowered his voice to a mutter ostensibly aimed at Doug but really intended for general consumption. 'Polishing their knobs, too, if you can believe it. He was young, and not bad looking.'

'I think that's outrageous.' Helen, easily inflamed, was glaring at Chris. 'You shouldn't be joking about it. That's actually the sickest thing I've heard in years.'

'I know, I know, they're animals,' said Chris, ruefully. Doug was asphyxiating with laughter.

'It isn't funny, Doug,' said Helen. 'It's sick.'

'*Sick*,' Leah agreed, although she felt none of Helen's indignation. Leah found it hard to get wound up about just people. Helen was always pestering Doug about the levels of pastoral care available to his men, as if joining the army were a traumatic experience in itself. Leah didn't really get that. She thought it sounded all right, the army. Limited space, limited possessions, limited freedom, lots of exercise. There was an economy, a purity there that appealed to her.

* * *

In principle, Tamsin's zeal for the Amad job was undimmed. She was undoubtedly making a difference. The Parkinsonian residents sufficiently liberated by the music to sway in time or even clap their hands, the loud sighs of recognition when she and Stavros the violinist started up 'White Cliffs of Dover', the more with-it residents who actively looked forward to the concerts, the time that a sweet shrunken lady rendered mute by acute aphasia had inched her way across the room to kiss Tamsin's hand in gratitude. However, the pleasure she got from all this was outweighed by the sheer tedium of the job.

After years of practising scales for hours on end, Tamsin imagined herself immune to boredom. But there were times when she felt that yet another rendition of 'Somewhere Over the Rainbow', with Stavros consistently failing to hit the octave note, might just finish her off. At least when you were practising you were improving. She and Stavros were not improving, they were merely repeating. Some days, Tamsin felt like a glorified CD player. And the residents – they couldn't help it, but they weren't improving, either. Sure, the music was making a difference, but what a temporary difference it was! This thought tinctured her boredom with alarm, an alarm to which Tamsin, as a self-avowed realist, felt she should be invulnerable.

In short she was embarrassed, by both the boredom and the alarm, and because she was embarrassed, she mentioned neither issue to Callum. Instead, she took her discomfort out on Stavros, who was, after all, no small part of her problem. She hated him for his musical inaccuracy. She hated him for fancying himself the star of their little show, for suggesting that 'maybe you play with a little more feeling, maybe, a little more passion' (here he demonstrated grotesquely, glissando-ing between each note and employing a palsied vibrato that made his cheeks shudder). She hated his cheap shiny suits, she hated the careful pleats in his trousers, she hated his extensive collection of maroon dress shirts, she hated the sandy noise his scalp made when he scratched it through his thick dark hair. She hated the way he bounced on his heels, just once, a single self-satisfied spring, before giving his flamboyant bow. Most of all, she hated him for being both hateable *and* a Greek immigrant from simple farming stock who had worked for thirty years to achieve a level of musicianship barely sufficient for a job she could do in her sleep – for being someone she should admire and pity, not despise.

The one gig she always looked forward to was her weekly afternoon slot at Hortensia Court care home in Tooting Bec. The Hortensia Court concerts had the advantage of being on Thursday, which was Stavros's day off. But the real reason Tamsin liked going to Hortensia Court was a woman called Antonia Platt. Antonia was just under six feet tall with straight dark-grey hair cut in a jaunty graduated bob, no glasses and near-perfect hearing. Even her name made her seem younger than the Mauds and the Doreens, the Muriels and the Janes.

The Hortensia Court piano was a Brodmann baby grand positioned in the large bay window of the dining room. After lunch on Thursday afternoons, the chipboard tables were stripped of their wipe-clean linen and pushed back against the dining-room walls to make room for ranks of chairs and wheelchairs. Tamsin played to an audience of about twenty residents, plus a few of the blue-smocked kitchen staff who drifted out between lunch wash-up and supper prep to enjoy a bit of Johnny Mercer and Irving Berlin. She noticed Antonia on her third visit to Hortensia Court, when she deviated for the first time from the programme prescribed by Amad to play Satie's three Gymnopédies. Several of her audience dozed off at this point, but others seemed to enjoy it, and to Tamsin's amazement Antonia, sitting in the front row, absently played along on her lap, her fingerings mirroring Tamsin's own.

At the end of the session, Tamsin hurried over to her. 'You're a pianist.'

'Was.' Antonia held up her hands. Six of her ringless fingers were long and straight and well manicured, and reasonably unspotted, given her age. Only the stiffly crooked little fingers were wrong.

'Dupuytren's contracture,' Antonia explained. 'I don't entirely understand it myself.' She showed Tamsin her right palm. Just beneath the little finger the flesh gathered and dipped, as if it were being pinned down from the inside. The skin had a stiff, burnished quality that reminded Tamsin of cocktail sausages.

A care worker approached with an institutional cup and saucer. 'You want some tea, Antonia my love?'

'No thank you,' said Antonia imperiously. 'This young lady—'

'Tamsin.'

'Tamsin and I will take our refreshment in my room.' The carer moved on to the next old lady and Antonia turned to Tamsin, girlish and uncertain now. 'That is, if you'd care to join me...?'

'I should like that very much,' said Tamsin, unconsciously adopting Antonia's formal idiolect.

Antonia led her up a flight of stairs, at the top of which were two doors. One was made of glass laced with a steel wire mesh, like a sheet of see-through graph paper. This door gave onto a long corridor. Sellotaped in its centre was a piece of A4 paper bearing three words printed in bold red capitals.

'Turn back John,' Tamsin read out loud. 'There's one of these on the front door, too.'

Antonia paused in the act of opening the other, wooden door. 'That's John Otterden. Four or five of those notices

133

are enough to keep him safely confined to the ground floor.' Her wry tone fell just short of contempt.

'My little oasis,' she announced, pushing open the door to her room. It was a large room similar in shape to the dining room below it, with another bay window letting in an abundance of late-afternoon sunlight. The walls were covered in faded posters and postcards of paintings by Klee and Schwitters and Nicholson. In the corner farthest from the window was a neat single bed with a bamboo cross tacked above the headboard. Over the mantelpiece hung a framed etching depicting a pair of gnarled, arthritic hands.

'Hepworth's hands, by Henry Moore,' said Antonia. 'I can't decide whether I find them comforting or depressing.'

They sat in the bay window and drank tea while listening to a cassette of Antonia playing Debussy. There were very few books in the room; all the available shelf space was given over to cassettes and CDs and vinyl. For about twelve years in her thirties and early forties, Antonia explained, she had enjoyed considerable success as a concert pianist in Belgium and Switzerland. Her collection included recordings of herself playing Debussy and Busoni and Ropartz. In 1952, Stravinsky himself had attended one of her concerts.

On her way out, Tamsin stopped at reception to ask all the questions she had been too delicate to put to Antonia herself, and discovered that her new friend was eighty-nine years old and entirely without living relatives. She had been at Hortensia Court just five months.

'She's not as all-there as she seems,' said Heather, the stocky receptionist. 'Came to us after a collapse in the street. She'd been trying to pay for stuff with old money, old money like shillings. Hadn't eaten anything in days.'

'No friends, no visitors?'

'None.'

Tamsin knew it was wrong, but she couldn't help being pleased by Antonia's utter aloneness in the world; she felt it made her own visits to the old lady all the more valuable. Every Thursday afternoon she stayed at Hortensia Court for an hour or so after the concert had finished. Sometimes they took tea in Antonia's bed-sitting room, but more often than not they stayed down in the dining room, Tamsin playing, Antonia listening, until it was time for the staff to reassemble the room for supper. Soon she was visiting Antonia on Saturdays as well as Thursdays.

Tamsin told Callum very little about her friend at Hortensia Court. She was worried he might guess – he was very perceptive – that Antonia was her favourite thing about the Amad gigs, and suggest that she quit, and satisfy her philanthropic urges by visiting Antonia alone. Tamsin herself had briefly entertained this as a possibility. But the truth was that, boring as the Amad job was, she appreciated the release it provided from the tyranny of practising. Instinctively, she avoided any conversational topic that might alert Callum to her waning determination. His steady faith in her abilities had been essential to her once, but lately she had begun to shy away from it, as she would an uncomfortably bright light.

So Tamsin found herself lying to Callum about her whereabouts on Saturday mornings, saying that she was practising at home in Notting Hill, or out walking along the canal by herself. This minor deception actually pleased her. She was betraying Callum not with Chris but with an old lady, which seemed, in some obscure, inexplicable way, to absolve her from her mental infidelities. This feeling was strengthened when Tamsin told Antonia, one Thursday afternoon in October when it was raining too heavily to leave, about how her father was the conductor Bertrand Jarvis, and how he had cheated on her mother Roz in the most cruelly calculating of ways.

Antonia was significantly less interested in Tamsin's musical pedigree or the injustice done to Roz than in Bertrand's new relationship with Valerie Fischer. 'Do they still live together, your father and this woman?' she wanted to know.

'Yup.' Tamsin raised her chin slightly, as if straining to detect some faint odour. 'They live in Holland Park, in the house where I grew up.'

'And are they happy?'

'I don't know. I don't want to know.' Tamsin put her cup down in its saucer and shifted her gaze from the window to Antonia's face before delivering her final line. 'I can't forgive him for what he did to my mother.'

She had spoken these words in this exact formulation so many times over the years that they had become a reassuring constant, an anchor for her very identity. *Steely*, Tamsin thought, the adjective presenting itself, like it always did at this point, as a rather satisfying description of the immobility she could feel in her own face.

'I had an affair with a married man once,' Antonia said quietly. 'During the war. He was much older than me, thirty-five, and I was eighteen.' She smiled sadly. 'He had two little children who were living in Wales, as evacuees, and his wife was pregnant with a third.'

'What happened?'

'I was a good Catholic – am a good Catholic' – Antonia crossed herself quickly – 'so I reported myself, and him, to the commanding officer. They relocated me to Belgium. I expect he's dead now.' Her hands were clasping her knees, the rayed tendons straining.

'So you did the right thing,' Tamsin breathed.

'Right!' said Antonia. It was impossible to say whether

she was agreeing with Tamsin, or ironically echoing her.

It was following this visit that it became Tamsin's private dream to make it possible for Antonia to play the piano again. She researched Dupuytren's contracture online and discovered that the condition was reversible, though not permanently, via several different surgical procedures. What she couldn't ascertain from the Internet was whether Antonia would be eligible for treatment on the NHS, or whether her age or supposed mental instability would complicate things in any way. Not wanting to raise the old lady's hopes unnecessarily, she resolved to check all the details with her own GP and with Hortensia Court before putting the idea to Antonia. Nor did she mention this plan to Callum. She imagined that one day Antonia might be capable of giving a concert herself, a concert to which Tamsin would invite Callum and her mother without telling them anything about Antonia or her fingers or the operation beforehand. She would let the music do its work; she would let them be moved by Antonia's playing (Tamsin had no doubt that the old lady would play wonderfully); and only then she would tell them that it was she, Tamsin, who had made all this possible, that this was the good that had come from the job they had both implicitly disparaged.

* * *

The junior officers' accommodation at Bulford reminded Chris Kimura of nothing so much as a glorified Travel Lodge. Chris lived in room 28 of 47, halfway down a windowless corridor carpeted in a tough, corrugated flooring fabric that continued into his little bedroom. All of his furniture – wardrobe, bedside table, queen-sized bed, small chest of drawers – had the same anaemic wood-effect veneer. The heavy curtains matched the petrol-blue of the carpet. In one corner of the room there was a tiny bathroom with a capsule shower and a raised floor that made Chris feel like he was stepping into a child's paddling pool. Some glitch in the shower's design meant the bathroom was permanently flooded. When he peed, Chris had to hold up his trousers with one hand so that the hems didn't touch the water.

All in all, it was a strange place to return to after a long afternoon's bayonet training with his platoon. (Thirty sweaty, cam-cream-covered men, most of them under twenty-five, plunging sharp steel into sandbags which had just raped their mothers.) Chris sat down on the edge of his bed then flopped backwards without taking his boots off. He could feel at least two new blisters that he was in no great hurry to inspect. The smoke detector winked its little red eye at him.

He was woken some minutes later from a dream about flying a fighter jet in defiance of a red alert signal on the dashboard by his mobile convulsing with a text message. He retrieved it from where it lay on his bedside table, between a half-eaten Mars Bar and a copy of *The Prophet* by Kahlil Gibran. The message was from an unknown, five-digit number.

Two weeks ago, all three platoons in C-Company had received routine health checks in preparation for their upcoming tour, including a urine test for STIs. Chris's immediate response to the message – 'On 13 Oct, you tested POSITIVE for Chlamydia' – was indignation. It was Leah who had suggested they ditch the condoms, claiming that the latex irritated her.

Suddenly desperate to shower, Chris bent to unlace his boots. His sweaty socks had softened the skin of his feet to a ridgy pinkish white. He hauled his left ankle up to rest on his right knee and gently prodded the little contact lens of his blister.

Then he remembered Lara. He had been inside her for less than five minutes, but maybe that was enough: he had had unprotected sex with a woman he barely knew.

Feeling guilty and tainted, Chris picked up the phone and found Leah's number. He sat for almost a minute with his thumb poised above 'call', then put the phone down and unbuttoned his flies. He reached into the slit in his boxer shorts and took out his penis, which was warm and moist. It looked like it always did, dun-coloured and slightly conical. No spots, no lesions, no swelling, no sign of a rash. Maybe there had been some mistake. He reached for the phone again and called Doug instead.

'Chillax, Crimbo,' he said when he'd finished laughing. 'It's only Chlamydia. I've had it twice.'

'But how do I tell Leah? I told her I was clean.'

'You don't,' Doug said. 'No symptoms. Or no obvious ones. One girl I knew said it made sex a bit painful.'

'Doug, it causes infertility.'

'No no no, you don't leave her with it, you just don't tell her you're treating it. Chlamydia's simple, one pill to cure. All you have to do is find some way of giving it to her without her noticing.'

Chris exchanged his left foot for his right and located the other blister. This one was bigger and tighter; he was surprised it hadn't burst. 'I'll have to tell her.'

'Just mash it up and put it in her drink.'

'Like spiking it? That's sick.'

He looked down at his penis, which was still poking ridiculously out of his boxers. He was seized by an irrational desire to cut it off. Instead, he pinched a slit in the blister using the nails of his middle finger and thumb. It expressed its little gout of thin, clear liquid and deflated instantly.

'So what are you going to say if you tell her, and she accuses you of cheating on her?' Doug was saying. '"I forgot I'd had sex"?'

Chris had no answer to this.

'Trust me, it's easy,' said Doug. 'I'll take care of it. Not to be a douche, but you're never going to get another girl as hot as Leah.'

'Wow, thanks, mate,' said Chris, and hung up.

But alone in his little regulation bedroom, Doug's logic didn't seem so quite absurd. Chris hadn't seen Leah in almost a fortnight; during that time, he had spoken to her just once, exchanged about five text messages, and barely thought about her at all. He certainly hadn't missed her. When he wanked, it was to mental images of Tamsin Jarvis or Scarlett Johansson. Now, though, faced with the prospect of losing Leah, of *being dumped* by her, he found himself desperate to preserve the relationship.

* * *

The weather stayed hot right into October. Then it was half term, and it rained, all week. 'It's sod's law,' announced Sophie to the supper table, earning an eloquent glare from her mother. 'What? I can say that, it's a recognised law. Miss Hinks used it in French the other day, about how all the most useful verbs are the irregulars. It's for when the exact thing you don't want to happen goes ahead and happens anyway.' Sometimes Sophie suspected her mother of being not very bright at all.

Seven days of rain had transformed Denham Hall. On Monday morning, the grey Victorian schoolhouse and its gently terraced grounds were as damp and fragrant as a new painting. The leaves of the two weeping copper beeches that flanked the main entrance had deepened to a vampish purple; the blue sky was downy with clouds; and out on the playing fields, the groundsman was laying down this year's geometry of touch lines and circles. The school buzzed with plans for break-time.

But at 10.30 a.m., in the middle of third period, a first-former slipped tremulously into 8S's English class to whisper to Mr Raddock that the whole school was expected to meet in the Assembly Room at break. At 10.50, with everyone duly assembled, the headmaster took to the podium. Mr Davenport was a thickset man in his late forties with faded brown hair and a Kitchener moustache.

'Someone has taken it upon him or herself to deface the wall of the toilets in the boys' changing room. I will not repeat what is written there. Until the culprit owns up, we will *all* stand here, hands by our sides – *hands by our sides, Wynter, and you too, Selby* – and if it takes the whole of break then so be it. I will not, repeat *not*, have this sort of *yobbish* behaviour at Denham Hall.'

Twenty-five minutes later the bell rang for the end of break and the school was released back to lessons, invigorated by the injustice of this communal punishment. To no one's surprise, the perpetrator had failed to come forward and confess.

'What I don't get is, it's majorly unfair, there's no way a girl could've done it,' whined Flick Chilcott, a swarthy, strong-jawed girl with a mania for horses. 'It was in the *boys'* changing room – we're not even allowed in there.'

All nine members of 8S were lined up in the corridor outside Room 16, waiting for Mr Bevan, their maths teacher, to show up and let them in.

'Does anyone know what it said?'

'I saw it,' boasted Des Kapoor with the eagerness of the constitutionally uncool. Everyone turned to look at him and he grinned, enjoying this rare moment of attention.

'What did it say?'

Des lowered his voice to a dramatic whisper. '"M. U. is a slut."'

There were nods of grudging approval. At least they had been kept in for something truly heinous.

'M. U.!' exclaimed Verity Trevena. 'I've got it: Milly Urquhart!'

'*Derr*,' Ludo scoffed. 'Who else is M. U. going to be?' Until not quite two weeks ago, Ludo and pretty blonde Verity had been 'going out', a state that in the pre-pubescent innocence of Denham Hall consisted of little more than hand-holding. Just before half term, Verity had publically dumped Ludo on the grounds that he was 'too juvenile'; since then, Ludo had seized every opportunity to 'rinse' her.

Michael Massey cleared his throat officiously. 'The question *is*, who wrote it?'

'Well, I think that's pretty obvious.' Sophie kept her voice casual. 'It's got to be Alex.'

She had played it just right; everyone looked piously appalled at the memory. At the end of the summer term Alex da Souza had stolen Milly Urquhart's swimming costume and worn it underneath his clothes for three whole days. He had been suspended for a week.

'But Alex fancies Milly,' frowned Rhiannon.

'Reverse psychology,' said Sophie with an air of unimpeachable authority, even though she wasn't entirely sure what this meant. Her classmates were impressed. Sophie was far from popular, but she was learning, this term, how to use her reputation as one of the cleverest.

Until recently, her teachers had agreed that Sophie Witrand was a model pupil. In many ways, she still was; there was nothing exactly *wrong* with her behaviour. It was her attitude that was no longer quite *comme il faut*. Teachers found it hard to fault her for asking perceptive, intelligent questions; but there was an element of performance to these questions, a delight in the discomfort her persistence could provoke. The other children, unfortunately, found these little showdowns between Sophie and her teachers highly entertaining, which only encouraged Sophie in her subtle insolence.

Mr Bevan in particular dreaded maths lessons with 8S. Luke Bevan was very young and very bald and had landed his job at Denham Hall not because he was good at maths or even that good at teaching, but because he had himself, just ten years ago, been a pupil at the school. He found 8S waiting outside his classroom in a state of worrying excitability. Sophie Witrand greeted him with a bold 'Hello, sir'. Already playing to the gallery, he thought. As he turned to unlock the door to the classroom, he saw Ludo Hall and Hugh Brodie raising their hands to shade their eyes as if from a blinding light, a cruel reference to his gleaming scalp. He didn't turn round. Being caught would give the boys equal pleasure.

Once the class was reasonably settled, he began the lesson with what he thought was a foolproof opener. He tugged down the scrolling blackboard to replace a diagram of the distance-speed-time triangle with a reasonable amount of blank, teal-green space, an action he completed with a flourish, affecting nonchalance. With loud, decisive jabs he planted two chalk dots on the blackboard, about a metre apart.

'All right, so here we have two points. A' – he labelled one – 'and B. What's the quickest way of getting from A to B? Yes, Verity?'

'Straight line, sir.'

'Very good.' Using a large wooden ruler, Mr Bevan connected the two points. When he turned to face the class again, Sophie Witrand was sitting straight-backed and alert with her right hand straining towards the ceiling.

'Sophie.'

'Sir. It's just – how do you know that that's the quickest way?'

'Sorry?'

'Can you prove it? I mean, it looks right, but how do we *know* that a straight line's fastest?'

'Trust me, Sophie, it is.'

'Then prove it.'

'I – listen, there is a proof, but it's really complicated. I mean really high-level stuff.'

'How high, sir? I mean, do you understand it?' The impertinent question was asked sweetly, with a troubled frown.

'Yes. Yes, of course I understand it. But I'm not going to waste precious lesson time teaching you something you don't need to know and you won't understand.'

'How do you *know* we won't understand it?'

'Sophie, there are A-level students who don't understand this.'

'Sir, please. I just want to know *why*. I find it really hard to remember things I don't understand.'

'Sophie, that's enough now.'

'What, sir? What am I doing wrong?'

Mr Bevan stared at her for a moment, then turned back to the blackboard, talking quickly and loudly to prevent any further interjections.

'Right, so as I said, the quickest route between any two points is a straight line. You already know how to calculate speed from distance and time, so today we're going to talk about vectors, okay, and a vector, a vector has both *direction* and *magnitude*.' He chalked these two words up on the board as he talked. In his haste he misspelled 'magnitude' as 'mangitude'. The class convulsed with silent laughter.

Sophie was sitting quietly now, her mission accomplished. A small part of her felt sorry for Mr Bevan, whose distress was obvious, but the mute approval of her classmates had been intoxicating. She hardened herself with the thought that if Bev couldn't take a bit of pressure from a twelve-year-old, he shouldn't be in the job. Today she felt extra-specially brilliant. In the History lesson that followed Maths, she refused to learn about John Knox on the basis of misogyny. After a long debate about feminism with Mr Atkins the history teacher, she agreed to settle down *only* if the next lesson was devoted to Emmeline Pankhurst, even though the Twentieth Century was off-syllabus. Then, after lunch, it was Art, a joke of a lesson taught by tubby Mrs Prokopowicz. The remit was to paint a still-life of bottles and vases arranged on a chequered tablecloth. At the end of the class Sophie produced a page of random splatters and argued with considerable cogency that hers was an 'abstract-expressionist' interpretation of the subject.

The last lesson of the day was Latin with Mr Dempster, one of the only teachers Sophie never felt like challenging. On some days Mr Dempster was chummy and approachable, happy to chat about football or the latest cinematic hash-up of Homer or Ovid; but on others, like today, he wore a look of the uttermost seriousness that defied anyone to cross him. So far, no one had dared.

Mr Dempster handed back the marked scripts of a mock exam the class had taken before half term. Sophie had come top, beating Karl Huber by just two marks. No one had done very well, however. They were going to have to put a great deal of work in between now and February, Mr Dempster told them soberly after explaining some of the problem areas on the paper. He set them a couple of translations to redo and installed himself at the front of the class with another pile of marking. 'Oh, and if anyone thinks they've been hard done by in the exam paper, then do feel free to come and see me about it.' It was this sort of thing that won him the respect of his pupils – the intimation that he knew himself to be fallible, that even though they had mostly flunked the paper he still thought enough of their abilities to allow them to contest his marking.

Sophie bashed through the translations fairly quickly, then began to check her paper. All of Mr Dempster's deductions – a tense error here, a missed plural there – seemed fair. But when she totted up the marks she found that he had miscounted: her score was 52, not 55. So Karl was top.

Trembling slightly, Sophie stood up and made her way to the front of the class. Everyone's eyes were on her. She could tell that they all thought she was mark-grubbing, the class swot looking to boost her already-sickening score.

'Sir, I'm afraid you got my marks wrong.'

'All right, Sophie, what should it be?' Mr Dempster uncapped a red biro and hovered the nib over the final page.

'Actually, it should be fifty-two. You gave me three extra points by accident.'

Mr Dempster chuckled into the silence. Then he grew serious. 'This is a first, an absolute first for me,' he said, speaking loudly enough for the whole class to hear. 'In eight years of teaching, I've never – I'm tempted to award you three points for truthfulness. But that's not what you want, is it?

'No, sir,' said Sophie, even though it sort of was.

'I hope the rest of you are listening to this.' Callum raised his voice even further. He was aware that his eulogy might later result in ridicule for Sophie, but he was moved by her self-sabotaging honesty. 'This sort of moral fibre is rare, very rare indeed.' He altered Sophie's mark to 52, then handed her back her script with a warm smile.

On the way out of the classroom, Ludo Hall bumped into Sophie, a little harder than was necessary. 'Weirdo,' he muttered.

Sophie grinned. She'd take weirdo. Weirdo meant you'd been noticed, that you weren't just some lumpy ghost. En route to the girls' changing rooms to collect her coat, she reflected on what a good day it had been. At break-time she had been clever; in the maths class she had been witty; and just now, in Latin, she had impressed Mr Dempster *and* provoked Ludo into speaking to her.

* * *

Chris, Leah, Doug and Helen were queuing for entry to a Clapham nightclub called Infernos. It was a cold night and neither of the girls was wearing very much. Chris stood behind Leah with his body pressed against her back and his arms round her waist to keep her warm. Her slender frame felt even more fragile than usual. On an impulse, Chris squeezed harder and leaned backwards until Leah's high-heeled feet left the pave-ment. It seemed to him that she weighed substantially less than his kitbag. For a silly moment, he wondered if maybe her bones were hollow, like a bird's. At any rate, feeling her breakability, seeing the delicate gleam of her cheekbone in the streetlight, Chris felt unpleas-antly aware of his own coarseness, his armpit smell and his hairy arse and, right now, the conveyor-belt of lager belches moving steadily up his gullet. He dispatched one as discreetly as he could, with a furtive, sideways motion of the head.

Inside, Infernos was full of leopard print and plastic light-up devil horns – all worn with a dash of irony, because the club was in fact a favourite haunt of the Chelsea public school set. The music enjoyed the same moratorium on good taste. Billed as 'disco' and 'boogie', the playlists consisted mostly of heartfelt rock ballads – songs universally acknowledged to be 'cheesy shite', yet nonetheless intimately familiar to everyone on the chewing-gum-cobbled dance floor.

All this was, of course, very much to Chris's liking; but this evening, he wasn't enjoying himself one bit. He and Doug had agreed that all four of them would go to the bar together for the first round, then find a table, where Chris would sit with the girls while Doug went up for the second round. The bar wasn't visible from where they were sitting, so Chris couldn't see how Doug was getting on. He had already been gone for at least fifteen minutes. Chris had visions of some boozed-up rugby player taking Doug to task over the capsule he was emptying into Leah's drink, or of the barman noticing, and calling the bouncer, or worse still, the police. Perhaps Doug was, even now, out on the street, trying desperately to reach Chris and Helen on their mobiles. Chris checked his phone. There was no reception.

And then Doug was back, bearing two bottles of Corona, a vodka tonic for Helen, and an antibiotic-laced orange and soda water for Leah. As he handed round the drinks, he treated Chris to a slapstick wink. Chris smiled weakly back. He felt cross with Doug for being so unsubtle, yet too grateful to show this irritation.

Leah trapped her drink's fluorescent green straw between two perfectly manicured fingertips and guided it towards her mouth. As if in slow motion, Chris saw the shadow of liquid rising, mercury in a thermometer, up the shaft and then over the little concertina of kinks at the neck of the straw. Leah was evidently thirsty; she sucked hard, draining an eighth of the drink in one mouthful. Chris scanned her face for any sign of distaste, but she was oblivious to the extra ingredient.

It took him a moment or two to realise that they were going to get away with it. Incredulity – *had it really been that easy?* – was followed by a perverse anticlimax, which was in turn replaced by a wave of relief. Chris did his best to resist this response. He was someone who always tried hard to feel the *right* thing; and relief, in this context, seemed very wrong. If anything, he thought, he should be feeling an intensification of the guilt that had gripped him in the queue for the club. On the other side of the table, Doug lowered his beer and grinned gauchely at him. Chris caught his eye, then looked away, wanting to dissociate himself.

The motivation behind Chris's moral rigour was a vague impression, never absent from his consciousness, that he had an audience. Even in the privacy of his own mind he was always performing, like the diarist who writes solely for himself with one eye on posterity. This sense of accountability was romantic rather than religious: he imagined himself watched by real people, not a deity. Chris wanted his whole being to be impressive to others, specifically one other, a perfected version of Tamsin Jarvis. For years after their encounter on the tube he had worried about how he must have appeared to her – nervous, indecisive, cowardly; and since then, she had occupied a front-row seat in his mental audience. Although he was not often directly conscious of measuring himself against her projected expectations, he wanted, in all ways, to feel himself worthy of her, and this informed both his actions and his thoughts.

But right now, in Infernos, with Leah rapidly drinking herself well again, he couldn't help it. Relief persisted. And sometime later, when two drinks became five drinks and the party moved from the table to the dance floor, it was superseded by an even cruder emotion: excitement. *Pain during sex* – hadn't Doug said that could, occasionally, be a symptom of Chlamydia? The recollection struck Chris like a revelation. *That* must be why things were so difficult between him and Leah in bed. She was sore because he had made her sore, and once she was better again – it took a week for the antibiotic to work – they would go back to the jubilant love-making of their first night together, the memory of which he had come to distrust as a dream.

Helen and Leah were dancing with each other, the sort of provocative bump-and-grind that apparently turned men on. Chris had never gone in for the lesbian thing himself. Watching them now, his dominant thought was that Leah looked too thin. Her arms were above her head, silhouetted by the hysterical strobe lighting. It was the swell of her elbows that bothered Chris; it was too marked, even bulbous, in comparison with her skinny forearms and biceps. But then the song changed to one of his personal anthems – 'We Are the Champions' – and this thought evaporated. 'And bad mistakes, I've made a few,' he sang happily, feeling as if the song were playing especially for him. Leah and Helen disentangled them-selves, provoking an extravagant mime of disappointment from Doug, who had been trying to get them to kiss. Chris stepped in between the girls and scooped Leah up into a crushing hug. Still singing, he spun her round and round, faster and faster, until she screamed for him to stop.

* * *

The following Thursday was Tamsin's twenty-sixth birthday. Jarvis family tradition decreed that all birthdays should begin with a breakfast of Eggs Benedict, but when Tamsin wandered downstairs at eight thirty, her mother was nowhere to be seen. She flicked on the radio, filling the kitchen with early church music. There were some birthday cards, including one from her father, whose handwriting was so bad that he always printed the address in capital letters. Tamsin didn't need to open it to know that it contained a card featuring a bland, tasteful close-up of a flower, presumably chosen by Valerie, from either the V&A or National Trust stationery range. The message would read, as always, 'Dear Tamsin, Have a good birthday and a drink (or two) on me, love B.' There would also be some money.

Tamsin briskly slit the envelope, glanced at the card (poppy, Georgia O'Keeffe) and removed the £50 note. She was about to deposit both envelope and card in the wastepaper basket when the front door opened and her mother's voice rang out.

'Tammy darling, happy birthday! Sorry, I just had to pop to the shops.'

The radio switched from Byrd to Scott Joplin. As Roz prepared the breakfast – slicing the muffins, splashing vinegar into the panful of simmering water – she sashayed jauntily to the music. Seeing this excess of good humour, Tamsin permitted herself a little unkindness.

'Ironic that Dad remembered and you forgot.'

Roz spun round, looking guilty. 'No no, I didn't forget, really, I just got my days mixed up.'

'Doesn't matter anyway, it's just a date,' Tamsin shrugged.

'No, it *does* matter. How about we party properly this evening?'

'That sounds nice.'

But Roz was shaking her head. 'Oh, Tammy, I've completely messed this up. I've just realised, I'm meant to be meeting someone tonight. But it's okay, I can cancel—'

'No no, don't do that. We can do it some other time, really.'

Tamsin was intrigued. Recently, Roz had been behaving rather strangely, receiving texts and calls from a mysterious someone or someones and staying out much later than usual. So far Tamsin had asked no questions, preferring to encourage her mother in her new-found independence. She had felt for a long time that Roz was too reliant on her opinion. This furtiveness seemed to signal a change for the better.

But as they stood watching the first egg filmily spinning in on itself like a miniature galaxy, curiosity won out.

'Tonight – is it a date? I mean – do you have a boyfriend?'

'No.' Roz lifted the egg out of the water with a slotted spoon and carried it, clouded and quivering, to the waiting plate. 'Not a boyfriend.'

Tamsin resumed her stirring duty in silence. That slight emphasis on the word 'boyfriend', the pinch of discomfort in Roz's face … could her mother be seeing a woman?

She felt surprisingly unsurprised – perhaps because the realisation made sense of a difference she had detected in Roz over the last few months. Her latest haircut was even more brutal than normal, actually shaved at the nape of the neck; she had developed a fondness for biker-style black leather jackets; and there was copy of *She Came to Stay* in the downstairs bathroom. While none of these things was inherently lesbian, they were sufficiently unlike Roz to jar, and now, Tamsin thought, she knew why. But she would respect her mother's privacy: she would say nothing until Roz indicated that she wanted to talk. This decision earned her a pleasing sensation of benign superiority.

Tamsin bent to kiss her mother's neat head as she carried her Eggs Benedict over to the table. 'Love you,' she said.

'Love you too, darling.' Roz looked delighted.

* * *

That night Callum and Tamsin arranged to meet for quiet birthday drinks at the Bar du Marché, a little French place in Soho that Tamsin liked, at 9 p.m.

Tamsin called Callum's mobile from the bar at 9.07 and was answered by a suave automated female voice informing her that 'this person's phone is not available'. Assuming that Callum had turned his phone off to conserve battery, and that he would be there at any minute, she settled down to wait.

To start with, it was pleasant enough to sip sparkling water at the bar in red lipstick and a new blue dress. She turned to look at a brown-haired couple sitting by the window. People watching: she would be observant, philosophical, shrewdly discerning. But the couple was unremarkable, and Tamsin couldn't hear their conversation, or guess at intimacy or irritation from the expressions on their faces. Bored, she checked the time, reapplied her lipstick, checked the time again. It was 9.15. She considered playing a game on her phone. At around 9.18 she became convinced that Callum was the victim of some terrible accident on the A40. By 9.23 she had persuaded herself that this fear was irrational. Now she just felt cross with him for making her wait on her birthday and for frightening her with the possibility of his messy death under the wheels of an HGV. In the space of a few minutes she had grown so indignant that even after Callum arrived at 9.26, breathless and apologetic with a perfectly reasonable explanation, she was unable to shake off her annoyance entirely.

'Soooo,' Tamsin said, once they were settled with a bottle of red at the other window table, next to the boring brown-haired couple. 'How are your little prodigies coming along?'

Callum missed the antagonism in her voice and answered enthusiastically. 'Ah, we had a grand session today. They're just about comfortable enough with the alphabet to tackle simple Greek-into-English now.'

The waiter arrived with their charcuterie platter. Dotted amongst the flat rosette of sliced hams and salamis were five or six fat green capers, still on their stalks.

Callum hated capers, but Tamsin loved them. 'Happy birthday,' he told her, picking up the biggest caper and offering it to her mouth.

As she ate, Tamsin indulged in a disgusted spasm of birthday stock-taking. What would her seventeen-year-old Nirvana-loving self have thought of twenty-six-year-old Tamsin sitting here in this chi-chi little restaurant, sipping a £22 bottle of Chianti with a prep-school classics teacher?

'Let me get this right. You're giving up your Tuesday and Thursday evenings to teach optional, unnecessary Greek to a bunch of already over-privileged kids,' said the twenty-six-year-old Tamsin, bitterly.

'Is something wrong?'

'Of course not.'

The alcohol in the wine had thinned Tamsin's lipstick slightly, making it bleed out over the edges of her lips so that her mouth looked big and blurred. Her fringe was due a cut; right now, it was a little too long, shading her big grey eyes and accentuating the sulkiness of her gaze. Callum thought how beautiful she looked when she was angry, although he knew from past experience to keep this observation to himself. He also knew that they were never going to agree about the school thing. But now a new, mischievous line of argument presented itself to him.

'Hang on a moment, Tam. I'm not sure you've got much of a leg to stand on any more. You're playing piano to a few select residents in highly selective, private nursing homes.'

'*Totally* different,' insisted Tamsin. Her cheeks were rapidly gathering sheen. 'Your pupils haven't worked all

154

their lives, haven't paid insurance all their lives, for the privilege of their education. Those kids have literally *everyone* on their side, everyone rooting for them and doting on them. The people I play for have been forgotten. They're just shoved away in those homes to rot and die, where no one can see them or smell them while they're at it.' Tamsin took a large mouthful of wine and then wiped her lips with the back of her hand. 'Oh, sod it,' she said when she saw the smear of red across her knuckles. She picked up her napkin and began to rub savagely at her mouth to remove the rest of the lipstick.

Callum took advantage of this hiatus to change the subject, sensing that if they went on like this, the mood might sour irreversibly. For a while, they talked peaceably enough about the wine, the possibility of snow at Christmas, Tamsin's suspicion that her mother was having a lesbian affair, the excessive media coverage of Prince William's relationship with Kate Middleton, a mutual friend's born-again baptism. But then Tamsin asked after a painting Callum was working on – an ambitious landscape, taken from one of the Ilfracombe photographs.

'Oh, *that* painting. It's on hold for a bit,' said Callum.

'On hold? Why?'

'I've had another portrait commission.'

'From who?'

'From the Halls, you know, Ludo Hall – the trouble-maker? I'm semi-tempted to draw a pair of devil horns poking out of his hair,' he joked.

Tamsin didn't laugh. 'It makes no sense. You like Lucian Freud, you like Schiele and whatsherface, Jenny thingy … Why spend your time on cosmetic pencil drawings of other people's snotty little children?'

'No, I see your point,' said Callum levelly. 'I enjoy it, though – it's sort of satisfyingly mindless – a bit like practising scales?'

'Mindless. Mindless.' Tamsin sounded as if she were trying out the word for the very first time. 'So you don't have a problem with increasing the stock of mindless art in the Home Counties.'

Callum shrugged. 'What can I say? The parents like it, it makes them happy, they pay me, I enjoy doing it.'

'And, what, never mind the fact that it's totally at odds with your whole view of art?'

'Tam, I don't have a "whole view" of art. I don't think many people do.'

Tamsin impassioned and indignant, Callum reasonable, teasing, ever-so-slightly superior: parts so familiar that they were barely aware of playing them. Usually, disagreement invigorated them; it had been there between them since their very first meeting, acting as a catalyst, a hook, the glue. They were not the sort of couple to exclaim, breathlessly, just how much they had in common. In the equation of their relationship, Callum was whatever Tamsin was not, and vice versa: they defined themselves in opposition to one another. She liked Stravinsky, he liked Mozart; she was a fervent socialist, he crept further right with every year that went by. Tamsin was wilful and impulsive in debate, drawing on a rat-tag array of frequently contradictory beliefs. Sometimes Callum found this frustrating, but mostly, he was amused by her inconsistencies. He was even – as someone who found conviction hard to come by – a little envious.

But lately their disagreements had become sharper, more serious. Feeling sad, Callum reached for Tamsin's knee under the table. Tamsin jerked it away.

'Are you okay?'

'Yes, I'm okay.'

'Tam?'

'Mmm?'

'We keep having these arguments.'

'Mmm.'

'Is something up?'

Tamsin met her boyfriend's worried gaze. It was the first time she had looked at him properly in over half an hour; for most of the evening, she had been resisting him almost as an abstract concept. Now she found herself faced with the solid physical reality of *Callum*, whom she loved: the defiantly unfashionable way his hair sprouted straight up from his scalp, the reassuring strength of his jawline, the soft bushiness of his eyebrows, which were barely a shade darker than his tanned skin.

The right eyebrow was a little unkempt. She reached up and smoothed it for him it with a sweep of her thumb. 'Everything's fine,' she said in a gentler voice. 'Promise promise.'

Callum caught her wrist as she withdrew her thumb from his eyebrow and squeezed it gently, feeling both disconcerted and relieved by this sudden mood change. Several of their recent tiffs had ended in this way, with Tamsin abruptly softening.

* * *

For all he had joked to Tamsin about adding devil horns to Ludo's portrait, Callum was actually rather proud of the progress he'd made with 8S's 'problem child'. Ludo was clearly better with smaller groups: in the Greek classes, he was attentive and alert. And the portrait had been something of a turning point. At his own home, with no classmates to impress, Ludo had been openly fascinated, asking so many questions that Callum had to dismantle his camera to demonstrate the workings of the single lens reflex. Pleased by the boy's enthusiasm, Callum resolved to start a photography club as soon as the exams were over.

So when he caught Ludo showing a copy of *Nuts* magazine to his classmates, Callum felt the transgression as a personal affront. 'Rest' was forty minutes of quiet-time after lunch, in which pupils were expected to pursue their own reading. Today, Callum was supervising both 8S and, in the next-door classroom, 4B. He returned from a stint with the younger class to find Ludo, Karl and Hugh hunched over a magazine. Des hovered behind them, trying to get a glimpse. Michael was the only boy reading a proper book.

As soon as Callum entered the room, Hugh threw his upper body forward to cover the boys' mysterious reading matter.

'Hugh, give that to me, whatever it is.'

'It's not mine, sir,' said Hugh, with a frantic glare at Ludo. Ludo was back at his own desk, apparently absorbed in *The Old Man and the Sea*.

'Not mine either, sir,' said Ludo, in a voice that perfectly confirmed his ownership of the magazine.

'I don't care whose it is. You were all reading it, all you boys.'

'But, sir, it's own reading,' said Ludo, sounding pained. 'We can read whatever we like, it's a free society, isn't it?'

'*Reading*,' scoffed Callum. He looked down at the magazine. The cover headline promised 'Summer's Boobiest Babes'. As the class watched, Callum flicked through page after page of balloon-busted impossibilities posing under such captions as 'Holly, 24, likes nothing better than licking a nice big lollipop!' His anger was rapidly overtaken by sadness. For these boys, for this generation, this was sex.

Des and Hugh were staring penitently down at their desks, but Ludo merely looked amused.

Callum held up a picture of a woman in a bathing suit

cut away to the navel, using a garden hose to spray her bare breasts. 'Look. *None* of this is real. Not the colour of her skin, not the size and shape of her breasts—' A couple of the children snickered uncomfortably at the word 'breasts'. 'Oh, come on, if you're old enough to look at this stuff you're old enough to talk about it. I'm doing you a favour here, I'm telling you not to develop a taste for this nonsense. I never want to catch *any* of you' – he was speaking directly to Ludo now – 'with this sort of thing again.'

He dropped the magazine in the bin and flipped up the lid of his laptop to signal to the class that the discussion was over. He'd only just managed to hold his temper; it was certainly the closest he'd ever come to losing it here at Denham Hall. Callum felt half-amused and half-ashamed to think that, in his last job, he had seen much worse, dealt expertly with much worse, every single day. Was he losing his touch? He should certainly never have allowed himself to feel that he'd 'cracked' Ludo Hall.

* * *

It was true, Tamsin conceded: Will Heatherington was generous. On the Saturday of Tamsin's birthday party he had opened up his huge flat to Callum, Tamsin, Chris, Leah and six of Tamsin's friends. Callum was in charge of food, enjoying the chance to cook on the brand-new induction hobs in Will's state-of-the art kitchen. On the large round dining table stood several bottles of good red wine, all provided by Will.

At first, Tamsin worried that her guests were too disparate. Her old schoolfriends Fran and Lottie worked in some obscure branch of consultancy, while Seb had a part-time job at a major theatrical agency to fund his pipedream of directing outré 1950s musicals. Tamsin wasn't sure how Seb's extravagant brand of camp would go down with her two Christian guests, born-again Julie and her fiancé Steven. It was Steven who had introduced Julie to God; in fact, he had baptised her himself, in a ceremony well-documented on Facebook. The sixth guest was Bethany, Tamsin's best friend from College days. Bethany wore deceptively expensive, drapey clothes in various shades of black and grey, and necklaces hung with large, bejewelled crosses. Her hair was a mass of tight black unmanageable curls which she referred to, loudly and often, as her 'jewfro'.

The meal began rather awkwardly. For the duration of the starter, Tamsin found herself stuck in the same banal conversation she always had with Lottie, an orgy of commonplaces about the march of time.

'Can you believe it's seven whole years since we left school?' Lottie would say.

Tamsin gave the requisite shudder of horror. 'Don't, just don't.'

'Seven years,' confirmed Lottie with grim satisfaction. 'In just three years time it'll be a whole decade. And, get this, the freshers starting uni this year were born in 1992. *1992!* That's like a year I can actually properly remember.' From here it was just a short hop to another exhausted subject: the quantum difference between their childhoods and the childhoods of the new generation, versed in smartphones and social networking from the womb. 'Think about it,' Lottie went on. 'We had cassette tapes; they won't even remember a time before the Internet. I got my first mobile when I was sixteen. Before that I had a pager. Can you believe it? A *pager!*'

But good food and wine gradually encouraged more communal conversation. Seb made everyone laugh with horror stories from the agency slush pile, recounting with especial relish the tale of one poor hopeful whose email address was hendonthewizard@burntmail.com. Then Bethany, after some prompting from Seb, confessed that she had helped to orchestrate the music for the latest Harry Potter film; and everyone, even the bored-looking Will, was full of questions about actors and premieres and life in the film industry.

Tamsin listened with a mixture of jealousy and pride. Until two years ago, Bethany had been as reliably unsuccessful as Tamsin. Now her career seemed to have unstoppable momentum. As Lottie and Fran, delighted by the idea of 'knowing the composer', busily took down details of a Southwark Playhouse production for which Bethany had written the music, Tamsin felt the seismograph of her jealousy spike new heights. She forced it down with the reflection that ultimately it was demeaning work – jingles for banks, join-the-dots orchestration for naff Hollywood film franchises. Only then was she able to enthuse about Bethany's success with what looked – and indeed felt to Tamsin herself – like real warmth.

During pudding, centre stage was occupied by Chris, whose career choice was a novelty to several of the guests. Before long, the chorus of general enquiries dimmed to an uneasy duet between Chris and born-again Julie. Now she wanted to know, *demanded* to know, how Chris could live with the idea that he would almost certainly return from Afghanistan as a killer.

Chris was unfazed. He had had this discussion, or variations on it, innumerable times before. 'The way I see it is, this war is happening. Someone has to be doing the killing, and frankly, I don't mean to brag, but I think that person might as well be me. I want the job done well, I want it done as cleanly and kindly as possible. Isn't that empirically better than someone who's attracted to the army because he's excited by the idea of violence?'

'I'm not talking empirically,' Julie said, by now very

hot. 'I'm talking about *you*. You personally. I don't believe you entered the army to prevent someone less intelligent, less measured, less whatever than you are from filling that place. So tell us: why do you want to go?'

Everyone had stopped eating now; all eyes were on Chris.

'I suppose,' he said slowly, 'I want to know what I'll do. I want to see how I behave in a truly elemental situation, when I've only got a split second, when everything else is stripped away. And I want to know that I don't value my own life more than what's right.'

Callum broke the silence that followed this little speech. 'Learn to love death's ink-black shadow as much as you love the light of dawn,' he murmured; and then, in response to Tamsin's puzzled frown, 'Tyrtaeus. He was a Spartan poet.' For some reason, this didn't seem to satisfy Tamsin, whose frown deepened to a full-bore glare.

It was almost midnight. There had been talk of dancing, but everyone agreed they felt too full and sleepy for that now; so apart from Will, they all set off together for the tube station. It was a cold night but the air was rich with the smell of vegetation from Clapham Common.

Bethany took Tamsin's arm and drew her away from the others.

'So, tell me about Chris, then,' she whispered.

'What do you want to know?'

'The thing with Leah, how serious is that?'

'Oh, you like him?' asked Tamsin, disingenuously.

'Come on, Tamsin, he's *gorgeous*.'

'I don't know. I just think he's a bit obvious.'

* * *

'So, I think everyone had a good time?' said Callum.

'It was *perfect*.' Tamsin turned to kiss his mouth,

pressing her tongue firmly onto his before pulling away to sit with her hand resting on his leg. She gave his thigh a brief squeeze. 'Thank you.'

Callum palpated the downy nape of Tamsin's neck between his thumb and middle finger in the way she especially liked, using the movement to soothe himself as much as her. On the tube ride home he had sensed, as he did so often these days, that Tamsin was somehow displeased with him. She had spent the whole journey quizzing Chris about literacy rates in the army, talking over Callum whenever he tried to join in. It was getting harder and harder to ignore the attention his girlfriend was paying to this younger, fitter, bigger man.

'All yours,' called Chris from the door of the bathroom.

'Sleep well,' said Callum as they passed in the corridor, enabled, by the enthusiasm of Tamsin's kiss, to summon his usual warmth for his earnest young friend.

In the bathroom Callum pissed while Tamsin washed her face. He watched her season a cotton pad with eye-makeup remover, staining the communion wafer with a bluish tinge. She applied it to her eyes with two fingers in a sideways sweeping motion that reminded Callum of a religious rite, an anointment or an ablution. Ablution: according to Chris, the officer cadets used this word for the communal bathrooms at Sandhurst. Chris wanted war to tell him a fundamental truth about his character. Or maybe even his soul: he wanted to leave Afghanistan with a judgement pronounced, for better or for worse. 'The Army as Religion' ... not a bad chapter heading, Callum thought as he joined Tamsin at the sink.

There wasn't really enough space for two of them; with Callum standing next to her, Tamsin had to tilt her head awkwardly in order to see the whole of her face in the toothpaste-freckled mirror. This tiny inconvenience, which she had experienced countless times before in the little bathroom, tipped her precariously balanced mood over into active discontent. She knew she ought to be grateful. On the sofa just now, she had kissed him as if she was. But she didn't feel grateful. She felt annoyed. Tonight, at her own party, Callum had embarrassed her with his cloistered aesthete's verdict on Chris's impending military tour. Quoting two-thousand-year-old poetry to a man about to face the twenty-first-century realities of lawless snipers and IEDs! It was the sort of intellectual arrogance Tamsin hated, smugly sure of itself yet totally disengaged from real-world events.

Ten minutes later Tamsin lay naked in bed with the covers pulled right up to her chin. She watched Callum wobbling on one leg as he reached down to thumb off a sock, an unconscious clown with a disaffected audience of one.

She went to speak, then thought better of it and closed her mouth; but Callum had heard her intake of breath.

'What is it?'

'Nothing, it's nothing.'

'Go on.'

'Why did you quote poetry like that?'

'Was it wrong?'

'I just think ... Chris was trying to explain something really difficult, something *real*, and it made you sound sort of pretentious.'

'Really?'

'Like you weren't taking him seriously.' Her tone was conciliatory, as if she were doing him a great favour by highlighting his shortcomings in this way.

'I don't think Chris felt that.'

'You think you know all about this stuff because you're writing some book,' said Tamsin as Callum climbed into bed beside her. 'But your version of it is so secondary, it's received, it's...' here she paused before delivering what she considered to be the greatest insult in her vocabulary '...*romantic.*'

Callum avoided Tamsin's indignant gaze, concentrating instead on removing a fraying jag of nail at the side of his thumb. If he too became angry, the night would end in another row. 'If anyone's being "romantic", as you call it, I think it's Chris. I know war is brutal and nasty, and for that reason, I would do everything I could to avoid it. Chris knows it's brutal and nasty too, but for him, that's part of the attraction. You see the difference?'

'Not really,' said Tamsin sullenly, but she seemed to be losing momentum. Callum risked a hand on her leg.

'I don't want to argue with you, hen,' he said, trailing his fingertips round to the smooth skin of her inner thigh. 'I want to kiss you ... here. But it's up to you, of course, it's your birthday.' He mimed a pair of weighing scales with his upturned palms. 'Argument?' he asked, raising one hand, 'or cunnilingus?'

Tamsin groaned – 'cunnilingus', as Callum knew, was a word she found both comic and disgusting – but she was smiling in spite of herself. The gratitude she had missed earlier rushed in. Here she was, doing her best to fuck up what should have been a lovely evening, and Callum, in his tender, patient way, simply wasn't going to let her.

'Argument?' he asked again, grinning now, because he could see his gambit had worked. 'Or cunni—'

'Don't say it!' Tamsin clamped a hand over his mouth.

Callum poked his tongue out between her fingers and waggled his eyebrows inquiringly.

Tamsin mock-sighed. 'Oh, go on, then. If you *must.*'

He kissed her once on the lips, then shuffled down to the end of the bed and slid off the edge so that he was kneeling on the floor. Tamsin assumed her position, lying diagonally across the bed with her legs resting on Callum's shoulders. With these preparatory movements, performed so many times they felt almost ritualistic, both Tamsin and Callum began to relax. They were practised at this. They were good at this. Callum was good, very good, with his tongue, and Tamsin was good at letting him know how good he was. In an ideal world she would have preferred to enjoy her orgasm in silence, but she understood the importance of allowing him to share her pleasure. So she mmmed and ahhhed and ohhed and oh godded and yessed and yessed and yessed until—

—until, in this instance, Callum's phone started to vibrate with an incoming call.

'Don't stop,' panted Tamsin. She was very close to orgasm. 'Don't stop, go on, don't stop.'

She willed herself closer to the edge, but each time the phone buzzed her climax receded a little further. It was no good; the feeling was going, gone.

'You might as well get it,' she said.

Frowning, Callum wiped his mouth on the back of his wrist and found the phone on the floor next to the bed.

'It's my mother.'

'Take it, I don't mind.'

'It's Saturday night, she'll be pissed.' He held the phone at arm's length until it stopped buzzing. Then he turned it off and resumed his position between Tamsin's thighs. 'Now, where were we?'

'Cal, I don't think I can any more. It's sort of gone.'

With the ebb of her arousal, the frustration Tamsin had felt in the bathroom returned to her, along with a growing clarity. There was a *smallness* in Callum that she had never seen before. Ironic, she thought, that Rugby-educated Chris should be so intensely aware of the real world; while Callum, whose own background had given him a much sharper taste of social inequality, was deter-mined to narrow his purview to Ancient Greece and schoolboy cricket and a moneyed bunch of Sloaney friends like Will Heatherington.

As Tamsin lay in Callum's arms, her mind hurtled on to new conclusions. Yes, she thought: Chris constituted a challenge to Callum's comfortable existence, which was why Callum was always trying, subtly, to undermine him. Suddenly it all seemed so *obvious*. The air of quiet intelligence she used to find so attractive in Callum masked a desperate need for control, born of an all-consuming insecurity that stemmed – *of course!* – from his sexual limitations. Until recently, their unconventional bedroom arrangements had always seemed a thing apart to Tamsin, an antechamber to both their lives. Now she understood that, for Callum, the problem with his penis coloured everything around him. She felt as if she were seeing him properly for the first time, as if she had at last discovered the organising principle of his entire being. It accounted for everything: the importance he placed on physical fitness, the multitude of hobbies at which he invariably excelled, the way he patronised her when they argued. Compensation, all of it compensation. He needed to dominate; he needed to maintain control. And only she, Tamsin, knew how weak he really was.

Callum's arm had travelled upwards, from her waist to her ribcage, and now Tamsin felt its weight as a more than just physical pressure. She wondered if she could move out from under it without waking him. His breaths, when she stopped her own to listen, were long enough to indicate deep sleep. She prised his arm up as carefully as she could and rolled her body over to the other side of the bed. In this virgin territory, the sheets and duvet had a delicious coolness. The back of her hand was still in contact with his arm; longing for the purity of complete isolation, she brought it over to her side of the bed.

Tamsin had guessed wrong. Callum was awake; he

felt it all. They were a couple who always slept as one, at least to begin with: if they woke up apart, it was because they had shifted away from one another in their sleep. Callum didn't need to check if Tamsin was awake. He knew that she had moved on purpose, moved all of her being, even her hand, so that no part of her was touching him.

* * *

Even before he understood what it was he was hearing, Chris was in a desperate mood. Last week in Infernos he had persuaded himself that once the infection had been treated, things would be different with Leah; yet here they were, staring at the ceiling after yet another session of silent and unsatisfactory sex. And now, like some cruelly calculated taunt, they were listening to Tamsin's moans gradually crescendo to a climax. Very clearly, they heard her imploring Callum not to stop whatever it was he was doing. Chris found it impossible not to supply the audio with visuals: Callum expertly fucking Tamsin from behind, grabbing onto her hips to pull himself deeper inside, perhaps, or reaching forward to caress a nipple. Then the camera angle switched to a close-up of Tamsin's contorted face, beautifully disfigured with a pleasure Chris couldn't begin to make his own girlfriend feel.

When it was over, the silence in Leah's bedroom had a different quality. For a while they remained on their backs, each too embarrassed to meet the other's eye. Finally Chris took a long breath in through his nostrils and shifted onto his side so that he was facing Leah's sepulchral side profile.

'Look, am I doing something wrong?'

There was a longish pause before Leah spoke.

'What do you mean?'

'You never come.' It came out more like an accusation than he meant it. Already he was wishing he'd never started this, but when Leah said nothing, he felt obliged to go on. 'The first time we were together, I thought maybe you did. But now I'm not sure.'

More silence.

'Leah?' Chris put a hand out and found her arm. 'We should talk.'

'What do you want to know?' she said. Now her voice was clear and faintly official, as if she were manning an information desk.

'Well … *have* I ever made you come?'

An even longer pause, then:

'No.'

'Not even the first time?'

'No.'

'So you faked it.'

Leah sat up and swung her legs off the side of the futon. For a moment Chris thought she was going to leave the room, but she simply repositioned herself at the foot of the mattress, sitting cross-legged on top of the duvet. The white linen curtains let in just enough of the night lighting in the courtyard shrubbery for Chris to make out her hunched silhouette. She had her head bowed so that her long hair hung straight down in front of her face. When she spoke, her voice was so low he had to ask her to repeat herself.

'I used to do that, to…' She tailed off.

'Fake it?' Chris prompted.

'All the time. And then with you, I thought I would just – I don't know exactly – be myself. I thought that if I did that then it might be different.

'But it's not.'

Leah shook her head. 'No.'

Chris made a noise halfway between a sigh and a

groan. 'And with other guys, could you, did they make you...?'

'No,' she whispered. Then, louder: 'It's okay. I get it.'

At first, Chris was too busy feeling pleased that no one else had succeeded where he had failed to grasp what she was saying. 'Sorry, you get what?'

'That you've. That you've had enough. It's okay.'

This time he understood. 'Hey,' he murmured, crawling over the duvet to join her at the end of the futon. 'Who's saying anyone's had enough?' He stroked her back, his hand bumping gently over the knobbles of her spine. 'We should have talked about all this ages ago, and now we have, and you've been open with me, which is great, and now we can start to do something about it.'

Leah said nothing.

'You've, you've had an orgasm before, right, on your own?'

At this point, Leah's self-imposed policy of total honesty failed her. The truth – that she had touched herself on three, maybe four occasions at most, that she hated the feel of herself down there, that she was too squeamish even for applicator tampons – seemed so cold, so horribly unwomanly.

'Of course, plenty of times,' she told him.

'Well, that's fine then,' said Chris, adopting a tone of breezy competence that he certainly didn't feel. 'You're going to show me what to do.'

Leah turned her head towards him sharply; it was too dark to see the expression on her face but he guessed, correctly, at alarm. 'Sshhh,' he told her, even though she hadn't said anything. 'Not now, I don't mean now. Now we're just going to curl up together, like this' – he helped her back into bed and drew her towards him – 'and I'm going to stroke you, like this, until you fall asleep. Okay?'

'Mmm-hmm,' murmured Leah through the tears that Chris couldn't see or hear.

*　*　*

Callum disapproved of colleagues who allowed their private lives to impinge upon their teaching. On the Monday after Tamsin's birthday party, however, he found himself struggling to maintain focus. For months he had been dismissing what he assumed were routinely paranoid thoughts about Tamsin and Chris; but these latest suspicions felt obdurate, immovable. He couldn't stop thinking about how he and Tamsin had argued, out of nothing, on her birthday and then again on the night of the party – about how she had ignored him on the tube journey back – about the attack she had launched on him for embarrassing her in front of Chris – about how she had shifted away from him so deliberately in bed, as if repulsed.

Deviating for the first time from his meticulously crafted lesson plan, Callum kept his classes busy with Latin word-searches until break while he hid behind his laptop with his thoughts. He needed to audit his jealousy, to systematically inspect each of its claims until he could determine whether or not his anxiety was justified. By the end of the second lesson he felt certain that Tamsin really did feel something for Chris. But what to do with this nebulous information? He had no conclusive evidence of her attraction to Chris, so if he confronted her with his suspicions she could simply say it was nonsense. All in all, it was probably not a good idea to talk to her about this. Callum knew himself very well; he knew that once the subject was live between them, he would be unable to leave it alone. Incontinent jealousy was bound to be a turn-off. And, worse, perhaps a confrontation would act as a trigger: Tamsin might agree, she might say yes, it's Chris I want, we're through.

The bell rang for third period. Callum roused himself from his worries for just long enough to dismiss 6C and settle 4B down in front of a fresh batch of word-searches. Then he returned to his computer, feeling blank. There was nothing to be done except wait, in silence, for Tamsin's crush to wax or wane. He played a few fitful games of computer solitaire, trying to comfort himself with the thought that as long as Chris was with Leah, he was safe. But that was faulty logic. He wasn't worried about the possibility of Tamsin cheating on him; he knew that was something her principles would never permit. The problem was one of proximity. They were seeing Chris all the time, at least once a fortnight – and the more opportunities that Tamsin had for unfavourable comparison, the more likely she was to become terminally dissatisfied by her relationship with him.

He had reached a dead end in the game he was playing; the two of diamonds was stuck behind a black King that was never going to shift. Callum clicked the little minus sign and the luminous green square sucked itself down to the bottom of the screen. Now he could see his desktop background: the panoramic shot of Arganite Bay, taken on the first day of that idyllic summer holiday. Was it really only three months ago? Callum found and opened a folder marked 'Ilfracombe-Aug' and scrolled through the rest of the photographs. There was Tamsin eating an ice cream. There was the beach. Here were the three nude photographs of her in all her beautiful, difficult glory. It was on that day, Callum remembered now, that they had had supper at the restaurant, and then later, in bed, that she had told him she was ready to move in with him.

During break he took a long walk round the peri-meter of the school grounds, stopping to scold, with uncharacteristic snappiness, a pair of second years who were crouched over a plastic marker cone, engaged in the muddy preparation of some sort of potion. He sent them back inside and tipped out the cone. In amongst the mud and leaves and stones was a small model of Spongebob Squarepants and one of those red cellophane fortune fishes. Callum used the outside tap on the back wall of the games shed to rinse out the cone. Then he held his hands under the tap until the cold water began to feel warm.

His misery was so engrossing that he lost track of time. When he arrived back at the main school, he was already late for his next lesson. The corridors were empty apart from Mr Kerry the janitor, buffing the wooden floors with the ancient electric polisher that always reminded Callum of a hovercraft. The grandfather clock outside the headmaster's study told him that the lesson had started not five but ten minutes ago; guiltily, he broke into a light jog, reaching his classroom twelve minutes after the end of break.

Twelve minutes: enough time to convince 8S that Mr Dempster was not going to turn up at all. He was never late; in fact, they couldn't remember a time when he hadn't been in the classroom before them.

'What are you doing, Ludo?' asked Verity. Ludo was behind Mr Dempster's desk, rooting around in the bin.

'Trying to find my magazine.' Unsuccessful with the bin, he started to shuffle through the piles of papers on Mr Dempster's desk. 'Bet he nicked it, the old pervert.'

'Ludo!' hissed Verity.

'What?'

Ludo straightened up to see Mr Dempster standing in the doorway, watching him.

'Sir, I was just putting something in the bin, that's not illegal, is it?'

'I don't care.' Mr Dempster sounded very tired. 'Just go and sit down, all of you. *Ecce Romani*, page 37, Latin into English. Go.'

The class exchanged glances. Mr Dempster had turned up late and now he didn't even care that Ludo was messing about with his things. Something was very wrong indeed.

Callum sat down at his desk and reached for his mouse. As soon as he touched it, the screen lit up with the photograph of Tamsin. He had forgotten to close the picture before leaving for break. And Ludo had been right here, his hands inches from the mouse...

He should have felt relief at such a narrow escape, but instead he found himself bleakly amused by the irony of it all. On Friday, he had caught Ludo looking at porn, and now the boy had almost discovered him in exactly the same posture.

Except, of course, Tamsin wasn't pornography. She was beauty, she was art. She was his life.

'Sir? Sir, are you all right?' It was little Rhiannon Jenkins.

Callum heard that she had spoken, but not what she had said. He stared at her.

'It's just' – Rhiannon went on, uncertainly – 'you look really sad, sir.'

'I'm fine, thank you, Rhee,' said Callum, realising as he spoke that he was not fine at all. Rhiannon's concern redoubled his emotion; he was close to tears, fighting that strange rictus in his lips in order to keep his voice normal. The whole class was watching him. 'I'm fine,' he told them, in what he hoped was a bright, reassuring tone. He bent himself over his laptop and tried to look busy.

On his computer screen, topless Tamsin lay on her beach towel and squinted up into the sun. He wished he hadn't been so brusque with the boys about that magazine the other day. He had been too hard, he decided; they were, after all, just curious. Callum thought about the girls in *Nuts*. He wondered if Ludo and Hugh and the rest actually found them arousing. If so, what would they make of a woman like Tamsin?

And the girls – what would *they* think of Tamsin? Would they want to grow into her? It seemed unlikely, when he remembered, with a pang, Tamsin's own reaction to this photograph. The sideways drag of her breasts, the tanned skin raked by paler stretch marks. At her bikini line, a few damp fronds of hair. He had read recently that waxing *everywhere* was becoming standard among fourteen- to sixteen-year-old girls and it had shocked him, slightly. Maybe he was being old-fashioned; maybe it was no different from shaving legs or armpits. But his mind returned to Tamsin, to the fuzz of her blondish-brown pubic hair, always surprising to him in its thickness. How he could cup it under his hand and feel its spring.

Callum glanced up at his class. Rhiannon, Hugh and Sophie had evidently all been watching him; as soon as he lifted his gaze, they snapped their heads down over their books. The idea of them looking at him while he looked at Tamsin gave him a strange feeling. Tamsin might not be pornography but she *was* erotic, and the erotic had no place in the classroom. He closed the image viewer and switched off his laptop.

* * *

To Tamsin's dismay, the decline of Antonia's mental faculties seemed to be accelerating. She still gave private recitals for the old lady every Thursday and Saturday, and they were still able to have reasonably detailed discussions about Ravel's relationship with jazz or the aesthetic value of Busoni's piano rolls. But where once Antonia had been opinionated, even domineering in these conversations, Tamsin now found herself having to provide forgotten names, to second-guess Antonia's meaning when she muddled her musical terminology. Tamsin began to suspect that, even if she could organise treatment for the Dupuytren's contracture, Antonia might no longer remember how to play.

She gave up on the idea for good one damp December Thursday. Thus far it had been a warm, wet winter; on the walk from the tube to Hortensia Court, a fine rain silvered her green wool coat. The nursing home was over-heated as always. Tamsin hung up her coat and glanced at her reflection in the hallway mirror. The smile-lines around her mouth were very pronounced today, and her hair looked dreadful, teased into a dull frizz by all the moisture in the air. Sometimes Tamsin felt like a different species from the shrunken old women with their terrible perms and that thin shiny skin on their swollen calves. On those occasions, it was hard to believe that simply by waiting fifty years her own body would be transfigured in exactly the same way. At other times, like today, her shrivelled audience made her acutely aware of her own mortality. As she played her way through 'The White Cliffs of Dover' and 'Lili Marlene' yet again, she experienced the strange sensation of existing in her own past. If she lived into her eighties or nineties, then those years would be her final present, her most real reality, and all of this – her smooth skin, the pleasures of running and dancing, sex, her fingers' extraordinary, unconscious agility over the keyboard – would be ancient history, remembered poorly, if at all.

At the end of the little concert Tamsin helped the staff to clear the room of all the residents apart from Antonia. When she returned to resume her seat at the piano, Antonia was sitting with her eyes closed, her long fingers pressing out the chords of a piano piece that only she could hear. Tamsin watched her for a while, noticing, with sadness, a few small external signs of the old lady's deterioration. Antonia had begun to apply her makeup badly; she used too much foundation, so that the bottoms of her glasses were permanently smeared.

Tamsin coughed quietly and Antonia opened her eyes. 'What were you playing?' she asked.

Antonia closed her eyes again. 'I was playing German music.'

'Lovely,' said Tamsin, pretending not to notice this evasion. 'Let's have some German then. Beethoven, then a piece by Franck that I think you'll *love*, then finish up with some Bach. But we have to be quickish, the concert starts at five.'

'The concert?'

Tamsin frowned; she and Antonia had discussed this on Saturday, at length, and she had reminded her of it again when she arrived just under an hour ago. 'The Berlin Phil. There's a programme on the television, remember?'

'Ah, of course,' said Antonia, suddenly in command of her world again. 'I've been looking forward to it all week.'

She remained composed throughout the recital, saying little but listening attentively to Tamsin's remarks at the end of each piece. When it was time to head up to her room for the concert, Antonia led the way, and while Tamsin found the right channel on the little wall-mounted television, she prepared the tea with all her usual elegance and efficiency.

But then, in the opening bars of Brahms's second piano concerto, as the camera swooped over the wind section:

'What are those long ones coming out of the sides of their mouths?'

'You mean – the flutes?'

Flutes: the word was evidently familiar to Antonia, something she knew she should know. Tamsin watched her squinting at the screen until comprehension bloomed – and with it, embarrassment.

'Well, they seem a lot longer than that to me,' Antonia said huffily, as if her mistake had been entirely justified. It was a face-saving move that Tamsin was only too happy to corroborate.

'Yes,' she said, playing along. 'I know what you mean. And the one on the right, it doesn't look *quite* as silver as a flute should do, does it?'

Antonia turned to look at her and now there was no confusion in her eyes, just pain and a gathering contempt. Tamsin had done the worst possible thing: she had humoured Antonia, and in doing so she had acknowledged the severity of her condition, consigned her to the same category as all the other residents of Hortensia Court.

'Let's enjoy the rest of this in silence,' said the old lady, settling herself neatly back in her chair and turning her face to the screen as the first movement approached its climax.

During the Lutosławski symphony in the second half of the concert, Antonia fell asleep, snoring lightly and erratically. Tamsin decided against waking her. When the orchestra finished, she immediately dimmed the sound so the loud sizzle of applause wouldn't disturb Antonia. Then she switched off the television and quietly left the room.

Outside it was nearly dark. The temperature had dropped so far that a fuzz of frost had already started to form on the garden wall of Hortensia Court. Tamsin reached for her mobile, instinctively, unconsciously, and found Callum's number. But just as Tamsin was lifting the mobile to her ear, she remembered: Thursday evening, Greek class. She killed the call before it reached voicemail and stared down at the little screen. A text message wouldn't do. She wanted to speak to Callum, to confess her mistake with Antonia and hear his voice absolving her. She tried her mother, but the line was busy; then Bethany, who had a midnight deadline and couldn't stop to talk.

Knowing that all her usual confidants were unavailable only intensified the need to talk to someone. Tamsin scrolled up to the top of her address book and began to work slowly down, considering and rejecting each name in turn. Aglé? Nope. Alastair? AJ? Nope. Baxter – who on earth was Baxter? Callum, James Carterton, Claudia, ChrisKim. *Chris*. She stopped outside a drab-looking Chinese takeaway called The Lunch Box and let her thumb dart forward onto the call button before her conscience could talk her out of it. By the second ringtone, she had changed her mind. It seemed like an absurd thing to be doing, calling Chris midweek to bore him with the minutiae of her relationship with an old lady he knew nothing about. But she was committed now; hanging up halfway through would look weirder still.

'Tamsin!' He answered the phone mid-ring, catching her off-guard.

'Chris, hi, sorry, am I disturbing?'

'No, it's perfect, I'm stuck in the office.'

She could hear that he was grinning.

'How's it going?

'It's all right,' Tamsin said slowly. 'Or actually it's

not really.' She had reached the glazed ox-blood tiles of the tube station already. There was an empty bench next to the entrance, but it was too cold to stay still, so she just carried on walking up the hill. 'Sorry. I shouldn't really be bothering you like this. I just had – I just had a bit of a shitty afternoon, and Callum's busy.' Her voice sounded as pathetic as she felt, making excuses for a call she should never had made. Yet her guilt didn't prevent her from enjoying the concern in Chris's response.

'Oh god of course, you poor thing. What happened?'

'Well, it's the job, with Amad, at the nursing homes. There's this one old lady, Antonia, we've sort of become quite close. But she's just—' She broke off, slightly breathless from the climb. She found she couldn't explain herself to Chris. With Callum it would have been easy to sketch out the complexity of her exchange with Antonia; but she and Chris were so new to each other that they had no private language, no common shorthand.

'Tamsin,' Chris said reverently. 'I think what you do is amazing, really, really amazing.'

'It's nothing, honestly, it's cushy, anyone could do it,' Tamsin murmured, allowing herself to be flattered and soothed by his admiration.

'No, they couldn't. I couldn't do it. I'm not patient enough. Or nice enough, for that matter.'

The urge to tell Chris just how nice she thought he was reminded Tamsin that they shouldn't be having this conversation at all. She had paused in the middle of the narrow pavement, earning an impatient look from a pregnant woman with her coat done up clumsily over her bump, like a badly wrapped present. Tamsin turned and followed the woman back down the hill to the tube station.

'Anyway,' she told Chris, 'I should go, I'm freezing –

but thanks, it was good talking – I guess I'll see you round sometime—'

'Next weekend? I'm with Leah on the Saturday, so maybe sometime on Sunday, maybe we could all hang out?'

The eagerness in his voice was gratifying and alarming in equal measure. Tamsin saw that her phone call had exposed a weakness in a structure that looked stronger than it really was: she had tugged on some crucial joist and discovered how little it would take to dislodge it. Frightened, she jammed it hastily back into place.

'You know I do think you're so good with Leah,' she said. 'It's lovely, I love seeing you two together.'

'Uh, thanks. I—'

'Well, see you round,' said Tamsin, and rang off.

* * *

Chris replaced his phone in his pocket and waddled his wheely-chair back over to his desk. He stared up at the big pale map of Kandahar province with its comforting complexity of signs and shading and tried to meditate on the unpredictable nature of insurgency, but the dull predictability of his personal life won out.

To start with he had been happy enough with Leah, but now he was bored. Following their conversation about sex, he had been filled, once again, with optimism. Their problems were nearly over: all that was required was patience and good communication. But things had got worse rather than better. Leah couldn't tell him what she wanted in bed; she didn't really seem to know, and whenever Chris pressed her for information she grew silent and stiff, quite literally, her thin body so tense that his touch – though she never rejected it – had for him an unnerving quality of assault. After a few weeks of this he privately admitted defeat, and now they were back to their old pattern of silent, perfunctory sex – or, increasingly, no sex at all. Chris couldn't help thinking that Leah was a hopeless case, repressed and frigid. His relief that the problem lay with her rather than him did nothing to reconcile him to the situation. He was bored and he wanted out.

Out, however, was not an option, for two rather complicated reasons. The first was that Chris didn't want to be the sort of person who dumped someone because of sex. Partly he felt it was unfair on Leah, but mostly it simply didn't fit with his chivalrous self-image. Even though no one had to know why he had broken up with her, he couldn't stand the thought of what people would think of him if they did. (He never considered that there was another, more palatable explanation for his unhappiness, i.e. that he didn't love Leah. Chris was so preoccupied by what didn't work in the bedroom that he failed to notice that nothing much was working outside it, either.) Also, it now occurred to him, there *was* someone who might guess at why he was ending the relationship: Leah herself. He ran the risk of seeing her realise why he didn't want her, the risk of inflicting pain on this fragile, brittle creature. It was not a role in which he wanted to watch Chris Kimura.

The second thing that made it impossible for him to leave was the conversation he had just had with Tamsin. *You know I do think you're so good with Leah*: incontrovertible proof that Tamsin herself didn't want him. Her words also confirmed something he had been worrying about, on and off, since the beginning: if he split up with Leah he might no longer be welcome at the Brewer's Court flat. He might never see Tamsin again. So, he was stuck. The best he could hope for was to impress Tamsin by behaving like a model boyfriend to Leah.

As he was glumly locking up his little office, Chris had an inspired idea. He would behave a like a model boyfriend, yes, but only until a week before his deployment. Then he could let Leah down gently, telling her that he didn't want her to suffer the heartache of having a lover in a war zone. No one could fault him for that. 'I can't do it to you,' he would say. 'You don't deserve that, Leah. You don't deserve this sort of burden.' He would confide in Tamsin and Callum that, although he was hurting, he knew he had to set Leah free.

By the time he reached the accommodation block, Chris had nearly persuaded himself that this was how things really were: that he was a good man in an impossible situation, forced by circumstances to sacrifice his own happiness to protect the woman he loved.

* * *

Over a month had gone by since the night of Tamsin's birthday party. Callum had managed to restrain himself from asking if she felt anything for Chris. He was resigned to waiting stoically for whatever his fate might be, and for the most part, he hid his anxiety well. His penis, however, was anything but stoic. His penis was giving him away. Over a month since Tamsin's birthday, and in all those weeks – a long time, even by Callum's standards – sex had not been possible, not once. Typical, thought Callum, that his genitals should fail him so completely just when he needed them most. No signal, out of reception, battery totally dead. Even solitary masturbation no longer worked.

And he worried about this, of course he did, but it was not – as Tamsin now thought – the key to his character. Or rather, it was and it wasn't. It was something that had troubled him nearly every day of his adult life, but in recent years it had dimmed to a low-level misery, the sort of background noise it was almost possible to ignore. There was some truth in Tamsin's theory that the energy Callum devoted to every other area of his life was a form of compensation: originally, his insecurity had fuelled his work ethic. By now, though, his work and his research and his photography and his sketching were pleasures in their own right. Apart from his recent fears about Tamsin and Chris, Callum was basically happy. He also knew that he owed a good deal of this happiness to Tamsin, who had made it all so much better by tacitly letting him know, over and over again, that his problem just didn't bother her.

(In fact, it was starting to bother her, much more than it bothered him – although she didn't know this yet.)

Callum found himself putting more energy into his work than ever. He was particularly committed to the scholarship form, now less than four months away from exams, making them flashcards and mind maps and even little podcasts to help with revision. Lessons with 8S became the highlights of his week. When he was with them, his mind kept returning to Rhiannon Jenkins, asking him if he was all right on that terrible day when he first acknowledged how close he might be to losing Tamsin. He wasn't stupid; he knew that the children could be brutal, even cruel, to each other and to their teachers. But he also knew that they liked him, and this knowledge was very precious.

He also found himself returning to the Ilfracombe photographs. In quiet moments, when the children were busy with their own work, he would flick through the three nude pictures of Tamsin, looking from Tamsin to the children and back again. He couldn't say why he was compelled to do this. Although there was something addictive about looking at the pictures, it wasn't arousal. It was more of an intellectual interest, he felt, in the contrast between Tamsin's known, loved, woman's body, and the unformed bodies of his pupils.

It seemed extraordinary to Callum that he'd never thought of his students in this way before. Their bodies were about to undergo the most significant change of their lives, far more dramatic than ageing. Sophie Witrand already had definite breasts, and he was fairly sure Verity Trevena had started growing as well. To be blind to this, or to pretend to be blind to it, was to deny a major aspect of their humanity. More and more Callum regretted his sharpness over Ludo's dirty magazine. That had been a denial, too – a denial of the boys' sexuality. These children were sexual beings and yet the system forced you to pretend that they weren't, to stuff them full of Ancient Greek and tell them nothing true about *now*. He wished he could talk directly to 8S, disregard the teacher–pupil barrier just as Rhiannon had so sweetly disregarded it when she told him he looked sad. But of course that barrier was a selective membrane. The children could say what they liked, but Callum couldn't.

* * *

When James Raddock the English master broke his collarbone two weeks before the Christmas holidays, Callum agreed to take on his teaching duties. It was fun to be teaching modern literature after years of *Ecce Romani*, and with most of Jim's classes he had free rein. He introduced 6A to Roald Dahl's adult fiction and got them all writing their own grisly short stories. He taught a giggling 5B to perform Robbie Burns with proper Scottish accents. In the evenings, back at home, he devoted far more time than was necessary to devising lessons and marking essays.

With 8S he had to stick to Mr Raddock's teaching plan, which consisted of learning the biographies of the Romantic poets and answering comprehension questions about their major works. For their final assignment of term, however, he couldn't resist deviating from the prescribed task. Instead of getting them to analyse the first two stanzas of 'Ode to a Nightingale', Callum asked 8S to write their own poem inspired by Keats. Most of the class turned in rather predictable rhyming ditties about robins and snow and Christmas and the blood of Christ, but there was a swashbuckling offering from Karl Huber about a golden eagle, and Michael Massey's four-liner about a city sparrow 'flicking its tongue at some crumbs' was so good Callum made him read it out loud. Sophie Witrand looked disappointed not to be asked to read her poem, which had, to Callum's surprise, been the worst in the class: a shopping-list of facts about a starling, surely taken straight from Wikipedia.

Callum thanked Michael Massey and walked round to the front of his desk, where he liked to sit in a relaxed, matey sort of way with his legs spread wide and his elbows resting on his knees, hands clasped.

'So, let's think about the Keats again. We start with his aching heart. And then when we get to the nightingale, Keats doesn't even call it a nightingale, he calls it a "Dryad". Yes, Felicity?'

Flick Chilcott – good with numbers but lousy with words – was frowning deeply. 'It's so stupid, sir. It's not a dryad, it's a nightingale. So why doesn't he just say so?'

'Remember we talked about metaphor? He's making a comparison between a nightingale and a dryad, because the nightingale's song is so beautiful it makes him think of a beautiful woman. That's the wonderful thing about language. You don't always have to describe things precisely as they are. I know, think about it like this.

You're not always taking a photograph. Sometimes you're painting, sometimes it's okay to blur the edges and switch around the colours a little bit. And that's what'll make your writing come alive. Get it?'

'I suppose so,' said Flick, who was really more interested in the elastic band digging into her wrist. There was a fuzzy knot of her dark hair wound round it, from which she was drawing individual strands with obvious pleasure. Next to her, Sophie Witrand was re-reading her poem, a look of pained concentration on her face.

That evening, Callum found a folded piece of paper in his mail tray outside the staffroom. It was a page ripped from a lined exercise book with a poem on one side and a message on the other. 'Dear Mr Dempster, I thought I should do another draft because after what you said it seemed to me that my poem probably wasn't exactly what you were looking for. Thank you for reading it, best wishes, Sophie.'

Sophie's revised version of 'Ode to a Starling' was now comically melodramatic. As far as Callum could tell, it was voiced for a murderer on the run from the law, contemplating his evil deeds and confiding his regrets to the starling. 'Your dark feathers are like my dark heart and I / Know that in time we two both must die,' ran the final couplet. Callum smiled, both at the poem and the gesture: he was touched by how seriously Sophie had taken his words, even if this new version was arguably worse than the first.

The next day was the last day of term, and the only day on which pupils were allowed to exchange Christmas cards. This restriction had been instigated three years ago, when competition over card tallies reached such a pitch that one pupil, Holly Shereton, refused to come into school for a week because she'd sent fifty-six cards and received only three in return. An element of the old competition still lingered, however. At the start of Callum's lesson with 8S, Ludo Hall and Rhiannon Jenkins were barely visible behind several ranks of cards, while Des Kapoor and Sophie Witrand were doing their best to arrange single-figure tallies to look as prolific as possible. Sophie caught Callum looking at her and managed a brave little smile; remembering her poem, he gave her a swift thumbs up that made her grin properly, then blush and dip her head.

He wanted to tell 8S how much he would miss them all over the three long weeks of the Christmas holidays. Instead, when the end of the lesson came, he reminded them to have fun when they weren't revising, and to email him if there was anything they didn't understand.

The bell rang for breaktime and the class rushed doorwards. Sophie paused by Callum's desk on her way out.

'Sir, will Mr Raddock be back next term then?'

'Almost certainly.'

'That's good. But – I wish we could have you for English all the time, sir.'

Callum smiled. 'Thank you, Sophie. I'll tell Mr Raddock you said that.'

Sophie looked panicked for a moment, then realised she was being teased and grew suddenly shy. 'Bye, sir,' she called, already halfway out the door. She reminded him a little of Tamsin: the awkwardness, the ardour. Though Tamsin at twelve, he imagined, would have had forty Christmas cards adorning her desk, not seven.

There was a little stack of blank cards on the desk in front of him: homemade cards featuring one of his own close-up, black-and-white photographs of frost fibres on a sprig of yew. These were for his colleagues; Callum had intended to spend break-time writing them. Now, on an impulse, he took a card from the pile and scribbled a message inside it. 'Happy Christmas, Sophie. You've been a joy to teach.' As soon as he'd written these words he regretted them. 'A joy to teach' – what a cliché. But it would look worse if he crossed it out, and he didn't have enough cards to use another.

All this took a matter of seconds: when Callum left the classroom, Sophie was yet to reach the swing doors that led out to the schoolyard. Callum sprinted down the long corridor to join her, and when he handed her the Christmas card, the pleasure in her face was worth all the indignity and impropriety of running to catch up with a pupil.

* * *

Following his new resolution to be (temporarily) the perfect boyfriend, Chris went all out with his Christmas presents for Leah. Tamsin helped him choose a cashmere cardigan and a simple gold necklace with a tiny diamond at its centre. On Christmas day itself, he had an enormous box of roses delivered to Leah's family home in Birmingham.

Each of these presents was, in its own way, repugnant to Leah. The cardigan was made in China. The diamond was untraceable, but she had serious doubts about it being ethically sourced. Her objection in these two instances wasn't so much the damage done to factory workers or diamond miners, but the thoughtless consumerism that cheap labour represented. It seemed to her like another form of pollution. She imagined all the wardrobes and cupboards and shelves of London filling up with the dark greasy sludge of unnecessary possessions, a contaminant sticking to everyone yet invisible to all but a few.

And then white roses, in England, in December: the carbon footprint was unthinkable. But the roses represented more than airmiles and high-end junk. The roses

CLAIRE LOWDON

meant that her boyfriend of nearly four months knew nothing whatsoever about her.

When Chris told Doug Ronson what he had bought for Leah, Doug was so impressed that he took down the address of the website the necklace had come from. He bought a necklace for Helen with not one but three diamonds, each bigger than the single diamond on Leah's necklace. Privately, Chris thought this one-up-manship a little tacky. He didn't know that the necklace was Doug's way of saying sorry for an un-confessed crime. Lately, Doug and Helen had both been very busy; it had been difficult for them to find time to see each other. On several occasions, in the middle of long, Helen-less stints, Doug found himself logged on to his old account on uniform-dating.com. Working quickly, as if Helen were about to come in and catch him at it – even though she was hundreds of miles away – he would select the first randy girl within easy driving distance, sidle into his Alfa Romeo with a pocketful of condoms, and be back in his own bed by morning. He told nobody about these trips.

Helen was careful not to show how pleased she was with the necklace. She wanted Doug to propose to her, and she had decided that the best way to effect this outcome was to behave as if all his attentions were nothing less than her due – to create, very subtly, the impression that she might tire of him at any moment. She needn't have worried: just as Chris was intending to break up with Leah on the eve of his deployment, so Doug was preparing to ask Helen to marry him before he left for Afghanistan. Each time he cheated on her this conviction grew stronger: the less Doug thought of himself, the more highly he valued Helen. He reasoned that his infidelities were purgative, that he was 'getting it out of his system' before he committed to one woman for the rest of his life. Yet a small sad part of him knew that it didn't matter

190

whether Helen were his girlfriend or his fiancée or his wife, because he would continue to have sex with other people whenever he thought he could get away with it. For ever and ever hymen.

Tamsin's present to Callum was an electric vegetable slicer that he'd been planning to buy for himself. She and Callum both disliked compulsory gift-giving, and usually they made a point of exchanging Christmas presents that were purely functional. This year, however, Callum had broken the rules: he had completed, in secret, his giant landscape painting of the cliffs at Illfracombe. On Christmas Eve, he stayed over with Roz and Tamsin in Notting Hill (Serena, who alternated parents each year, was at Bertrand's). In the middle of the night, he hung the picture on the wall at the foot of Tamsin's bed with a sheet draped over it, so that she could uncover it in the morning after opening the stocking that Roz still liked to prepare for her.

Tamsin should have been delighted with the picture, but instead she felt angry. In a sense, Callum had cheated; next to the painting, her own present looked thoughtless and mean. The picture also reminded her – just as Callum hoped it would – of what a good time they'd had together on holiday. But rather than endearing him to her, this only served to emphasise the contrast between their current situation and the way things had been in Ilfracombe. The painting made it impossible to ignore what she had been ignoring for months: that she no longer liked Callum in the same way that he liked her. For several days Tamsin was miserable. Then she went back to being angry with Callum for forcing this terrible knowledge upon her with his stupid unnecessary beautiful heart-breaking picture.

* * *

'And the penultimate question – penultimate, thass a fancy word for second last, for all you thick shits out there – the penultimate question for this round is, in what country, sorry *county*, in what *county* is Leeds Castle?'

It was New Year's Eve: a bumper quiz-night at the Ploughman's Rest.

'An' again,' bellowed Dave, the quiz-master. 'In what county is Leeds Castle? I'll give you a clue – it's not in Yorkshire cause Yorkshire's a fuckin' shithole!'

'Remind me why this is funny?' Tamsin asked, glaring at Will. It had been Will's idea to come to the quiz; later, they were all going on to a house party in Fulham, but Will had persuaded them to start the evening here in the Ploughman's in Putney. 'Best pub quiz in town,' he'd assured them. 'The guy's a liability, honestly, it's hilarious. A total prick, you'll love him.'

Tamsin hated being associated with Will in his red chinos and deck shoes. The two friends he'd brought along were, if possible, even worse: Jemima was a pashmina'd stick figure who insisted on drinking champagne, while Angus had made an embarrassingly conspicuous entrance halfway through the first round, wearing tweeds and a deerstalker with a skateboard tucked ironically under his arm.

'It's in Kent,' whispered Chris excitedly. 'Weird but true, Leeds Castle's in Kent.'

'Great, you sure?' asked Callum, who was in charge of writing down the answers.

'Hundred per cent,' said Chris with an urgent nod. Another reason why Tamsin wasn't enjoying herself: from the very first question, Chris and Callum had been locked into a little world of two, both of them blissed out on good-natured competition and admiration for each other's formidable general knowledge. Tamsin had only been able to help with one question so far, and to her mortification, she hadn't known the answer to the only music question of the night (the year of Mozart's birth).

In between rounds Dave would do a tour of the pub, stopping to repeat questions on request. When he reached their table Callum shook his head to indicate that they'd got them all, but Dave stopped anyway. He was tall, and quite good-looking: a wide, square face with clear blue eyes.

'What about number 14, you got number 14?' Dave put a hand on Leah's bare shoulder and leaned in to their group. ''Cause if you didn't, I got a clue for that one. The clue's Canesten, geddit? You got it?' He glanced towards Leah, clearly hoping for a reaction. 'Funny thing about Canesten. I had to use some once, for sort of cock-rot chafing problem with me jock strap. And I was in the changing rooms, and a mate wanted to borrow some toothpaste so I said yeah sure, in that bag, and he brushed his teeth with the fucking Canesten!'

Dave looked down at Leah with undisguised lasciviousness. Then he winked, over her head, at the rest of the group.

'Gor, I hope you lot win, then you can send her up to get the prize and we can all have a good look at those lovely legs.'

Will laughed and elbowed Leah, who looked as if she were about to cry. Chris was hunched over the answer sheet with Callum, oblivious to the discomfort Dave's attentions were causing his girlfriend.

'Anyone know number three, African river? Come on, guys, we *must* be able to get this one.'

'I'm going for a cigarette,' Tamsin announced loudly. 'It's not like you lot really need me anyway.' She paused to give someone a chance to protest, but nobody did. Then she caught Leah's eye. 'Want to come too? They've got heaters, we can take this—' She lifted a nearly full bottle of white wine from the table. Leah looked over at Chris, nodded once, and got to her feet. Jemima ran a smug hand through her blonde hair and settled herself closer to Chris.

The beer garden was almost as loud as the pub itself: crowds of smokers packed under four huge mildewed umbrellas, their faces tinted red by the outdoor heaters.

After a cursory search for a chair, Tamsin gave up and pulled Leah down onto a little stone ledge outside a back entrance to the pub kitchen. Bunched up shoulder to shoulder, both girls suddenly felt how strange it was for them to be alone together like this. Tamsin offered Leah a cigarette, knowing it would be refused.

'Warm enough? You don't have to stay, I just thought you looked like you wanted out...'

'No,' said Leah. 'I mean yes, I did. Thank you.'

'S'okay.' Tamsin took a long drag on her cigarette and washed it down with a mouthful of wine straight from the bottle. 'Do you want some of this?' She tipped the bottle towards Leah, expecting her to refuse again.

But Leah took the bottle with a grim little 'thanks'. She drank deeply, three big mouthfuls, before handing it back to Tamsin.

'That bad, huh?'

Leah missed the humour in Tamsin's voice and answered her seriously. 'It's just – I don't know – I can't really—' She sounded very upset. Tamsin reached over a hand to squeeze Leah's knee.

'No, I know, it drives me crazy when Cal goes all know-it-all. The two of them, it's like some private club.' Tamsin paused, registering the oddness of this conversation in which she and Leah were now suddenly on the same side, united against their boyfriends. Of course, she quickly reminded herself, she had never *not* been on Leah's side. It was a point of personal pride with Tamsin never to despise women who were more attractive than she was. Apart from jarring with her feminist ideals, it struck her as a) ugly and b) a sign of weakness.

Yet these principles had never prevented Tamsin from feeling grotesquely oversized next to Leah. Tamsin lifted herself off the step slightly in order to rearrange her belt, tucking her small soft belly down and under the buckle. Now she felt neater, more contained. Although, she thought, glancing over at Leah's legs, for the first time ever she wasn't entirely certain that she wanted to swap figures with the younger girl. Even in thick black tights Leah's legs were alarmingly thin. She had her knees pressed tightly together but the flesh of her thighs bowed inwards, not touching at any point.

'He's so *good* to me,' Leah was saying, as if being good to someone were on a par with domestic abuse. 'We've never had an argument, he's...' She wanted to say, *he's the only person who knows I'm terrible in bed and he doesn't seem to mind*, but this wasn't possible, not with Tamsin, not with anyone, really. 'Sorry,' she said. 'You guys – you're friends—'

'No, no, go on, it's fine, you can say anything,' Tamsin murmured. The solicitude in her own voice sickened her slightly: she knew that her interest stemmed more from her feelings for Chris than concern for Leah.

'Those presents, at Christmas,' said Leah.

Tamsin nodded.

'They make me feel *sick*. It's like, I've been trying to live as cleanly as possible lately, get rid of anything un-necessary – and he hasn't even noticed. I can't get rid of them because he'd be so hurt, but *I'm* hurt, too, because it's like, it's like he hasn't even seen me.' She held her hand out for the wine and took another long pull. 'Then sometimes – often – often I think it's me.' She looked up at Tamsin. 'Do you think that's right? What do you think?

You and Callum, you just seem to – I mean I hear you argue, but that sort of seems more normal. I'd never have the, I don't think I could, I wouldn't be able to do that. I don't know why. There's something wrong with me.' Leah pushed her sleeve back and began to massage the crook of her elbow with her thumb, softly at first, then with increasing vigour until she was scratching hard at her skin. 'What do you think?' she asked again, more urgently this time.

Tamsin was alarmed by the note of deference in Leah's voice: clearly she had real power here. Whatever she said was going to be taken very seriously indeed. It sounded as if it would be easy enough to convince Leah to break up with Chris – which of course would be a terrible thing to do. The only right course of action was to plead Chris's case.

'Well…' she began, sipping thoughtfully at her cigarette, 'In my experience with guys … just because someone doesn't get you doesn't mean they don't care about you.' She didn't quite believe herself, but she pushed on anyway, doggedly saying all the right things. 'Chris is just being a bloke, but I know he really cares about you. With those presents, he really wanted to get it right.' This was true: Chris had been touchingly anxious over the presents. That feeling she had had when she called him to tell him about Antonia – the feeling that he might be attracted to her in some way – it was pure fantasy, surely, and Tamsin felt foolish whenever she recalled it. He was obviously in love with Leah. 'I'm sure of it, Chris loves you,' she said at last. 'And that's the important thing.'

Leah was very quiet. When Tamsin looked round at her, she saw that she was crying heavily. She put her hand on Leah's thin back and understood how selfish her reasoning had been. Doing the right thing in order to keep her own moral slate clean was, in this instance, the wrong thing for Leah. Now it was simply a question of truth and not-truth, and the truth was that Leah was really unhappy in her relationship – just as she, Tamsin, was in hers.

'Chris loves you,' she said again, slowly, 'but you don't love him, do you?'

Leah shook her head and didn't stop shaking it for a long time.

'Then dump him. Dump him! Look, it's not easy, but honestly…' Tamsin was possessed by a sudden urgency – a feeling that if she didn't act now, then she never would. 'I know. Let's make a deal. You break up with Chris and I'll break up with Callum.'

'What?' Leah lifted the wine bottle away from her lips. 'You want to break up with Callum? That's awful, what happened?'

'I don't know.' Tamsin shook her head. 'Well, I do know, but it's too complicated to explain. It's just over. At least, it nearly is. Which is the same thing, isn't it?' There was a sad little pause. Then Tamsin forced her face to brighten. 'Hold on,' she said, jumping to her feet. 'Wait there, I'll be right back.'

There was an outside bar that was really a garden shed, trimmed with raffia to simulate a tropical beach hut. Tamsin bought four double shots of tequila and wiggled her way back through the tightly packed drinkers to where Leah was clutching the now-empty wine bottle.

'Our secret New Year's resolution.'

Leah took her first shot and nodded.

'To freedom,' said Tamsin, feeling euphoric, school-girlish.

'Freedom,' mumbled Leah. She gulped down her shot, coughed twice, and went back to scratching her arm. By now it was pink, and peppered with blood flecks.

197

Eight

Leah was first to go through with her side of the bargain. As soon as she decided to leave Chris, his presence became so unbearable to her that she couldn't understand how she'd stayed with him for four whole months. The problem was, she had no idea how to leave someone. For a fortnight or so, she hoped that her obvious aversion to him might prompt Chris to ask her what was wrong. But Chris didn't seem to mind her froideur. No, scratch that – he didn't even notice it. Leah began to feel that no matter how badly she behaved, Chris would remain his gallant, good-humoured self. She had an unsettling idea of herself as a storybook ghost, translucent and insubstantial, her hand passing pathetically through any object she tried to hold on to.

Halfway through January he rang to tell her he wanted to make a reservation for the two of them at a Michelin-starred restaurant in Clerkenwell. Leah was in her bedroom, folding laundry on the futon. She took the phone over to the window and answered the call with her forehead pressed against the glass.

'What do you reckon? It's meant to be really cool, they do all sorts of weird bits like the nose and the trotters.'

Chris was developing a taste for gourmet dining. If Leah objected to the expense, he would reply that it was his money and this was how he wanted to spend it. Then he would make a quip about how bad the food was going to be in Afghanistan. 'I'm filling up on the good stuff while I can,' he would say. This was unanswerable, so Leah found herself suffering overpriced, cream-and-butter-heavy meals whenever Chris came to London. After two of these dinners she had secretly made herself throw up, something she had promised herself and her parents and her childhood GP that she would never do again.

Now, standing at the window, it was the thought of this restaurant as much as the thought of Chris that emboldened her to say, 'Actually, I don't think I want to.'

'What, you'd rather just have a quiet one? That's okay, we can go on Sunday instead, maybe lunchtime?'

'I mean I don't want to go at all.'

'Oh. Right, okay,' said Chris. 'So … what do you want to do?'

The words were already there; she'd played them in her mind a thousand times. It was just like diving into an outdoor swimming pool: you focused on the mechanism of the dive, not on how cold the water was going to be. One little sentence, a single articulated exhalation – that was all she had to do—

'I don't think this is really working for me any more.'

'What? Sorry, I didn't catch that – you're breaking up – my reception's a bit dodge—'

Trembling now, she said it again. This time he heard her.

'Oh. Right. I see. Right.' There was a short spate of muffled coughing. 'I see,' he said again.

'Sorry,' said Leah. She knew she should say something more than just 'sorry', but she couldn't think what. She

199

looked out of the window for inspiration. There was a patch of grease on the glass where her forehead had been. Leah put her index finger in the middle of the greasy patch and smeared it round in a spiral. Somewhere she had read that if you drew spirals it meant you were sexually frustrated.

'Leah? Are you still there?'

'Yes. Sorry. Yes, I'm here.' She was starting to feel panicked.

'Can I – can I ask why?'

She tugged her sleeve up over her palm and wiped the window clean. 'I don't know. I'm really sorry. I – I'd really like it if we could stay friends?'

Leah didn't punch the air when she hung up, but she did clench her fists, one quick pulse of triumph. She decided she would treat herself – though this was absolutely the last time ever – to a purge. Actually, she felt a bit sick after the stress of the phone call, so this wouldn't even really count. Really she was just helping nature along, she thought, as she dug in her pocket for a pony-tail band.

*   *   *

If, on New Year's Eve, someone had told Chris that in three weeks time Leah would break up with him and spare him all the bother of ending things himself, he would have been delighted. But rejection almost always smarts more than we rationally think it should. Although Chris had long since concluded that the problems in their sex life had everything to do with Leah and nothing to do with him, he now found himself plunged into his old paranoia, still staring at the phone five minutes after Leah had rung off, unable to work out whether it was her frigidity or his incompetence that had ruined things.

Because if it wasn't the sex, then what possible reason could Leah have for splitting up with him? He had done nothing different; he had been, since the very beginning, generous and attentive and outwardly adoring. Apart from sex, and the incident with the Chlamydia – which Leah knew nothing about – he felt his performance had been fairly exemplary. But she had dumped him. *She had dumped him.*

Feeling very sorry for himself, he called Doug.

'It's over,' he said before Doug had finished saying hello. 'Leah, she broke up with me.' As he said these words he felt oddly cheered. He was the injured party, he realised, the jilted lover whose friends would be moved and concerned by his stoicism.

'Yeah, well, me too,' said Doug bitterly.

'What?'

'Helen dumped me.'

'*Fuck*.' Chris was immediately ashamed of his own self-pity. 'But – you guys are perfect, that's not – is she crazy?'

'Don't give me any sympathy.' Doug sounded furious. 'It's all my own fucking fault, I was online, I was using that website again.'

'The one where you met Helen? How come?'

'I wanted sex. Simple as. I'm a cunt and I wanted sex. And there was this girl who was really putting it out there. Only problem was she didn't have a proper photo up – just a shot of her legs in these boots that came right up over her knee. Jesus. So I told her I wanted to see a picture of her first, and she said the only good one she had still had her ex-boyfriend in it. And it was me.'

'What? I don't get it.'

'Oh for fucksake, the girl was Helen! It was a picture of me and Helen! She was baiting me, she was testing me, must've been on to me for a while—'

201

Chris managed to suppress his laughter. 'Doug, how many times—'

'I don't know, three, maybe four. Go on, you can laugh. I can see how this would be funny if I hadn't made the biggest fucking mistake of my whole fucking life.'

'I wasn't laughing.'

'No, it's fine,' said Doug, sounding very tired indeed. Chris wondered if he was crying.

'Doug, mate. Here's the deal. You're a fucking idiot and you're going to come up to London tomorrow afternoon and we're going to get you absolutely shitfaced. Non-negotiable.'

'Thanks, man,' said Doug. He sounded terrible. 'What happened to you and Leah, then?'

'Nothing important. It doesn't matter,' Chris said, realising that this was true.

* * *

Callum had no idea what Tamsin and Leah had agreed to on New Year's Eve, but in the first few days of January he felt more powerless than ever around Tamsin. His jokes were beginning to bore her; and this, he thought, was a very bad sign. It didn't help that Roz had friends staying, so Tamsin was spending all her time with him in Brewer's Court. He knew he needed to make himself scarcer, and therefore more valuable.

The first day back at Denham Hall came as a great relief. If he was powerless in his private life, then here, in the classroom, he had supreme control. Form 8S were more biddable than ever now that the exams were so close.

'Right, I want you to do the second part of this practice paper, exam conditions, no dictionaries allowed,' Callum told the class after they'd handed in their holiday work.

'Sort of like the eve of a battle, isn't it, sir?' asked a wide-eyed Hugh Brodie as he stood in line to collect his paper.

Callum bit back a smile and nodded his agreement. This was what he liked about the job, he thought as he as he sat down at his desk. The heightened emotions of a world peopled by pre-pubescents – a self-refreshing world that came to a dramatic, tearful end once a year, when goodbyes were said and leavers' ties distributed and unkeepable promises of everlasting friendship made as the top-year pupils went their separate ways. A world in which a good teacher was a sort of god. Callum was well aware that it was also, in a sense, a dream world – but it was a dream he was more than happy to inhabit, perhaps, he realised, for ever.

There were twenty minutes left on the clock. Idly he opened up his laptop and found the three nude pictures of Tamsin. There she was on her beach towel, squinting up into the sun, her big breasts slewed sideways. So different from the models in *Nuts* magazine. He wondered if 8S had ever seen natural breasts, mothers excepted. Perhaps they would be shocked, even disgusted, by breasts like Tamsin's. Tamsin herself had hated the beach towel picture. Would it be possible to prevent that self-revulsion developing in his pupils by educating them about what their bodies might become? By showing them *real* female beauty, teaching them to look, shaping their tastes.

There was something oddly appealing in that idea, impossible though it was. Staring now at the photograph of Tamsin standing in front of the sea, Callum fell into a long reverie in which he was delivering a lecture to 8S. He was teaching the children about the camera's relationship to the female body – specifically, the best lighting conditions for capturing the shape of a breast. Example

1A, the photograph of Tamsin, blown up to life-size on the smartboard behind his head.

And then there it was: an erection, his first in nearly two months. In what seemed like no time at all he was almost completely hard. Callum was so surprised that he didn't stop to think about where it had come from. He looked at Tamsin's breasts, then at the oblivious heads of the children, Verity Evanson's neat white parting, Flick Chilcott's thumb poking through the cuff of her damp, chewed jumper. Imagine if they could see what he could see. Callum was now so stiff that the pressure against the thick fabric of his flies was actively uncomfortable. A ridiculous phrase – 'irrepressible erection' – came into his head and played itself over and over, absurdly exciting him further. He had an *irrepressible erection*. Nine pairs of eyes on Tamsin's tits, full of shy excitement. He would make them look. Callum nudged his erection with his knuckle and it felt glorious.

'Mr D?'

At the sound of Hugh Brodie's voice, Callum's erection rapidly deflated.

'Yes, Hugh?'

'Sir, I know you said not to do the English into Latin on question 4c), but I want to know, what if the other one looks really nasty?'

Callum hastily closed down the photograph of Tamsin and motioned for Hugh to come and show him the problem, hoping the boy wouldn't notice the tremor in his hands.

He spent the rest of the day suspended between shame and giddy relief. His impotence had granted him false immunity: because there had been no erection, he had allowed himself to believe that his impulses were not sexual. Yet he knew better than anyone that arousal was not always accompanied by erection.

Today, though, there had been arousal *and* erection, a wonderful erection. It was still possible. He still functioned, and that was, indisputably, good news. Each time he remembered the erection he felt jubilant – an elation qualified by an ill-defined sense of wrongdoing.

Cycling home that night, Callum tried to parse his fantasy more definitively. What was the locus of his excitement? Perhaps it was the idea of looking at Tamsin's body in an inappropriate space that turned him on. Some people fantasised about masturbating in public; this must be a variant of that.

But his behaviour had been undeniably reckless. From now on, he told himself, there would be no more mid-lesson viewing sessions.

* * *

At the end of January, Callum and Tamsin were still together. Every Monday Tamsin told herself that she would do it at the weekend; and then it was Friday, and then it was Saturday, and then it was Sunday and she hadn't done it. There was always some reason for her deferral, although these reasons were never good enough to save Tamsin from feeling like a coward on Monday mornings. Now it was mid-February, and today, Saturday, was Valentine's day. Obviously you couldn't break up with someone on Valentine's day.

'It's Valentine's day today,' she said brightly as she entered Antonia Platt's bed-sitting room. 'Look, I brought us some cake.' Tamsin showed Antonia the soft mushroom-clouds of two raspberry and white chocolate muffins, topped with a sprinkling of tiny pink sugar hearts.

The television was showing a Wallace and Gromit movie. Tamsin turned the volume down but left the movie playing in the background, to fill the long, difficult silences that increasingly punctuated her visits to Antonia.

'Oh, you're wearing gloves?' Antonia asked. 'I haven't started that yet. I'm going to wait until the weather gets a little colder.'

'With any luck it should be getting warmer,' Tamsin said mildly. She had learned never to sound as if she were contradicting or correcting the old lady. Antonia's condition had worsened rapidly over the last couple of months, and as meaning receded, she was becoming extremely sensitive to tone of voice. Before Christmas, her blank moments – like the confusion over the flutes – had been intermittent. She had a tendency to repeat herself, but back then it was still possible for Tamsin to cut in after a sentence or two and say, 'Ah, yes, I remember you telling me about that.' About a month ago, Tamsin had stopped bothering. It was easier and nicer for both of them if she simply let Antonia tell the story again, and again. Tamsin also found herself answering incessantly repeated questions as if she had never heard them before. Last week, for example, she had given Antonia her address in Notting Hill four times, each time agreeing with credible surprise that it was indeed a great coincidence that Antonia had been born just a few streets away from Ashcombe Mews.

Tamsin sensed that her presence was often stressful for Antonia, because although Antonia knew she had to make conversation she was unable to think of anything to say. And so lately Tamsin had begun to repeat herself, too, returning to the same subjects several times in each visit, sticking to a script she knew Antonia could follow. Certain topics – music, clothes, food – were safe, always guaranteed to prompt a memory that was clearly pleasurable to Antonia, if a little jumbled. Other topics – her past and especially her family – were to be avoided. Any discussion that referenced, however obliquely, Antonia's parents, was bound to end unhappily, with Tamsin informing a tearful/disbelieving/indignant Antonia that Professor and Mrs Platt had been dead for quite a while. 'Well, I'd like you to do some asking around, because if that's so, no one's thought to inform me,' Antonia had huffed the last time this subject had, mistakenly, arisen.

'That's a very pretty skirt you're wearing,' Tamsin said now. Antonia's clothes were always beautiful: silk shirts and Liberty prints, beautifully tailored jackets and cashmere twinsets.

'Thank you.' Antonia looked delighted. She pinched up a bit of the fabric (a sort of rough shot silk) between thumb and forefinger and rubbed it to test the quality. 'It *is* nice, isn't it? I can't think where it's come from. It certainly isn't mine.'

'Hold on a moment...' Tamsin stood up and moved round to the back of Antonia's chair. 'Antonia – there's something wrong with your shirt, I'm afraid. I think you've got it on back to front.'

'Have I? Have I really?'

'Quite impressive, actually,' said Tamsin, starting to undo the buttons. 'Must've been a real squeeze getting this over your head.'

Halfway down Antonia's back the shirt's fabric bulged oddly. It was her bra, also on back to front. When Tamsin removed the shirt, she saw that Antonia had done the clasp up underneath her small breasts, which were being squashed by the bra straps in what looked like an extremely uncomfortable manner.

'And while we're at it, we'll just...' Tamsin murmured, undoing the clasp of the bra. Unsupported, Antonia's breasts were slack and low, but their skin was surprisingly smooth. Antonia seemed quite happy for Tamsin to be undressing her. As Tamsin helped her back into her bra, Antonia took a shaky hold of her hand and held it to her chest, pressing her cheek sideways onto Tamsin's forearm as if it were a pillow. She rubbed her cheek up and down, evidently enjoying the pleasure of this contact with warm young flesh.

'Mmmmm, aren't you just lovely,' she said.

But later, when the muffins had been eaten and conversation had run dry and they were watching the end of the Wallace and Gromit movie, Antonia grew agitated, and there was nothing Tamsin could do or say to placate her. The problem was the evil penguin, who in the tradition of cartoon villains everywhere was being sent to stripy-pyjamaed, iron-barred gaol.

'But that's disgusting,' Antonia said. 'That's outrageous. Is there no one on the penguin's side?'

Tamsin tried to explain that the penguin had committed a crime; then, when that line of argument failed, she pointed out that it was all made up anyway.

'Nonsense. It's the principle of the thing,' Antonia spat, looking really angry now. 'What we need is – what we need is – an elderly gentleman to represent him!'

'Yes,' agreed Tamsin. 'That's just what we need.'

'Well? Aren't you going to do something, girl? Are you just going to sit there?'

Tamsin stood up slowly, propelled by the force of Antonia's will, by the perverse logic of her madness.

'That's it, go on, don't drag your heels now.' Antonia was waving Tamsin towards the door with furious flicks of her hands, as if she were shooing some unwanted animal from the room.

'But, Antonia, I just—'

'I said go on! Go away! Leave me alone!

Tamsin gave up and made her way downstairs to the front door, stopping en route to let one of the care workers – Magda, the redhead – know that somebody should probably go and check on Antonia.

'Okay. Sank you. I see her in a little moment,' said Magda with a smile that implied she would do no such thing.

Outside it was raining heavily. Usually Tamsin was someone who raged against the weather whenever it didn't go her way, just as she did with train delays, or inconveniently timed traffic lights. But today the rain felt grimly appropriate: yet another piece of misfortune in the washout that was her life. Career, Callum, Hortensia Court. All at once she thought of her mother, and felt a righteous little hiccup of anger. It wasn't fair: she'd been there for Roz, year after year, staying in for her, passing up all sort of opportunities, and now she, Tamsin, was in trouble, where was Roz? Out, all the time, with god knew who. She had to admit that her mother's absence accounted for some of her reluctance to follow through with her New Year's resolution. If she broke up with Callum, there would be even more evenings when she found herself alone in the house in Notting Hill, eating some basic pasta supper instead of Callum's wonderful food, passing the time with crap TV or by playing the piano, not well enough, and then, at the end of all this, crawling into bed in the room next door to her mother at the age of twenty-six.

Just then, her phone went. If it was her mother or Callum, she thought as she took the phone out of her handbag, she would press 'silent'. Lately she had been pressing 'silent' on most of Callum's calls. Realising this now made Tamsin feel guilty, and the guilt made her even more irritated and unwilling to talk to whoever it was who was calling her.

It was Chris.

Tamsin hadn't seen Chris in over a month, not since just before Leah had dumped him. Callum had been out for a commiserative drink with him after the split, but had come back early, saying that Chris's friend Doug had been hideously drunk, and that Chris himself wasn't much better. Tamsin took this as evidence that the break-up had been hard on Chris.

'Tamsin? Tamsin, hi, it's Chris here, Chris Kimura.'

'I know that,' Tamsin giggled, her bad mood immediately lifting. 'I can see who's ringing.'

'I tried Callum first, but I just get this dead tone—'

'No, no, that's right, he's got a new number. I can give it to you.'

'Actually, it doesn't matter who I talk to really – I was hoping to see you both – the thing is, I'm leaving for Afghan in a week.'

'Wow, that's – how do you—'

'*Fantastic*,' Chris cut in. 'I feel fantastic. I know I shouldn't say this, but I can't fucking wait. It's like, we've been building up to it for so long. The bureaucracy. Three times now I think the date's been pushed back. I was starting to feel Kafkaesque.'

'What-a-what-esque?'

'Kafka, sorry, German, well Czech really—'

'Oh, him, right, with you.'

Tamsin found she was grinning. With Callum, it had got to the point where the poor guy couldn't even mention Roald Dahl without the literary reference feeling pretentious and unnecessary. When Chris did the same thing, she didn't mind. Fleetingly she noted the unfairness of this.

'So, the thing is, I'm actually on my way up to London,' Chris was saying. 'My parents are flying in this evening, I'm going to have supper with them – but I wondered – you and Callum – I really wanted to see you guys before I go, say a proper goodbye and all that.'

'Why don't we all meet at Callum's?' Tamsin suggested.

smiling was difficult he was damn well going to man up and smile anyway.

But as soon as the conversation moved away from Leah it became painfully spasmodic. Chris and Tamsin had so rarely spent any time alone together that they almost felt like new acquaintances. They were both nervy, taking it in turns to talk too much. Tamsin would mono-logue for several minutes about Amad and Hortensia Court, then exclaim that she'd been going on about herself for ages and what did any of this matter anyway in comparison to Afghanistan? After insisting that Tamsin's work *did* matter, it would be Chris's turn to take to the floor, speechifying on about preparations for the upcoming tour, with Tamsin nodding slowly throughout to show that she understood how serious it all was. Eventually he too would grow embarrassed by the sound of his own voice, and so Tamsin would take over again.

And throughout all this a subtle pressure building between them, a steady thickening of the air.

'So ... would you like to see the rest of the house?' Tamsin asked after a particularly awkward pause, wincing inwardly at the overtones of her mother. But Chris imme-diately brightened.

'Can you show me your piano?'

Tamsin lead the way through to the music room. It was the largest room on the ground floor, dominated by the Bechstein grand in the middle of the floor. Against the far wall there was also a battered old upright and a newish cedar-wood harpsichord inlaid with mother-of-pearl butterflies. On the window seat lay assorted sheet music, some of Serena's reeds, an old accordion and a ukulele. Plenty of conversational fodder: the accordion alone kept Chris occupied for the best part of ten minutes, face twisted in concentration as he tried, under Tamsin's patient instruction, to change fingerings at the same time as he compressed the bellows. Tamsin remembered the first time she had brought Callum back to Ashcombe Mews. He, too, had been fascinated by the accordion, but in contrast to Chris he had used it as a prop, incorporating it into a long-standing private joke in which Callum was a lecherous Frenchman called Georges. At the time Tamsin had found the whole Georges-with-an-accordion routine charming, but now it struck her as silly and even a little bit selfish. This was her music room, her instruments, her world – yet Callum had immediately claimed it with his clowning. Chris, on the other hand, was taking her seriously, listening, enraptured, to everything she said.

Once all the other instruments had been exhausted, Chris turned to the grand piano. The inevitable question was asked, and Tamsin obliged him far more willingly than usual, with a showy blast of Scott Joplin.

At the end Chris applauded enthusiastically. Then he got up from the window seat and came over to stand behind Tamsin at the piano. Leaning over her shoulder, he began to riffle through the thick stack of books and manuscript paper on the music stand. Tamsin breathed in the tang of his unsubtle aftershave: a brash, commercial brand which she professed to dislike, though now she found herself responding to it pathetically, helplessly, just as the adverts promised she would. A lyric from one of the '101 Golden Oldies' songs drifted treacherously into her head. *It's not the pale moon that excites me ... oh no ... it's just the nearness of you.*

She coughed loudly to break the spell. 'What are you doing, are you looking for something in particular?'

Chris let go of the music and stood up straight. 'Doesn't matter. Bit cheeky of me really, I was just wondering if you had any Chopin. He's my favourite, I think his music blows everyone else's right out the water. But you're probably sick of people getting you to play stuff for them.'

'No no, it's fine, I can play you some Chopin,' murmured Tamsin. 'I know a couple off by heart, actually...' She ran her hands silently over the piano keys, sketching out the music in her memory. Her acquiescence was out of character: usually, Tamsin had no time for Chopin fans. She considered most of his music too obvious and too easy, a cheap thrill for people who didn't really know how to listen. But right now Chopin seemed like the perfect choice. How bold and brilliant of Chris not to care about picking something so unoriginal!

She played the E-flat major nocturne with lashings of rubato, thinking, as the simple melody filled her up, that all those years spent championing Berg and Webern were a sham, that this was the true music, the best music, the only music. With each swell her awareness of Chris's proximity intensified. The fact that she couldn't see him heightened her sense of a connection formed by the music alone, a beautiful, invisible bond joining her mind to his.

When Tamsin finished playing this time, Chris didn't clap. For what felt like several minutes they remained silent, Chris standing, Tamsin sitting, the back of her head no more than an inch from his stomach.

Very gradually – almost imperceptibly – Tamsin began to move. It was less a case of deliberately leaning back than of simply allowing her head to respond to the charge that was drawing it towards Chris's unseen body. And all the while she was justifying the inevitable contact to herself: what did it matter if the back of her head touched Chris's jumper? Hardly an erotic configuration. It could have happened by accident, after all; she couldn't see him, so how did she even know he was there?

But she did know he was there, almost to the millimetre; and when contact finally came, her body responded instantly – her skin flushing, wetness sparking between

215

her legs. She leaned back further, making sure Chris knew that this was not, after all, an accident. After another long pause Tamsin felt his fingers in her hair. Neither of them spoke, but they both felt that a question had been asked, and answered.

Then Tamsin stood up, so abruptly that Chris wondered whether his touch had been unwelcome after all.

'Sorry it's so cold in here,' Tamsin said. She turned to face Chris with an uninterpretable expression on her face. 'It's for the instruments, we try to keep it coolish. We could go into the sitting room but it's such a tip in there – my mum uses it for her office. But upstairs, let's go upstairs, it's warm – do you want to go upstairs? – you can see the garden from my bedroom window, it's actually quite nice—' She was talking very quickly.

Chris followed her dumbly out of the music room and up to the first-floor landing, mesmerised by the way the stairs exaggerated the sway of her hips. In the doorway to her bedroom Tamsin paused and smiled at him from under those wonderful heavy eyelids of hers – a significant smile, full of sensual promise, he thought.

'I'm just going to nip into the bathroom, won't be a moment. You go on in.' She gestured towards her big double bed, which was covered in a sun-bleached patchwork quilt.

Chris sat down on the edge of the bed and took advantage of his temporary solitude to do some rapid moral arithmetic. He knew it was reprehensible, but if Tamsin tried to kiss him he wasn't going to stop her. He would remain the passive party until he was absolutely, one hundred per cent certain of her intent – and then, Callum or no Callum, he would go for it. After all, he thought as he quickly checked his armpits, it might be his only chance. Even though the probability of him being killed in Afghanistan was very small (as he kept telling his mother, he was more likely to die in a car accident), the fact remained that in ten days' time he was leaving for a war zone. He wasn't going to breathe his last breath having passed up the opportunity to hold Tamsin Jarvis in his arms.

His jeans pockets yielded an enormous quantity of small change, which he stacked in three neat columns on the windowsill, and then, mercifully, the thing he was looking for: a piece of chewing gum, squashed and slightly fluffy but still in working condition. He sat back down on the bed, chewing rapidly in order to activate as much of the mint flavour as possible.

Tamsin, meanwhile, was busy ransacking the bathroom cabinet in a futile search for some toothpaste. For lunch she had eaten a Mediterranean wrap thing from Pret a Manger, stuffed with tabbouleh and a rather potent tzatziki. Tamsin hadn't really thought about her breath in years; with Callum, that sort of thing had long since ceased to matter. A first kiss, though, was not supposed to taste of garlic.

Unfortunately the tube of Colgate lying on the shelf above the sink looked as if it had been ironed flat; Tamsin sucked at the nozzle so hard that the vacuum hurt the tip of her tongue when she pulled away, but the tube was completely empty. At least she had some decent underwear: on her way to the bathroom she had snatched a pair of lacy black knickers from the pile of clean laundry on the landing, which she now hurried to exchange with the pair of greying M&S girl-boxers she was currently wearing. Tamsin tugged off the tracksuit bottoms and the old pants in one go. She was just stepping into the clean pair when she noticed a flash of red in the crotch of her discarded pants. The wetness she had felt at the piano: not arousal, but her period. Sighing, she found a tampon and sat down on the loo to clean herself up. Tamsin herself had no qualms about having sex during her period, but she couldn't tell how Chris would react, and she didn't want to risk his discomfort or, worse, his disgust. So they would kiss, and nothing more. Perhaps it was better like that.

But her desire was losing velocity; there were too many things going wrong. Although Tamsin didn't believe in 'meant to be', she couldn't help feeling that if this was meant to be, it wasn't meant to be like this. And so, en route from bathroom to bedroom, she changed her mind. The transgression became resistible once more; and Tamsin – already forgetting the role that biology and bad breath had played in her decision – entered the bedroom feeling as if she had just passed a difficult test of character. Instead of sitting down next to the expectant Chris she went straight over to the window and began to chatter, slightly hysterically, about the garden, her mother, her job again – anything and everything to erase the delicious tension that had built up between them.

Poor Chris sat and listened, nodding and murmuring when necessary, horrified that he had misjudged her intentions so badly. Did she realise that he had imagined she was coming on to him? The thought made him feel a bit sick. What if, when she leaned her head against him, it had been entirely accidental?

After fifteen minutes that felt more like an hour, he stood up to leave.

'Oh, are you going?' Tamsin asked. She was still bright-eyed with the triumph of not having kissed him.

'Yeah, I'm meeting my parents at six,' Chris lied. He wasn't meeting them till seven.

'Well, okay.' She shrugged goofily and drew him into a long, tight hug. 'I don't really know what to say,' she said into his sleeve. 'Good luck, and stay safe, and – I'll see you in six months?'

'Six months or sooner,' Chris said. 'I should get a good two weeks' worth of leave, I can't be certain when – I'll let you know when I know.'

'You do that,' said Tamsin fervently, standing back and giving Chris a small smile. Now he saw that she was crying. He hugged her again, more confidently this time.

'Say goodbye to that boyfriend of yours for me,' he told her. 'He's a great guy, I'll miss him.'

'You're both great guys,' said Tamsin, and something in her voice – a slight emphasis on the word 'both' – undid all the doubts of the past half hour. The imminence of his departure made him suddenly bold.

'Tamsin, can I ask you something?'

Tamsin smiled and shook her head. 'Not now,' she said, lifting a finger to his lips. 'Ask me in six months' time, okay?'

Chris kissed the finger faintly. 'Okay,' he said. 'I will do.'

* * *

Callum failed to observe his self-imposed ban. Since his unexpected erection on the first day of term, he had found himself looking at the photographs again and again. When he was alone, or in bed with Tamsin, it was possible to put the fantasies from his mind. But in the classroom, with the unsuspecting children bent over their work and the photographs calling to him from the little folder marked 'Ilfracombe', an irresistible compulsion overtook him – a compulsion he both welcomed and feared.

He reminded himself that what turned you on and what you actually wanted to do were two very different things. If he thought about real sexual interaction with a child, just as sort of test, he felt a definite physical revulsion. It was *wrong*, and he didn't want it.

It was true, though, that his fantasies were becoming more extreme. Once when Callum looked at the photo, he imagined Tamsin standing naked in front of the class as he invited each member of 8S to come up in turn and feel her breasts. As his excitement grew, he pulled a pile of books onto his lap to give himself something to push against. By the end of the lesson the moisture from his cock had leaked right through his putty-coloured trousers, and he had to untuck his shirt to hide the stain until it dried.

He compiled some PowerPoint presentations on the history of the female nude and briefly persuaded himself that this might be a legitimate lesson to teach 8S when their exams were over. One presentation discussed changing ideals of female beauty, from Greek and Roman statuary through Botticelli's Venus to Rubens. Another dealt with the tension between art and pornography: Edward Weston's early nudes, Georgia O'Keeffe, Stieglitz, Man Ray. Mistrustful of his motives, Callum soon abandoned the idea of actually showing these pictures to the class and instead embellished them for his own pleasure, with the photographs of Tamsin included in the examples. He also added Courbet's *L'origine du Monde*, which he had initially rejected as too explicit. Next to this, for contrast, he set a picture of the Venus de' Medici, zoomed right in over her smooth marble crotch. In quieter lessons he would flick through these slideshows from start to finish, accompanying each photograph with a silent commentary that grew more obscene as his arousal increased.

Sometimes he pictured the girls examining the naked Tamsin while dressed in only their knickers and vests. Those sweet thermal vests that children wore, lace-edged with the puncture-points in zig-zag patterns. Maybe a little rosebud, shiny synthetic silk, in the middle of the scalloped V-neck.

Callum took comfort from the fact that in these fantasies, the girls were always reasonably developed – he was interested in *breasts*, and real children didn't have breasts. It was also a good sign that the girls were partially clothed: that he never imagined them completely naked.

He didn't realise how much he was censoring himself.

* * *

After exams were over, the whole of 8S was due to go on the annual post-scholarship trip to Normandy to visit various WW1 memorial sites. Touchingly, the class had cheered when Callum announced that he'd be joining them on this trip.

The Wednesday following Valentine's Day was the last double Latin lesson that the whole class would attend before the first examinees – Hugh Brodie and Verity Trevena – went off to sit their scholarships. The atmosphere in the classroom was tense.

While the class did a final English into Latin unseen, Callum turned his attention to the customised sweatshirts he was designing for the Normandy trip. Usually the sweatshirts came from the school's outfitters – just the uniform dark green tracksuit top with 'Normandy' and the relevant dates embroidered above the school crest on the left breast. But Callum was in charge of ordering them this year, and to his pupils' delight he had chosen hooded sweatshirts in a cool mid blue, with the signature of each member of 8S printed in red on the back.

At the end of the lesson, after the translations had been discussed and another pep-talk delivered, Callum called a picture of the finished design up onto the electronic whiteboard for the class to approve. 'Any objections, speak up now, because I have to order by five o'clock today to get them in time for Normandy. Just think, next

221

time we're all together, we'll be heading for the ferry at Dover.'

'That's if I don't die of stress in the exams first, sir,' said Verity, who was prone to melodrama.

Callum laughed absently as he scrolled down to the website's order form.

'Hold on, they want shirt sizes. If you could all just line up by the door – this won't take a minute, I just need to see the label inside your collar—' It was straightforward enough with the boys: their school shirts were measured in chest-size cm, just like the sweatshirts Callum was ordering. But the girls' blouses only gave 'S', 'M' and 'L'.

What would worry Callum later, when he recalled the next thirty seconds, was the speed with which his brain had worked, the agility with which it avoided the simple, obvious solution.

The simple solution would have been to take a guess. He could see that Flick was about the same chest size as Michael, for example. They were just hooded sweatshirts. It wasn't as if they needed bespoke tailoring.

But he could also see, in his mind's eye, those soft cotton vests, full of promise and sweet new flesh.

'Boys, you're all done now, you can go to break.'

His conscious mind didn't even register it as an opportunity but he was seizing it anyway. Now he was back at his desk, rummaging through the drawers – there was the ruler, there was a ball of string, a marker pen – he was dividing up the string into five-centimetre sections—

Even the feel of the string was exciting to him. He wondered if he could trust himself to do this. Of course he could trust himself to do this. He wasn't some sex fiend; he was just taking some straightforward measurements, from *children*, for godsake, he didn't fancy children. He needed measurements and all he had was string so he was using string. Necessity, invention, mother of.

'Sir – what are you doing?' asked Flick.

He started; her voice had woken him as if from sleep.

Callum put the string back in the drawer. 'Girls, if you could all go up to sick-bay and get Nurse to write down your measurements. I'll collect them from her later.'

The girls tripped out into the corridor. Putting a hand up to his forehead, Callum found he was sweating. It was break time, but he couldn't face the staffroom today. Instead, he took this alarming new information about himself for a brisk walk around the grounds. The problem – he saw it so clearly now – was not whether he could have trusted himself to measure them, but that he'd even considered it as an option. It was not an option. A male teacher – *any* teacher – in today's world of knee-jerk litigation, measuring the budding chests of four twelve-year-old girls with a piece of string – it was insanity. He'd have been jobless in minutes.

Callum stood at the edge of one of the football pitches and watched a group of third-years, nine- and ten-year-olds, playing British Bulldog. Some of the girls – Tiffany Dunthorpe, with her high freckled forehead and silky blonde hair – were really quite pretty. He made himself watch them, think about them. To his relief, he felt nothing.

Perhaps he had allowed himself to get too close to 8S. Perhaps that was the problem.

Or perhaps, Callum thought as he turned to walk back to the school, perhaps there was no problem. He had done nothing wrong: he had stopped. If there was anything really the matter with him, he would not have stopped. He had self-control. Maybe all this meant was that these unusual desires were stronger than he'd realised at first. And now he knew this about himself, he really would put an end to it. No more photographs, no more imaginings. It had been a strange interlude in his interior life, that was all. He remembered a phase in his early twenties when he had fantasised almost exclusively about pregnant women. This was surely comparable. A phase that would pass.

Before fourth period began he went up to sick-bay to get the girls' measurements. Callum was so worried that the girls might have told Nurse Bailey about his bizarre behaviour with the string that he found himself fabricating alternative explanations. He could say that the girls were confused; that the string was for an exercise with the football team, that it had nothing to do with the sweatshirts.

From the absent-minded way that Nurse Bailey smiled at him, though, he saw he had nothing to worry about.

'Here you are, Mr D,' she said, tearing a piece of paper from a little spiral-bound notebook. Jennifer Bailey was in her mid-fifties but she was so fat she looked at least ten years younger. 'A good thing you sent them to me, actually. Sophie Witrand's got quite a substantial pair of breasts under that jumper of hers and she's still not wearing a bra. Tells me her mother says she doesn't need one and I can assure you that's absolutely *not* the case.'

'Right,' said Callum weakly. 'Er, thank you for these.'

At the end of the afternoon, he called Tamsin.

'Cal? What's up, you sound a bit strange.'

'Just ... had a bit of a tough day today. Let's meet for supper.'

'I'm having supper with my mum tonight.'

'In town?'

'At home.'

'I can come and join you, can't I?

'Course. Why *not*?'

Callum made it back to London in just enough time

to catch the florist on Kensington Park Road, where he bought a big bunch of Paperwhite narcissi for Tamsin and Roz.

'Callum, darling, they're gorgeous,' cooed Roz. 'Now we can throw out these ratty old roses.' She gestured towards Chris's roses, still in their vase in the middle of the kitchen table. 'I *know* they're not from you, because you've always had such beautiful taste in flowers.'

'Mummy, you know you sound horribly snobby,' said Tamsin.

Callum was frowning comically at the roses. 'So who's your secret admirer?'

'They're from Chris, you know he was here on Saturday,' said Tamsin impatiently.

'And he brought you flowers on Valentine's day, the poor ignorant fool,' Callum tutted. 'Little did he know that in the land of Tamsin there is no crime more terrible than flowers on Valentine's day!'

'Oh for god's sake, Callum, he was about to go to Afghanistan, *Afghanistan.*' Tamsin began to lay the table, loudly and imprecisely. 'Have you called him yet?'

'No, but I will do.' Callum came up behind Tamsin and wrestled her into a reluctant hug. 'Don't you worry,' he said. 'Chris'll be fine.' He felt strangely comforted by Tamsin's distress: that she was making no effort to hide it surely minimised its significance. Besides, he couldn't help but relish the prospect of six months without Chris.

These thoughts made him almost jovial. During supper he flirted cutely with Roz and even dared to ask her who it was she was seeing.

Roz looked quickly at Tamsin. 'Who told you I was seeing someone?'

'Educated guess,' grinned Callum. 'Honestly, Roz, just a guess.'

'Hmmph,' said Roz. 'Although – as it happens –' she looked at Tamsin again '– I am seeing someone. An old friend, in fact. We're – how should I put this? – we're rediscovering each other.'

Tamsin gave Callum a meaningful glance. 'That's great, Mummy,' she said lightly. 'When do we get to meet ... this person?'

Roz looked uncomfortable. 'I'm not sure I'm ready for that yet, darling. You know, when you've been hurt as deeply as I have, the next time something, love, romance, whatever, comes along – well, it makes you very cautious.'

'It's fine, we understand.' Tamsin reached over to squeeze her mother's shoulder. 'Don't we, Cal?'

'Of course,' smiled Callum, enjoying the complicity this little interrogation had engendered between him and Tamsin.

But the sense of closeness was short-lived. After supper, the three of them trooped through to the sitting room to watch a re-run of an old Inspector Morse mystery. Roz sat down first on the two-seater sofa, and Tamsin – immediately, deliberately, Callum thought – sat down next to her, leaving the three-seater for him to sit on.

'Oh no, you two have this one, much cosier,' said Roz, starting to get up.

Tamsin put a hand on her mother's knee and pushed her down again. 'It's fine, we're fine, we can manage an hour or two apart,' she said testily.

Tamsin took in very little of the Morse: instead, she spent the next two hours deep in contemplation, staring at the screen with unfocused gaze. Mostly she was day-dreaming about Chris, as she had been since the weekend. She wanted him and he wanted her: that much she knew now, for certain. And she was very glad indeed to have walked away from the situation on Saturday. To think that she had so nearly stooped to her father's level! But she hadn't: that was the whole point. She had been tried, and she had not been found wanting. Before anything happened between her and Chris she was going to break up with Callum. When, though? Obviously things couldn't go on like this for much longer. She was being unfair to him, she could see that. But he had those scholarships coming up, and then that trip to France: whatever she might think of his spoilt little pupils, she knew how much he cared about the job, and she didn't want to make things unnecessarily difficult for him.

'When's your Easter holiday start?' she asked during one of the ad breaks.

'End of March,' said Callum. 'Why, do you want to go away somewhere?'

'No, I was just wondering.'

So that was it, she promised herself. It was going to be horrible but she *would* do it, without fail, at the beginning of his holiday: that way he'd have a good three weeks to sort himself out before term started up again. It was surely the kindest way. And then there would be almost five months before Chris came back – a decent interval.

It felt like a reality now, in a way it hadn't before. She was really going to sit him down and tell him she didn't want to be with him any more. The thought of this conversation – how painful it would be for both of them, but especially for Callum – aroused a strong, almost indignant protectiveness in Tamsin – as if the threat posed to Callum's happiness came from someone other than herself. At the end of the programme she padded over to his sofa and sat down on his lap.

'You are staying over, aren't you?' she asked, kissing him gently on the cheek.

Callum was surprised but pleased. Then he was worried, in case this meant that Tamsin wanted to have sex tonight. While Tamsin showered he sat on the edge of her bed, fully dressed, with one hand rubbing at his crotch in order to give himself a head start, careful not to let his mind go anywhere it shouldn't, thinking exclusively of Tamsin's big, *womanly* tits.

That was when he saw it: on the windowsill, arranged in three tidy stacks, a large amount of small change. At first he couldn't work out why this was so disturbing. But women never had that much change. They had purses – he could see Tamsin's purse now, poking out the corner of her open handbag – and so they spent their change. Whereas men just carried on filling up their pockets until it was time to undress. Then they emptied those pockets and – in some cases – stacked the coins, just like this, into neat little cylinders. Callum tried to tell himself he was being paranoid, for the second time that day. Why shouldn't Tamsin have a lot of spare change on her windowsill? Those columns, though: they were somehow peculiarly male. And Chris had been here at the weekend. Yet he could hardly accuse Tamsin of having an affair on the basis of a pile of coins.

The shower was turned off. Callum darted forward and took Tamsin's purse from her handbag. He popped open the coin pocket: two pennies and a five-pence piece.

'Tam,' he called. 'You got any spare change? I meant to pick up a copy of *The Times* on my way here, there's this thing in it by Pete, you know, my friend Pete Danneman?'

'Try my purse, should be some in there,' came the reply.

Callum left a short pause before answering. 'Nope, not enough.'

'Well, that's it, that's all I've got.'

'No change anywhere else in your bedroom?'

'God, Callum, I don't know, try the pot on the dresser?'

Callum waited until he could hear the hum of her electric toothbrush before sweeping the coins off the windowsill. He put them in his own pocket and, calling out to Tamsin that he wouldn't be long, set off out of the house and up the street towards Denbigh Road. He wasn't sure where he was going. Certainly not to buy a newspaper. To calm down, then, and to consider his options. What did he know? Nothing for certain; and yet somehow he *was* certain. Callum felt sure that the money was Chris's, and that it meant that Chris and Tamsin had slept together. He had never imagined she would actually cheat on him. It was a good enough reason to leave. But he didn't want to leave. And although his proof was stronger now, it was still far from irrefutable. Perhaps the real question was: did he even want to catch her out? What did it mean to him if they had indeed slept together?

Through the thin cotton of his pocket lining, the coins were cold against his thigh. He thought that if it was only sex he could just about cope. After all, Tamsin wasn't exactly getting that from *him*. But how often is it ever just sex? How long had they been doing it for? If they weren't in love already, how much longer would it take before they were?

All of this, Callum realised with a slight shock, was beside the point. He wasn't going to leave her, and he wasn't going to tell her what he thought he knew. Confrontation would be messy and inconclusive at best. So he would stay and he would say nothing. At least Chris was going away. For that he felt more grateful than ever – a dirty, uncomfortable gratitude, given that his rival's destination was a war zone. He turned and walked slowly back to Ashcombe Mews.

'You get it?' Tamsin wanted to know when he re-entered the bedroom. She was sitting up in bed playing Tetris on her mobile phone.

'Nuh-uh,' said Callum. He was still in shock from his discovery. It was an effort to keep his voice steady. 'I found the paper but I couldn't find his piece, I must have got the wrong day or something.'

'Mmmm.' Tamsin was absorbed in the game.

Callum undressed and got into bed beside her. He raised his hands to his face and sniffed. Even though he'd washed them twice he could still smell the money on his fingers. It was strong and sharp, almost like pickled onions.

'Nooooo!' said Tamsin. 'Look, Cal, look how unfair that is, I had three of those zig-zag ones in a row! And I was so close to my best score!'

Callum inspected the little screen. 'It's an outrage,' he said solemnly.

Tamsin smiled and kissed his temple. She was being more affectionate than she had been for weeks, Callum realised sadly as they curved their bodies round each other in preparation for sleep.

'Callum?'

'Mmmm?'

'What happened today?'

'What?'

'You said you'd had a bad day. I should have asked.'

'Doesn't matter.'

'I'm such a bad girlfriend.'

'No you're not.'

Nine

Normandy in mid-March: a freakishly early spring, warm enough for the hardier members of 8S to swim in the river behind the large converted barn they were staying in for the week. There was a nearby farmhouse that supplied them with fresh eggs; otherwise, the barn was the only building for several miles. On the other side of the river was a track used for racing small horse-drawn chariots: the driver rode standing up with a whip in one hand and the other hand holding on to the edge of the chariot for support. They went extremely fast. 'A very old French pastime,' Mr Dempster explained. 'Highly dangerous, of course, but also quite exciting, because it's not so far from the sort of thing the Romans would have been getting up to.'

For Sophie, the week in France seemed like the start of an adulthood she hadn't known she wanted until now. It was the longest she'd ever been away from her parents: the longest she'd ever been responsible for her own personality, unregulated and unchallenged by her mother. The scholarship exams were finally over, and all she had to do between now and September was 'develop as a person'. These were her mother's words. For Mrs Witrand, developing as a person meant practising the clarinet more often and getting better at French. For Sophie, it meant becoming *someone* at last: someone with opinions and tastes and defining characteristics. In the ferry on the way over, she joined Rhiannon and Verity on a trip to buy nail varnish at the cosmetics section of the duty-free. While Rhiannon and Verity picked out tasteful pastel shades, Sophie plumped for a weird olive-green colour.

'Are you actually sure you want that?' asked Verity. 'It's blatantly one of those ones you buy and then never wear, I've never seen anyone with that colour nail varnish before.'

'Then I'll be the first,' said Sophie happily.

Perhaps it was the simple fact of being away from school, but for whatever reason the other girls seemed much nicer than usual. On the bus ride from Calais to the barn, Flick leaned over to Sophie and offered her a headphone.

'Here, have a listen. I think you'll like it, it's sort of old-fashioned.'

Sophie frowned. 'Are you taking the piss?'

'No no, I mean it in a nice way. Listen.'

The song was 'Son of a Preacher Man' by Dusty Springfield. Sophie could hear immediately that it was cooler than the Beatles. Her kind of cool. She nodded along.

'You're right,' she said. 'I do like it.'

One day they hired bikes and took a break from WW1 and just cycled round the countryside.

'I feel so free,' Sophie said to herself as they cycled past a big blue lake. It seemed like a pretty sophisticated thing to say, so she said it again, out loud. Ludo Hall heard her and gave a funny look, but she didn't mind.

That day they ate their packed lunches at a couple of

picnic tables near a campsite in a little beech wood dotted with yellow aconite. Rhiannon dropped her Dairylea triangle on the ground under the table and bent down to fetch it. When she sat up again she was laughing.

'What's the joke, Rhiannon?' asked Mr Dempster.

'Nothing, sir,' said Rhiannon, unconvincingly. 'I was just laughing coz I dropped my cheese, and now it's all covered in twigs and things.'

When Mr Dempster went over to the other table to discuss the route with Mr Raddock, Rhiannon explained in a whisper to Sophie and Flick what it was she'd *really* been laughing about. Mr Dempster was wearing tight lycra cycling shorts: apparently, when he sat down, his penis bulged up between his legs. 'Wait till he comes back, then pretend to drop something and have a look,' Rhiannon advised.

'I actually already noticed it when he was just standing up at that junction earlier when we stopped for our drink,' said Flick excitedly.

'I think it's a big one,' said Rhiannon.

'Do you think he has to get it measured when he buys those shorts?' Sophie joked, and was gratified by the other girls' approving laughs.

'Sssh, he's coming back,' hissed Rhiannon. 'Get ready to drop something.'

But Mr Dempster had only come over to tell them it was time to eat up and get back on the bikes.

* * *

In the evenings, the teachers took it in turns to cook. The children found this hilarious, especially when it was clumsy old Mr Mably's turn. (In fact, he managed a passable spaghetti Bolognese.) The culinary star of the week was Mr Dempster: his *coq au vin* scored highly, mostly on the grounds that it contained alcohol in the sauce and 'cock' in the title.

Sophie was one of Mr Dempster's kitchen helpers for the *coq au vin* meal, so once they'd finished eating her chores were over for the night. While the plates were being washed up she slipped outside to catch the last of the sun. It was very low in the sky, blazing through the thin leaves of the young hazel trees that lined the river banks. The water flickered with a richer shade of gold. Sophie squatted down on the bank and stared at the river until she could see the trout. They were always there, only you had to wait for your eyes to catch up.

'Sophie?'

It was Mr Dempster.

'Everything okay?'

'Yes, thanks.' Sophie stood up. 'I just came out to enjoy the sunset.'

'It's beautiful, isn't it?' said Mr Dempster. He came and stood next to her, looking out across the river. 'Do you remember me telling you that when I see beauty like this I feel ... well, something close to religious? And I promised you that I'd explain that better if you asked me about it again. But you never did.'

Sophie plucked a blade of grass and began splitting it into strips with her thumbnail. Briefly she thought of her siblings and the spaghetti-grass game. She was deliciously conscious of the fact that she was standing by a river in France at sunset talking about religion with a grown-up man.

'It's all right, sir,' she said. 'I knew what you meant.'

'What did I mean?'

'Well ... I *think* you meant that you don't really believe in God. Otherwise you would have just said yes you did.'

Mr Dempster smiled. 'You're a clever girl. So ... *is* there anything you want to ask me?'

Sophie thought. 'Just one thing.'

'What?'

'Do you get scared when you think about dying?'

'Good question.' Mr Dempster frowned, and Sophie could tell he was deciding whether or not to tell the truth. 'I suppose the answer's yes, sometimes. But it scares me much more to think about the people I love dying.'

'I get that too,' said Sophie. 'Even though I do actually believe in God. Sort of.' With her right index finger she drew a small cross on the inside of her left palm: her private method for undoing any potential blasphemy in case God did, after all, exist. Then she did it again to atone for the sin of making fun of Mr Dempster over lunch, especially as he was being so nice now.

Her soul thus absolved, Sophie threw her head back and breathed in deeply. 'You know what, sir? When I remember this week I think I'll remember it as two colours, green and gold, just dancing in front of my eyes like the sun in those trees.'

'Mmmm, very impressionistic,' said Mr Dempster.

Sophie had heard the stifled amusement in his voice. 'Did that sound really stupid?'

'No, no, not at all.'

'Okay,' said Sophie, not quite convinced.

They stood in silence for a bit. Then Sophie grew bored, thanked him for the chat, and ran back inside to join the others.

*   *   *

Callum stayed by the river for another twenty minutes or so, listening to the water and the beeping of the first few bats. He no longer worried about his fantasies, or the photographs, or the string. If he did think about his old urges, it was merely to observe, with a vague, wry sort of relief, that he had been 'cured' by that evening at Tamsin's when he discovered the coins on the windowsill. The pain of her betrayal was purgative in its intensity, obliterating everything else. All his energy went on survival now: on not, under any circumstances, thinking about Chris. There was certainly no space for excitement.

This trip was a welcome distraction. It was nice to see his students in a new context, to watch them clumsily becoming themselves. Sophie's forays into intellectual sophistication were particularly endearing. It was a strange age they were entering. Callum remembered his own early adolescence much more clearly than later periods of his life. During those four years, from thirteen to seventeen, he had experienced his strongest, most unified sense of self. He thought of himself as he was then. The teenaged Callum would have disapproved of sticking by a woman you knew to be cheating on you – but the teenaged Callum didn't know how complicated things could be. That when the thing finally happened, your monstrous capacity for jealousy might not, after all, consume you; that you might find a way to go on loving alongside the terrible fact of betrayal. The trick was simply to turn your thoughts away. As soon as Chris came into his mind, Callum replaced the thought with something else. It was tiring but it was possible; he could do it, he felt, indefinitely.

Like now, for instance. He could feel Chris's presence encroaching on his consciousness, so he threw himself outwards, back to the river and the bats and the clouds with their bellies lit highlighter orange by the setting sun. He thought about the woman at the bike-rental place with her tongue stud and her asymmetric fringe; about something funny that Hugh Brodie said at supper; about Karl Huber's preternatural ability for languages; about Sophie Witrand, standing beside him in the fading light, asking him if he was scared of death. He thought about dying violently, a broken bottle, a knife in his guts. He thought about anything, anything at all, anything apart from Chris's mouth on Tamsin's mouth and Chris's hands on Tamsin's body and Chris's (big, hard, infallible) cock in Tamsin's cunt and their mouths and their heads and their bodies and their hands and their breath and their mouths and their tongues.

* * *

Chris checked his watch. Over four hours since he had stepped off from the base with his patrol: they were running well behind schedule. The sun was too high, approaching the dangerous heat of midday.

Mirwais Kalay was the last settlement on this morning's patrol, but they should have reached it long before now. Chris had been to this Kalay twice before, both times on market days. Now it was much quieter. It was a smallish settlement, made up of about thirty compounds loosely clustered around a central crossroads. There were fewer than twenty villagers in sight. Despite the heat, a handful of vendors were still operating from blankets on the ground, heaped with dusty vegetables.

So far, the patrol had been successful, apart from the timing issues. They had encountered no resistance this morning, and the locals they had spoken to had been reasonably positive about British presence. Yet Chris couldn't help feeling disappointed about the lack of action. Although he felt guilty about wishing for violence, the truth was that he had spent most of the past four weeks feeling slightly cheated. It was hard not to see his tour to date as series of let-downs. He'd trained to deploy as a full-strength platoon, but on arrival he'd been informed that the platoon would be splitting into two multiples with just fourteen soldiers in each. The idea was that the multiples would alternate between patrolling and defending a set of small checkpoints. Every couple of weeks, the two multiples switched tasks.

Chris had spent the first fortnight in the checkpoints, getting increasingly bored with short local patrols and trying to keep his patience with the constant solicitings of his corrupt Afghan National Army commander, Sergeant Abdullah. Sergeant Abdullah was in charge of the eight Afghan soldiers that made up the ANA supplement to Chris's multiple. He was a fearsome sight, hefting an American M249 machine gun and draped mayorally in belt after belt of ammunition. He was also a predatory homosexual. This had been the big surprise of the tour so far – that the puritanical Afghan culture had a series of loopholes which more or less allowed for homosexual activity. As far as Chris could tell, anything an Afghan male got up to on a Thursday didn't really count. It was on Thursdays that Sergeant Abdullah was most likely to leer at him and murmur 'Bes-yaar khoob', translated for Chris by the giggling interpreter as 'very good'. Sergeant Abdullah also kept a small white kitten in the leg pocket of his trousers, which he liked to stroke suggestively in the direction of his favourite members of the British unit – most notably eighteen-year-old Private Marrak from St Ives, whom Abdullah had nicknamed 'Anar gul', or 'flower of the pomegranate tree'. Marrak was so traumatised by all this that Chris actually arranged for him to swap places with Private Barker from the other multiple.

The business with Marrak was the most interesting thing that happened in all of those first two weeks; so when changeover time came round, Chris was eager to get out on patrol. The other multiple swaggered into the checkpoint buzzing with stories of the ferocious firefights that Chris's lot had been hearing in the distance for the past few days. Chris was nervous but excited. Lately, his most childish daydream had been irresistible: the one in which he and his men were in mortal danger, with everyone looking to him for salvation as he bent friend and foe alike to his will through cunning and audacity. Chris had never spoken about this fantasy to anyone. Obviously he didn't *really* want his men to be in that kind of danger. He was, however, pleased to think that he would at last have the chance to find out whether he actually had it in him to soldier – to confirm that he wouldn't fall apart at the first hint of real danger, forsaking his men and thinking only of his own safety.

But the enemy seemed to have taken an impromptu holiday, and now he was facing the prospect of a return to the checkpoints with little to show for his time on the ground. He was becoming increasingly concerned that the current lull in fighting might come to define the whole tour in his area. Even here, in Mirwais Kalay – known to be a particularly vulnerable location – Chris felt he was going through the motions. As he spread his troops out to cover the different approaches to the Kalay, he sensed that the men were just as fed up as he was. Muscles were aching, attention was wandering, the heat was bearing down. It was time, Chris decided, to head back to base.

He radioed Corporal Robinson, his second-in-command. 'Two two bravo, this is two two alpha, close in on my location for face-to-face, over.'

Robbo's Dorset burr came crackling back at once: 'Two two bravo, roger, on my way.'

Chris looked down the litter-strewn street. Robbo was only thirty metres away – he had clearly been heading over already. Beyond him he could see the rear men of the patrol spread out in a loose arc, some kneeling, some prone, covering the way they'd just come. Chris could tell from the rhythm of Corporal Robinson's walk that he wasn't happy. He liked the corporal, but a pissed-off NCO, especially one as experienced as Robbo, was an unnerving thing for a junior officer.

'All right, Robbo?'

Robbo tapped his wrist. 'We need to get back to the PB. I know we said we'd stop here, boss, but fucking ... new blokes not carrying enough water because they can't hack the weight.'

'Yeah, agreed,' said Chris, thinking guiltily of the last few mouthfuls of water he was hoarding in his one spare canteen. He had made the same error as his men: just three litres instead of the usual six. They'd only expected this patrol to last a couple of hours. No point in carrying weight you don't need, he'd thought – although now he realised that this was false economy verging on recklessness.

'I've told the ANA we're not sticking around,' he told Robbo, wondering if some of the older man's ire was actually directed at him, for underestimating the length of the patrol and taking it too slow. 'We've shown our faces here, that's the main thing. Um, you happy with the route back?'

Robbo nodded silently. He was taking a long suck from the extended drinking straw that led to the hydration pack in his rucksack, his deep-set eyes dramatically shadowed. Chris watched him drink with envy.

'Okay then,' he said. 'I want you to take your team to the far side of these compounds to cover us over that stretch of open ground to the treeline, like we did last time. We'll bring you up once we're over, all right?'

'Roger, boss, I've already got Davies and Mitch covering it with the gun.'

'Good man, move the rest over and we'll look to move in five.'

240

As Robbo set off back to his team, Chris reached for the straw of his hydration pack, before remembering with resignation that it was empty. He was starting to feel a little light-headed. He turned to Rami, his 'terp. Rami was watching a motorcycle in the distance kicking up a hazy wedge of dust, making no attempt to disguise his boredom.

'Rami, did you see where Sergeant Abdullah went?'

Rami gestured down the street towards the little group of sellers sitting in the shrinking shade next to their blankets of produce. Almost the entire Afghan contingent appeared to be haggling with two of these vendors over sweets and cigarettes. As far as Chris could make out, only two of them were watching the road they were supposed to be covering.

'Fuck'ssake...' he muttered.

At that moment Chris's radio cackled and he heard Robbo's voice in his ear.

'Two two alpha, two two bravo, in covering position. You're good to move, over.'

Chris paused, then reached for his radio on the left shoulder strap of his rucksack. He selected the short-range option: the situation was slightly embarrassing, and he didn't want HQ to overhear.

'Two two alpha, roger, ummm ... we'll be a couple of minutes more. Looks like the ANA are doing a bit of shopping, over.'

'Two two bravo, roger, cracking timing. Tell them to get a move on, we're in the open out here. Over.'

'Two two alpha, roger, out.'

Chris heaved himself to his feet and shuffled his load into place. For a few seconds, it felt as if the top of his head was evaporating. He forced himself to focus his vision and set off down the street with Rami in tow.

Sergeant Abdullah, absorbed in his haggling, barely

noticed their approach. Chris turned to Rami, then remembered that he was meant to talk directly to the Afghan, not the interpreter.

'Sergeant Abdullah, we are leaving now.'

Rami translated this. Abdullah looked at Rami, then to Chris, then answered directly to Rami.

'He's buying cigarettes,' Rami explained.

Chris was annoyed but he knew that his next move required careful formulation; the Afghans were tired and crabby, and he couldn't afford a confrontation. It was hard to think in this heat. As he was trying to devise a tactful but persuasive response, he vaguely heard a vehicle approaching, larger than a motorcycle and revving higher than most local cars. Then came a squeal of brakes and a scream foreshortened by an audible thud. Chris whipped round, his hands tightening on his rifle, his right thumb resting against the safety catch.

All heads were turned towards the noise. People were starting to gather near a corner at the end of the street. Chris could hear angry shouting and the sound of a child wailing.

Sergeant Abdullah was immediately decisive. He looked at Chris, nodded once, then turned and said something to his soldiers. Three of them moved off in the direction of the sound. Chris followed with Rami, reaching for his radio, feeling very unsure of himself.

'All call signs, two two alpha, uh, possible, uh vehicle incident at my location, wait out.'

As he rounded the corner, Chris saw a lightly bearded Afghan man in his early forties, clearly furious and shouting directly into the face of an equally irate man dressed in Afghan National Police uniform. Chris recognised him as a local police commander he'd had dealings with once or twice before. Next to the two men was the ANP commander's four-by-four. The driver was still sitting behind the wheel, watching dispassionately. Another police commander was busy trying to keep the gathering crowd away from the argument. Some of the onlookers were more interested in what was happening behind the four-by-four. Chris stepped forward to get a better look: a limp figure in a burqa was being half-carried, half dragged into an adjacent compound by a younger man and an adolescent boy. A little girl in a frayed red scarf stumbled after them, tears darkening the dirt on her cheeks. She was shrieking one word over and over again, something that sounded like 'more, more, MORE'. Chris's first instinct was to push through the crowd to see how badly injured the woman was. But contact with a Western male would only cause her more trouble. For a heat-addled second, he found himself wondering whether he had any women in his team who could check on her.

One of the ANA soldiers had been talking to the policeman marshalling the villagers. Now he walked over to where Chris was standing next to Sergeant Abdullah and began reporting back in rapid Pashtu. Rami translated: the ANP ranger had hit a local woman, and the husband – the lightly bearded man currently arguing with the ANP commander – was angry.

Rami was in the middle of this explanation when the husband's gesticulating hands came into contact with the ANP commander's chest. None of them had been watching directly but all of them registered the contact. The ANP commander reacted violently, forcing the man back with a vicious swipe from his rifle. All attention was focused on the two men. What had been a complex and confusing situation was suddenly reduced to a single point of tension. The crowd grew animated with indignation as the ANP commander forced the injured woman's husband to the ground. He kicked him three times then stood over him with his gun pointing at the man's chest. Now

243

everyone was very still and silent. Chris stifled a cough, as if the slightest noise might provoke the policeman into actually pulling the trigger. But he simply yelled a few more words at the man on the ground, then made a dismissive gesture and stormed back to the four-by-four. Without offering any acknowledgement to the British and Afghan troops, he signalled to his driver and the car pulled away. The little crowd of villagers closed in round the beaten man.

Sergeant Abdullah looked at Chris and then spoke to Rami, gesturing after the departing vehicle.

Rami turned to Chris. 'He says something bad about the police.'

Abdullah shrugged and started off to join the rest of the ANA, leaving Chris staring confusedly at the raggedy bunch of locals. A few of them were looking over in his direction now, calling things out in Pashtu. They sounded angry. He knew that he should go over and talk to them, to reassure them that the commander would be reported and punished. But he didn't know how to approach this situation and he was terrified of making it worse. His throat was very dry. What if the locals turned their aggression on him and his troops? What if that provoked the ANA to similar violence? And even if he managed to stop a fight from breaking out, any discussion with this lot was guaranteed to last a long time. He didn't have a long time. His men were waiting for him. They were low on water.

Robbo came through on the radio, sounding worried.

'Boss, Robbo, I'm getting atmospherics here – farmers clearing out of the fields to our East. We need to get moving, over.'

Chris looked over at the locals. He realised he could still hear the child's crying – or had it just started up again?

'Two two alpha, roger,' he said. 'Uh, we're leaving. Moving to link up with two two charlie, over.'

He killed the radio. 'Rami? Go tell Sergeant Abdullah we're moving NOW.'

*   *   *

On the last day of the trip they went to the Somme. For Sophie, the graveyards and the trenches they had seen so far had all just about made sense, but the scale of the Thiepval memorial had her stumped. There were too many names. If you looked at one or two or even ten or twenty you could imagine them as actual people, but when you looked up, and then behind you and then across at another pillar they stopped being people and became just names. Sophie wandered round the memorial in a semi-trance, feeling pleasantly dwarfed by its incomprehensibility. Then she felt worried that the thing she was feeling was pleasant when it should be horrifying. Then she felt pleased that she was sensitive enough to worry about that. Then she felt worried about feeling pleased, and so on until the thought ran away from her into infinity. Just like the names, she thought, and that thought was so clever she couldn't help being pleased. She could tell that some of the others were whispering about her because she was spending such a long time in silence, just looking, but she decided that was okay.

In the visitor's centre there was a guestbook for people to record their responses. Ludo Hall made a beeline for the pen, but Mr Mably stopped him.

'No thank you, Ludo, I don't need all nine of you scribbling god knows what all over the place. Let's have one person, one *sensible* person, to write something respectful on behalf of everyone. Sophie, you come and do it.'

Sophie stood and thought for a long time before selecting what she felt was the perfect word. Lately she had been thinking that she might like to be a writer when she was older.

'Surreal,' Ludo read out loud when she'd finished writing.

'Because it's like your mind can't even really process what actually happened out there,' said Sophie. 'It's like it happened on another planet.'

Several people giggled at this.

'That sounds fair enough,' said Mr Dempster. 'It is pretty hard to take in, isn't it?'

The teachers moved away to examine a display of personal items found in the trenches, but most of 8S stayed crowded around the book, reading out other people's entries in foreign accents.

'Surreal,' said Rhiannon, faux-thoughtfully. 'That's just like Hugh Grant, "surreal but nice", like *Notting Hill*. Was that your *inspiration*, Sophie? Were you quoting Hugh Grant?'

Verity and Flick laughed. Sophie felt wounded; Rhiannon had been reasonably pleasant to her all week, so this reversion to her usual mocking tone came as a blow.

'Why don't you write the whole thing out, "surreal but nice"?' Rhiannon was saying.

'Because that wasn't what I wanted to say. It wasn't nice,' Sophie said.

'But you're meant to be our *spokesperson*, Sophie,' said Rhiannon. 'That's so un*fair* of you to just totally ignore what *we* want to say.'

Ludo Hall held out his hand. 'Gimme that pen.'

'No.' Sophie shook her head.

'Well then, *you* write it,' said Ludo. 'Go on, I bet you don't have the guts. You're such a suck-up, you never do anything—'

'Watch me,' said Sophie, bending over the book again. Her nose was hot with unspilled tears. In her best hand-writing, she added the words 'but nice' to her comment.

'There,' she said, standing up straight; and before the others could see how upset she was, she marched off to join the teachers by the display cabinets.

After supper that evening, Mr Dempster closed all the shutters in the main sitting area so they could play Murder in the Dark. If you drew the ace you were the murderer and if you drew the king you were the detective. When the murderer tapped you on the shoulder you had to die, but you got to choose your own grisly ending. Mr Dempster encouraged them all to be creative with their pretend deaths. People got poisoned and strangled and shot and beheaded and exploded. While Des Kapoor was dying from head injuries, perhaps a little louder than was strictly necessary, Sophie tripped over someone's ankle.

'Are you dead?' she hissed. If you found a dead person you were supposed to shout 'Murder', but this was the last game of the evening and she didn't want it to end.

'No, I'm just hiding,' came the whispered reply.

Sophie put out a hand and touched a bony forearm. 'Who is that?'

'It's Ludo. Who're you?' Ludo's hand found her knee and squeezed.

'Sophie.'

Ludo said something she couldn't hear.

'What?' She put her head down to where the sound was coming from. Ludo's mouth was right next to her cheek; she could feel his breath on her skin.

'I'm sorry about calling you a suck earlier.'

'That's okay,' Sophie whispered back.

Then Ludo tapped her on the shoulder and she cried out once and died happy, the touch of his hand on her knee still tingling long after he'd crawled away to murder Hugh.

Mr Raddock had brought his book of war poetry with him: every night, at the very end of the evening, once they had all used the bathroom and changed into their pyjamas, they gathered in the sitting area to hear someone read out a poem. Tonight it was Ludo's turn. He read Wilfred Owen's 'Anthem for Doomed Youth', clearly and well. Sophie's eyes never left his face. The WW1 soldiers who lied about their age would only have been two or three years older than him, she thought. She imagined Ludo lying in no-man's land with his pale face even paler than usual and dark jammy blood oozing from a hole in his head. She imagined being his girlfriend back home in England, trembling as she opened the dreaded telegram.

When Ludo read the line 'What candles may be held to speed them all?' she found she had tears in her eyes. It was the first time a poem had ever made her cry, she realised, feeling very proud of herself indeed.

*   *   *

Three days later: another reassurance patrol, the last before Chris's multiple returned to the checkpoints. Showal Kalay was the second village on their route. Chris had been looking forward to returning to Showal: the last time he was here, he got into a heated discussion with a local trader who wanted the British troops to go home and leave the local people in peace. Since then, Chris had had time to think up a set of simply worded, sympathetic but firm defences of the British mission that he was keen to try out on the old trader. But today he felt too distracted to navigate such a sensitive debate. Ever since the incident in Mirwais with the ANP and the injured woman, he had thought of little else.

After walking away from the situation that day, he had ordered his patrol to continue straight back to base. He didn't report the fight between the ANP commander and the woman's husband, because any account of this would have to include his failure to intervene. Why hadn't he stepped in to protect the husband? The heat? His reluctance to make a bad situation worse? No explanation satisfied his conscience. Chris wasn't sure what the right course of action would have been, but he was certain that he had not taken it. When Robbo asked him what had held him up, Chris told him only that a woman had been knocked down and he had been unsure whether or not to attempt to help her.

'Bloody burqas, they're always getting hit,' Robbo had said, with the air of one long since inured to this kind of thing. 'No peripheral vision, see? And there's fuck all we can do about it, they're tainted goods once we've touched them. You just have to leave them to it. Honest, boss, you did the right thing.'

His one chance so far to display some integrity and he had, unequivocally, failed.

Showal Kalay was busy this afternoon. They had teamed up with another multiple for this patrol; as well as their usual reassurance duties, they were detailed to search several compounds for weapons and drugs following intelligence received from some locals. One of these compounds was here in Showal. The search team were clearing the compound now, while Chris and the Afghans patrolled in the market place. The old vendor he'd spoken to last time was sitting in exactly the same spot as before. Chris watched him from a distance. He was selling poultry: the filthy live birds were crammed into small cages stacked on top of one another, while the merchant himself sat cross-legged on a mat next to this rustling, squawking pile. He was currently re-stocking the small heap of freshly butchered chicken in a Tupperware container on his right. On his left, a chicken's arse pointed directly upwards, its head in the dust nearby and its body wedged into a hollow breezeblock like an egg cup, neatly containing its last convulsive shudders and directing the squirts of blood downwards. The stink of blood and chicken shit had a nasty edge that cut through the background smells of dust, diesel, sun-ripened groceries and litter. Chris moved away, feeling slightly nauseous. In his memory he kept hearing the sound of the woman being hit: that aborted scream, the force of the thud. He didn't know why he was so shaken by it. Worse happened here every day; it was ridiculous to be this squeamish over a road accident.

His radio retched: it was NCO Pfeiffer, the commander of the search team, asking to speak to him in person. Chris left Sergeant Abdullah in the marketplace with the other Afghans and started to make his way over to the compound that was being searched. To get there, he had to walk over a small embankment leading out of the centre of the Kalay. The ground here was sufficiently raised for Chris to look over the wall of one of the outlying compounds. There, oblivious to his appearance, was a bareheaded woman in her thirties carrying a bucket of water across a courtyard. Before he could even process why this sight was so surprising, Chris had a shock of voyeur's guilt – a sense of having committed a violation, as if he'd glimpsed the woman not just bareheaded, but naked. He realised that this was the first time he'd seen the face of an adult Afghan woman. The young girls went everywhere bareheaded: they were often strikingly beautiful and even more brazen than their brothers about approaching patrols to demand sweets and pens. But at the cusp of puberty, the gender vanished. It was rare even to see females in burqas outside their compounds. And somehow, Chris thought with alarm, he had absorbed – in just four weeks – the values and taboos of this godawful country to such an extent that it now felt wrong to look at a woman's face.

He was so preoccupied with thinking about all this that as he neared the compound where his men were, he cut through a gap in a wall. As soon as he'd done so he stopped, horrified at his own stupidity. This certainly wasn't the route his troops had taken with their metal detectors.

He made to walk backwards – and immediately put his foot on the pressure plate he'd just stepped over. There was just time, before the explosion, for another rush of shame and self-reproach. What a basic fucking error!

And then he seemed to be jumping upwards with enormous power as some strange dark object flew past him to hit the compound wall behind his head, and then he was on the ground, and because of the jumping and the loud noise he understood that there had been an explosion. He wasn't in pain, though, so perhaps he'd just been spectacularly lucky.

His men were coming towards him. He wanted to call to them that he was okay but for some reason his voice wasn't working. He could hear Robbo, taking charge, yelling at everyone not to move around so much before they'd checked the ground for more IEDs. A man was kneeling heavily on his groin, and now Chris knew he'd been hurt, because a textbook scrap of battlefield first aid drifted into his mind: *apply weight to pinch off femoral artery and slow the bleeding*. Was he bleeding? He must be: another guy was sliding a combat tourniquet up his leg and winding it viciously tight with the windlass. And here, *here* was the pain, and there was his own voice, screaming for morphine. Somebody dropped a boot on the ground nearby. There was something wrong with it;

it looked as if it had been burned. But why would anyone be changing their socks at a time like this? Chris stared at the boot. It seemed oddly familiar. The second-from-top eyelet on the left hand side was broken. Now why was that significant? He wanted to remember but thinking was so hard, and it was nicer, after all, to just go to sleep...

Ten

A week after his return from Normandy, Callum was sitting alone in his classroom marking a pile of Year 5 homework when a large woman wearing a multi-coloured sweater with small pom-pons round the neckline knocked on the door.

'Mr Dempster? You remember me? I'm Elsa Witrand, Sophie's mother. Have you heard?' she said, striding towards his desk. 'Sophie got a scholarship! Nothing major, just an exhibition, in fact – but we're delighted.'

'That's wonderful!' Callum got up to shake her hand. 'Though I'm hardly surprised; she and Karl Huber are streets ahead of the rest of the class, in Latin at least.'

'Yes, she did particularly well in her Latin paper,' gushed Mrs Witrand. She pulled her long brown plait over one shoulder and rubbed its scrubby tip between her fingers. 'And I know she's just loved your Greek classes. In fact, I think you're something of a hero for Sophie. She hasn't stopped talking about your trip to France all week.'

'Well, I was really just a tag-along on that trip. But I'm very pleased to hear that Sophie enjoyed herself,' said Callum. 'She's a special young lady.'

'Which is why I was wondering,' Mrs Witrand continued, fixing him with a stare, 'if you'd be willing to do one of your pictures for us, of Sophie. The Halls said you did a terrific portrait of Ludo, and I actually saw the one of the Knight twins and their dog, I thought that was really charming.'

'Of course, I'd love to,' said Callum warmly. 'Just Sophie, or a family group?'

'Oh, you don't want to draw an old bag like me,' Mrs Witrand laughed.

She was flirting with him, Callum realised. He was popular with a certain type of just-past-it mother – of which Elsa Witrand, with her bobbly sweater and her oversized earrings, was a prime example. At twenty-five, he imagined, she must have been a real handful: big-hipped and pink-faced and forthright. Now she just looked heavy, as if every movement, even that flick of her plait, was an effort. Trying to be as tactful as possible without getting drawn into the flirtation, Callum suggested taking photographs of a range of different groupings, so that the Witrands could choose which one they liked best. But Mrs Witrand was adamant: the picture was to be of Sophie alone.

'I think it'll be such a lovely reminder for her, of her time at Denham Hall. She really has flourished this year, you know.'

Callum pulled out his diary so that they could pick a day for him to come round and photograph Sophie. In the end, that evening turned out to be a good time for both of them. The Witrands lived just outside the village; it was barely a five-minute detour from Callum's usual route home.

* * *

The Witrands' house was a large nineteenth-century cottage with a recently re-thatched roof. The whole of the front of the cottage was covered in an ancient wisteria vine, with hard grey stems that looked soldered together wherever they crossed. Callum parked his bike against a huge staddle stone and rang the doorbell.

Mrs Witrand ('Elsa, *please*') was wearing a red apron embroidered with the words 'No. 1 Mum'. 'Thank you *so* much for doing this. Sophie's feeling a little shy, but I'm sure you're used to that from your, ah, subjects. Do come on in.'

'I'd like to take the pictures right away, if that's all right,' said Callum. 'While there's still a bit of natural light left.'

He was shown through to a cosy wood-beamed sitting room, where Sophie was slumped in a floral armchair.

'No one told me about this,' she said by way of greeting.

'Sophie!' her mother snapped. 'Don't be so rude.'

'Sorry, sir,' Sophie said, looking dolefully at Callum. 'But I didn't even know this was happening until like five minutes ago.'

Callum squatted down next to Sophie's armchair. 'So you're not keen, then?'

'I look rubbish in photos.'

'All the best-looking people are un-photogenic,' said Callum.

'Well, I photograph terribly, so I'll take that as a compliment!' tittered Mrs Witrand. Sophie glared at her mother.

'We'll do loads of pictures,' Callum told Sophie. 'We won't stop until we get one we're all happy with, okay?'

'Okay,' Sophie said grudgingly.

'Is there anything in particular you'd like Sophie to be wearing, anything you want to do with her hair, perhaps...?'

'Come here, Sophie,' Mrs Witrand beckoned her daughter to her and tugged her long, light brown hair out of its ponytail. 'I think we'll just have her hair down,

I want it to be as natural as possible. Natural and *time-less*. Actually, that one you did of the Knight twins, they both seemed to be – well, I think they had bare shoulders. It was a lovely effect. Very classic.'

'That's easy enough, if that's what you want – and if Sophie's comfortable with it,' Callum said. 'I'll need you to get changed into a towel, maybe use a couple of clothes pegs for security?'

'Lovely,' said Mrs Witrand briskly. 'Sophie, you go upstairs and get a towel round you.'

Sophie trudged out and reappeared in her towel some minutes later, still looking miserable. Mrs Witrand fastened it shut behind her back with two big plastic clothes pegs.

'I hear you did rather well in those exams of yours,' Callum said as Sophie took her place on the stool.

Sophie smiled shyly. 'I only just found out at the end of the day, no one else at school knows yet.'

'So I gathered. And you got an A+ in the Latin paper.'

'I know, I couldn't believe it! I honestly thought I'd bished up the English into Latin, did I tell you, it was super hard, sir, honestly I'd say it was as hard as that one you gave us that you said would be harder than anything we'd get in the exam.'

Callum kept her talking while he snapped away. After he'd taken about twenty pictures he flicked back through them to see if any would do.

'Sophie, if you don't mind – there's a bit of towel sticking up, just by your left armpit – could you tuck that under for me?'

Blushing, Sophie rearranged the towel.

'In fact,' said Callum, putting his camera down and stepping up beside her, 'I think this needs to be a bit lower all the way round – we'll have to undo those clothes pegs – are you happy for me to...? He glanced up at Mrs Witrand.

'Yes, go on, go ahead,' said Mrs Witrand.

'Sorry if my fingers are cold, I'll try not to touch you.' Very carefully, Callum unclasped the clothes pegs and turned the top of the towel down by half an inch. He leaned back to check the effect. Sophie was looking at him with her serious grey eyes. You could see the shape her face was going to take as she grew older: quite a strong jawline and sharpish cheekbones, with a clear, high forehead. For now, though, the clarity of that structure was still softened by baby fat. Callum thought of the dark room he occasionally used in Brixton, that thrilling wait as the image slowly swam its way into sight. Her mouth in particular was childish, with a full bottom lip tucked under the top, almost as if she were biting it.

A rich, deep excitement was stirring inside him. Callum acknowledged it calmly, without surprise. He had thought all that was over weeks ago. Now it seemed as if it had never gone away. And this time, it didn't feel dirty. He was aroused but he was also obscurely moved. He realised he wanted to do a proper portrait of Sophie – not just what she looked like but who she was, right now, in this sweetly fleeting in-between state.

He undid the clothes pegs for a second time and rolled the towel down another half inch, one eye on Mrs Witrand to see whether she was still fine with this. Callum knew he was pushing a boundary now, but he had to include a hint of her little breasts – just the first soft swell at the very top of her chest, not quite a cleavage yet, more like the blueprint for one.

'Is that okay?' he asked Sophie.

'I suppose so.'

'Of course it's okay, you look lovely,' said her mother.

'You do,' Callum agreed. He returned to the camera, feeling something that he recognised, to his shame, as triumph.

257

Afterwards, over tea and flapjacks, they looked at the pictures on Callum's laptop. Sophie was quietly rather pleased. She had hated it when Mr Dempster was adjusting her towel; she knew he must be noticing all the horrid podginess on her chest and near her armpits. But Mr Dempster had taken the photos in black and white, which made everything look much nicer. Her shoulders were the real surprise. She had never even noticed them before, because whenever she looked in the mirror she was too busy worrying about her breasts or her chin. There was no other way to put it: they were beautiful.

'Gosh,' said Mrs Witrand. She sounded less sure than she had done in the sitting room. 'They're certainly very ... sophisticated.'

'If you're not happy with them I can come back tomorrow,' Callum offered.

'No no, it's not that – they're terrific, thank you – it's just – Sophie, you look so grown up!' She pulled Sophie into her huge chest and held her there until her daughter began to protest.

'I think we should go with one of these three,' said Callum. 'If you give me your email I'll ping them over to you now, and then you can let me know when you've decided on one.'

* * *

It was 9 p.m. by the time Callum got back to Brewer's Court. When he first entered the flat, he assumed that Leah must have had friends over, and then gone out: there were no lights on anywhere, but he could see, in the streetlight, two bottles of white wine glinting on the coffee table. One was empty, the other about three-quarters full. He switched on the lights and was about to go through to the little kitchen area to make himself something to eat when a noise like a very long cough made him pause. He listened hard and heard the same strange noise again, even longer this time. It was coming from somewhere in the flat.

He found Leah in the bathroom, retching drily into a toilet bowl already full of thin, blond vomit. When he switched the lights on she looked round at him once. Then she cringed back towards the toilet and hid her head in her arms.

'Leah? Are you OK?'

After a bath that Callum insisted on running for her, Leah changed into pyjama bottoms and a big woolly cardigan. Reluctantly, she agreed to join Callum in the sitting room for a glass of water. Callum was shocked to see how loose the pyjamas were on her. As she walked towards him, the outline of her legs rose and fell sharply against the fabric. She was extremely thin. Callum was reminded of a fairground stilt-man, those broom-handle legs inside the baggy trousers.

'You've lost a lot of weight,' he said gently as she sat down. He felt guilty for having failed to notice the change in her before now.

Leah said nothing.

'Here.' Callum poured water for her, and then some wine for himself. 'I'm going to have some of this, if that's all right. I'm guessing you've had enough. You know, I didn't drink you thank.' It took Callum a few seconds to hear his mistake. 'Sorry,' he smiled. 'Think you drank. I didn't think you drank.'

Leah didn't smile back. She realised that Callum was being very kind, but there was no way she could explain to him why she was so unhappy. Right now she didn't even trust herself to talk. She felt horribly drunk. Unconsciously she pushed up the sleeves of her cardigan and started to scratch the eczema inside her elbows, which was already raw and glistening from a savaging earlier that evening.

'Shit, that looks nasty.' Callum caught hold of her wrists and held her two arms away from each other. 'You mustn't do that. You'll hurt yourself.'

Leah's chin dimpled with the effort of not crying. Her lips were dry from all the vomiting and the bottom one had cracked in two places. She could feel her blood pulsing tightly behind one of the splits.

A tear leaked out without her permission. She sniffed hard, but it was no good: it was merely an advance guard, not just for more tears but for words, more words than she'd said at once in days, maybe even weeks. The little bit at the centre of Leah that wasn't drunk listened to the words with a detached horror. She could hear that they sounded slightly mad but she was too far away to do anything about it.

Callum fetched the box of tissues and did his best to make sense of what Leah was trying to tell him. As far as he could understand, the problem was something to do with control. Leah was out of control and the whole world was out of control and yet no one seemed to realise it.

'Leah, is this something to do with you and Chris?' He hoped it was; if Leah was heartbroken it would make this extraordinary outburst much less alarming.

'Chris?' Leah looked confused. 'No, not about me an' Chris. Iss about *me*, there's something wrong with *me*.'

She was scratching again. Callum took hold of her wrists and held them firmly above her knees, trying to keep pace with this sudden change of direction.

'What's wrong with you? Leah? What is it?'

Leah shook her head.

'Come on. You can tell me.'

'Can't.'

'Yes you can. Come on. What sort of thing?'

There was a very long silence. Leah had her head twisted to the left and down so that there was no way Callum could meet her eye. Finally she said, in a voice so low he almost missed it, 'It's to do with sex.'

'Okay,' he said steadily, trying not to sound surprised. 'What about sex?'

'I don' wan' to say.'

'Okay,' he said again. 'I understand.'

Leah just cried harder. Callum shuffled up closer and put his arm round her, pulling her head sideways onto his shoulder so that they couldn't see each other's faces any more.

'Shall I tell you something?' he murmured, as if talking to a small, frightened child. 'There's something wrong with me, too.' He felt her shoulders tighten. 'So how about we do a swap?' Callum went on. 'You tell me and I'll tell you. Your thing can't be worse than my thing.'

'It *is* worse,' whispered Leah.

'How do you know that when you don't even know what my thing is?'

Callum's mobile phone rang, making them both start. 'Hold on, let me just see who—' It was Tamsin. He held the phone in his palm for two more rings, then silenced the call.

'S'okay, you should get that,' said Leah.

'No, I shouldn't. This is much more important.'

The phone stopped vibrating; then, almost at once, it rang out with a second call from Tamsin.

'Looks like she really wans to talk t'you,' Leah said, getting unsteadily to her feet. Callum silenced the call again and grabbed Leah by the forearm.

'And I really want to talk to *you*. Okay?'

He could tell she was pleased: nervous, reluctant, but pleased.

'Right,' Callum said as Leah sat down again. 'You were going to tell me about whatever it is that's worrying you.'

Leah took a deep breath and closed her eyes. She felt it surge up inside her like vomit. 'Okaymmm-jussgonnasayit,' she said, 'vvvneverhadnorgasm.'

'Never—'

'*Never*. See,' she spat, suddenly angry, 'that *is* worse than yours, issnit?'

'I don't know,' said Callum slowly. 'Do you still want to know my problem?' It occurred to him that once, not long ago, it would have been impossible for him to tell Leah – to tell anyone – about his impotence. But it seemed almost trivial now in comparison to his troubling, semi-articulated new secret.

Leah nodded.

'It's a bit of a cliché. Erectile dysfunction. I can't get it up.'

Leah looked confused. 'But you and Tamsin—'

'—hardly ever have sex. Or not *sex* sex.'

Her eyes widened. Then she started to laugh. 'Sorry, mmm sorry, mmm not laughing at you, mmm laughing at us, it's juss, iss juss so *shit*.'

'Have you ever talked to anyone about this before?' Callum wanted to know.

'Nohreally. Chris a bit. But I lied, I said I could, you know, when I was on my own—'

'But you can't?'

She shook her head.

Callum shifted one knee onto the sofa so that he was facing her. 'Listen,' he said, taking both her hands in his. They were cold, and there were angry red calluses at the base of her index and middle fingers. 'The thing is, with me and Tam—' Callum stopped, aware that he was about to lie, or if not lie, peddle a truth that was long past its sell-by date. But it was better for Leah this way.

'Wha'about you and Tamsin?'

'With me and Tam, it doesn't actually matter. I love her, and she loves me, and when you find someone like that, someone who just accepts you as you are – I'd actually even say it's brought us closer together.'

He smiled encouragingly at her and his smile made Leah want to cry again. She had insider information. She knew that Tamsin wanted to leave Callum – and now she thought she understood why. The idea that Callum should be sitting there telling her that Tamsin didn't mind about his problem, that he should actually believe it had brought them closer together, struck her as unbearably sad. For a minute she considered telling him everything. Then she took a large gulp of water and forced herself to smile back at him.

Leah and Callum sat up talking until almost midnight – so it wasn't until Callum was in bed, reaching for his phone to set a morning alarm, that he remembered Tamsin's call. Not wanting to wake her, he sent her a text message. Sorry I missed you. What's up? xxx Then he read for fifteen minutes while he waited for a reply. When nothing came, he switched the bedside light off and was asleep in moments.

The next day, three more missed calls and a text from Tamsin, sent at 1.17 a.m. Where are you?? Had a ghastly evening, I needed you. It was 6.30 a.m.; he could hardly call her now. He texted again as he munched on a banana. Sorry, was with Leah – she was really upset about sth. So sorry. Hope you're feeling better, what happened? Xxx

At break time, the staffroom was noisy with talk of the holidays: just three and half days to go now. Callum took refuge beside the broken coffee machine and turned his phone on to see if Tamsin had replied.

Can I come over later? I need to talk.

263

I need to talk: those four words shot out of the phone and embedded themselves in his stomach.

'Callum Dempster!' roared a voice on his left. It was Mr Davenport, the headmaster. Like most of the teachers at Denham Hall, Callum didn't particularly like Niall Davenport, but he didn't dislike him, either. In eighteen months of working together they had only seriously disagreed once, over Callum's insistence on calling all the pupils by their first names.

'Cheltenham gave Karl Huber the top scholarship, marvellous news!'

'That *is* good news.'

'It is, isn't it?' Mr Davenport scuffed his moustache on the back of his hand to clear it of biscuit crumbs. 'And we heard from Bryanston last night – nothing for Hugh Brodie, but a minor for Verity Trevena. Going to do wonders for our rep. And they all did extremely well in their Latin papers. Even Brodie got a B+. You've worked a miracle, Dempster. How long've you had with them, a year and half?'

Callum could feel the rest of the staffroom listening in, some admiringly, some enviously. 'Ah, just a half a year, actually. I took over from Dennis in September.'

'Amazing, Dempster. A miracle worker,' said Davenport, clapping him heavily on the shoulder.

Weirdly, this little interlude seemed to clear Callum's mind. When he returned to Tamsin's text, he felt quite calm. It was simple: if missing one evening's worth of calls was enough to provoke his girlfriend into breaking up with him, then the relationship was dead anyway. At the same time, it wasn't over until it was over – and until that point, he would behave as he had always behaved towards Tamsin. He raised his phone and began to text.

Come for supper. I'll cancel tonight's Greek class. Love you xxx

Her reply came back almost instantly.

Thank you xxx

Three kisses! Tamsin hadn't bothered with text-message kisses in some time. So his worries were pure paranoia. He fairly bounced out of the staffroom, trying not to look too chuffed in case his colleagues thought he was hyped up over Davenport's eulogy.

* * *

The previous night, while Callum was comforting Leah, Tamsin's father had texted her to try and persuade her to meet him for coffee. The text had spooked Tamsin. She hadn't heard from Bertrand in years, apart from at Christmas and birthdays. Also, she'd changed her phone about six months ago, and she certainly hadn't given the new number to Bertrand.

She tried her mother as soon as the text came through, to see if he'd been hassling her as well; but Roz was out, yet again, and too busy to talk. Then she called Serena, her chief suspect.

'Bean, it's me. Did you give him my number?'

'What? Hello? Who is that?'

Serena was in a bar. Tamsin could hear boozed-up voices and a song, something by Florence and the Machine, coming tinnily through the earpiece. Tamsin had just spent the last hour sitting at the kitchen table, killing time by looking at the Facebook profiles of friends she hadn't seen in years. On the sideboard, a slice of three-day-old lasagne awaited. The mental image of her pretty little sister in the middle of a group of happy, successful, real live people was galling.

'It's Tamsin, your sister, remember me? Did you give Bertrand my number?'

'Oh, *Tamsin*, Tammy, hi! You're not going to believe

this, I'm at this drinks party thing, and that guy Will, you know the one who used to live near us, the one who's friends with Callum – he's here, he knows my friend Jojo! Isn't that the weirdest coincidence?'

'Not really,' said Tamsin.

'He's actually very nice about you, Tam, he seems like a nice guy. And' – here she dropped her voice to a loud whisper – 'he's really hot!'

'Of course he's nice about me, he's nice about everyone, he's the biggest sleazebag in London.' A disturbing thought occurred to Tamsin. 'Look, Bean, whatever you do, don't fuck him. I mean it.'

'Since when have you given a monkey's about who I sleep with?'

'Bean, tell me honestly, did you give Bertrand my number?'

There was a long pause and some clunking noises as Serena moved somewhere quieter. When she spoke again, she sounded furious.

'For fucksake, you're like *obsessed* with this whole Dad thing! It's been nearly ten years, d'you realise that? And actually some middle-aged guy having an affair with a colleague, which is effectively what happened – it's not such a big deal, it's—'

'So you did give him my number.'

'No, as it happens, I didn't. And *as it happens* I think you're being a complete twat about the whole thing. You should be proud to be his daughter. Did you even *know* that he's conducting some of the LBO concerts this season?'

'Wait. You're actually working with him now?'

'Why is that so surprising?'

'Fuck. *Fuck.* Never mind. Have a nice evening,' said Tamsin with full-bore sarcasm. Then she hung up.

Tamsin made a furious noise deep in her throat, somewhere between a growl and a small screech. It sounded absurd in the silent kitchen, and hearing it angered her even further. It was at this point that she rang Callum for the first time. When the call went through to voice-mail, she hung up and called again, immediately. Still no reply. Feeling really wretched now, Tamsin flipped up her laptop and allowed Facebook to reclaim her. Although she knew, even as she was doing it, that this was a bad idea, she typed her sister's name into the search box. For the best part of half an hour she clicked through photo after photo of Serena in various lovely outfits, oboe in hand, smiling out into paused applause. The pleasure of self-abjection led her from Facebook to her father's Wikipedia page, and then finally, fatally, to Google, where the search terms 'Bertrand Jarvis' conjured up over a hundred thousand results, from concert reviews and photographs and interviews through articles reporting on his OBE and speculating on the future of his stellar career.

When Callum's text arrived just after midnight, she missed it because she was watching – at top volume – a YouTube clip of her father guest-conducting the Berlin Phil on the opening night of the Proms four years ago. Tamsin had actually taken Roz away on holiday, to Corsica, to avoid all the media hype leading up to this concert, which was broadcast live on BBC 2. Now Tamsin watched the entire Prom straight through from start to finish. It was the first time she had seen her father conduct since she was seventeen. There was no question of his greatness: even on screen, Tamsin could sense the magnetic effect he was having on the players. For the encore, he had chosen 'Jeux de vagues' from Debussy's *La Mer*. When she and Serena were still small enough to fit in the same bath, their favourite treat was for Bertrand to 'make waves', his big hands churning up the water while he whistled snatches of the Debussy melody to an accom-paniment of delighted shrieks from his girls. Tamsin listened to the first thirty seconds of the encore then snapped the lid of her computer shut. Either Bertrand had picked the Debussy on purpose, or he'd forgotten about those bathtimes, and 'Jeux de vagues' was just like any other piece of music to him. Either way, all ways, she hated him.

It was 12.30 a.m. There was a text from Callum, but when she tried calling him she ended up with voicemail again. This time she found herself listening to the voicemail right through to the end, just to hear his voice. 'Hello, you've reached Callum Dempster's mobile. Sorry I can't take your call at the minute, but here comes the beep, you know the drill.' It was a faintly irritating message that she'd been nagging him to change for some time, but tonight all she could think about was that she missed him. She realised, more sharply than ever before, that she'd grown very used to having Callum in her life.

For half an hour she sat at the kitchen table in silence. The lasagne lay untouched on the sideboard. She called Callum and listened to the voicemail for a second time. Now Tamsin found herself subject to the law by which desire increases in inverse proportion to availability. She smoked her last cigarette as slowly as she could before ringing Callum again, but there was still no reply. Finally, sometime towards 1.30, she sent him a text and dragged herself off to bed, deliberately not muting her phone so that she'd wake up if he called her back.

She couldn't remember the last time she'd gone to sleep while still waiting on a call or a text from Callum. The first thing she did when she woke up was to check her phone, eagerly, like someone in the first stages of a crush. Opening his message to find that he'd missed her calls because he'd been with Leah, she felt a twinge of indignation that wasn't entirely unpleasant. So he'd been helping someone else instead of her! Suddenly all she wanted was to see him and to be held by him and to tell him every-thing about Serena and her father, because Callum would understand, better than anyone else in the world.

Can I come over later? I need to talk.

Even as she pressed send, Tamsin was aware that this was not a sensible way to behave. She was meant to be leaving Callum in less than a week. Relying on him for comfort in this way was hardly kind. But there was no one who knew her like he knew her; and besides, she thought, breaking up with him was going to be horren-dous anyway. Just one evening, just one more night – what real difference could that make?

* * *

Sophie's day passed in a thrilling whirl of temporary celebrity. Her scholarship had been read out at Notices that morning, and the whole school had clapped. Everyone, even first and second years she'd never even spoken to, seemed to want to congratulate her. At lunch-time Verity and Karl sat next to her and whispered that they too had scholarships. Sophie wasn't to spread this news, though, because Hugh hadn't got anything and they didn't want to hurt his feelings. Obviously he would find out in Notices tomorrow; but for today, it was their delicious secret. Sophie felt blissfully conspiratorial, a member of a brilliant and privileged elite.

They watched DVDs in both Science *and* Latin, and best of all, extra Greek got cancelled. She enjoyed the Greek sessions, but her next-door neighbour Nathan had a new computer game that she was dying to play on and his mother always called him down for supper at seven o'clock. Except Nathan's family didn't have supper, they had 'tea'. Nathan was only eleven and a good deal smaller than Sophie, but she still had a bit of a crush on him.

Although he was no Ludo Hall, there was a certain cocky worldliness about him that Sophie liked and found herself trying to emulate. When they played together she consciously changed her speech to sound more like his, turning *running* into *runnin'* and *wanted* into *wan'id*. The best thing about Nathan was that he treated her like she was another boy. They played army together and climbed trees and did dares about how much wild garlic they could eat without being sick, and when it was too dark or too cold to stay outside they went up to Nathan's little loft-space bedroom and sat on the beanbags munching Quavers and playing Mario Kart until they could see the virtual racetrack every time they closed their eyes.

But in the girls' changing rooms, locked into the end toilet cubicle with the sounds of home-time chatter echoing ceramically around her, Sophie's good day came to an abrupt end. In the gusset of her Little Miss Chatterbox knickers was a viscous substance with a light brown tint, printed in a tapering strip about three centimetres long. Her first thought was that she'd forgotten to wipe herself properly, but the brown stuff was too far forward for that, and too creamy-pale. Could it be her period? That, too, seemed unlikely; this fudge-coloured smear was so different from the shocking crimson she'd been expecting. So, she thought: it must be an illness, possibly something very grave. Brown seemed ominous, an indication of impurity and decay.

Sophie knew she should probably tell her mother about this, but the humiliation of the worms was too recent. She couldn't stand the idea that her parents and her doctor might think her unclean, the sort of person who was always having problems *down there*. And maybe, please God maybe, it would be gone by the morning. She dried her eyes with a tightly scrunched pellet of toilet paper.

Then she tore off three more sheets and folded them into a pad exactly the width of her gusset. She hoiked her knickers up as far as they would go to keep this improvised sanitary towel in place and sat on the edge of the loo seat, waiting until the last of her happy, undiseased peers had left the changing room before opening the door of the cubicle.

She didn't feel like seeing Nathan any more. When she got home she went straight up to her room and stayed there till supper. She was monosyllabic with her mother and so short-tempered towards James and Harriet that even before pudding was served she had been declared 'over tired' and prescribed a non-optional early bedtime.

*   *   *

Thanks to the Normandy trip, it was nearly a fortnight since Tamsin had been to Callum's flat. As she pushed open the front door, she was surprised by a sense of homecoming. The place smelled terrific; there was some sort of rich meat stew slow-cooking on the stovetop. Callum was already back. When he heard her come in he stood up from the little desk by the window and carefully laid aside a large drawing board.

'Hey you,' he said as he came towards her. Tamsin let him take her into his arms, resting her head on his shoulder and making no attempt to bring the contact to a premature end.

'It's good to see you,' she said, meaning it.

Callum poured drinks and came back through into the sitting area to find Tamsin inspecting his drawing. He had just started the portrait of Sophie: so far the picture was little more than structural markings, but the photograph he was working from was up on the screen of his open laptop, zoomed in slightly over Sophie's face.

'She's pretty,' said Tamsin.

'Isn't she?' agreed Callum. 'And seriously clever, too. Actually she reminds me a bit of you.'

Tamsin bent down to the laptop and zoomed out to get a look at the rest of the picture.

'Whoa, that's a bit risqué, isn't it? You can practically see her nipples.'

'I often do the kids with bare shoulders, you know that,' said Callum. 'Let's put some music on.' He nudged her away from the computer screen and replaced the picture of Sophie with his iTunes library.

Over Callum's delicious lamb stew Tamsin told him about the text she'd received from Bertrand and her conversation with Serena. One of the things she had always liked most about Callum was how seriously he took her problems: the way he listened and the calm intelligence with which he considered all sides of an issue, never judgemental, never partisan, always emotionally discerning. When it came to her family, he was wise enough not to directly criticise Serena or even Bertrand.

'So do you think you want to see your father?' he asked gently, once they had finished discussing Tamsin's deteriorating relationship with Serena.

'No,' said Tamsin, emphatically.

'Then that's fine. You absolutely don't have to. You don't even have to reply to his text if you don't want to.'

She gave him a grateful smile. This was the most amazing thing of all – that although she knew he thought it might be a good idea for her to see her father again, he didn't ever try to force this point.

Afterwards, Tamsin curled up on the sofa to read the Style section left over from the Sunday paper while Callum worked on the drawing of Sophie. The album Callum had chosen to play – Charlie Parker's *Talkin' Bird* – had long since finished, and the flat was filled with that lovely silence peculiar to two people doing separate things in companionable solitude. Leah was out; they had the place all to themselves. Sitting there listening to the shush of Callum's pencil moving over the rough-grained cartridge paper, Tamsin felt as if it could have been any night of their relationship – any happy night before her doubts set in. Perhaps it had been a bad idea to come here after all. Today was Tuesday; Friday was the last day of term; and on Saturday, she was going to end it. But her resolution felt more precarious than ever. Each time she thought of Chris she felt a lurching excitement that surely meant it was him she really wanted to be with – and yet, right now, the idea of leaving Callum filled her with a sensation that was – well, a sort of homesickness.

Tamsin had promised herself she wouldn't allow any sort of sexual contact between them; but later, when Callum dared a goodnight kiss, she found it impossible not to respond. She still wanted him, she realised unhappily. What that *meant* – well, she would worry about that later, not now, not when they were kissing like this, tightly and deeply, their tongues a perfect fit, filling each other's mouths with the wonderful restless desperation of desire.

This kiss was confusing to Callum as well. He had been miserably certain that now he knew Tamsin and Chris had slept together, it would be harder than ever for him to keep his cool in the bedroom. But the fact that the worst thing that could possibly happen had, finally, happened was strangely liberating. He couldn't begin to match up to Chris. Yet, rather than crushing him, this knowledge brought the calm of utter abnegation – and with it, obtusely, confidence.

Tamsin undid her jeans and slowly trod them down her legs until she was standing in just her T-shirt and pants. It was a long time since they had done this and the unfamiliarity was exciting. She undid the buttons of Callum's shirt. Then a little chain of kisses down from his sternum to the top of his trousers. She was kneeling on the floor in front of him now, facing a slight but unmistakable bulge in his suit trousers. Tamsin helped him tenderly out of the trousers but left his boxer shorts on. Callum's rare erections were shy creatures; abrupt exposure often scared them away. Much better to let Callum take his shorts off in his own time. It was a bit like playing hide and seek with a little child: you knew exactly where they were hiding, but you pretended not to see.

But when Tamsin – now free of T-shirt and bra – pressed her naked body into Callum's, taking care not to look down as she came towards him, she found that the boxers were already gone. Squashed between her lower belly and the top of Callum's thigh was Callum's rapidly stiffening penis. Moving slowly, Tamsin moistened her palm and took his erection lightly into her hand. Callum let her rub him for a long time, until his cock felt properly hard. Although they were both very excited, they knew how fragile this situation was. Tamsin led Callum down onto the bed and positioned herself on top of him. They smiled at one another in wonder as his cock slid into her, undiminished. Tamsin leaned forward so that the tips of her breasts were brushing Callum's chest. When he began to return her movements with small thrusts of his own, she picked up her pace, enjoying the feeling of fullness and the friction on her clitoris. She moaned quietly as she rocked back and forth. This too was an art she had perfected: articulating her pleasure without impinging on Callum's easily broken concentration.

Callum was doing his best not to think of anything, to stay totally inside the feeling of soft warm wet tightness around his cock. But it was impossible not to be conscious of the fact that they were having sex – *they were having sex, they were actually having sex!* – and this thought was, inevitably, accompanied by the fear that sex would be unsustainable for much longer. It was a mental pathway Callum knew to be lethal: he could already feel his cock softening slightly. Quickly he tried to think of something else. The first thing that came into his mind was the drawing he'd been working on – specifically, the swell of Sophie's budding breasts. He felt his penis regain stiffness. She's only *twelve*, he reminded himself, and his cock began to shrink again. But now that he was trying not to think about Sophie's breasts it was impossible not to – and to his comingled delight and dismay, it was also impossible to stem his growing excitement. He thrust harder. As his arousal mounted, he gave himself up to the pictures in his mind, seeing Sophie's nipples now, still soft and puffy and so very pale, little pink peaks on top of that firm new flesh, probably tender, even painful, with growing, swelling, thickening, he closed his eyes and Tamsin's nipples were Sophie's nipples, he felt the heat of those young soft nipples in his mouth, marshmallows, and when Tamsin pushed her hand down between their bodies to rub herself as they fucked he imagined it as Sophie's small hand reaching down to his cock. With that thought he came with a shout and a long, full-body spasm, clutching Tamsin to him as the last of his orgasm ripped through him.

Tamsin carried on rubbing herself after he'd finished until, a minute or so later, she came too. She flopped forward to rest her full weight on Callum and let out a long, contented sigh.

In the bathroom he washed his hands and ran them, still wet, over his cock. The euphoria of having had successful sex with Tamsin at last was complicated by what he'd been thinking about as he came. As he patted it dry on a towel, the sight of his big ugly adult penis appalled him. Ten minutes ago he had forced, in his imagination, an innocent twelve-year-old hand to touch this wrinkled, purple-brown monster. To calm himself, Callum repeated a now familiar mantra: his thoughts were just thoughts, and no one had been hurt, and no one need ever know he had thought them. What you imagined and what you wanted were two different things. Bringing Sophie Witrand into the bedroom didn't mean he *actually* wanted to bring Sophie Witrand into the bedroom.

But, *but*, what a delicious idea. Sophie in bed with him and Tamsin, tucked up between them in her pyjamas. They could educate her. They could teach her everything, corrupt her awkward innocence, witness her first baffled orgasm—

Callum looked down at his penis again. His hand was massaging it gently. It was barely even soft and it was beginning to get hard again. He wanted to laugh. To be getting hard again, just fifteen minutes after orgasm! He felt like superman, filling up with pride and gratitude, gratitude towards Tamsin but above all towards Sophie, because now he *knew*, there was no point pretending any more, that this terrible impulse had always been there, and although it was terrible it was also wonderful, it was beautiful, it was love.

'Cal? You all right in there?'

Guiltily, Callum stuffed his semi-hard penis back into his boxer shorts and padded back into the bedroom.

'Shouldn't you go pee?' Callum asked, keen to have the room to himself for a moment or two. He needed to cool down, refocus himself on what mattered right now: Tamsin, and the fact that finally, after weeks out in the tundra, she seemed to be ready to let him back in. He marvelled briefly at how unrelated that part of his life – his world with Tamsin – was to this other, different realm of desire. They were separate, yet he wanted, he needed both.

'If I *have* to,' Tamsin grumbled. 'You're so bossy, you know.'

Really she was touched: Callum was clearly remembering how easily she got cystitis, and worrying about that. She took her time in the bathroom, as he had done, examining her thoughts along with her bed-messy reflection. It was just so confusing. All she knew was that she didn't know what she wanted. Was she changing her mind simply because Callum had managed to have sex with her? No, she reassured herself, it wasn't that – the confusion had started long before they reached the bedroom. But the sex had definitely left her feeling closer to him.

'What was even up with Leah?' she asked later as they lay in bed.

Callum hesitated before answering. 'You promise not to mention this to *anyone*?'

'Promise.'

'A whole bunch of things, and she'd had far too much to drink – but I think the thing that was *really* bothering her was the fact that she's never had an orgasm.'

Tamsin shifted to face Callum. 'Are you *serious*? Not even by herself?'

'Nope. Never, nothing.'

'*Fuck*. I can't believe she told you that. What do you even say to something like that?'

'I told her about me.'

'You mean, about your...' Even naming it as a problem was difficult between them.

'Yes.'

'Okay. Wow.'

'I thought it might help.'

'Mmm.'

Callum tried to draw Tamsin towards him but she struggled up to a sitting position instead.

'Tam, you all right?'

'Yeah. It's just … it feels a little … that you can talk to some other girl about our sex life, when you can't even talk to me.' She was hurt, she realised – hurt by someone she had been pitying, as a victim of her own imminent cruelty, for months. And the pain was all the greater because she had just been wondering, as they lay there, whether she might want to stay with Callum after all.

'Tam, Tam, let me, let me explain—' Callum was sitting up too, now, stroking Tamsin's back in an ill-judged attempt to calm her down.

'I don't want you to explain, you don't need to explain, I want you to stop touching me' – she jerked forward, out of his reach – 'and I want to go to sleep, okay?'

Thus in a matter of minutes all their new-found closeness was undone. They both lay awake for some time, in silence, on separate sides of the bed. Tamsin mentally composed long, eloquent rants about the injustice that had been done to her. Disconcertingly, she realised she was feeling jealous of the intimacy that existed between Callum and Leah. But fuck that, she thought: they were welcome to each other, because on Saturday she was breaking up with Callum, for good. Tamsin even wondered whether Leah had had all this in mind when they made that silly pact on New Year's eve – forgetting that the pact had been entirely her own idea.

To start with, Callum's thoughts were quieter and sadder. He was used to this by now: rapprochement followed by rejection. And, he realised, Tamsin had a point. He didn't talk to her enough. He couldn't, especially not now. If she had any idea where his mind had been this evening she would despise him.

To his shame, just the thought of the thoughts he wasn't meant to think rekindled his arousal. Earlier, in the bathroom, his perversion had been exhilarating; but now it disgusted and frightened him, as it had done when he nearly lost it with the string. The unfamiliar problem of an un-willed erection made him feel contaminated, out of control. Callum forced himself to imagine Chris and Tamsin together, surely a foolproof dampener. But it didn't work. Sophie, Rhiannon, Verity, Flick: he refused to look but he could still sense them there on the edges of his vision, ready for him, waiting.

His sleep, when it finally came, was uneasy. In the still-conscious borderland of his dreams he saw Tamsin sitting at a desk in an unfamiliar office. He couldn't talk to her because his tongue was too flat, flat and thin as paper. He tried to pinch it and pull it out of his mouth to show her, but each time it slipped out of his fingers. And although he knew it wasn't real, that he was actually just lying in his bed with his hands tucked firmly underneath the pillow, he carried on rummaging pathetically in his mouth for his horrible flat tongue, unseen by the dream-Tamsin behind the desk.

* * *

In Chalfont St Peter, Sophie was sleeping in two pairs of knickers, with a fresh wodge of loo roll to staunch any leakage. When she woke up, the paper was stained with the same light brown substance as before. She lifted it to her nose. It smelled like something in the art room, but she couldn't remember what. She balled yesterday's dirty pants into a plastic bag and hid it at the bottom of the bin.

* * *

279

During fifth period on Wednesday morning, Callum unwittingly showed 8S his three naked pictures of Tamsin. Not only did he do this without meaning to, but when he left for lunch at the end of the lesson, he had no idea that the whole class had seen the photographs.

This is how it happened.

Once 8S were settled at their desks, he handed out a worksheet of humorous Latin cryptograms. He needed them busy so that he could continue to worry about the state of his relationship with Tamsin. She had been asleep when he left that morning for work. Callum had called her twice since then, and received no reply. It was the first time they'd ever gone to bed on an argument and he wasn't sure it was going to be possible to put things right.

But Callum had spent the last four lessons worrying about Tamsin and he felt he deserved a break. Last night, in bed, his disturbing new pupil-related potency had disgusted and frightened him. Now, in the light of day, with 8S sitting entirely unharmed in front of him, his qualms seemed squeamish. What problem was there with imagining or even looking? No one was getting hurt; it was all safely in his head. Besides, it was weeks since he'd looked at any of the pictures in class. The fear he'd once had – that this was some sort of compulsion, even addiction – was obviously unfounded.

Soon his screen was filled with a close-up of Tamsin's breasts, cropped from the picture of her standing in front of the sea. The left breast was softish, with the areola melting indistinctly into nipple. The right nipple was stiffer, with several of the empty hair follicles around the areola also puckered into points, like little stitches in the skin. They were, indisputably, the breasts of a fully-grown woman. There was a Henry Moore in the Tate he'd always loved, called, simply, *Girl*. *Girl*'s breasts were necessarily smooth, because she was made of polished stone. Her nipples were pinpricks, engraved with the lightest of touches. The lack of detail beautifully captured the half-formedness of adolescence. Unlike Tamsin's, *Girl*'s breasts were small and high and almost pointed, as if they were still pushing outwards, potent with growth. *Puissant*.

And yet something in *Girl*'s diffident, uncertain posture recalled Tamsin on the beach, shy and proud all at once. He wondered what it would be like to photograph the 8S girls in this posture. Naked on the beach like Tamsin, nervous and goosefleshed, their small nipples stiffened into beads ... He imagined asking them how it felt to be looked at. Did they like being looking at? Did it make them feel ashamed? Did they ever think about being watched, naked, in the bath or the shower?

Girl, Callum decided, would make a perfect addition to his slideshow on representations of the female body – something else he hadn't looked at in weeks. He opened up the presentation in PowerPoint and found a jpeg of Moore's sculpture on Google. He selected the picture and pressed Ctrl+C to copy it. Then back to PowerPoint: Ctrl+V to paste. Instead of the picture, the words *Sextus et Marcus currunt prope piscinam* appeared – text from an exercise sheet he'd been assembling earlier.

Callum assumed, correctly, that he'd failed to press the 'C' of Ctrl+C during the copying stage. What he didn't realise was that he'd actually pressed Ctrl+D, a command unknown to him. The 'D' was for 'display', as in 'display on smartboard'. Now his entire desktop was visible to the class on the big screen behind his head.

And so as Callum copied the picture of *Girl* for a second time and added it to his slideshow, 8S gradually became aware of these strange images flashing up on the smartboard. Flick Chilcott actually said 'Sir?', to ask what it was all about; but Callum didn't hear her, and when

Flick raised her hand Ludo pulled it straight down again. He mimed for her to be quiet and pointed at the smart-board. Callum was cycling through the whole slideshow. By the time he got to a painting of a woman's private parts, huge and hairy, 8S were explosive with suppressed laughter. This picture remained on the screen for several minutes. Several of the others – especially the photographs – stayed up even longer. The pictures of Tamsin stayed up longest of all. Ludo nudged Hugh and drew his attention to Mr Dempster's face. Callum's mouth was slightly open and his breathing was obviously disturbed. Hugh struggled so hard to suppress his giggles that some snot came out of his nose in a milky bubble.

Then the bell rang and Callum closed down the presentation and the smartboard went blank. Distractedly, he collected their cryptograms and sent them off to lunch.

In the corridor, 8S were euphoric.

'Omigod, like what even *was* that?'

'That was literally the *best lesson ever*!'

'He was so getting off on it, did you see his face?'

'No no no, did you see that hairy fanny, wasn't it the grossest thing you've ever seen?'

'I know, he's obviously a major perv.'

'*Sssh!* KV!'

They fell briefly silent as Mr Dempster strode by on his way to lunch, oblivious. As soon as he had gone the laughter began again.

'That woman at the end, I'll bet you anything she's his girlfriend,' said Ludo, smugly. 'The picture where she was lying down on the towel, right? You could see a copy of *Ecce Romani* in the corner.'

'Oh, so he actually *is* a perv.' Rhiannon gave a delighted shudder.

'What are we going to do about it?' Verity wanted to know.

'What do you mean?'

Verity looked prim. 'Well, it wasn't very *professional* of Mr D, was it?'

'No, it was freaking hilarious!' said Des.

Hugh was miming a pair of huge breasts with his hands. 'Just say that is his girlfriend, can you imagine what it must be like when they do it? I bet she could knock Mr D out with those!'

Everyone laughed at that.

* * *

Everyone – except for Sophie. She could see that the Latin lesson had been very funny, but she didn't feel like laughing. All she could think about was the loo roll in her pants, about what would happen if it slipped out and gave her away. She kept movement to a minimum and spoke only when asked a direct question. Just looking at the other girls made her feel filthy, infected, grotesque. When she changed her tissue paper after lunch, she noticed that the stain was getting darker.

The most sinister aspect of Sophie's mysterious sickness was that there was no pain. On the second night Sophie knelt by her bed and prayed for the strange brown stuff to stop. In the morning it was still there, lighter, perhaps, but just as disturbing.

* * *

Tamsin was in a trendy Shoreditch cocktail bar with her friend Bethany, getting drunk on passionfruit mojitos. She had considered confiding in Bethany about the whole Chris-and-Callum thing, but residual loyalty to Callum prevented her from doing so. Instead, she talked around the subject, telling Bethany about Chris going to

Afghanistan, and how Leah had dumped him just a few weeks before he left.

'Sorry, just a moment—' Bethany swiped her thumb across the screen and became instantly absorbed in the email.

This aspect of Bethany's professional success irked Tamsin more than any other: her friend would drop whatever conversation she was having, no matter how serious, to answer her email. Tamsin now made a point, perhaps childishly, of checking her own, decidedly non-urgent emails on her lethargic old Nokia whenever Bethany picked up her iPhone. As Bethany thumbed out a reply to her email, Tamsin waited for the progress bar labelled 'Checking for new mail' to crawl its way up to full.

'Beth, you're not going to believe this—'

'Just a minute, nearly done—'

'No, actually this is too weird, I've got an email, I've got an email from Chris!'

Bethany put down her phone immediately. 'What does it say?'

'I can't see, my phone's so bloody slow – hold on, I'm just opening it now – the subject line starts with 'Please don't', but I can't see the rest of it—'

'That's so *strange*, we were literally just talking about him.'

Tamsin felt herself grinning idiotically. This was what she would think about on Saturday, she promised herself. This excitement, this light-headedness, *Chris*.

Then she looked down and saw the full subject line: 'Please don't panic: injured but safely back.'

'*Shit*,' she breathed. 'He's been hurt.'

It was a group email, sent to an undisclosed recipient list. Chris was at Selly Oak Hospital in Birmingham, recovering from an IED blast that had seriously injured his lower left leg.

No infection, no major blood loss, but – no foot.

They had amputated a week ago, on the day of the explosion. Now it was just a question of waiting for the wound to heal so that he could have his prosthesis fitted. By Afghanistan standards, the outlook was good; he would certainly have the option of returning to his career in the army if he wanted to.

He was very shaken but basically doing okay.

He'd love to see anyone who could spare the time to see him.

Tamsin and Bethany read the email in silence, heads bent close together over Tamsin's tiny phone screen.

'Tam, I'm so sorry,' said Bethany quietly, putting her hand on Tamsin's knee. 'You guys, you're close, right?'

'Woah,' said Tamsin. '*Woah*.'

'You'll have to go and see him.'

'I know,' Tamsin nodded. 'I'll go tomorrow.'

* * *

The next day was Thursday. Tamsin was wide awake by 6.30 a.m., badly hungover yet galvanised by an unshakeable sense of purpose. She checked the Selly Oak visiting hours: the earliest she could see Chris was 2 p.m. At 8.30 a.m. she called Hortensia Court to reschedule her afternoon session for the morning. By 10 a.m. she was sitting behind the piano, groggily bashing her way through 'Some Enchanted Evening'.

Three songs into her programme, Tamsin noticed that she couldn't see Antonia. Her usual seat in the middle of the front row was occupied by a new resident: a bald woman deeply tanned from chemo, with a single wisp of hair in the middle of her head and hoop earrings that made her look like some sort of genie. At the end of the song, Tamsin scanned the room properly. Antonia definitely wasn't there. Tamsin knew she was probably just sleeping, or having a late breakfast. But something, perhaps her hangover, perhaps the thought of Chris, lying broken in his hospital bed, was making her panic. With each song she played, she became more convinced that Antonia had died. And although Tamsin had said to herself more than once that this would be the best thing for Antonia – to die, and be spared the indignity of further deterioration – the idea of never seeing the old lady again was unexpectedly painful to her. She played to the end of the programme as fast as she reasonably could, slowing down only for the closing number, 'We'll Meet Again'. This song was a favourite with the residents of Hortensia Court, many of whom hummed along to the melody, their combined efforts producing a tuneless drone that Tamsin found both irritating and slightly creepy. Today, though, she was moved by her own playing, almost to tears. In the final repeat of the chorus she held the sustain pedal down and swelled the melody to a heaving rallentando that would have made Stavros proud.

As soon as she'd finished she rushed out to the reception area to talk to Heather.

'Where's Antonia? Is she ill?'

Heather was typing something very quickly, the keyboard splashing rhythmically under her long nails. 'Oh no,' she said breezily, somehow still typing while she talked. 'She's just keeping away from "group situations".' She pronounced these two words with audible inverted commas, as if 'group situations' was a new and complex term that Tamsin might not quite understand.

'But she loves the piano.'

Heather shrugged. 'Sorry, love, not my decision.'

'So she's just sitting up there in her room,' Tamsin said furiously. 'Can I at least go and talk to her?'

'Course you can,' Heather said, but when Tamsin was

halfway to the stairs she heard Heather calling her back. 'Sorry, love, she's not actually up there any more. We moved her – she's down there now.' She tipped her head towards a corridor just to the right of the reception desk.

'Right. Which room is it?'

'Near the end, you won't miss it, all the doors should be open.'

This was a part of Hortensia Court that Tamsin had never seen before. All the doors were indeed open – presumably so that patrolling staff members could keep an eye on the 'inmates', as Antonia used to call them. The corridor was too hot and it had a meaty smell. The bedrooms Tamsin glanced into were filled with obscure equipment for lifting and cleaning the residents, most of whom seemed to be asleep. But there was one old lady sitting in a chair by the window, her hair still almost completely black, calling 'help, please help … someone … anyone.' Outside in the corridor, a few doors down, one of the careworkers was arranging syringes and cotton wool on a wheeled trolley. Tamsin coughed to get her attention.

'Excuse me – sorry to interrupt – but there's a lady in there, saying she needs help?'

The careworker stood up. She was taller even than Tamsin, with long blonde hair and big shoulders. 'That's Doris,' she said, as if this were sufficient explanation. 'She's always like that, there's nothing to worry about. Who are you looking for?'

'Uh, Antonia, Antonia Pratt?'

'Last door on the left,' said the blonde woman.

Although Tamsin tried not to look into any more rooms on her way down to the end of the corridor, one woman in a bed with cot-like sides caught her eye. She was sitting propped up by several pillows, her head rolling about. Her skin looked like pale wax or plastic, with an almost luminous quality, as if it might glow in the dark. The wrinkles on her face were so thick that Tamsin couldn't see her eyes. Because she wasn't wearing dentures, her toothless mouth was just a small dark hole with rounded edges. Her tongue poked out from one corner, light pink and bloodless. It was alarmingly pointy: it looked tensed, alert, the last flickering outpost of the woman's sentience. Tamsin took all of this in in a matter of seconds; but she knew that the image would stay with her.

She found Antonia sitting on the edge of her bed dressed in a raincoat, as if she were about to go out. The dried hydrangeas from her old room were on the windowsill, and a few of her postcards had been stuck up above the bed, but compared to before, the set-up was depressingly spare. Worst of all, there was no music player.

'Antonia, what's happened to your records?' Tamsin asked after she had introduced herself and explained that they already knew each other well.

'You know,' said Antonia thoughtfully, 'the trouble with men is—'

'Yes? What's the trouble with men?' Tamsin pressed. These days conversation with Antonia had a riddling element. Tamsin was convinced the old lady was usually saying something that made at least some sense; you just had to do a little bit of interpreting. Right now, for example, she might be trying to say that some men, perhaps Derek the handyman, had taken her stereo system away. And occasionally she still had periods of lucidity, when Tamsin could see in her face that she knew exactly what she was saying. These were the saddest times, because it was then that Antonia seemed briefly to intuit where she was and what was happening to her.

'The trouble with men is that they can be terribly funny about the meaning ... the meaning of the word *prime*.'

Antonia looked at Tamsin as if seeing her for the first time. 'And who are you?' she asked sharply.

'I'm Tamsin,' said Tamsin. 'I play the piano. I've played for you before, lots of times, and I was playing for some of the other residents just now.'

'You're not very good.'

Tamsin smiled. 'I'm afraid I have to play those old war songs.'

'You were never that good,' said Antonia, looking straight into Tamsin's eyes with what looked like real recognition. It was as if she had momentarily managed to place Tamsin and this was what she had remembered: that her piano playing was no good.

'Why not?' Tamsin asked quietly, willing Antonia to come out with some nonsense.

'Your phrasing. It's always so...' A look of disgust crossed Antonia's face. '*Predictable*.'

'At least I'm not crazy,' said Tamsin, very slowly and clearly.

'What do you mean?' asked Antonia. She sounded frightened.

Tamsin knew that it would be unkind to go on; but she had been wounded and she wanted to inflict pain in return. In a few seconds, she told herself, Antonia would have forgotten anyway.

'You're losing your mind,' she said, dropping her voice to a whisper in case the nurse was still outside in the corridor. 'Half the time you don't even know what you're saying.'

A terrible understanding entered Antonia's eyes, mixed with raw animal alarm. Then her whole face began to shift. For a second or two Tamsin thought she was having a seizure, but it was just her dentures, which she was pushing forward with her tongue.

'Antonia – no, don't do that' – Tamsin lifted her hand

to her face and mimed a pushing motion towards her own mouth. Like a child, Antonia copied her, nudging the dentures back in. She sucked them into place with a loud slurp.

'That's better,' said Tamsin, relieved that Antonia seemed to have moved past her vicious revelation. She was already regretting her cruelty.

'Where am I?' Antonia was trying to stand up. 'What is this place? I need to catch a train, I'm going to, you know when you just – and they don't wait – they go if you, you know what I mean.'

Tamsin tried to ease her back down onto the bed, but Antonia was surprisingly strong. 'No thank you, young lady, I don't need your help,' she snapped, elbowing Tamsin out of the way. 'You can infintigate the t, the t, the tizer but I'll have you know that my father, he's got a degree in that bridge, you know that bridge, I DON'T WANT TO GO, DO YOU HEAR ME? EFF YOU YOU BLOODY SHITTING WHORE!' She was shouting at the wall but Tamsin felt every word as if it were aimed directly at her.

'Is everything all right in here?' The blonde nurse was at the door. She strode over to Antonia and took her firmly by the arms.

'Thank you,' said Tamsin shakily. 'She just, I don't know what—'

'It's okay,' said the nurse, raising her voice over Antonia's protests. 'It wasn't your fault, don't worry about it.'

'Can I, do you want me to do anything…?'

'No no, you go on, I'm just going to sit with her until she's calm enough to take a pill.'

'Right. Thank you,' Tamsin said again as she backed out of the room.

When she was halfway up the corridor, Antonia's

shrieks abruptly stopped. Now all she could hear was the hum of machinery and Doris, calling repeatedly for help.

* * *

It was the second last day of the Easter term. The sunny, windy weather matched the restless mood of the pupils. Sophie Witrand was in particularly high spirits. She had changed her tissue paper three times so far today and the last two times it had been practically clean. Had it been her period, or some sort of infection? It didn't matter. The main thing was that it was finally clearing up; if it recurred again in a month's time, she would deal with it then.

At break-time they were sent to the changing rooms to clear out their lockers. Shelley, the cool gap-year student overseeing proceedings, let them listen to the radio while they tidied. Sophie played the clown, crooning along to Robbie Williams's 'Angels' and rocking her hips as if she were making slow love to an invisible man. Everyone was being friendly towards her. Milly Urquhat even gave her half a packet of chewing gum, only slightly squashed, that she had found behind the back of her locker.

In double Art Mrs Prokopowicz gave them free rein – pencils, paint, clay, pastels, whatever they wanted. Sophie plumped for a Chinese brush and a pot of ink and a seat directly opposite Ludo Hall, who was making some sort of monster out of clay. But her calligraphy was so absorbing that after five minutes she forgot he was even there.

'Hey, Sophie.' Ludo's whisper startled her. 'What're you eating?'

Sophie blushed guiltily. 'Chewing gum.'

'Give us some, then.'

Sophie glanced round to check that Mrs Prokopowicz wasn't watching. Then she fished the little packet out of her pencil case and offered it to Ludo under the table.

He held up his clay-covered hands. 'Just put a piece in my mouth, will you?'

'Really?' stammered Sophie.

'Yeah, get a move on, before Prokko comes,' said Ludo impatiently. He opened his mouth and leaned across the table towards her.

With trembling fingers Sophie pinched out a piece of chewing gum and placed it on Ludo's tongue, a sacrament. She did her best not to touch him in case he found that disgusting but she could still feel his breath, warm and wet on her fingers. Their eyes met. Then it all grew too much for Sophie and she hurried back to her calligraphy, bowing her head low to hide her ecstasy.

On the way from Art to Latin she deliberately walked by herself, replaying the glorious moment of contact over and over in her mind. It was, she thought, the best thing that had ever happened to her, better even than getting the scholarship. She was so blissed out that she remained quite calm when Mr Jensen stopped her in the corridor and told her that the headmaster wanted to see her in his office – a summons that would usually have terrified her.

She sobered up quickly enough when she entered the headmaster's study to find her mother sitting next to Mr Davenport.

'Mum? Why are you here? What have I done?'

Her mother got up to give her a quick hug. 'Darling. You haven't done *anything*. It's very important you remember that. *You haven't done anything wrong.*'

'Uh, Mrs Witrand, if I may...?' said Mr Davenport. He was stroking his moustache with his thumb, over and over again, as if he were trying to rub it off.

'Yes, of course,' said Mrs Witrand, sitting back down. Sophie hadn't seen her mother looking this serious since James had eaten all the chocolate eggs the night before Easter Sunday.

'What's going on?' she asked.

'We just want to ask you a few questions,' said Mr Davenport. He motioned towards a wingback armchair. Sophie sat down on the edge of the cushion. 'Some questions about Mr Dempster.' He had a pad of paper on his lap and a pen in his hand.

'Darling,' said her mother, 'if you feel at all uncomfortable, at any point, I want you to let me know, all right?'

Sophie frowned. 'All right.'

'Good,' said Mr Davenport. 'First of all, I understand that you saw some unusual pictures during your Latin lesson yesterday. Is that correct?'

'Yes,' said Sophie.

'Can you tell me what the lesson involved?'

'We were just doing our work, and then these, these pictures started coming up on the smartboard. It looked like Sir didn't realise it was still connected up to the computer.'

'I see,' said Mr Dempster. 'Why didn't you alert Mr Dempster to this fact?'

Sophie thought. She could hardly say it was because they had all found it so funny – and anyway, *she* hadn't been laughing.

'I suppose we were a bit embarrassed.'

'Why was that?'

'The pictures – they were pictures of naked people.'

'Paintings, or photographs?'

'Some of both.'

'Can you remember any of the photographs?'

'We-el,' Sophie began uncertainly. 'There was one of a woman on a beach.'

'And was she wearing anything?'

'Um, a pair of pants. I mean, I think they were actually bikini bottoms.'

'Anything else?'

Sophie shook her head.

'Thank you.' Mr Davenport made a note on his pad. 'And is it true that last term he also showed you photographs from a pornographical magazine?'

'Yes, but that was different—'

'How did it happen that time?'

Sophie thought. Really it was Ludo who had started all that stuff with the magazine. But she didn't want to get him into trouble. She looked at her mother and shrugged miserably.

Mrs Witrand stepped forward. 'Ah, Mr Davenport, do you not think that's probably—'

'Yes, sorry, I've heard enough,' said Mr Davenport. 'You have the card and the photograph?'

'Right here,' said Mrs Witrand, reaching into her handbag and drawing out a brown A5 envelope. When Mr Davenport opened it, Sophie was surprised to see the photograph Callum had taken of her just five days ago, and a Christmas card.

'Hang on, that's the card Mr D gave me!' she said, suddenly recognising it. 'Mum, where did you find that? You're not meant to go into my letters box, that's private!'

'I'm sorry, darling.' Her mother sounded very upset. 'Just – we'll talk about all this later, okay?'

'Sophie.' Mr Davenport was holding the card out towards her. 'To the best of your knowledge, were you the only pupil who received a Christmas card from Mr Dempster?'

'I think so,' said Sophie. 'But—'

Mr Davenport cut across her. 'Thank you. Thank you, Sophie. You've been very helpful. I just need you to do one last thing for me.' He tore off the sheet of paper he'd been making his notes on and held both pad and pen out to Sophie. It was a gorgeous silver bullet ballpoint, warm from Mr Davenport's grip.

'If you just take a seat over there—' Mr Davenport motioned to his desk.

'At your desk?' Sophie asked, uncertain she had heard correctly.

'That's right. Your mother and I are going to leave the room for a bit, leave you in peace, and while we're gone, I want you to write a short ... essay for me. Just description. I want you to describe the lesson in which you saw those photographs. And, Sophie...?'

'Yes, sir?'

'Don't be afraid to write exactly what you were feeling, how you – how the class – experienced the situation. Do you understand me?'

'I think so,' Sophie nodded. She could sense that this was all very serious but she wasn't entirely sure why. Perhaps letting them see those pictures had been 'unprofessional' of Mr Dempster, but Mr Davenport seemed to be making an awful lot of fuss about it.

Still, the headmaster had chosen *her* for this obviously important task, and she was determined to do it well. The problem was that she couldn't think of where to begin. She could hear her mother and Mr Davenport talking in low voices in the next room, and the clink of coffee cups against saucers.

'These last few days she really hasn't been herself,' her mother was saying. 'I feel terrible that I didn't put two and two together until Mrs Trevena called. Thank God Verity had the courage to speak up. And then, when I knew ... it just all *clicked*. The Christmas card, everything. I mean, Francis and I both thought that picture was a bit *revealing* – but you just think, he's an artist, what do we know, perhaps it has to be like that because of the lighting or whatever. I blame myself, really. I was right there in the room. But you trust people, don't you? You just do.'

'I really can't apologise enough,' said Mr Davenport. 'You've been so understanding, I'm very grateful to you indeed. To you and your husband.'

Sophie looked down at her piece of paper, beginning to feel panicked. Her mother and Mr Davenport might come back at any minute and find that she hadn't written anything. She realised that all of this meant something very bad for Mr Dempster, but she didn't have time to think about that now. The headmaster had charged her with a serious task which was, more importantly, a chance to shine, to demonstrate the fierce intellect for which she had just been awarded a scholarship by Oundle School. But her mind was a blank; she didn't even know what style she should write in. Mr Davenport had said an essay, but there was no question to answer.

Then she thought of the advice Mr Dempster himself had given them about writing – about how it was more like painting than photography, how you had to make it come alive. Well then: she would do it in the present tense, like some of the reportage pieces she read in her parents' Sunday supplements – sort of as if she were reporting back from a war zone. A few possible sentences drifted into her mind. She was, she thought to herself, *inspired*. It was an exciting feeling, mixing with her relief over her newly unstained knickers and the thrill of feeding chewing gum to Ludo Hall. She felt brilliant and powerful and very, very clever.

Sophie screwed up the nib of the ballpoint pen and began to write.

It is the lesson after break. When Mr Dempster enters the classroom on this fateful morning, he makes an announcement that we are to solve a sheet of Latin cryp-

tograms. The class is pleased because it is quite a fun task. But all is not as it should be. Before long someone notices that projected onto the screen behind Mr Dempster's desk is a picture of a naked Greek statue. The children have seen ancient art before and this does not shock them. But soon the images become more disturbing. The children want to look away but they can't, something is gluing their eyes to these shocking images. Most horrifying of all is a painting of a woman's reproductive parts in close up. There are also lots of photographs, mostly not so bad in fact, like the one of a woman's back made to look like a cello.

The last photograph is different from the others however. To start with it is in colour, and the woman is not very beautiful. She floats over the class, staring down at the children with hungry eyes. She is totally anonymous. The children don't know who she is or where she has come from. Afterwards, they will wonder what propelled her to prostitute her body for the camera in such a manner. The more pessimistic among them will come to fear the worst: drugs. The image stays on the screen for a very long time. The children sit in horrified silence, too frightened to move. At the end of the lesson they leave the classroom feeling older and wiser than they entered it. A little bit of innocence has been lost and their lives will never be quite the same again.

When Mr Davenport and her mother came back into the room, Sophie was just re-reading her little essay for the third time. She was really quite pleased with it. It was nicely atmospheric, she thought.

Mr Davenport took it from her and read it through, nodding as he went. When he had finished he handed it to Mrs Witrand.

'This will do fine,' he said sadly.

Sophie was confused. 'Is it okay?'

'Yes,' said Mr Davenport. He sounded very tired. 'It's very good. Thank you. You've done everything I've asked quickly and maturely. I'm sorry we had to involve you in this at all, Sophie. I'm going to leave you with your mother now.' He put out his hand to take the essay back. Mrs Witrand held up a finger to show that she was still reading. After a few moments she looked up and passed the essay over to him with a single tight nod.

As soon as the headmaster had left the room Mrs Witrand opened her arms and rushed towards Sophie.

'Darling, my darling, well done,' she heaved.

Sophie moved her ear away from her mother's hot breath. Funny how when it was Ludo's it was delicious but when it was your mum's it was repulsive. Then she realised her mother's back was shaking gently.

'Mum, are you *crying*?'

* * *

The guy in the bed next to Chris was a triple amp who always kept his curtains closed when he had visitors, so Chris didn't see Tamsin until she was standing at the foot of his bed. She was wearing a simple grey wool dress with a very high hemline made decent by the fact that her black tights were completely opaque.

'You came,' he grinned. He had been dreaming about her for weeks and now she was here she was even more beautiful than she had been in his mind.

'I came.' Tamsin sat down on the chair beside his bed. She put her hand out and placed it over Chris's where it rested on top of the powder blue waffle-knit blanket.

'Honestly,' said Chris, his voice thick with emotion, 'I have to tell you – this morning, when they said you were coming, I had to get them to say your name twice, it was just too good to be true. I sent that email out to about twelve people and of all them it was you I wanted to see the most. Am I, I'm not, am I embarrassing you?'

Tamsin was blushing but she shook her head.

'Actually, I'm sorry, you know, I don't even care if I am,' Chris went on. 'You get to a point when it all sort of becomes very clear. I wasn't going to tell you this, but out there – most guys take a photo with them, so you can show it to the Afghans and tell them she's your wife, even if it's just some random woman. In their culture it's weird for a man my age not to be married, it'd make them suspicious.'

'And your photo was…?' Tamsin asked softly, although she already knew the answer.

'You. I printed one off Facebook, that one where you're sitting on the grass with your mum.'

They smiled at one another, but the eye contact quickly grew uncomfortable and they both looked away, feeling self-conscious. The intimacy that had come so easily in the first few adrenalised moments of seeing each other again receded. Tamsin searched in vain for something to say. She had spent the whole train journey preparing for this meeting – doing her best to forget about what had happened at Hortensia Court by concentrating intently on how she would behave with Chris. She would show him, calmly and compassionately, that nothing had changed between them, that it didn't matter to her whether he had two feet or one foot or no feet.

Now she was here that confidence was nowhere to be found. In many ways the ward itself was much less awful than she had anticipated. Tamsin had been expecting dimmed lighting and weeping relatives and frail, wan amputees, but the majority of the soldiers looked reasonably cheerful, playing on gameboys, listening to radios, talking to friends and family – even, in some cases, doing gentle exercises beside their beds. What she was unprepared for was their vitality. No one was pale or sickly. They were all suntanned. So tanned their wrap-around sunglasses had left a spectral outline, a negative afterimage. Even the men who had lost two or even three of their limbs had clearly been, just weeks ago, at the absolute peak of fitness. It was this contrast, the sheer distance they had fallen, that made the wrongness of it all so much greater.

Chris himself seemed remarkably unchanged – thinner, certainly, and covered in little cuts and scars, but otherwise he was so exactly as Tamsin remembered him that she couldn't help wondering whether she'd read the email wrong. Had he really lost his foot? Embarrassingly, she couldn't stop her eyes flicking down to the end of the bed, where his legs were and his left foot supposedly wasn't.

'Have a look if you like,' said Chris, noticing her gaze.

Tamsin didn't really want to see it – she had never been very good with blood – but she was afraid that she'd hurt him if she didn't, so she lifted the edge of blanket.

'Go on, it's fine,' he encouraged her.

She took a deep breath in and looked. His leg ended about six inches below his knee, but to her relief the wound was entirely hidden by a mass of clean white bandages. There was a plastic tube sticking out of the bandages leading down to some point below the bed. It looked empty.

'Fluid drainage,' Chris explained. 'But it seems to have dried up. I'm making great progress, apparently.' He heard the bitterness in his own voice and hastily corrected it. 'Bandages are coming off tomorrow, I'll be in rehab at Headley in no time. And actually I didn't lose much more than the foot, but they took the amp up a bit higher because that's best for the prosthesis. They've got this whole thing down to a fine art, it's amazing really.'

Tamsin had replaced the cover and was looking at him wonderingly. 'I don't know how you can sound so cheerful about it.'

Chris lowered his voice. 'Seriously, when you see some of these guys—' He pointed over to the curtains on his right, then motioned just below one shoulder and above both knees. 'A couple of years ago he probably wouldn't even've made it. Whereas me, I'm like the model amputee. Perfect Paralympics material. I'll probably be faster with a peg leg than I was with a real one.' He nodded at his bedside table, which was decorated with a few cards and a cuddly toy parrot. 'I had some mates in yesterday,' he explained. 'Doug Ronson, I think you met him once or twice? He brought me the parrot, and a box of plasters, oh, and this, too.' He reached behind his pillow and drew out a copy of a magazine: *Runner's World*.

'I don't understand, why didn't they – I mean, why would your friends—' Tamsin looked distressed.

'Oh, god no, sorry, it's fine,' Chris hurried to reassure her. 'It was a joke, it was really funny at the time. Everyone gets this sort of shit. Just standard banter. The parrot's a bit of a cliché, in fact. At least two more on this ward. And you see that blond guy, two beds down? His friends nicked his crutches when they left on Tuesday, he thought it was hilarious.'

Chris smiled gamely at Tamsin. He could see she was impressed. He didn't mention that he was yet to get through a night without lurid waking dreams of writhing limbless on the hot, sandy ground, bombs exploding around him and everyone shouting and running away, leaving him behind to bleed and wriggle like one half of an earthworm. The psych had diagnosed mild PTSD, but Chris didn't want Tamsin to know this. He didn't want her to think of him as being any more damaged than he obviously was.

'Do you want to talk...?' Tamsin asked.

'Actually, if you don't mind, I feel like I've kind of been over it enough lately.' Chris reached down to scratch his leg. 'They've been great here, I was in and out of consciousness for the first forty-eight hours or so and one nurse actually kept a diary for me, just noting down everything that happened, who came to see me, what decisions were being made and all that. When I came to, properly, I spent ages going over what had happened, trying to make sense of it all. I felt – I feel – so fucking *stupid*.' He stopped himself. 'Pointless. Not going there. All done now. And seeing you, I just actually want to hear about *normal* things, about your life, your job, your music, anything you want to talk about, really.'

'Of course,' Tamsin breathed. 'You can tell me about it some other time. We've got all the time in the world.'

They were talking as if Callum had never existed. It was a fiction that, Tamsin knew, couldn't continue indefinitely. But now was surely not the time to go into all that.

'Soooo ... what do you want to hear about?' she asked.

'Anything. Anything at all ... What did you do this morning, before you got here?'

Tamsin was sceptical. 'You really want to hear about my day?'

'Yep. As long as there's no sand involved I'm a happy camper.'

'Well ... I woke up pretty early ... with a hangover, as it happens, I was out last night, with Bethany – Bethany?'

Chris thought. 'Shortish, massive hair?'

'That's her. She's a huuuge fan of yours, you know. You seem to have quite a dramatic effect on women.'

'And now I can accessorise with a prosthesis I'm going to be doubly irresistible.'

Tamsin looked stricken. 'Shit – I'm so sorry – I didn't – I didn't think—'

'Tamsin.' Laughing, Chris reached over and put his hand just above her knee. He gave her thigh a reassuring squeeze. 'Just joking. Really.' His face grew serious. There was something he wanted to tell her, something that he was sure she must be wondering about – just as everyone on the ward was wondering it, about each other but especially about the guys like Tomkins, because if you'd lost both legs then chances were you'd lost more. He'd heard plenty of lads swear they'd rather die than come back without a cock. Chris wanted to reassure Tamsin that he was still perfectly intact, but he didn't know how to begin that conversation. And now he had been silent for too long, and she was chattering on, getting into her stride, telling him, just as he had asked her to, all the little details of her day.

Tamsin's account of Hortensia Court omitted mention of Antonia. Instead she told Chris about the residents humming along to 'We'll Meet Again', and made him laugh with a quick sketch of Gerry, a good-looking old man who never joined in with the humming, but instead used his hands to beat out fast and complex rhythms on the sides of his wheelchair.

'Sort of like a very elderly Dave Grohl,' said Tamsin.

Chris grinned. 'But what about – I forget her name, but you've told me about her before – there was an old lady, wasn't there, who was really musical?'

Tamsin's face tensed. 'Antonia. She's – yes, you're thinking of Antonia.'

'What's wrong?'

'No, no, she's still alive...' Tamsin hesitated. She was touched that Chris had remembered Antonia, and touched by his concern – but also slightly wrong-footed, because she didn't want to explain about Antonia. 'It's just ... she's so much worse now.'

Chris leaned forward, looking deeply concerned. 'It must be horrible for you. You're very fond of her, aren't you?'

Tamsin nodded. Chris was staring at her earnestly and it was making her feel terrible. She looked down at the waffle-knit blanket. She had poked three of her fingers through the holes and the middle one was turning dark from restricted blood-flow. Chris was just so conspicuously *good*. If she told him what she had said to Antonia he would be repulsed by her – quite rightly, of course. How could a man who'd just given his right leg for his country – a war hero, no less – be expected to understand, let alone forgive, the smallness she'd succumbed to at Hortensia Court a few hours ago?

'It's wonderful to see you,' said Chris, taking her hand in his again. 'You know, I really do mean it when I say you've kept me going.'

'It's good to see you too,' Tamsin murmured, just as tenderly, but even as she spoke a difficult realisation was growing inside her. Chris was looking at her with nothing short of adoration. He had carried her photograph around Afghanistan with him ... Yet she couldn't help thinking of Callum: she could tell *him* anything at all, in the knowledge that his love for her was set hard. With Chris, she might never be able to risk revealing her worst self to him. For example: even to start explaining what had happened that morning she would have to disabuse Chris of his belief that she was a musical prodigy who just happened to be so altruistic she chose to spend her talent not in the concert halls of Europe but in the nursing homes of suburban London. She perceived for the first time what a myth she had allowed him to construct around her real character – and how difficult it might be to dismantle that edifice. Because when he knew her, *really* knew her, he might not even want her. Whereas Callum – Callum was a sure thing.

'I can tell you now,' Chris was saying. 'It seems so easy to be honest all of a sudden. I've loved you for years, I never forgot you after that night on the tube. And then you were so happy with Callum, so, uh, I just sort of fell into that thing with Leah. I never loved her. It was always you. It's, well, it's *always* been you.' He was radiant, beatific; yet to her dismay Tamsin found she couldn't match his euphoria with her own. She'd wanted this moment for such a long time and now it was here, it felt all wrong.

'There's something else,' Chris went on. He lowered his voice to a whisper. 'It's a bit awkward – I thought you'd want to know.' He beckoned her in closer to him and glanced around to see if anyone were watching or listening. 'I've lost my foot, but otherwise I'm fine.'

Tamsin began to reassure him that the foot made no difference to her – helplessly aware that by doing so, she was putting her pen to a contract she was no longer sure she wanted to sign. But Chris stopped her mid-sentence.

'No, that's not what...' Chris nodded downwards, between his legs. 'I mean *everything*' – he gave her a significant look – 'is in working order.' The significant look modulated into a suggestive one.

Now she understood; and because she had just been thinking about Chris's implacable goodness, the understanding came as a shock. It seemed incongruous, even wrong, that he should be thinking about sex at a time like this. And although she told herself, in the same instant, that she was being grossly unfair – that the man had just been through an unimaginable trauma, that he had every reason to be talking to her in this way – she felt a lurch of disgust. At the worst possible moment, she realised, she was changing her mind about Chris. She didn't want goodness, she didn't want ardour, she didn't want risk, she didn't want – abhorrent, unsayable, but true – an amputee. She wanted what she already knew. She wanted Callum.

Tamsin sat back in her chair and bit her lip. 'You know, Chris, I think – it's been wonderful to see you – but you should know, I'm still with Callum. And I shouldn't really be here, talking like this, not yet. I need to sort things out with him first.'

Chris nodded fervently. 'Of course, I understand.'

Then Tamsin stood up and took the coward's way out, kissing Chris's cheek, smiling her goodbye – with no intention whatsoever of seeing him again.

* * *

As she walked across the hospital car park, it was all Tamsin could do not to break into a run of pure joy. There was no part of her that mistrusted this latest revision of her emotions. She had spent the last year in a state of perpetual uncertainty but she knew that this was it: this was the answer to all the months of confusion. *Callum* was the answer. Everything that had so irked her about him lately seemed suddenly trivial. Even the fact that he had confided in Leah about his problems had lost some of its sting. She knew he loved her – she had always known that – she had just undervalued that love, until now. It almost felt – although obviously this was nonsense – as if Chris had been sent to them on purpose to show her her true feelings. She wanted to call Callum with the good news, but that was impossible: first, he was probably teaching, and second, how to explain all of this over the phone? Tamsin realised with disappointment that today was an extra-Greek Thursday. Then she had an idea: she would take a train to Denham and surprise him at the end of school. She would tell him everything, all about her doubts, about Chris, about her epiphany in Selly Oak. He had to know how close he had come to losing her, because things weren't perfect; there was a lot of work to be done. But the main thing, the glorious central thing, was that she knew now that she wanted him.

Tamsin half-jogged the rest of the way to the train station, where she found, to her delight, that she was just in time to catch the delayed 15.22 train: she would be at Denham Hall by 6 p.m. She wasn't sure exactly when Callum would finish teaching, but she was more than happy to stand and wait for as long as it took him to appear. Halfway between Solihull and Warwick, she had another brilliant idea – to book a B&B in Denham, and take Callum out for the night. There wasn't enough signal on her phone to search the Internet for places to stay, so she called her mother and asked her to find one for her. Roz was bemused but compliant, ringing back five minutes later to say that she'd booked them into a nearby boutique hotel with gardens landscaped by Capability Brown, her treat, they should go ahead and enjoy themselves.

Tamsin arrived at the school just as the last carloads of children were leaving after the end of normal lessons. She stationed herself under a large beech tree outside the main entrance. It was the first time she had been to Denham Hall. Behind her was a large, tree-studded lawn. At its fringes, little wooden signposts asked people to 'please keep off the grass' in tasteful gold letters. It was the sort of ostentatious luxury that would usually have riled Tamsin, but right now, standing under the beech tree with its new leaves still only half-unfurled and the first hint of dew sending up those mysterious evening smells, she could understand why Callum liked working here. She would tell him that when she saw him, she thought, resolving to be much more tolerant of their differences. She couldn't wait to see the look on Callum's face when he came out and saw her standing there. Tamsin fell into a deep reverie of contentedness, imagining all the things she would say to him.

The heavy whirr of some bird taking off in the bushes behind her startled Tamsin out of her daydream. She glanced up and noticed a boy slipping out of a side door in the main school building. As she watched, he ambled across the front of the school towards a lower, more modern building with a blue door marked 'Boys'. He was taking his time, stopping to do a lazy leapfrog – more of a leg-over – on every one of the little concrete parking bollards he came to. When he stopped to tie his shoelace on the fourth bollard, Tamsin hurried over to him, hoping to find out what time the class would end.

'Excuse me?'

The boy looked up at her from a racing-start position over his shoelace. He was twelve or thirteen years old and already very good-looking, with slightly slanting hazel eyes and the most gorgeous rust-coloured hair.

'Um, hi,' said Tamsin, feeling stupidly awkward in the face of this unexpected beauty. 'Sorry to bother you – but do you know when Cal— I mean, Mr Dempster's – Greek class finishes tonight?'

The boy checked his watch, an obvious affectation that made Tamsin smile.

'Well, it was meant to finish at seven pee em, but actually it's been cancelled,' he said. 'Everyone else's mum came to get them at normal home-time but my mum never picks up her phone so I just have to wait.'

'Cancelled? How come? I mean – do you know where Mr Dempster is?'

The boy stood up straight and looked at her properly

for the first time. A mischievous grin broke out across his face. 'So are you Sir's girlfriend then?'

Tamsin smiled. 'How did you guess?'

'Oh,' said the boy with deliberate airiness, 'he showed us a picture of you yesterday. A really nice one.'

Tamsin was doubly flattered – that Callum had wanted to show her to his students, and that this beautiful boy had been impressed. 'Which photo was that?' she asked.

'On the beach,' said the boy. Grinning widely, he sauntered off on his way to the changing rooms.

Tamsin walked slowly back to her position under the tree, wondering what all this could mean. She had almost dismissed his behaviour as childish nonsense when it hit her. *On the beach*.

The only photographs Callum had taken of her on the beach were those three nude pictures.

She told herself that it was impossible, he would never *do* that to her, he would never do something like that to his pupils, he was just too professional and upright and that simply wasn't *Callum* – but if he had, *if* he had, then that was truly disgusting, it would be the worst possible violation of her—

The boy was back, walking across the front of the school in the other direction. Without really thinking Tamsin found herself jogging over to him. She blocked his way and put a hand on his shoulder to stop him slipping past her.

'Tell me,' she said in a hard voice. 'What photograph did he show you?'

Clearly frightened of her anger, the boy mumbled something and looked down. Tamsin took him by both shoulders now, digging her thumbnails in. She didn't care if she hurt him.

'Look at me,' she said. 'Just tell me yes or no. Did he really show you one of *those* photographs?'

The boy's face told her all she needed to know. She let him go and began to stumble dazedly back to her tree. Then she noticed a young man, surely a teacher, walking over to a line of parked cars, his arms full of books. She strode up to him.

'Hi. Sorry to bother you – but can you tell me where Callum Dempster is?'

The young man turned towards her, raising his armful of books in what looked almost like a defensive gesture. 'Are you a journalist?'

'What? No, of course not.'

'We're not meant to talk to the press.'

'I'm not the press, I'm Callum Dempster's girlfriend. Why would I be the press?'

The young man put the books down on the roof of the car and rubbed his very bald head with the palm of his hand. 'All I know is that he's been dismissed.'

'He's – what? That's ridiculous. What for?' But even as she heard her own indignant question she was looking through it, to impossible possibilities.

The bald man opened his car door. 'I don't think – it's not my place to say – we haven't been told exactly—' He stopped, took the books from the top of the car and slung them over onto the passenger seat. When he turned back to her he seemed calmer.

'Look, I'm really sorry. I liked your husband,' he said, as he sat down behind the wheel. 'I expect he's in a pretty bad way.'

'He's not my—' Tamsin began, but the man had already closed the car door.

* * *

Tamsin hailed a taxi to Denham station, bought a new ticket and made her way onto a London-bound train, using only the smallest portion of her mind to complete these external transactions. The rest of her brain was sifting, at speed, through a mass of evidence she'd been unconsciously carrying around for months. Callum's impotence, now seen in a sinister new light. The photograph of the little girl she had seen on his computer. Hadn't he even said – and this thought nearly made her retch – that she reminded him of Tamsin? The speed – *guilty* speed – why hadn't she seen it before? – with which he'd covered up the photograph after she commented on its slightly sexualised quality.

She wondered if there had been a mistake. But what excuse could there possibly be for showing a topless photograph of her to the children he was trusted to teach? (Tamsin's outrage bypassed the relish with which her informant had recalled the picture; but when she later remembered it, this only added to her sense of violation.) To think that just four hours ago she had been planning to spend the rest of her life with this man. Right now she didn't even want to speak to him, let alone see him.

By the time she got to Notting Hill it was 8.30 p.m. A fat man stopped her as she emerged from the tube station. It was a cool evening but there was a thick glaze of sweat on his pale skin, lending him a luminous, waxy look. His belly, breasts, nose and chin all drooped down towards the ground, as if he were slowly melting. He wanted to know the way to the Prince Albert pub. When Tamsin gave him the directions, he asked her to repeat them; and then again, for a third time. Then she realised that he wasn't lost at all: he was just keeping her talking in order to stare at her chest (admittedly very prominent today, under the tight grey wool of her dress) for as long as possible.

'You're sick,' Tamsin snapped at him, and set off down

311

Pembridge Road, feeling that all men everywhere were disgusting sex-obsessed perverts. Even Chris, lying maimed in his hospital bed, had sex on the brain! What she needed was alcohol and an ally. Tamsin stopped at a little off-licence to pick up two bottles of red and a packet of Camels. She would go home to her mother and they would smoke and they would drink and she would tell Roz everything, about her and Callum, about Chris, about the nightmare discovery she had just made at Denham Hall...

Pushing open the front door of Number 8, she was met by a delicious smell of Indian food. So her mother had ordered in curry. Tamsin was just about to call out in greeting when she heard voices in the kitchen: Roz was evidently not alone. She listened for a few moments. Now she could hear that the voices weren't talking, not really. She stepped quietly through the hallway until she was just a few feet from the open kitchen door, still out of sight. They were murmuring and sighing and – that was unmistakable, that tiny, high-pitched sucking sound – they were kissing! Her mother's mystery lover, at last! To Tamsin's surprise – and even, she realised, disappointment – it was clear that this person was not a woman after all, but a man with a burry deep voice. But she was still curious. She cleared her throat loudly to alert them to her presence.

'Hello, I'm back—' she called as she entered the kitchen. Then she stopped.

'No. No way.' Tamsin heard herself start to laugh, a horrible dry humourless laugh. '*Fuck*. I don't *fucking* believe this.'

She was already backing away as her mother came towards her. 'Tamsin,' Roz said lamely. 'You're meant to be in Denham.'

'Tammy—' said her father, stepping forward to join her mother.

But Tamsin was gone.

* * *

'I'm so sorry, Tammy. You poor poor darling, I literally can't imagine how ghastly that must've been for you.'

In desperation, Tamsin had called Serena; and in direct contravention of all her expectations, Serena was being lovely.

'I juss can't believe it,' Tamsin snivelled into her phone. 'I mean, who KNOWS how long's been going on, 'slike she's been sneaking around behind my back for MONTHS, maybe even years – and after all I've DONE for her – and now I can't go back in, iss like iss where I live and I can't even go BACK there.' She sniffed back a large quantity of snot and tears and drank it down. It tasted a bit like chicken stock.

'Have you called Callum?' Serena was saying – gently, entirely reasonably – but this only made Tamsin cry harder. 'Tam. *Timtam.* Listen. I can't really understand you, you're too upset. I'm coming to get you. Just tell me where you are. Are you near Mummy's?'

It was just about possible to pick the word 'Portobello' out of the mess of Tamsin's reply.

'Portobello, that's great,' said Serena. 'Make sure you're walking south, all right? Back up towards the station. Then when you get to the Bayswater Road, walk right and stay on the right side of the road. I'll meet you halfway.'

Tamsin was so surprised she almost stopped crying. 'Wha, you're walking all the way from Clapham?'

'No, I already told you—' Serena began impatiently,

then continued in a softer tone. 'Sorry. I'm at a party, in Holland Park, I'm literally just round the corner. But I don't have to stay. I'll come and meet you and then we can either go back to the party or go somewhere just the two of us and talk. It's totally up to you.'

'Oh, Bean, you're amazing, thank you so much,' snuffled Tamsin.

She opted for the party, for music and alcohol and people she didn't know and didn't care about.

* * *

Although Tamsin didn't know it – would never know it – she and Serena would pass, on their way to the party, the very pub in which Callum was sitting. After his dismissal he cycled home out of sheer numb habit. It was only 3 p.m. when he arrived back, but he grew worried that Leah might come home early and find him there. He turned his phone off and went out for a walk. Then he became paranoid that he might bump into someone he knew, so he ducked into a pub he was certain none of his friends would ever consider drinking in. No artisan ales, no wasabi nuts. The Live And Let Live had obviously not cleaned its carpets in several years; it still smelled of stale smoke from before the ban. All of the drinkers were over fifty. Only one of them was a woman. Callum ordered a pint of Stella and sat in a corner facing a television showing the Grand Prix. Whenever anyone came close to him, he feigned intense absorption in the race.

It had all happened so quickly. After lunch, he had been summoned to a meeting with Mr Davenport and two of the governors. Mr Davenport appeared agitated and struggled to maintain his usual headmasterish bluster. Twice he muttered that it was all a 'terrible shock'. It took Callum several minutes to understand that yesterday, when he was looking through the presentation, the computer had been connected to the smartboard.

'We wanted to let you know as soon as possible,' said the older of the two governors, 'so that you can look for another position. Not, of course, one involving contact with children.'

The whole ghastly process took less than an hour. His laptop was searched; the slideshow and the three incriminating images of Tamsin were discovered; and this, along with the photograph of Sophie and her written testimony (typed to ensure anonymity), constituted sufficient evidence for him to lose his job.

Callum listened in a state of cold shock. He argued against the allegations even though he knew this was futile; no school would dare to continue employing him in the face of such charges. It was true, he said, that he had put together a presentation about the nude in photography, including a photograph of his girlfriend Tamsin. It was true he had been under considerable personal and emotional strain at the time. But his motives had been entirely educational, designed to develop artistic sensibility in the children. Besides, he had decided *not* to show them the pictures. They had only seen the slideshow by accident.

'But you did show them pictures,' said Mr Davenport. 'Two terms ago, you showed them pictures from a pornographic magazine.'

'*One* picture,' said Callum weakly. 'Just one. They were – I found them – the boys were looking at the photographs right there in front of the girls. It seemed, I don't know, somehow harmful to just ignore the issue.'

'Can you prove it?'

'No, of course I can't *prove* it.' Callum was finding it hard to stay calm. He could hear how weak his case sounded. 'I shouldn't need to. They're children. They're *children*. I would never do anything to hurt a child, surely that's obvious.'

Much was made of the cropped picture of the Venus de' Medici, which – according to the lady governor – looked worryingly like a young girl's pudendum.

'I never thought about it like that,' Callum lied weakly. 'I mean, it's a famous work of art, how can that be wrong?'

'Stupid, Dempster, stupid,' said Mr Davenport sadly.

'Will you be involving the police?' Callum wanted to know.

Mr Davenport look appalled. 'Good god no, we're not inhuman. And think of the school!'

It was agreed that the official reasons for Callum's dismissal would be 'irreconcilable professional differences'. He would get a good reference on the understanding that he would never apply for another job working with minors. The governors were clearly expecting gratitude for their generosity, but Callum found himself unable to meet their eyes, let alone thank them.

He forced himself to drink his beer very slowly. Every time he thought of Sophie he wanted to cry. If he thought about Tamsin, it was even harder. He didn't trust himself with alcohol tonight.

At 10.30 p.m. he left and caught the bus back to Edgware Road, arriving home just after 11 p.m., when he was certain Leah would either be out or asleep. He crept back into his bedroom like an intruder and lay on his back on top of the duvet, fully clothed.

* * *

'You didn't tell me Will Heatherington was here,' hissed Tamsin.

Less than an hour had passed and she and Serena had

already resumed their habitual hostile positions. They were conducting their argument in fierce whispers in the hallway, next to a large heap of coats that had overflowed from the designated hooks onto the sweeping mahogany banister. When they entered the party and removed their own jackets, Tamsin had commented, unfavourably, on the number of fur coats – obviously real – in this pile. Serena had retorted that they were family heirlooms and why shouldn't they be worn; and there they were, business as usual.

Now Serena took the antique pewter tankard Tamsin was drinking from and sniffed its contents.

'Do you even know what's in this punch?'

'Whisky and cider,' said Tamsin.

'Well, you shouldn't be drinking it by the pint then, should you?'

'Don't change the subject. Why didn't you tell me Will was here?'

'What, you expect me to give you a rundown of the whole guestlist?' Serena snapped back.

Tamsin could see that she was being unfair: she had told her sister nothing about Callum, so Serena had no way of knowing that she didn't want to see anyone or anything connected to him. She dropped this line of attack and tried another.

'Have you slept with him?'

Serena bulged her eyes in frustration. 'No, but I might,' she said.

'I think it's pretty disturbing that he's here at all,' Tamsin muttered darkly, as a tiny girl in a crotch-skimming paisley print playsuit walked past them on her way to the loo. 'Look at her, she can't be older than eighteen, she's practically a kid.'

'Her name is Portia, she's twenty-three and she's a successful banker,' said Serena impatiently.

'He's at least a decade older than everyone here apart from me, don't you think that's creepy?'

'Ten years is nothing, Callum's eight years older than you, Dad's what, ten, eleven years older than Mummy—'

'AND LOOK HOW THAT TURNED OUT,' Tamsin shouted.

'Keep your voice down, you're making a complete tit of yourself,' Serena glared. 'I *knew* you'd overreact when—'

She stopped herself but not soon enough. Tamsin had heard, and tipsy as she was, it didn't take long for her to make the necessary mental leap. She leaned back against the banisters for support.

'You *knew*. You *knew*,' she said, her eyes widening. 'That's why you sounded so cool about it on the phone. I just got the biggest shock of my adult life and you don't even break a sweat because *you already knew*.' She was holding Serena by the shoulders now, just as she had done earlier to the boy at Denham Hall. This time, she actively wanted to inflict pain.

'Tam, let go, you're—'

'I don't give a shit if I'm hurting you. I can't believe *all three of you* knew about this.'

'We were going to – it's just we knew how you'd—'

'How long? Actually, no, don't tell me,' said Tamsin, abruptly loosening her grip on Serena. She held out her hand for her drink. 'And don't speak to me again this evening, please.' She snatched the tankard roughly out of Serena's grip and marched past her into the heart of the party.

For three hours, Tamsin successfully avoided both Serena and Will. She drank the punch, she talked for a long time to a boy who was very excited about some start-up selling a product he called 'sausage jam', she drank some more punch, she smoked a cigarette, she danced limply to the never-ending playlist of Swedish House Mafia.

She had just stepped out onto the crowded first-floor balcony to light her second cigarette of the evening when she heard Will's voice loudly calling her name.

'Tamsin Jarvis, I had no idea you were here!'

Tamsin whipped round to face him. 'Vyoo fucked my lilsister?'

'Is Callum about?'

'Just answer me.'

'Not that it's any of your business, but no, I haven't had that pleasure.'

'You're vile,' said Tamsin, illustrating this remark by spitting a gob of tobacco-induced phlegm over the balcony.

Undeterred, Will squeezed in beside her, resting an elbow on the wrought-iron railing and placing his other hand on her waist. 'Where's Callum?'

'Don't know and don't care.' Tamsin tried for tough but she felt her mouth begin to quiver. She took a long pull on her cigarette to steady herself. 'We're over,' she told Will, looking straight at him.

For a moment, she saw real concern in his face. But after second or two of calculation, recalibration, his features arranged themselves into a more conscious – and therefore less convincing – expression of sympathy.

'Well, that's *dreadful* news. I thought you'd go on for ever.'

'So did I,' said Tamsin. She began to cry.

Will put his arms around her. He was very tall – taller than Callum, taller than her – and Tamsin allowed herself, briefly, to enjoy the feeling of being dwarfed by him. He smelled delicious: some spicy yet subtle aftershave, very expensive, no doubt.

An unfamiliar female voice said, 'Is everything all

right?' Tamsin pulled back from Will and saw that the speaker was one of the other smokers, a plump girl with auburn hair and a lightly hooked nose. She looked more curious than worried.

'She's fine,' said Will firmly, leading Tamsin off the balcony and back inside. Instead of going downstairs again, though, he pushed open a door on the landing and ushered Tamsin into a small room with two large sofas and an old box television set. He sat her down on the nearest sofa and handed her a big cotton handkerchief.

'I didn't know anyone under forty still used these,' joked Tamsin through her tears.

Will ignored this. 'I suppose you want to talk about it,' he said, sitting down next to her. 'Well, I'm listening.'

Tamsin shook her head. 'Not really. Not with you.'

'Good, I hate all that sort of stuff,' said Will briskly. 'You know, you're even prettier when you're upset.'

Tamsin looked grimly triumphant. 'I knew it. You've got a seriously disturbed lidido, libdido – oh fuck it, you know what I mean. Uh, zit okay if I blow my nose on this?'

Will waved his hand to show that he didn't mind. 'Just tell me one thing, who dumped who?'

Tamsin glanced up from the handkerchief. 'He – actually he doesn't know I've left him.'

'But you have, definitely, left him?'

Tamsin felt a light pressure low down on her inner thigh, just above her knee: Will's hand, resting there in a gesture that seemed intentionally ambiguous, halfway between comfort and come-on, wide open to interpretation. *Her* interpretation. It was up to her, Tamsin realised. Will was the most unscrupulous man she knew; if she wanted to do this awful thing, it was very unlikely that he would stop her. She opened her legs a little further, moving the thigh that he was touching a few inches closer to him. His hand stayed put. Callum had hurt her more than she thought possible; this, surely, was the ultimate way to repay that hurt. Besides, there was no small satisfaction to be had from the idea that she could sleep with the very man Serena was after. Tamsin closed her eyes, trying to think. Sharp fragments of her extraordinary day – Antonia, Chris, the little boy outside Denham Hall, her *parents* – made themselves painfully felt. She opened her eyes. Thinking was not good. Better not to. Not to think, just to do.

Tamsin put the handkerchief down and turned her body towards Will's. Their faces were close enough for her to smell the whisky on his breath.

'You're a very bad friend,' she whispered.

'Yes, I am,' said Will. 'And you're a very bad girlfriend. Ex-girlfriend. Whatever.'

Will's left hand had been joined by his right, and he was lightly massaging Tamsin's breasts through the fuzzy grey wool of her dress.

'I'm just helping you take your mind off things,' said Will. 'Callum never has to know.' He leaned forward and kissed her mouth softly.

'Unless I tell him,' said Tamsin, through the kiss.

Will snapped his head back. 'You bitch,' he said, half-admiringly. Then he pushed Tamsin backwards and she reached up to grab his shirt, drawing his body down roughly on top of hers, welcoming his weight, the way it crushed her into the sofa.

* * *

Callum stayed in bed all the next day, which was Friday, the last day of term. He wanted to hear Tamsin's voice but he couldn't face telling her what had happened, or even that he had lost his job. Obviously she would have to know eventually. But for now he decided to behave as if he were still at school and call her only at the usual times: mid-morning, during break; then at lunch; and then at 3.30 p.m., which was always a free period for him on Fridays. Tamsin probably didn't know that, but it seemed best to do the thing properly. When school finished, at 6 p.m., he rang again. And then again, and then again. Worried now, he tried Roz, who was curiously cagey; she said she had seen Tamsin on Thursday night but had no idea where she might be now.

Callum gave up and rang Will, but his friend wasn't picking up, either. He waited half an hour, tried Will two more times, and then, in desperation, sent him a text to explain that he'd lost his job. Will called back within minutes, full of sympathy, insisting on taking Callum out.

They met in the bar of the Covent Garden hotel, where Will treated Callum to the enormous seafood platter and round after round of expensive martinis.

Callum found himself running with the line the school had given him. '"Irreconcilable professional differences",' he said bitterly, taking a large mouthful of martini. 'Otherwise known as, the headmaster fucking hates me.'

'Sounds sketchy to me – probably illegal, even. Do you want to lend me your contract? Be happy to have a read. I mean, employment law's hardly my thing, but I've got friends...' Will tailed off; Callum was shaking his head emphatically.

'No. No. I'm glad to be out, I've had it with schools. I'm going to – well, I don't know what I'm going to do, but not that.'

So this was the lie he would be telling for the rest of time, he thought miserably: that he had grown disillusioned with the thing he loved most in the world, that he had all but voluntarily chosen to leave the place he was happiest. The question he'd been trying not to ask himself since 2 p.m. yesterday pushed its way to the front of his mind: was he, as the school had clearly decided, unfit to teach? At one end, there was harmless casual fantasy, a vague predilection. And then at the other there were things that were unequivocally bad, like child pornography or actually doing something that caused distress, or pain. He was certain he would never be guilty of that. But there were infinite gradations between those two poles: terra non-firma that he wanted, and didn't want, to explore.

'And to make it all worse,' he said, talking quickly and loudly to obscure this murky line of thought, 'I can't get hold of Tamsin. I don't know where she's got to, her mother doesn't know either.'

'Oh, I'm sure she's fine,' Will said uneasily. 'Another one of those?'

* * *

Callum heard from Tamsin the next day. It was an email – brief and trite, full of break-up boilerplate. She thanked him for their wonderful years together and informed him that she needed to be alone right now. No doubt this wouldn't come as a surprise to him; it had been ending for a while. She was sorry to be melodramatic but she felt it would be too painful for them to see each other again. He could keep anything of hers that he found in the flat.

Callum wanted to write and ask her *why*, but – he thought – he already knew. It was his sexual shortcomings that had driven her away, like all the girls before her. That, and the ridiculous blunder he had made when he let on he'd confided in Leah about his problem.

In the end, he sent her a single-line response: 'Is there anything I can do to change your mind? If not, no need to reply.'

She didn't reply.

Eleven

Callum was surprised to find himself unbroken. Angry, yes; ashamed, yes; but not broken. He got a temporary job working on a building site off the Tottenham Court Road and found he could get by, for the time being at least, on hard physical labour and the exhaustion it brought at the end of each day.

He had lost his job and the love of his life but there were moments when he felt strangely calm. Although he missed them all – Sophie, Rhiannon, Michael, Hugh, even Ludo Hall – it was simpler without them. From now on he would live a clean, uncomplicated, solitary life, without sex, without, as far as possible, other people. Children he would avoid above all – not because he didn't trust himself, exactly, but because it had been too much.

The greater pain of losing Tamsin was tempered by an unexpected lightening. At first he thought this was because, as she'd pointed out in her horrible email, the relationship had been ending for a while. Then it occurred to him that he was relieved because now he would never have to lie to her, would never have to risk her finding out why it was he had left Denham Hall. She might not love him any more, but at least he had given her no reason to hate him.

* * *

One month after his dismissal, Callum had a phone call from Leo Goulding. He had almost forgotten: Leo and Bex were getting married that Saturday, and he was meant to be going to the wedding – with Tamsin.

'I take it you've heard,' Callum said as cheerfully as possible, doing his best to spare Leo's understandable discomfort. 'I'll be there, but I'll be on my own. Tamsin and I broke up.'

'No, I know that.' Leo was clearly unhappy about something. 'Actually, Callum, what I want to say – I'm not sure the telephone's the best – could we meet, maybe, for a quick coffee?'

Over burnt filter coffee in the Tottenham Court Road Starbucks, Leo explained that he wasn't sure if this was the right thing to be doing but it was surely better than the worst-case scenario, which was Callum finding out at the wedding, you know what weddings are like, too much gossip and too much booze, and as he and Bex didn't know how he was going to react they thought it was better—

'React to what, Leo? Just tell me!'

Leo swallowed. 'Tamsin and Will,' he said miserably. 'I heard rumours, I thought it couldn't possibly be true, but I called Will and shat all over him just to be sure – and it turned out that – they slept together. I'm so sorry.'

Callum nodded numbly. 'Do you know, do you happen to know when?'

'About four weeks ago. Will swears that Tamsin said you guys were already over when they – but he knows that doesn't make it any better – he's actually devastated, Cal, I don't think he'll forgive himself for this.'

'That makes two of us, then,' said Callum quietly. 'I'm afraid I won't be coming to your wedding after all. Thank you for letting me know.'

'Are you sure? I feel like a shit, I feel – if Will weren't best man I'd tell him to bugger off, but it's a bit late in the game—'

Callum stood up. 'It's fine. Give my very best to Bex. I hope it's a wonderful day for both of you.'

He managed to get himself home. He called the super at the building site to inform him that he wouldn't be coming back to work. Then he sat down on the sofa and stayed there for three whole weeks.

During all that time Leah shopped, cleaned and cooked for him, in near silence, asking no questions. He discovered that she had an extraordinary talent for cooking rich food: huge fried breakfasts and creamy soups, macaroni cheese and chocolate mousses. Callum ate himself right out of fitness, taking a melancholy pleasure in the softening of his thighs, the spreading at his waist.

* * *

Callum had had no contact with Tamsin since her sign-off email, so he didn't know she was living in Balham with her old schoolfriends Lottie and Fran, or that she had been miserable since the night she had slept with Will.

And he didn't know that she knew, or half-knew, why he had left his job, and that this was why she had sent such a cursory sign-off email. The fear of having her fears confirmed made it impossible for Tamsin to talk to him. If the truth was what she thought it was, she didn't want to hear it.

She felt as if she'd been caught in the vicinity of an enormous explosion: a blast that left her apparently unharmed, yet suffering serious internal damage.

CLAIRE LOWDON

For several weeks, Tamsin spoke exclusively to Lottie and Fran. She went to work, came home, ate, watched bad television, went to sleep, got up and did it all over again, ignoring Chris's calls, when they came, and Serena's, and Roz's, and Bertrand's. Her family seemed to understand that she needed time, but Chris's messages grew baffled, then hurt and eventually bitter. In his last message he accused her of leading him on. When she finally did call him, six weeks after her visit to Selly Oak, to say that she had sorted her life out and was ready to see him again, he told her very politely that he had fallen for one of the physios at Headley Court and that she was welcome to come and visit whenever she felt like it.

It was shortly after this blow that Will texted her, late one night – a shameless booty call, but one Tamsin felt too weak not to respond to. They fell into a queasy relationship, held together by guilt and reasonably good sex.

* * *

One particularly sleepless night Callum crawled into bed with Leah and put his arms around her. She didn't say anything but, a little while later, when he turned over on his other side, she turned with him and curled her body into his.

From then on, they slept in the same bed as each other every night. Life gradually became bearable once more. Callum went out and found a temping job that just about paid the mortgage. He started to see some of the old crew again. Leah was his girlfriend now, so she came with him. She still wasn't eating properly but as far as he could tell she had stopped making herself sick. She seemed contented enough. Although they kissed sometimes, they didn't try to have sex. The arrangement suited them both. Callum took care that he and Leah never went anywhere where Tamsin and Will were likely to be. He had heard – from Leo again – that when it became clear that his friendship with Callum was definitely over, Will had started sleeping with Tamsin once more.

'They're – well, they're a couple now, I suppose,' said Leo. 'It's funny to see Will with a girlfriend. Are you okay, should I stop?'

'No, go on. I prefer to know.'

'Actually there's not much more to tell.' Leo frowned, thinking. 'Except ... I don't quite believe in it, somehow. It won't last. I almost get the feeling that Will's doing it as a sort of *atonement* – to make it so that what he did wasn't just a meaningless one-off. So that he didn't screw you over for just a fuck. Am I making any sense?'

'Not really,' said Callum.

* * *

Tamsin's reaction to the news that Callum and Leah were an item was not entirely rational. Again, she remembered the pact she had made with Leah on New Year's Eve and became convinced that Leah had orchestrated the whole thing. She couldn't stop thinking about Leah and Callum, wondering if they were happy together, if Callum was happier with Leah than he had been with her. Tamsin thought about how thin Leah had become and decided that Callum liked her because she looked like a child.

She was very unhappy indeed. She still fundamentally disliked Will; and despite all of the evidence against him, she found she was missing Callum.

Several times she thought about calling him; but even

in those moments when she felt equal to the truth about his dismissal, she lacked the courage to speak to him. She herself had behaved too badly. So she didn't call, and didn't call, and after a while, it was too late.

Twelve

He has paid for the flat – a beautiful airy two-bed in Putney Bridge – so he could certainly afford to pay for a removal company.

But he wants to help her move in.

She thinks it's a stupid, sentimental gesture – especially stupid because his precious back 'goes' more and more often these days, and because the flat is on the third floor of a tall building with no lift. She understands, though, that having accepted the flat, she also has to accept his indulgent, demonstrative kindness.

She hopes that he'll leave her in peace once they've finished lugging her stuff from the car, but instead he produces a bottle of expensive-looking champagne and starts rooting around in her packing boxes, hunting for glasses.

'I'll do that – I know where things are—'

He stands up and stretches, palms pressed to his lower back like a pregnant woman. Then he picks up the champagne and nicks the foil with a well-practised thumbnail.

'Sorry, it's probably a bit warmish,' he says as he eases the cork from the bottle. 'But I thought we should christen this place with some bubbles.'

Irritated, she holds out two mugs.

'To you,' he says, bringing his mug (Keep Calm And Play Piano) to touch hers. 'To your first house. Oh, and to your ... your qualification. What is it again exactly, a diploma?'

'Yes, a diploma. You don't have to do that, I know what you think.'

'Come on, darling, that's hardly fair. It's just ... I didn't know much about what music therapy, ah, involved before. Your mother and I both think it's fantastic. We're very proud of you.'

'Mmmm.'

* * *

He is plaiting her hair: a complex, many-stranded confection inspired by a character from a programme they discovered two weeks ago. They are already halfway through the third series. They take their television very seriously these days.

When he's finished he stays sitting behind her, rubbing her back and shoulders.

'Did you think about my suggestion?' he asks gently.

'Yes,' she says, just as gently. They are always gentle with each other. 'I did think. And I think – I think I'd rather stay here.'

He nods even though she can't see him. 'I thought you would.'

There is a long pause.

'I will miss you,' she says eventually.

'You too, hen. We've had a good run, haven't we?'

In bed that night he lies behind her, passing his lips lightly over the nubbles of the plaits. He thinks she's asleep but then suddenly she speaks.

'Did you hear from your mother today?'

He shifts onto his back.

'Yeah. She was too blissed out on the morphine to make much sense. She knew who I was, though, and she understands I'm coming home. So that's something. The doctor's confirmed that she's diabetic. Apparently they don't want to operate yet. Best option is to try and get her dry, then pray that the enzyme supplements start to kick in. But I know my mam. She won't stop drinking.'

'I'm so sorry. Oh god. That's horrible.' She sounds distressed.

He feels the old, familiar urge to protect her. He rolls back onto his side and strokes her hip reassuringly.

'I think I've always known I'd end up going back. I'm actually quite looking forward to it.'

*　*　*

Good evening, ladies and gentlemen, I think that after that excellent character reference from the groom I need no introduction myself, except to say that being best man today is an absolute honour. You'll be pleased to hear I've taken my duties very seriously indeed. I did my best to get the groom legless at his stag do – though, as you can see, I was only half successful. (Sorry, had to be done, sorry.) So, I've known this young man quite a long time now – we were buddies here at Sandhurst, and many of you here today will know that the friends you make in that year are friends for life. We've helped each other through some pretty rough times, and I'm not just talking about hangovers. Without wanting to get too soppy on you all, I should mention that this legend helped me through the toughest break-up of my life, and if he hadn't kept me from going nuts it's seriously possible that I might never have persuaded my girlfriend – now, by some unholy stroke of luck, my fiancée – to take me back. I am one lucky bugger, but he's one lucky bugger too, because the bride, ladies and gentlemen, is an absolute angel. In fact, as many of you will know, she's the angel responsible for getting him back on his feet again. She's done a bloody good job, he can run as fast as I can, no joke, although somehow he's sitting pretty in a well-heated office while I'm still rotting away in a ditch in Wales. The good ole British Army are labouring under the delusion that he makes a rather good Intelligence Officer, but anyone who's seen him on a night out in London town will know that that's possibly most mendacious job title in history. Seriously, though – the job suits his formidable abilities to a tee. He's one of the finest minds I know, and one of the finest men, and if anyone deserves the beautiful bride, he does. And so, ladies and gentlemen, please join me in a toast: to the very happy couple!

* * *

He is forty-eight years old and seriously unattractive: weak-shouldered and pink-faced, with thinning white-blond hair and disturbingly small ears. He can't believe his luck when she lets him buy her a drink. Five months later, when she agrees to move in with him, he wonders if it might be some sort of hoax. He is suspicious when she turns up on his doorstep in Battersea with a single packing box.

'Is that it?'

'That's it.'

'That's all your stuff, in that box?'

He has a solicitor's sceptical mind. Is she a gold-digger? It seems unlikely; environmental law is hardly the most lucrative or glamorous profession. Plenty of better-looking, wealthier men would count themselves lucky to land her.

There must, he thinks, be a catch.

* * *

The new archivist at Glasgow University Library has a reputation for aloofness. No one knows much about him, apart from the fact that he used to live down South. There are rumours that someone close to him, either his girlfriend or his mother, has just died. Some people say that he's very well off and he doesn't need to put in all that overtime. Other people say he's taking advantage of the University's resources to work on a project of his own, something huge and ambitious.

She sees him walking to work across Kelvingrove Park. One evening she sort of follows him home, but only because she was going in that direction anyway. The gossip was right: he lives in a beautiful Victorian townhouse just off Sauchiehall Street.

She brings him tea in the mornings and they get talking. The book is something to do with military history. She offers to help him hunt down some obscure documents he can't get hold of.

As she twists her hair up, she thinks she can feel him watching her.

* * *

There is no catch. She is just happy that he shares her certainty that the world is heading for environmental apocalypse; that he is a vegetarian; that he is undemanding and unadventurous in bed; that when she tells him she doesn't want children, he nods and says 'fair enough'.

* * *

He guesses that the librarian is a few years older him, maybe forty-three or -four. She has a lot of green clothes and a way of pinning her hair up with a chopstick that he quite likes.

He takes her out for coffee with the intention of telling her not to waste her time on him, but ends up asking her out for dinner instead. Before he knows it, they're in bed together.

He is just unhooking her surprisingly sexy bra (later he will learn that she bought it that afternoon, especially for their date) and wondering how to prepare her for the inevitable disappointment when she announces that she has something to tell *him*. She isn't a virgin, but she has very little sexual experience; this will be the first time she's slept with someone in over five years. He will have to be very gentle with her, and make allowances for the fact she is bound to be terrible in bed.

Perversely, they are each calmed by the other's nervousness. He still finds sex difficult, but it is easier than it has ever been before.

One day he tells her that he used to be a teacher, but there was a misunderstanding and the school fired him. When she wants to know what exactly the misunderstanding involved, he tells her that he had tried to speak honestly and openly to the children about sex.

'I felt somehow ... hypocritical. That there're all these images in the media but we're still too buttoned-up to give our children any help to, to navigate that labyrinth. So I tried. But obviously I got it wrong.'

It is part of the truth, at least.

He doesn't tell her that every time they sleep together, he is thinking about twelve-year-olds. *A* twelve-year-old.

She is instantly outraged on his behalf and it makes him feel terrible.

*　*　*

They meet in a Turkish restaurant near Earls Court. It is two months since her last course of chemo. Her hair is growing back, but she keeps her rakish flat-cap on inside. She is very thin. Conversation is difficult for both of them.

At last he says gently, 'Was there something in particular you wanted to talk about? It sounded from your message as if...'

She pushes her broad bean pilav away, untouched. 'How did you lose ... we never actually – why, why did you stop working at Denham Hall?'

This is not what he expected. 'I had a disagreement with the headmaster,' he says lightly. There is no need to go into all that with her now. 'All water under the bridge. I'm glad I left, actually. Why do you ask?'

'Oh, no real reason, I was just wondering,' she says. Her plan was to tell him what she knew, to ask him for the truth at last. Now she realises she isn't going to.

He is looking at her. 'I don't quite understand, what was it you wanted to tell me?'

'I wanted to ... apologise,' she says. 'About the way things ended between us. And to say ... well, that I made a mistake. Leaving you. Was a mistake.' This she has certainly not planned to say. She is breathing heavily and her cheeks are flushed.

'Are you okay?' It is very painful for him to see her like this.

'Apart from the whole John Malkovich thing, yeah, I'm good,' she quips, rallying.

After that they talk more freely about their lives. He tells her more about his house in Glasgow, his life with the librarian. She says how pleased she is for him and describes, with lashings of black humour, her six-year affair with a married man (now over). They talk about the glowing reviews his book received and reminisce about mutual friends.

When they say goodbye, they hug for a very long time.

*   *   *

'He's out at church. He should be back in about forty minutes if you're willing to wait.'

She looks at the young woman on the doorstep, the huge pregnancy distorting the ribs of her knitted sweater. Her sleeves are rolled up to her elbows, displaying goose-fleshed skin on her forearms. 'You're cold,' she says. 'Why don't you come inside?'

The girl looks oddly relieved. She reaches an arm out and checks her watch.

'Thank you, but I think I should get going. We're just passing through, I only stopped by on the off-chance. Could you tell him that Sophie Witrand remembers his lessons very fondly? Tell him that I studied Classics at UCL. Tell him I read his book. Tell him I ... actually, just tell him that.'

Thank You

Andy Pierre, Ruari Owen, Diana Moss. Katie Greening and Tannith Perry. Olly Rowse, Lettice Franklin, Peter Straus and Clare Reihill. Kate Tolley, Kate Gaughran, Rebecca McEwan, Anne O'Brien, Luke Brown. Simukai Chigudu, for the rap. Polly Wilkinson, Gemma Cusworth, Hannah Richards. Emma Shearn, Emma Boswood, James Chapman, Liza Rogers, Mark Wright, Natalie Hind. Steven McGregor, Jaspreet Singh Boparai, Philip Hancock, Christopher Reid, Keiren Phelan. My family, and Bas.